3

MALE MODEL

BOOKS BY DAVE BENBOW

Daytime Drama

Male Model

Man of my Dreams
(with Jon Jeffrey, Ben Tyler and Sean Wolfe)

Published by Kensington Publishing Corp.

MALE MODEL

A NOVEL

Dave Benbow

KENSINGTON BOOKS
www.kensingtonbooks.com

KENSINGTON BOOKS are published by

Kensington Publishing Corp.
850 Third Avenue
New York, NY 10022

Library of Congress Control Number: 2003116201

ISBN 0-7582-0629-1

First printing: July 2004

10 9 8 7 6 5 4 3 2 1

Printed in the United States of America

For Cindy Pieratt Blass.
The most incredible woman I've ever met.

Acknowledgments

I'd like to thank everyone at Kensington Books for their unflagging enthusiasm and commitment towards my books and me. But special thanks must be given to my dashing editor, John Scognamiglio and Louis Malcangi for yet another stunning cover—is it *so* wrong that I tell everyone it's me? Their hard work only serves to make me look brilliant (which they know I'm not).

Heartfelt gratitude goes to my fabulous agent Sally Wofford-Girand, and the many amazing people I've had the pleasure of working with, and learning from, during my retail days: Allen & Ally Haines, Jerry & Lois Magnin, Clif Taylor, Sue Balmforth, Jon & Mindy Peters, John Omler, John Butler, Edward Blanchard, Michael Carey, Marilyn Miller and Robb Ginter.

And, finally, while I'm extremely grateful and thrilled that the "big box" bookstores and major online retailers have developed a growing gay and lesbian catalog, I'd like to remind book lovers everywhere not to forget to support our own. Terrific businesses like the InsightOutBooks gay & lesbian book club (insightoutbooks.com) and local GLB&T bookstores (such as A Different Light in West Hollywood) provide unconditional support and promotion of gay and lesbian writers and are the reason my books have been successful. The owners and staff of these unique and much needed businesses are an important link to our community's past, present, and future. They are your friends and neighbors, and they depend on *you* for their livelihood.

MALE
MODEL

1

The constant flashes from the paparazzi were mini explosions that lit up the impressive stone facade of the Cameron Fuller store on Rodeo Drive with staccato bursts of bright light. As each new limousine discharged yet another celebrity, the cameras went into overdrive. *Flash! Flash! Flash!* The clicking sound from over fifty cameras, combined with the roped-off onlookers' cheering of each new arrival, was deafening.

Oprah. Brad Pitt. Jennifer Aniston. Sandra Bullock. Jennifer Garner. Quarterback Colt Jennings. Reese Witherspoon. Travis Church. Clay Beasley. Gwyneth Paltrow. The Rock. The Fab Five from *Queer Eye for the Straight Guy.* Drew Barrymore. Cameron Diaz. It was a cross section of early 21st century fame that had the starstruck onlookers spellbound.

And all the dazzling celebs were at this store for one reason. To pay homage to the hottest fashion designer of the moment.

Cameron Fuller.

The name alone had been in the vernacular of clothes conscious Americans for years. Along with Ralph Lauren, Calvin Klein, Tommy Hilfiger and Tom Ford, he had helped shape the way Americans dress, sleep, and smell.

Tonight was the formal launch of Cameron's newest fragrance, Pacific Coast Highway, a clean, spicy scent that had gotten remarkably high marks from every focus group that had sampled it. The marketing team was optimistically projecting sales of over twenty million dollars before the end of the year.

Cameron had impulsively decided only weeks before to launch the scent at his new Rodeo Drive store, instead of at the Warehouse, his venerable Soho area New York emporium, as had been originally planned. The reasons he gave publicly were that the ad campaign and the fragrance itself promoted a California lifestyle, so where better to launch it than California?

The actual and true reason for the California launch was known only by him, and one other person.

Standing in the grand rotunda, at the top of the stunning curved Italian marble staircase that was strategically centered in the great hall of his beautiful store, Cameron Fuller himself looked around and was pleased by the turnout. He was elegantly dressed in one of his own Manhattan Label single-breasted navy suits. A crisp white shirt and sedate purple rep tie worked perfectly on his tall athletic frame.

A worried crease appeared on his normally smooth brow. On top of everything else that had gone wrong tonight, he had just had a disturbing conversation with one of his oldest friends. With determination, he forced the dark thoughts from his mind. Tonight was supposed to be a happy night.

He had called in all his markers, and every celebrity who owed him a favor was there. He hadn't given these people free clothes for years without expecting some payback, and tonight was it. He could tell by the reporters' excited questions that the notices about the launch in tomorrow's papers would be glowing.

Cameron saw his wife's father, Silas Cabbott, standing stiffly with a small group of other board members. The tension between Cameron and the board had been palpable lately, and Cameron hoped the great success of this party, as well as the launch, would smooth things over. He attempted to aim a tight smile at his father-in-law, but the old man ignored him, obviously still enraged from their earlier argument.

Cameron turned away from Oprah Winfrey and Drew Barrymore to catch the eye of his Pacific Coast Highway spokesmodel, who was across the rotunda. A new discovery, the model was everything Cameron had envisioned. He had a sexy, casual air that made you think he could go surfing, hiking, or snow boarding and still look good in a tuxedo. The hot model was lost in a sea of reporters who were firing off questions at him faster than he could answer them.

Cameron winked at him, and was just starting to walk over to rescue him from the throng when he felt a strong tug at his elbow.

"Cameron, I don't know how you do it, but you manage to pull it off every time."

Annoyed that he was being diverted from his mission, Cameron looked harshly at the woman beside him. "Yes, Suzette. I try," he said through tight lips.

She raised a champagne flute in his honor. "To my husband. Who else could pass off horse piss as cologne? *Salut!*" She drunkenly tipped the glass to him, then brought it to her lips. As she drank, she spilled a fair amount of the Dom Perignon onto the top of her black Dolce and Gabbana sequined minidress.

Cameron stared at her in bemused disgust and detachment. He eyed her dress, noticing for the first time that it was a competitor's design. "Jesus, Suzette. Couldn't you at least have worn one of my dresses tonight?"

"I don't like anything you make." She tipped her glass up again. "Besides, don't you want to congratulate *me*?" she asked, too brightly, her almond-shaped eyes flashing.

"What for, my dear?"

"Because I'm going to bury you, you sanctimonious bastard! You swore an oath to me! You swore you'd never tell, but you did! You won't have anything left when I'm done with you! Ha, ha!" She laughed, spinning around. Her carefully arranged, sun-streaked hair flew out, and then obediently returned to its original position. "You're going to be left with *nothing*!" she derided him, her face becoming pinched and spiteful.

"It's been a hard night, and I think you've had too much to drink, Suzette. Maybe you should lie down. Let me escort you back to the VIP room," Cameron said, trying to take her fashionably thin arm. He just hoped to God no one was paying attention to her.

"Is everything okay, Cameron?" asked Rafael Santiago, Cameron's Director of Creative Services, and right hand man. He had stepped up to the arguing couple unnoticed.

"Yes, Rafe. Everything's fine. I'm taking Suzette to the VIP room. She's had a little too much celebration," he explained, falsely cheerful.

"Take your hands off me!" Suzette slurred the words as she tried to pull away from Cameron. "I'll tell you when I've had enough! And not versa vice!" she said, her famous temper flaring. She tripped on her own feet, which were shod in a simple but obscenely expensive pair of gold Gucci strappy stilettos. Stumbling, she fell toward Cameron, who took firm hold of her and tried to lead her to the stairs.

"Suzette! For God's sake, sober up!" hissed her father, Silas. He had come up behind the small group silently. Suzette shooed him off with an airy wave.

Blake Jackson observed the scene between Cameron and his wife, and was concerned. Blake had been an uncomfortable witness to the earlier nasty argument. Now, Cameron looked embarrassed, and Suzette was obviously too drunk to be left alone. He knew he should go to Cameron's side and help him with his shrewish wife, but he doubted he could get through the crowd in time. The camera flashes started up again, temporarily blinding him.

Blake had been pushed by the crowd up against the railing above the stairwell. When his eyes cleared and he could see again, he looked down the staircase at the even larger crowd milling around on the floor below.

Quite the turnout, he thought. *Simply amazing. All these people here to meet some male model no one had ever heard of before tonight.*

He looked up again and saw that Gwyneth Paltrow happened to be standing next to him, and again a flood of camera flashes went off in his face. At that exact moment, a woman's scream built in pitch and intensity until it could be heard by everyone.

As the spots vanished one by one from Blake's eyes, he looked toward where the scream was coming from. Oddly, it now seemed to come from below. He focused on a blur of black that was falling, rolling and tumbling down the Italian marble staircase. It was a woman's body, and Blake could hear her head thunk against each one of the cold stone risers as she tumbled. The screaming suddenly stopped. Silence fell over the entire area as people watched in fascinated horror, and the woman's descent continued all the way to the bottom of the wide staircase. Spots and smears of bright red could clearly be seen on steps as she passed them, tumbling toward the bottom.

"Suzette! My God!" There was a flash of movement at the top of the stairs as Cameron Fuller leaped down the staircase two risers at a time. Every photographer in the store had now trained his or her camera on the terrible drama happening on the marble steps. Photo flashes burst like fireworks in the three-story space.

Suzette's body came to a stop in a twisted heap at the base of the stairs. Both her arms were bent at odd angles, and a large laceration on her forehead was pumping blood into an ever-widening pool about her. She did not move.

Halfway down the stairs, Cameron slipped on a bloody wet spot, almost falling over himself. He regained his balance and proceeded more cautiously down the staircase. At the bottom, he squatted down, picked up Suzette by her lifeless shoulders, and cradled her to his chest.

"Call 911! Someone, please! 911!" he shouted at the crowd.

Dozens of people whipped out cellphones and dialed.

Blake stood rooted in shock where he was. Even though he was far above, away from Cameron and Suzette's huddled forms, he knew she was dead. Cameron looked up frantically and caught Blake's eye. They stared at each other helplessly for a beat, then Blake turned away from the grisly scene as the photographers pressed forward to snap off shots of the tragedy below.

"Did she fall?" one of the photographers breathlessly asked him, snapping off a long series of shots with his automatic camera. "Or was she pushed?"

Blake ignored him, and fighting his way out from the gasping, gawking crowd, walked over to an enormous potted palm tree and held on to it for support. He closed his eyes tight, but the photographer's words kept ringing in his ears.

Did she fall, or was she pushed?

2

"Ohhhh! God, baby, that's it!"

"Yeah? *Mmmmmm* . . . Yeah!" Blake pulled out slightly, then thrust back in, the gasp of delight from his sex partner telling him that what he was doing was not only welcome but wanted. His hands had a firm hold of Brady's tapered thirty-two-inch waist, and he pulled him back into each push, in effect bouncing Brady's perfect bubble butt up against his pelvis. The muscles in Brady's broad worked-out back flexed slightly as he adjusted his stance.

"Oh, *maaaan!*" Brady sighed deeply. The palms of his hands and his knees were getting rubbed raw from the rough natural sisal carpet, but he didn't care. He hadn't been plowed this good in weeks. Sex with Blake had always been good, but this was, like, another world!

"*Daaayum!* You feel so good, Brady," Blake murmured, picking up the pace a bit. The sensation of having Brady's beautiful ass slam into his crotch was bringing him to the brink.

"I'm gonna come, Blake!"

"Me, too!"

"Together! . . . *Ohhhh!* . . . Yeah! . . . Now . . . !" Brady's voice trailed off into a long, sustained whoosh of air.

"*Ohhhh,* damn . . . ," Blake added as he slipped out, tugged off the condom, and shot all over Brady's back. At the same instant, Brady came as well, valiantly trying to come in his cupped hand.

Afterwards, the two men lay on the scratchy fiber rug catching their breath. Blake began to laugh hysterically.

"I've never understood why you always laugh after you come," Brady observed dryly, stretching his arms above his head. He reached for his balled up navy blue T-shirt with the yellow West Hollywood Sheriff's Department logo on it, and brought it under his prematurely gray head, like a pillow.

"Tension release, I guess," Blake laughed. "I can't believe we just did that! Jesus."

"I know. Oh, well . . . if you can't have rockin' sex with an ex-boyfriend, then who can you have it with?"

"True," Blake agreed. "Sex was never the problem with us. It was the whole 'relationship' thing we couldn't make work."

"I know. Not that I didn't try." Brady leisurely reached up to his left ear and deftly removed the small gold hoop that had been there. He reached over to his shorts and shoved the tiny earring into his pocket. Men were not allowed to wear earrings while on duty, and last week Brady had forgotten to remove his before reporting for work. He'd been written up for it.

That small task completed, he rolled over on his side and propped himself up on one muscular arm. He looked intently at Blake through warm brown eyes.

"I know," Blake said softly.

"Well, maybe we could try again. I miss you, Blake. Don't get me wrong. I like being your friend and workout partner. But maybe we should try for more, again."

"Brady," Blake began, turning to face his ex-lover, "we tried it. It didn't work. And yes, I'll admit that I miss you, too. What I don't miss are the fights. I don't know . . . I just can't see it working out," he said, being honest.

"Well, think about it. That's all I ask. Just think about it, okay?" Brady gently pleaded. Even though he was easily six feet, two hundred twenty pounds, and a tough looking sheriff's deputy, he could seem very childlike in his needs.

"Okay, I will. I promise." Blake glanced at the clock and was shocked by the time. "Jesus! I'm gonna be late! I gotta get in the shower."

"I don't have to report in for another two hours. Want me to join you?" Brady hinted suggestively.

Blake laughed. "No, thanks. You caused enough trouble for one day, deputy. By the way, your chest presses today were sad." Blake got up and trotted out of the living room and into his bedroom.

"Fuck you!" Brady called after him good-naturedly. "You know I pulled a double shift yesterday! I couldn't keep up with you."

"Jealous, much?" Blake shouted back, turning on the shower. "You just wish you had my body!"

Brady sighed deeply, and sank back to the floor. "You have no idea how badly, and not in the way you think," he said quietly.

3

Three thousand miles away, another shower was being turned on. The scalding hot water shot out of two large facing nozzles set about six feet apart. The heavy glass door swooshed open and Cameron Fuller stepped into the enormous stall. Made entirely of imported beige Italian tile, the stall was ten feet by ten feet square. A low flat bench had been created along one side, and the platinum chrome fixtures gleamed with the shine of daily cleanings by Josephina, the trusted housekeeper.

Cameron Fuller was forty-six but looked to be only in his late thirties. A few nips and tucks here and there had helped with the subterfuge, but he had always looked younger than he was. In fact, when he was first starting out in the rag trade, he would sometimes get doors slammed in his face because the vendors couldn't believe this kid could deliver what he promised. Now his handsome face was the iconic image of Cameron Fuller USA, CF America, CF/Active, and Cameron Fuller Manhattan Label. He was quickly becoming one of the world's hottest clothing conglomerates, and along with his wife Suzette, he was used extensively in advertising and commercials for his company.

His hair was starting to gray, and to his surprise, he discovered that he liked the gray. It gave him a mature, distinguished air. His honest-to-God violet eyes blazed like amethysts when he was interested in something, which was all the time. His Romanesque nose was centered on a rather squarish face that, without his expansive mouth and dazzling smile, would have seemed rather blockish. A small scar marred his chin, but, oddly, it made him appear even more masculine.

Originally from a small town outside Toronto, Cameron was six feet one inch tall, and kept in remarkable shape with grueling work-out sessions supervised by his Nazi-like trainer, Rolf. Rolf pushed him beyond his limits every day, yet Cam kept coming back for more.

Because he saw—and liked—the results.

His stomach, flat and cut into a solid eight-pack, rested below squared off but beefy pecs. Thick arms with beautiful musculature ended in broad shoulders that supported a thick neck.

He had a body to die for.

And right now, he just wanted to shower away the stress of the spring collections, web site snafus, the looming and troubled new cologne launch, and the disaster that was his private life.

"Cameron?"

He ignored the call, began to lather up.

"Cameron?"

He scrubbed the loofa hard into his taut skin.

"Cameron! Answer me!"

"What?!" he finally shouted back.

A shadow fell across the glass, and Cam knew that Suzette had entered the bathroom. He refused to look at her.

"A little late for a shower, isn't it?" she questioned archly.

"A little. I slept in. I only had time to do the treadmill. I *was* up late last night, if you recall."

"What I recall is that you didn't make an appearance at Simone and George's. You promised me, you bastard!" she snapped.

"Sorry. I had to work late at the office. I do have a fragrance launch coming out soon, you know."

"Work late, my ass! If you're going to fuck around, just have the balls to admit it!"

"Suzette, I'm not fucking around." He sighed. *Here we go again.*

"Please. I'm not that stupid, Cameron Fuller. You may have the world fooled into thinking you're Mr. All America, but I know better!"

"Is there a point to this, Suzette?"

"Yes. Two points, actually. One," she pointed a fleshless finger at him, "when I find out who you're screwing, I swear to God, I'll be charged with murder one. And the second point is, you wouldn't even *be* here if it weren't for Daddy's money. He got you started. Don't you ever forget that!" She had once again played her trump card.

"How *could* I forget it? You remind me of it at least once a day."
He turned his back to her and rinsed off the suds.

Ignoring him, she railed on. "And I should think that the least you
could do would be to show up at a party for me. Just once. For *me!*"

Cam said nothing, hoping she'd run out of steam soon and leave.
Out of the corner of his eye, he glanced at her.

She was standing in the exact center of the huge bathroom, thin
hands on even thinner hips. At five feet six inches and a perfect size
two, she slavishly maintained her body with a workout routine that
rivaled his own. She had intricately highlighted honey blond hair that
fell to just below her narrow shoulders. Cam couldn't remember it
ever looking any different. All one length, it was a timeless cut, and
it worked for her.

Her gaunt, forty-six-year-old face had a pinched look to it, as if
she was in need of a good meal. Which she was.

She, too, had had the odd lift and tuck, and was a big devotee of
botox. Pale blue eyes observed everything in their path, and thin lips
rarely curled up in a genuine smile.

Once every six weeks she took Cameron's private jet to L.A. for
an eyebrow tweeze by Anastasia, the eyebrow tweezer to the stars.
She would return to New York the very same day, hating to spend even
one night in Los Angeles, a city she loathed.

Suzette Cabbott Fuller had been the veritable poor little rich girl.
She was the daughter of multimillionaire blue blood Silas Cabbott.
Her mother, Clarice Wedgeway Cabbott, had been a celebrated beauty
and a famous hostess. Sadly, Clarice Cabbott died giving birth to
twin infants, Suzette and her seconds-younger brother, Stanton.

Suzette and her sibling were raised by a series of nannies, and
while Stanton had grown up rather well adjusted, she had not. As is
often the case with overindulged children, she had never outgrown
her childish ways. Her temper tantrums were legendary, and more
than one fiction writer had based an unflattering character on her.

She was dressed for her lunch date with Liz Smith already. Head
to toe black Prada. A Gucci silver chain belt casually looped about
her waist. A large black Hermès Birkin bag hung limply in the crook
of her bony elbow.

Cam almost laughed. His own wife. Going to lunch with a reporter and not wearing a stitch of his own clothing label.

So typical.

"What? You're not going to mention the apartment, too?" he asked, not caring that he was taunting her now.

"The apartment. The house in Tuxedo. The beach house in Kauai. All of it paid for by daddy!"

"Au contraire, my dear." Cam twisted off the shower spigots and reached over for a thick ecru Cameron Fuller Newport towel. "I believe I paid for all of those. I do make a decent living, you know. Your father only put up the *down payments* on each of those when you decided that you *had* to have them. He was paid back quickly. And, even more to the point, when exactly *was* the last time you even *saw* the Kauai house?"

"The weather there messes up my hair. That one, you wanted. Not me," she said dismissively.

"Whatever. Fact is, yes, there have been times when we needed your father's money. But we haven't needed it for a long, long time." He toweled off the excess water and briskly rubbed himself down. "The money your father loaned us is almost completely paid back. At thirteen percent interest, I'd like to point out. He will be receiving the final payment I owe him in three months. Then both he and you can get *off my back.*"

Suzette fumed silently. She knew that once Silas received that last loan payment, there would be no need for Cameron to keep him on the board of investors. It was her second biggest fear.

Cameron enjoyed the momentary shift in power. "And, I'd also like to mention that your father's investment in my company has proved lucrative to him as well as me. I've never heard him complain about the size of his check each March."

Cameron's mention of March referred to the end of his company's fiscal year. Profit checks were sent out to the investors the third Friday of each March. It was known throughout the company as "Green Friday." The famous designer shook his head vigorously, shaking out the excess water. "For Christ's sake, despite *my* wishes, he runs the board of investors!" he spat out. "Something that will stop soon enough."

"Daddy has saved your ass repeatedly with his financial expertise! He deserves to be on that board!" Suzette shrieked, her temper flaring.

Cameron sighed. "I'm well aware of the contribution your father has made to the company and to us personally."

"Well, Mr. America," Suzette said, her thin ruby lips twisted in scorn, "just remember that when we sit down with the lawyers to split it all up. And I've decided I want the Tuxedo house completely. You never go there. You don't want it and we don't need to share it. I want the Aspen condo. I also want this apartment," she said, counting off the properties on her jewel-encrusted fingers as if she was counting pennies. "You can have the beach house."

Cam snorted. "That's mighty big of you. Tuxedo's worth, what? Fourteen million dollars? Aspen? Nine million. This place? Twelve million? I think the last I checked, the beach house was worth three million dollars, and that's only because of the beach front property."

"You want out? You *pay*," she hissed.

Cameron frowned, then turned his back to his wife. Little did she know how willing he was to pay. Anything to get her and her impossible father out of his life. But, only after the spring collection was safely in the stores and his new cologne, Pacific Coast Highway, was successfully launched.

After that, he'd have the massive cash flow needed to pay back the enormous personal note he had owed his father-in-law for too long. Silas Cabbott would then be unceremoniously dumped from the board of investors, and Cameron could finally run his company the way *he* wanted.

He'd also be able divorce his wife, something that caused Cameron to smile every time he thought about it. Total freedom in only three months. He could hardly wait.

He turned around slowly and stared his wife dully in the eye. "Trust me. I want out."

"Good. Let's set up another meeting with the lawyers for right after we get back from L.A. How I let you talk me into staying in that awful town for two whole days, I'll never know." With that, she whirled about abruptly and calmly strode out of the bathroom.

4

Blake had to haul ass.

He was late, and his obligatory daily stop at Starbucks would not help his time crunch. The Monday morning manager's meeting was scheduled at the store for precisely 9 A.M., and Steve Barton, the store's fidgety manager, did not take kindly to tardy section leaders. He would make a big show of pointing out the latecomer's error and scowl at the transgressor for the rest of the day.

"Venti Mocha Frappacino, extra whip," Blake said urgently to the bug-eyed counterperson. After illegally parking his five-year-old Jeep Cherokee in a red zone, he had literally dashed into the Starbucks on Santa Monica, across the street from the shiplike 24 Hour Fitness gym.

"Venti Mocha Frap, extra whip!" the counterperson repeated loudly to the "steamer" in back.

Nervously glancing at his watch, Blake realized he was definitely going to be late now. He would be the whipping boy at the meeting, and he knew that at the very least he would also be the recipient of a private chat with Steve about showing more respect and setting a better example for the associates.

Blake sighed and ran fingers through his thick dark hair. He was clearly the most handsome man in the coffee shop. And while he noticed the quick, appreciative glances in his direction from the women and the men waiting in line, today they did nothing to improve his frenzied state of mind. His athletically tall frame was the perfect size forty-two regular, and he wore clothes with the ease of a runway model. Daily two-hour workouts maintained the six-pack abs and

muscular body that he'd had when he was on the swim team in college.

At thirty-one, his square, chiseled jaw line was softened by ruddy
cheeks he'd inherited from his Polish mother and ice blue eyes that
were a gift from his father's German side of the family. His dark skin
was courtesy of a Native-American branch somewhere in the wood-
pile. Thick lashes and a well-groomed brow line complemented the
glorious dark hair that tumbled casually down to his shoulders.

Unfashionably long hair, some thought. But Blake liked the fact
that while almost every other gay man had the standard Boy Scout
haircut, he stood out.

Dressed for an active working day in worn low-rise Cameron
Fuller Montana Rough Wear jeans that fit like a glove and a soft red
flannel CF/Active shirt, he put out a vibe of relaxed confidence that
was irresistible.

"Venti Mocha Frap, extra whip?" called out the counterperson,
who, taken slightly aback by the beautiful man in front of him, almost dropped the beverage.

"That's me." Blake took the hot cup from him gratefully, and raced
back out to his truck, only to find a one hundred and ten dollar ticket
waiting under his windshield washer.

Well. That was a damn expensive cup of coffee, he thought grimly.

Twenty minutes later, Blake pulled into the underground parking
structure beneath the Cameron Fuller store. As temporary Director
of Creative Services, he was allowed to park in one of the rare and
enviable employee parking spaces under the store. His boss, Spencer
Douglas, had taken a few weeks off to have some liposuction done.
Blake, as the most talented of the creative services team, had been
asked to step up and fill Spence's shoes while he was out. Blake had
pressured Steve for the use of Spence's space, reasoning that since he
was in and out of the store so much, it didn't make sense for him to
have to spend fifteen to twenty minutes running to the regular employee lot way down Canon Drive, four blocks away, each time he
had to leave.

Just before he entered the depths of the garage, Blake looked up
and drank in the stunning beauty of the store, something he never
tired of doing. That he worked in such a beautiful building, doing a
job he loved, always caused his heart to swell with pride.

*   *   *

Built at a cost of over twenty-seven million dollars, The Cameron Fuller store stood like a sentinel at the corner of Rodeo and Little Santa Monica. An impressive structure of stone, concrete, glass, and steel, it perfectly reflected the vision of Cameron Fuller. The traditional arches that curved over the six display windows fronting Rodeo Drive would have looked at home on an old New York brownstone. Contemporary chrome and glass had been fitted into them to combine the craftsmanship of the old world with the excitement and energy of the new.

Rising three floors above the ground, and extending two below, the Cameron Fuller flagship store had already made the "ten best" lists of several retail marketing magazines, and had won three separate awards for innovative architectural design. Within its expensive walls was the world and lifestyle vision of its founder, Cameron Fuller.

Cameron had spilt his fashion sensibilities into several main categories. Each group fit a particular consumer niche, suiting a different type of customer.

CF America was his mid-range, more traditionally preppie line. Core basics such as khaki pants, fine-point oxford cloth shirts, ties, navy blazers, tailored twill skirts, and silk shirt-dresses were the staples of this line.

CF/Active was Cameron's underwear and sport collection, and while it had the essentials for tennis, basketball, and golf, the designer had ventured into more cutting-edge choices for biking, hiking, and water and extreme sports with fabrics such as fleece-wear, nylon, stretch cotton, and the hottest trend in fashion retail, microfiber. CF/Active was his fastest growing line, and had been embraced by celebrities worldwide.

Manhattan Label was his extravagant and deliciously expensive top-of-the-line group. Handmade blazers easily went for four thousand dollars and up, and the Manhattan Label evening gown collection was a first choice pick for savvy stars on award nights.

Montana Rough Wear was his trendy "western," or "work," line, full of denim, plaids, and suede half jackets, with two hundred fifty dollar jeans and three hundred dollar denim shirts, standard. Montana Rough Wear was Blake's favorite line of Cameron Fuller clothing. Each time a new shipment arrived at the store, he would try on one of everything, just to see how it fit.

And these fashion treasures were housed in the beautiful stone structure on Rodeo Drive. It was a Disneyland for the clothes conscious consumer.

The ground floor of the store was a mecca of women's fashion. From the affordable juniors CF America line to the pricey Manhattan Label collections, Cameron's vision of what a stylish woman should wear was on glorious display. Twenty salespeople wandered purposefully among its racks, mannequins, cashwraps, and dressing rooms offering the ultimate in service to customers.

The second floor was given to the men's collections. Cameron's original success had been with a small line of uncommonly comfortable dress shirts that he and his wife had sold out of the back of her car (granted, it *was* a Mercedes Benz 450 SL) during his salad days. After establishing himself with a small collection at a local Madison Avenue haberdasher, and achieving significant sales as a quality label, he had quickly branched out into suits, shirts, and casual wear. Cameron had truly hit his stride with a knit polo shirt adorned with his now-famous logo of a small blue outline of the continental United States filled in with red and white stripes on the left breast pocket. Cameron's better-cut version of the staid polo shirt proved so staggeringly successful he had almost single-handedly put the Izod Lacoste company into bankruptcy.

From those knit shirts, he had built an empire.

While most of his divisions were under the supervision of a few trusted designers, his men's wear collection was still something he continued to oversee personally, often drawing the original sketches himself. In the store, men's suits were in a well-appointed, cloistered area where the three salesmen waited on TV celebrities, movie moguls, and rock stars.

Sportswear was front and center at the top of the cut Italian stone staircase, which had been hand-built by a team of Italian master craftsmen brought over from Italy specifically for the purpose of constructing it.

His Montana Rough Wear collection, the rugged and absurdly expensive casual line, was sectioned off in a large room decorated and propped out to look like a modern lakeside cabin.

At the top, the third floor was the domain of the Home Arena. A relatively new venture of Cameron's, the Home Arena was turning out to be so successful that smaller Home Arena boutique shops were already being planned for the major department store chains that carried the Cameron Fuller line.

Furniture, bath linens, bedding, fabrics, and wall coverings were displayed in various themed rooms. These theme rooms were the lifestyles that Cameron wanted to project as being hip and trendsetting for that current season. The home collections were changed out twice a year, spring and fall, and the spring change out was one of the topics to be discussed at the manager's meeting this morning.

The meeting was already in progress in the employee lunch room when Blake tried to slip in unnoticed. He might have made it had Steve not looked up for a second from the notes laid out in front of him.

"Ah. Blake. So glad you could join us," he said in a condescending tone. His pinched expression looked entirely appropriate on his balding head. He was a short man, only five feet six inches, and had the typical Napoleon complex. Arrogant and self-aggrandizing, he wore round wire-rimmed glasses and was slightly underweight, despite living on a diet of fast food and root beer.

Steve only wore seersucker suits, as Cameron Fuller himself had once casually told him they were flattering to his frame. Today, dressed in a Cameron Fuller blue seersucker with Cameron Fuller braces and wingtips, he had the studied look of an accountant from the 1940s.

"I believe that nine A.M. means nine A.M. Not nine twenty-six," he said with a sneer, looking over the tops of his glasses.

"I know, Steve. I'm so sorry. Big accident on Santa Monica near me. Totally messed up my timing today," Blake lied.

"Huh. I came down Santa Monica this morning. I didn't see any accident," Steve countered, folding his arms in front of him like a schoolteacher.

The jerk.

Blake smoothly covered: "Must have happened after you passed, then. So, what have I missed here?"

After staring sternly at Blake, Steve returned to his notes. "I was saying that Cameron and Suzette will be visiting us tomorrow, as we all know. I want the new spring shoes out and the holiday and cruise shoes put back in the stockroom. After he's left, Sven, we'll bring them all back out, on sale. Whatever doesn't sell then, ship to the outlet store."

Sven Lundstrom, the footwear manager, nodded in agreement.

"Kelly, women's spring Manhattan Label won't arrive until late this afternoon, so plan on keeping a few people here tonight to help Spence's crew get it up, and don't forget the steaming." The steaming he was referring to meant each individual garment had to be completely free of wrinkles before it could hang on the showroom floor. Thus, each piece was carefully steam pressed by hand before any customer saw it.

"Okay, Steve, we'll get it done. Don't worry," answered Kelly Gecko, the beautiful and whippet thin women's buyer.

"Now, Blake." Steve's attention was again on Blake, who had pulled out his large binder with all his notes in it. "Spence is due to return next week. Finally." The relief in his voice was obvious. "Clearly, spring home change won't be done by Cameron's walkthrough, but make sure you have detailed plans to show him. He'll want to see everything, and I mean everything. Carpet samples, paint chips. Have everything there. Also, the store will have to be immaculate. I assume your crew is pulling overtime this week?"

"Yes," Blake said. "We're splitting into two shifts, and we'll all stay as late as we need to. Men's is pretty well tied down now. There are a few weak areas in women's that I want to go over with Kelly after this meeting, okay, Kell?"

Kelly nodded her perky blond head.

Blake continued speaking. "The presentation for the spring home collection is ready and I think Cameron will like what I have to show him. As you remember, Rafael was out here from New York two weeks ago, and we went over it at least twenty times."

Rafael Santiago was the Creative Director for the entire home collection, and Spence's boss. He was also Cameron Fuller's right-hand man, a point he let no one forget. Based at the New York headquarters, Rafael often flew out to L.A. to check up on the store, and make the creative services team's lives a living hell. Once in L.A., however, he usually spent little time in the store, and too much time in the many bars of West Hollywood, trolling for twenty-year-old frat boys, his weakness.

Drumming his fingers restlessly on the tabletop, Steve glared at Blake. "Good. I'll want to see those plans some time today. Is that possible?"

"You got it."

"Good." Steve then addressed all the managers. "We will have extra staff on during Cameron's visit, so please adjust your scheduling as needed. Kelly, make sure you have all the size twos ready for Suzette."

"I've already pulled one of everything aside," she responded coolly.

Suzette Fuller was a notorious shopper, and even though she could have anything with a Fuller label delivered directly to her sumptuous Fifth Avenue apartment, she loved to shop in the stores themselves. She claimed it let her experience the store through the eyes of a typical customer, but in reality she loved to model the clothes in full view of whoever was there. She had a compulsive need to be complimented.

She also loved to order the sales associates around, which she did without grace or style. She was an infamous bitch who had reduced veteran salespeople to tears on more than one occasion. In-store visits by Suzette were absolutely despised. This was partially due to the fact that after running the staff crazy with demands, Suzette never actually *bought* anything.

Racing through his notes, Steve crammed his hour-long speech into thirty minutes. He rambled on about mundane things having to do with promotional tie-ins, rate of sales and sell-through. Blake tuned out and mentally went over his "to do" list for the day.

He had been working, quite happily, at the Bloomingdale's in Century City, and had been wined and dined by Rafael Santiago. Rafael had been having a hard time finding qualified staff for the new Rodeo Drive Cameron Fuller flagship store, and Blake's windows for the fall season at Bloomingdale's had caught his eye. After requesting to see his portfolio, he had offered Blake a job on the spot over lunch at the Chateau Marmont. He wanted Blake to be the windows manager and head up the third floor Home Arena.

Rafael had promised Blake a certain amount of creative freedom with the windows, and promised a pleasant working atmosphere. He had also offered to increase his current salary by fifty percent.

Rafael had made it clear that his own vision would be the direction the store followed, and that Spencer Douglas would have responsibility for the overall appearance. Blake would report to Spencer, who in turn would report to Rafael. Blake knew it would be a huge challenge, but he felt he was up to the task. That, and the fact that, as an employee of Cameron Fuller, he'd get a sixty percent discount.

Blake had excitedly taken the job.

What Rafael *hadn't* told him was that he was a control freak who micromanaged everything he was involved in. He phoned Spence several times a day to check up on what the creative services, or visuals, team was doing, and to triple-check on things that Spencer had patiently explained only hours earlier. And since Spencer was on leave, Blake had had to take up the slack with Rafael.

He dreaded the thrice daily phone calls from Rafael, who had also neglected to mention he was a low-grade schizophrenic who sometimes forgot to take his medication. Blake had had to spend an entire three days with Rafe two weeks earlier to go over the spring Arena changes, and he thought the experience would kill him. Rafael had flip-flopped on some key issues several times and Blake was still not sure if what he had down on paper was what Rafe wanted, but he figured he'd follow what he understood, and hope for the best. This was a dicey idea when it came to Rafael, but Blake had no choice.

When the staff meeting finally broke up, Blake tried to beat a hasty retreat before Steve could nab him. He might have made a clean escape if it hadn't been for Sven pestering him about some shoe display tables he needed from the warehouse. His two-minute chat with Sven caused him to be directly in Steve's eye line, and Steve had motioned for Blake to join him for a second.

Christ, thought Blake.

Kelly saw Blake walking out of the room, and waved him over with a smile. "So. What did the führer have to say?"

"Responsibility. Role models. Standard dress-down speech number three." Blake shrugged. "Pompous ass. Whatever. Now, about the areas in women's . . . I think we need to work on juniors today. I want to fold down the knit sweaters and move them to the front. Then let's hang the new jean jackets where the sweaters were. Can you spare a couple staffers to help Chelsea?" Chelsea Watkins was the creative service staffer in charge of women's.

"Sure. I'll put Karen and Dylan on it. We're not really going to be here late tonight, do you think? I really want to get my presentation for Cameron in shape, and I need more time." Kelly batted her blue-green eyes at Blake.

"I don't know. Depends on how well things go today. I think we'll be here at least until midnight. I still have to finish the windows tonight. Pizza's on me, though."

"God. I hate these visits. Whenever Cameron comes to town, Steve just wigs out and makes it unbearable for all of us. Is crazy Rafael coming in, too?" Kelly asked, knowing about the ever-growing strain on the relationship between the creative team and Rafael.

"Unfortunately, yes. I wish I could have my first visit with Cameron be smooth. With Rafe around, I doubt it will be." Blake quickly noticed, and straightened, a crooked stack of sweaters as the pair walked onto the sales floor.

"Oh, Cameron's usually pretty cool. I forgot this was your first visit with him. He's been busy dealing with plans for the London store, and the new fragrance. Hasn't been out here much this past year."

"I know."

"Well, it's show time." Kelly giggled as she straightened her cute Cameron Fuller day dress. In a bright print of yellow and green it showed off her recently acquired Cabo San Lucas vacation tan. Her low-heeled Manolo Blahniks clacked on the polished wood floor as she walked with Blake. The store was now open, and customers were coming in through the heavy plate glass doors and a few already had clothes on hangers in their hands.

"See you at lunch?" Blake headed towards the stairwell and his basement level office.

"You bet. By the way, why *were* you late?"

Blake blushed.

Seeing the color spread across his handsome face, Kelly knew there was a good story to be told. "Oh, *you!*" She laughed. "You *will* tell me all about it at lunch," she threatened, wagging her middle finger at him.

Blake just smiled and went down the stairs.

Despite having to deal with Rafael, Blake really did love his job. His position at Cameron Fuller was a prestigious one, and he got to be creative all day long. As a kid, Blake had always had to be making something. Creating something.

He built elaborate cities in the backyard for his sister's Barbies and his own G.I. Joes, though he secretly preferred the Barbies (they had better outfits). Then, he would level these fanciful cities in pretend earthquakes. He had built pretend cable cars out of empty shoe boxes and strung up yarn all over the house to slide them on, driving his mother half insane.

And now, he got paid to build sets and dress mannequins. He liked to joke that he finally was getting paid to play with six-foot Barbies all day.

His main responsibilities for the store were coming up with window display concepts, planning them out, sketching them, cost-estimating them, budgeting them, and overseeing their construction and final installation.

After Blake came up with a concept, he would then compile a "window presentation book." This presentation would contain an explanation of the inspiration for the window concept, sketches of what the final windows would look like, paint and fabric samples, mannequin recommendations, and a detailed budget breakdown. Blake would send this presentation off to Rafael, and wait for the revisions to come back.

And they *always* did.

Sometimes Blake would have to redesign one set of windows four or five times before Rafael finally approved them. Even then, when Rafe saw the finished windows, he would usually bitch about some small detail, claiming that he had not approved it.

Blake still grimaced when he remembered designing and getting full approval from Rafe to build some "Greek isles" windows that were to highlight the last "holiday" men's collection. After Blake had spent forty-five thousand dollars and countless hours building a replica of a contemporary Greek villa with white stone walls, custom-made washed linen cushions on the faux stone benches, and stunning gauzy blue-striped billowing curtains to hang in the fake wood window frames set in the faux walls that stretched over all six Rodeo Drive-fronting windows, Rafe had paid a surprise visit and demanded that they be ripped out and changed to a "W" Hotel theme in twenty-four hours.

Blake and his team had had to repaint everything, strip out the curtains, get new white covers made for the benches, buy new mod small tables and chairs, and put in hastily purchased light fixtures to make the windows more modern.

Up for twenty-six straight hours, Blake made the new deadline with thirty-three minutes to spare. It had cost an additional fourteen thousand dollars to get it done. Rafe hadn't cared about the toll on the creative services team, or the expense. He just wanted the windows changed. All because he had spent the previous week at the W Hotel in Waikiki, and thought it stylish.

Blake went through some variation of this madness every six weeks.

He was also was in charge of the third floor Home Arena. He was responsible for making sure it was stocked with product, assuring that the displays always looked fresh and exciting, maintaining the floral arrangements, replacing sold off merchandise, and supervising the twice-yearly room change.

Actually, it was the perfect job for a compulsive-obsessive gay man.

As Blake breezed into the creative services office, he saw Chelsea Watkins and Dusty Stricklin sitting at the large open table thumbing through the new issue of *Vogue*. The creative services office was actually a large open space Spencer had commandeered from storage. A vast room, it held his desk and the desks of his crew, plus a multitude of mannequins, fixtures, clothes racks, and props. Highly crowded and cramped, it was chock-full of fantastic things that always made people stare in wonder the first time they entered this special place.

"Morning, ladies and gentlemen," he said, sinking into Spencer's Aeron chair at his overflowing desk.

"Good morning, Blake," the two said in unison, as if he were Charlie and they were the angels.

"Whatcha doin'?"

"Looking at the spread on Cameron's spring collection in *Vogue*. He got amazing coverage. The clothes look great, and they got Gwyneth Paltrow to wear them. Yow. There's even a few shots of her with your favorite, Travis Church," Dusty teased. Dusty was a lanky Texan with dirty blond hair who had worked with Blake at Bloomingdale's. A good hard worker, Blake had convinced him to join the team at Cameron Fuller.

"Well, let me see that!" Blake rolled his chair over, and pored through the pages.

Blake had often joked that the only man for him was Travis Church, the ultra-hot actor who starred in the new hit UBC sitcom *Us Two,* and who had gotten his start on the steamy daytime drama *Sunset Cove*. Travis looked amazing in the formfitting clothes for spring.

"I remember when he came in here a few weeks ago," Chelsea said, pointing an orange-painted fingernail at a hot photo of Travis lying on his back on a poolside chaise longue, shirt unbuttoned, pants half unzipped. "Such a nice person. He was with that other soap guy, Clay Beasley, from *The Insiders*. Two *very* handsome men."

Blake smiled. He knew Clay from the gym. And he knew that Travis and Clay were lovers. It was an open secret in West Hollywood circles.

So, alas, Travis would never be his.

After gawking at the sexy editorial for a few minutes, Blake had to crack the whip.

"Okay. Let's get to work . . ."

5

Suzette Fuller strolled down Madison Avenue listlessly looking at the window displays of the pricey stores. It was an uncommonly mild winter day in the city, and the Prada cashmere wrap coat she wore so beautifully was perfect for the temperate weather. Hands in her coat pockets, head held high, and with a slight breeze blowing her hair back, she was the jaunty epitome of a chic New Yorker.

The sun was out, shining bright, and her large black sunglasses shielded her eyes, not only from its harsh rays, but also from connecting with anyone who passed her. She sensed that she was being recognized by many of the people passing her on the busy sidewalk, but her body language and attitude kept them from interrupting her mission. She was simply not in the mood to play celebrity today.

She had let her car and driver go after her lunch with Liz Smith, because she wanted to walk down her favorite street and browse. This was her secret form of personal therapy. She would study the clothes and displays, her expert eye calculating how each garment would look on her, or where she would place an interesting antique in one of her four homes.

But, today, the therapy wasn't working for her. Her private thoughts were far from the dazzling and expensive baubles she was strolling past. She could not stop thinking about one person.

Cameron.

Sighing heavily, she tried to force her scattered thoughts to solidify. She didn't hate her husband. She knew he thought that, and right now it was okay with her. It was easier to deal with *that* than the actual truth.

Their marriage was over, and she was savvy enough to realize it. In fact, she was surprised they had stayed together as long as they had. The common denominator they had shared as young twenty-somethings was now a faded relic, much like a photograph turned yellow with age. Their common love had seemed a good enough reason to get married on that long-ago spring day, but now, in hindsight, Suzette saw that she had spent the best part of her life with a man who hadn't given her the things she needed most.

She had only goaded Cameron this morning because that was the pattern they had fallen into, and it made her feel temporarily better about her tenuous position in his life. Lately, she couldn't help but notice her husband's excitement about his future life. A life that *wouldn't include her.* That stung terribly, and she repeatedly lashed out at him.

Despite what most people thought, Suzette Fuller did possess a conscience, and the slight pangs of guilt she felt about her behavior this morning *almost* made her vow not to treat Cameron that way again. However, Suzette knew herself too well. She recognized that she was simply irrational when it came to her husband. The arguments would happen again, so why make a promise she already knew she wouldn't keep?

She stepped up to another store window and wearily peered in, gazing at the beautiful clothes. Her initial excitement about the window shopping excursion was fast declining as she contemplated her life. She sighed heavily again.

Added to her misery was the fact that her father was going to be forced out of the company soon, and she didn't know what to do to stop it. Everything seemed so out of her control. And Suzette liked to be in control at all times.

She was also cross that she had to fly to L.A. this afternoon. If she didn't have an eyebrow appointment scheduled for tomorrow in Beverly Hills, she would have canceled her participation in the trip. The thought of spending two days with her husband in Los Angeles was simply too grim to ponder. She knew exactly what would happen: behind closed doors, they would fight, they would scream; well, she would scream, he would just stand there like a dullard and look hurt, and then they would pretend everything was fine and dandy in public. It would be too grueling for words.

The only good thing about this little junket was that, for two days, Cameron wouldn't be able to fuck whoever it was he was seeing on the side. That thought made her smile cruelly. She knew her husband was having an affair. Suzette didn't know who Cameron was sleeping with, but she'd sniff the answer out. She'd found out about the other three, hadn't she?

Her attention was suddenly drawn to a mother and daughter arguing as they walked by her. "They make you look like a prostitute," the mother hissed at her daughter, pointing down to the young girl's tight low-rise jeans.

"Oh, Mother," sighed the exasperated teen.

In a rare moment of self-reflection, Suzette paused to wonder: what kind of relationship would she have had with her own beautiful, cultured mother? Had Clarice Cabbott lived, would they fight and bicker, like the mother and daughter who just passed her? Or would they have had the relationship Suzette had longed for, one of love and respect and nurturing? More important, what kind of mother would she herself have been? Would her own children love her . . .

"No!" Suzette chastised herself out loud, startling the pretzel vendor she was passing. She had almost broken her cardinal, sacred rule. Suzette never—*never*—allowed herself to think about the babies she never had. It was just too painful.

Shaking her head to clear it of ruminations best not undertaken, she quickly returned her attention to thoughts of her husband. And life after he left.

Despite her strong, take-no-prisoners demeanor, if Suzette Cabbott Fuller were forced to confess her darkest secret, it would surprise everyone. She was absolutely terrified to see what her life would become when she was no longer Mrs. Cameron Fuller. Who would she be? All her life she had been either Silas Cabbott's screwup daughter, or Stanton Cabbott's tag-along sister, or Cameron Fuller's shrew of a wife.

Perhaps that is why I'm so crazy when it comes to Cameron, she mused as she approached an exclusive jewelry store. Scared to let go of a bad situation, she held on tightly to something that didn't work, because the alternative was so frightening to face: an uncertain future. That was why she was being so greedy when it came to splitting up the property and houses. If she demanded too much, it would stall the proceedings, buying her more precious time to figure out what to do next.

In her more lucid and calm moments, Suzette realized that she and Cameron simply didn't work as a couple anymore, and that they had to move on. Wouldn't it be better? Wouldn't her true life begin, then? Wouldn't she then be able to find some happiness for herself with someone who would love her completely and totally?

But, then again, the thought of her husband in the arms of another drove her insane with anger. He was marked territory. *Her* territory. The fact that she herself was no stranger to adultery, had had many sizzling affairs during her marriage, didn't register as hypocritical to her. In Suzette's egocentric reasoning, it was perfectly fine for her to seek comfort outside the bounds of matrimony, but not for him. After all, hadn't she always been there for him? For over twenty-five years? He wouldn't be the man he was without her! When she considered this, Cameron being with someone else, Suzette usually flew into an unstoppable rage, and would furiously vow to *never* let him go.

So, the woman who was always in control, the woman who never questioned herself or her decisions, flip-flopped back and forth on the most important issue of her life like a petulant six-year-old. One moment she was fine with Cameron leaving, the next not. The eternal drama of it all was wearing her down. She wasn't sleeping well, she popped tranquilizers as if they were candy, and her already sour demeanor reached testy new depths. She was redefining the word "bitch," and knew it, but simply didn't care.

"Isn't that Suzette Fuller?" she heard a female voice whisper nearby.

Glancing up, Suzette saw two matronly women with bad perms ambling slowly past her, checking her out, but trying hard not to show they were checking her out.

"Yes, it is! She's so . . . slim!" replied the other woman, a tad jealous. "And so pretty . . ." Then they were gone, melted into the jostling, faceless crowd strolling the sidewalk.

Suzette ruefully half-smiled and returned to staring at the display window she was in front of. She lived a blessed life, and was the envy of millions of women. She was wealthy, famous, and, finally, beautiful. But none of it was due to her own efforts. She was who she was because of the hard work of either her father or Cameron. On her own, she had done nothing of value except get married. It was so very different from what she had planned on as a small girl.

She almost chuckled recalling that she had wanted to be a vet. She had *loved* horses when she was little, and she had spent hours in the stables of her father's country house grooming and tending the five horses they kept there. Her equestrian skills were average, but under the tutelage of several top trainers, she actually began to win ribbons in the prestigious horse shows of her set. It had been the happiest time of her life.

Standing in front of the deluxe jewelry store, as the midday traffic honked and whizzed past, Suzette no longer saw the diamond and pearl necklace she had been gazing at. Instead, in her mind's eye, she saw herself, eleven years old and sitting atop Camelot, her favorite childhood horse . . .

The strikingly pretty child in the perfectly tailored riding habit was dusty from her exertions, and her ponytail had come loose. Flyaway strands of dark hair fluttered in the breeze as she watched her father and brother slowly stride up to her. Clutching her hard-won ribbon proudly, Suzette held her head high and smiled from ear to ear.

A tall, impressive figure with the dignified manner of a man comfortable with his position in life, Silas Cabbott more often than not terrified the hell out of his daughter. He approached her stiffly, his hands clasped behind his back. His coat and tie were impeccable, as always, and his cold eyes scanned his offspring on her perch on the chestnut mare.

"Look, Daddy! Look, Stanny! Look what I got!" Suzette excitedly exclaimed, holding out the pretty long ribbon.

With barely a movement Silas indicated he saw it. "Third place." It was said with all the disdain he felt toward his daughter.

"But, Daddy . . ." the young girl tried to explain.

Silas cut her off brusquely. "I had to stand in those bleachers, next to the Bromptons and Ambassador Smith, and watch you let that horse have his head all over the course. It was a dismal display, Suzette. Barrett and Rosemarie have worked with you and worked

with you, and that's the result? You should consider yourself lucky that you got the ribbon that you did. You certainly deserved worse."
Her father hadn't noticed the sudden effect his harsh words had on his daughter. Her shoulders slumped and the proffered ribbon was slowly pulled away and hidden behind her back. "Third place is simply not good enough, Suzette. Cabbotts do not come in third." During this lecture, Silas grew even stiffer, and a bit taller. "I don't ever want to see you come in third again. Do you understand me, young lady? If you can't win, or do it right, you won't do it at all. Stanton has never come in third in anything in his life, have you, son?" Silas wrapped a loving arm around his handsome son.

"No, Daddy," Stanton replied.

Nodding proudly at his son first, Silas then looked back at his daughter. "I think it's time to accept that equestrian events aren't your strong suit, Suzette. Let's find something—anything else—that you can excel at, besides embarrassing me."

"No, Daddy! I love horses! I'll do better! I promise!" Suzette pleaded, hot tears filling her eyes.

"No, Suzette. You simply aren't good enough. It's a waste of my money and your trainer's time." He turned around, showing her his back, signaling the conversation was over.

Suzette fought to keep the tears from falling. "But, Daddy . . ."

Silas whipped around, his face a mask. "I said no. This was your last show." He started to walk away, but stopped and looked back at her. "Oh, do stop sniffling, Suzette," he commanded. "Look at you. You're a mess. Comb your hair! You're covered in dirt. You're a Cabbott, for God's sake! Act like one! If I hadn't witnessed your birth, I swear to God, I'd think there was a mixup at the hospital . . ." he let the sentence hang and walked away.

Stanton wiggled out from his father's grip and ran back to Suzette as she sat crying on her horse. "I thought you did great, Susie." He gave her a bright smile.

"You . . . you did?" she said, wiping her damp eyes with her sleeve.

"Yes. I thought you were the best one out there! Everyone applauded you the most."

Suzette jumped down from Camelot and rushed to hug her brother, whom she loved so much.

With a soft tranquil look on her face, caused by the memory of that tender hug, Mrs. Cameron Fuller was pulled from her reverie when someone accidentally bumped into her.

"Oh, excuse me," mumbled the tourist over his shoulder as he and his plump wife continued to plod down the sidewalk, a stiff folding map of the city held open wide in their hands.

"Well, I should hope *so,*" Suzette sniffed haughtily. Picking up her pace, she resumed her walk down the fashionable avenue. It occurred to her as she crossed Sixty-fourth street that after the infamous "third place" incident, she never again rode a horse.

6

Blake stood about fifteen feet away from the window, and, hand on chin, squinted harshly. He cocked his head to one side, then the other. Finally he waved his right hand.

Inside the window, Chelsea moved the mannequin to the right about six inches. Blake held up his hand sharply: *Stop!* She did, and he retreated another five feet back to stare again. He nodded his approval, and walked back to the main front doors.

He raced through the foyer and around the planters to the hidden access door that led into the the roomy display windows. Each of the six windows was over fifteen feet tall and ten feet wide. It was eight feet from the thick plate glass window to the back wall of the display space. Tracks for spotlights and floodlights hugged the interior lip of the fly walls, and there were also tracks overhead for downward pointing light cans.

These six boxes truly were Blake's world.

The concept for the windows they were working on this night centered on the newly arrived spring collections—a sort of "introduction" to them.

The spring runway shows had just been held in New York the week before. So, large, blown-up photographs of the models strutting down the runway had been framed in enormous burl wood frames and hung on the cream-colored flannel-covered back wall. In each of the six windows, a single Adele Rootstein mannequin was placed offset to the large portrait in the same outfit seen in the photograph. Simple cream-colored stickers would go on the front of the glass saying:

CAMERON FULLER

MANHATTAN LABEL

SPRING

A very simple, classic window, signature Cameron Fuller.

Unfortunately, the upholsterer had been late finishing the flannel walls this afternoon, so here it was, one o'clock in the morning, and Blake and Chelsea were still tweaking the mannequins into place.

The day had been unbelievably long. The team had worked steadily all day prepping the store for Cameron's visit. They had finished up in women's by eleven-thirty, and after letting Kelly and her helpers leave, Blake and Chelsea spent the remaining time in the windows. They would surely be there for at least another two hours.

But it had to be done. Cameron was due in at opening time tomorrow, and things had to be perfect for him.

Rafael had been in the store all afternoon driving everyone crazy with his endless list of things that had to be done. He had left explicit instructions on how he wanted the windows to look, then had fled the store precisely at five to hit happy hour at Rage, a gay bar and dance club on Santa Monica Boulevard. He told Blake his plan was to pick up some young stud and have a wild night in his Chateau Marmont suite.

Blake climbed the short step on the left side of the entrance foyer, and into the first window, passing through that one into the next, and finally into the third one, the one where Chelsea was working.

"Looks perfect there. Pull her jacket back a bit here," he demonstrated, pushing the mannequin's light wool cream-colored blazer back off its hip. "And find a thin necklace over in jewelry. She needs a spot of shine."

Chelsea yawned. "Okay." She had been playing around with this mannequin's clothes for the past half hour. The outfit or "rig" as it was known in the business, was a cream-colored leather miniskirt, a lime green silk blouse, and the blazer. Cream leather pumps and a large handbag completed the look.

"I think we're set on the women's side. I want you to recheck the lights here while I start on men's."

"Okay." She turned to get a ladder that was leaning up against the back upholstered wall. "Where do you want the pin spot aimed?" she asked.

"On the blouse. I want to punch the color," Blake replied as he leapt down to the floor.

"You got it." Chelsea was soon clambering up the ladder to adjust the lights, and thus she missed seeing the black limousine pull up and stop outside the store.

Blake didn't notice it either, and he climbed up into the other bank of windows, on the opposite side of the entrance hall. He had pulled his hair back into a ponytail with one of the many elastics he kept stuffed in his pocket.

He manhandled the bulky men's mannequin into place, and using a power screwdriver, screwed the form's floor mounting plate into place through the carpeted floor. From this steel plate, a twelve-inch-high metal rod rose up, to be fitted into a slot in the mannequin's ankle. The plate and rod support kept the body from falling over.

Satisfied the mannequin was in position, Blake walked out of the window, through the foyer, and out the glass front doors into the street. He stood in front of the window, squinting at it, trying to decide if the look was right.

So intent was Blake on his windows that he didn't even notice the tall man leaning against the limo watching him. Blake took a few steps back, getting some distance between him and the window display, and studied it critically for a minute or two.

"Try pivoting the body about a quarter turn to the left. His stance will have more attitude that way," called out the leaning figure.

Startled, Blake spun around to face the man. In the dim light of Rodeo Drive's streetlights, it was hard to clearly see him. Blake's first response was going to be "Huh?" but, before the words could come out of his mouth, he realized the stranger was right. He looked back at the display and calculated the amount of turn he would need to make.

"Thanks," he called back to the man. "You're right. You in the biz?"

"Sort of," chuckled the stranger. He started to move toward Blake. "Why don't you go back in and I'll let you know when you hit the right turn," he offered.

As he came closer, and into the direct light of the street lamp, Blake realized who he was.

"Uh, sure, Mr. Fuller," he stammered, flustered.

"Please. Call me Cameron. Or Cam." The famous designer stood waiting. "Go on, hop in. I've helped do this sort of thing before." He grinned easily.

Blake moved. Quickly.

Suddenly very nervous, he ran back into the building and jumped up to the window access door, then ran through to the window box. Seeing Cameron outside through the glass, he bent down and pivoted the mannequin around until he saw Cameron put up his hands. *There!* He watched Cameron back up a few feet and study the display.

Damn! Who would ever believe this? Blake thought. *Cameron Fuller helping me do windows!*

Cameron held up his hand in the "okay" sign, and motioned for Blake to come outside and join him.

Blake did.

"Looks good. We just did this exact same display at the main Soho Warehouse store. Looks good there. Looks good here," Cameron complimented.

"Thank you, Mr. Fu . . . Cam." Blake beamed. This was a thrill. And who knew that Cameron Fuller was so fucking handsome in person?

Cameron gazed at the window dresser standing nervously next to him. "I have on that same shirt," he said, pointing at Blake's chest.

Blake was still wearing the CF/Active flannel shirt he'd worn all day, though It had come untucked from his jeans in places from his exertions. Blake shot a glance at Cam and noticed he did indeed have on the exact same shirt. Only his was neatly tucked in, and covered by a sheered lamb's wool short jacket. Cam also had on faded Montana Rough Wear Jeans and a pair of scuffed work boots. He looked like an ad for . . . himself.

"Well, it looks better on you than it does on me," Blake said, truthfully.

"Hardly, but thanks for complimenting an old man." Cameron smiled his trademark toothy grin.

Blake held out his hand. "I'm Blake, by the way. I do the windows and the Home Arena," he explained.

"Ah, yes, Rafe told me about you. Said you were doing a bang-up job. I can't wait to see what you've done upstairs."

There was an awkward pause. "So," Blake said, "what are you doing out here at one-thirty in the morning?"

"My wife and I just got in a couple of hours ago. I slept on the plane, and now I'm not tired. Time changes always screw me up. Thought I'd come down and look at the store before everyone is running around trying to impress me. I like it when things are quiet. I didn't think there'd be anyone here. Why are *you* working so late?"

"We have a grand poohbah visit tomorrow," Blake said, grinning. "And we didn't get these clothes in until today, the upholsterer ran late, blah, blah, blah."

"I understand completely."

"Well, I should get back in and finish them so you're properly impressed tomorrow," Blake said.

"Why don't I help you?"

Blake wasn't sure he heard right. "What?"

"Why don't I help you? I used to do this all the time back in the old days when we opened the first store. I always liked it. I'm wide awake. Let me help you."

Was this a joke? Cameron Fuller, grunting in the windows to prep for a visit by himself? Blake didn't know what to say. So he said what he felt.

"We can always use an extra pair of hands."

Cameron looked back at his limo. "Do you have a car here?"

"Uh, yes, in the garage. Why?"

Cameron motioned to his driver. "I'll send him back to the hotel. You can drop me off. Is that okay?" He faced Blake, and his violet eyes shone brightly.

"Of course, of course." As he watched Cameron Fuller speak to his driver, Blake happened to see Chelsea standing in her window, mouth hanging open in disbelief.

Two hours later, Blake and Cameron were finishing off the last window. They had let Chelsea go an hour earlier, and the two of them were wrestling a male body into place, only it just never looked right. They tried ten different positions, and nothing seemed to work. Finally deciding the pose of the mannequin was the problem, Blake went and dug up a different form while Cameron stripped down the one they'd been working on.

Blake stumbled in lugging the awkwardly stiff form, and Cameron, noticing his struggle, went to help. Together they dragged it over into position. In the action of doing this, Blake's hand briefly touched the top of Cam's, who, curiously, didn't move it away.

Sweating profusely from the exertion, the two men took a five-minute breather.

"I forgot how hard this all is. Remind me to get you a raise," Cameron puffed.

"Don't think I won't," Blake responded, breathing hard himself. He motioned to the new mannequin. "I think this one works much better. We'll be out of here in twenty minutes, I promise."

"No sweat. I've enjoyed this. Really." He smiled warmly at Blake, who blushed a shade.

They had spent the last two hours working, talking, laughing. It was surprisingly easy to talk to him, marveled Blake. The man was a millionaire, if not yet a billionaire, and he was as down to earth as anyone he'd ever met. Not only that, he was a hard worker. Blake would have hired him any day.

And those eyes!

Damn those eyes. They mesmerized Blake. The color, the way they saw everything. In fact, everything about Cam was attractive to Blake. Not that it would do any good.

While there were the standard rumors swirling around Cameron Fuller, simply because he was in the rag trade, no one had ever come up with definite proof that he walked both sides of the street. He was married, and apparently happily so, to the same woman for the past twenty-five years. Never a hint of scandal, never talk of extramarital affairs.

"Well, speaking of sweat," Blake said, lifting his arms and seeing the dark circles forming near his armpits, "I'm burning up. These lights are so damn hot."

"I know. Me, too," Cameron agreed. He had long since ditched the jacket along with his flannel shirt. He was working now in an extremely white V-neck tee. A tight tee that showed off his amazing upper body, Blake had noted.

In fact, being in close proximity to such a virile man had turned

Blake on big time. He wondered if it would be inappropriate to call up Brady on the way home, try to sneak in a quick one.

"You look good sweaty," Cameron noted, his tone intelligible. "Like a model. Have you ever done that? Model?"

Blake laughed. "No. People always told me I should, but it never really interested me."

"You should reconsider. You have a great face, a fantastic body, and you move well. You'd be a sensation at it."

"I'll take that under advisement. As it is, I have a job, and one I might lose if Rafael doesn't like what he sees tomorrow."

"You leave Rafe to me. He'll love it. I promise."

There was a charge in the tiny room, one that Blake had trouble defining.

Was Cameron Fuller coming on to him?

Not possible, he told himself.

But, *was* he?

And if so, what was Blake going to do?

Cameron broke the mood by going back to work. Blake did likewise.

Thirty-three minutes later, they were in Blake's Cherokee heading toward the Beverly Hills Hotel. It was four-fourteen in the morning and traffic was practically nonexistent. Blake drove in silence while Cam stared dully out the window.

"Listen," Cameron finally said. "Thanks for letting me help you. I really enjoyed that. You have no idea how much." He gazed at Blake with such a look of intensity that Blake had a hard time pulling away from his stare.

"No, I should thank you. All the changes you made? Perfect. You really know what you're doing."

Chuckling, Cameron said, "Tell that to my investors."

"Well, it was my privilege. No one will believe it when I tell them."

"Oh, don't tell them. Anyone," Cameron said directly. "Let's keep this between you and me."

Not understanding the meaning, but knowing he'd better do as requested, Blake nodded.

"It's just that I get so few opportunities to play. When it does happen, I like to keep it for myself. Private, you know?"

"No problem."

They were fast approaching the hotel. Cameron put a hand on Blake's thigh. "Do me a favor. Pull down this street. I'd rather walk back up to the hotel. It's a beautiful night."

Surprised at the odd request, Blake did as instructed, and steered the Cherokee over and down the next cross street. He pulled over to the side and placed the SUV in park. It was a completely dark street, and the only view was of a long, tall, impenetrable hedge that ran about four hundred feet next to the street, down to the next driveway. They were all alone.

"Thanks again, Blake. I had a great time. It's not too often I get dirty and sweaty like that. I really needed it," Cameron said sincerely.

Blake noticed that Cam had still not removed his hand from his thigh. Finding it strangely hard to speak, Blake merely nodded in agreement.

"And now, I guess I'll head in," Cameron murmured softly.

Yet, he just sat there.

Blake realized he had stopped breathing. His heart was racing.

Then, as if both men had discussed it in minute detail earlier, they leaned in to each other in perfect unison and pressed lips to lips.

Blake actually felt an electrical charge course through his body as the pressure on his lips grew harder. He allowed Cam's tongue to enter his mouth, and in return, he followed suit. He felt warm, trembling hands come up to his face and pull him closer. Soft groans came from both of them as they made out like teenagers in the front seat of Blake's car.

Blake boldly reached down, and tugging on Cam's compressed hard-on, maneuvered it around until it was freed and straight up inside the worn denim. Then he allowed his hand to rub up and down, first hard, then softly, and then hard again. Cam's heavy breathing gave away his pleasure, and spurred Blake on.

"Oh, you have to stop . . . I'm so close . . ." Cameron uttered, but he did nothing to move away.

"I can't stop," Blake replied between kisses.

"I wanted this . . . God, you're so damn sexy . . ." Cameron reached a hand over the center console and grabbed at Blake's erection.

"You, too! I can't believe I'm . . . *mmmm* . . ." He reacted strongly to

Cam's rubbing. Blake redoubled his efforts, his hand fluidly rubbing up and down against the hard zipper and worn cloth. He could feel the tremors in Cam's body as he gave himself over to the sensations.

Cameron let out a low muffled cry, then convulsed in slow twitches. He didn't make another sound as he ejaculated in the denim. He just closed his eyes tightly and grimaced.

Blake, close himself, pulled back and let himself calm down.

"Oh, my God," whispered Cameron as he caught his breath. He turned to Blake sharply, and taking Blake's face in his hands, gave him a deep, lingering kiss that conveyed both his excitement and gratitude. "I have to see you again," he said urgently.

"Oh, man. Cam, this just got out of hand. Aren't you *married?* I don't think I . . ."

"No! Don't say no, please. Let me take you to dinner tonight. We'll talk. I'll tell you everything. Things aren't always what they seem. Please? See me. Please?" the famous designer pleaded.

How could Blake say no?

"Yes. Okay. I'd like that, too," he admitted.

Cameron broke out into a huge smile, and adjusting himself, opened the door and started to get out. "I'll see you at the store tomorrow?"

"You bet. Big day."

Cameron smiled. "I hope it is." He gave a slight wave, and shut the door.

Blake sank back into his seat and watched the retreating figure of Cameron Fuller walk up the hillside to the hotel entrance.

Several hundred yards away, in a private, unmarked bungalow of the hotel, Suzette sat up in bed, her back resting on a flotilla of soft down pillows. She glanced at the clock again. With each passing minute, her anger grew. She reached over, picked up the remote, and clicked off the TV.

Sighing in frustration, she tossed the electronic device aside as she looked around the spacious bedroom of the bungalow for the thousandth time. Pink and green. The entire bungalow was decorated in pale peach and sea foam green.

Suzette hated it. It was so . . . *California.* The deco touches of the exclusive suite of rooms also angered her. The round curves and beveled detailing that were the trademark of the luxury hotel set her teeth on edge. She needed clean lines, hard edges, and a sleek palette of creams and beiges.

How am I supposed to sleep inside a goddam avocado, she seethed inwardly. *And where the fuck is Cameron?*

He'd left her hours ago, after their late supper in the Polo Lounge, and after yet another argument, to go check out the Rodeo Drive store for a few minutes. She could easily pick up the phone and call him on his cell, but she chose not to do so. Why let him know she cared? Besides, it was more satisfying to get angry.

Realizing that he probably wouldn't be coming back tonight, Suzette settled back into the pillows and prepared herself for the darkness. *I wonder if he just took another suite to avoid me,* she thought. *It wouldn't be the first time he's done that.*

Deciding that had to be the answer, Suzette prepared herself for what little sleep she would get. Breathing in deeply three times, she slowly reached her hand out and found the switch on the bedside lamp. Closing her eyes tightly, she turned her wrist, clicking off the light.

Now bathed in darkness, Suzette snuggled down under the covers. She had left the bathroom door ajar, with the light on in there, but the illumination was dim. She opened and closed her eyes three times, just to check the light levels, and reasonably comfortable with the amount of light creeping into her bedroom, she finally allowed her body to relax.

Suzette Cabbott Fuller had a deathly fear of the dark.

Ever since she was a little girl, she had hated the dark. She would scream and cry if the lights were turned off in her room. Nannies and governesses quickly learned always to leave at least one light on. Silas knew of Suzette's terror, but instead of being sympathetic, he perceived it as a cowardly trait in his daughter. When he found out the staff was coddling his child by allowing her to give in to her fears, he ordered them not only to turn off each and every light every night but to install blackout curtains in her room as well.

No child of his was going to grow up fearful of anything.

So Suzette's cheery lavender and white room became a black void after bedtime. She would whimper and cower under her bedcovers, shaking from fright every night. It was only after Stanton would sneak in and crawl into bed with her, softly calming her, that she would stop crying and relax. She could sleep only if he was there, hugging her tight, protecting her from the monsters that surely lay in wait.

Cameron knew of her deep-seated fear, and he had filled the void left when Stanton died. She could sleep knowing he was next to her, warding off the bad things. When he wasn't beside her, she rarely slept. Instead she tossed and turned as old traumas bubbled to the surface.

He's doing this on purpose, she decided. *He knows I can't sleep without him here, so he's staying away just to spite me!*

Working herself into a state, Suzette was just about to turn the bedside light back on when she heard a clicking sound come from the front room, the living room. Instantly alert, she strained to hear what it was, her heart racing. The sounds of the front door opening and then softly closing were sweet relief to her. Cameron was back. Thank God.

When the famous fashion designer walked into the bedroom of the bungalow, he found his wife sound asleep, under the 350 thread count sheets. Exhaling gently from relief that a scene was going to be avoided, he went into the bathroom, stripped off his clothes, including the newly stained jeans, and brushed his teeth.

When he was through, Cameron was careful not to shut the bathroom door completely, leaving a decent amount of secondary light to enter the bedroom. He padded naked to the king size bed and slipped under the sheets. Turning on his side, away from his wife, he thought happily about the amazing man he had just met and what he had allowed to happen.

He was revitalized, feeling that something wonderful was about to happen to his life. He had given in to his passion and for once did not regret it. No, he was surprised to discover, he was looking forward to further explorations with Blake Jackson. He grew rock hard as erotic thoughts of the handsome window dresser aroused and tantalized him.

Sleep did not come quickly to Cameron.

It did not come quickly to Suzette, either. Each of her five senses on high alert, she had feigned sleep as her husband prepared for bed, done for no other reason than she just didn't want to have an accusatory screaming match just before bedtime.

She could sense an almost electrical charge in the room, clearly emanating from Cameron. Something unexpected had happened to him, she was sure of it, but what?

He was practically bursting with energy, a contented aura about him. Her eyes flew open in shock when a terrible certainty suddenly popped into her mind. *He didn't go to the store at all,* she realized. *He's been whoring around!* She had just closed her eyes when a new, horrible thought came to her:

What if his new secret lover was here in L.A.?

Sleep completely forgotten, she began to plot strategies to uncover the truth, and decide what she would do about it. The first thing she had to do was find out who Cameron was seeing. That would be easy.

The harder part was figuring out how to stop it.

7

The elevator doors opened on the executive floor of Cameron Fuller USA, and a trio of extremely well dressed men exited the car. Each of them was wearing a Cameron Fuller Manhattan Label suit, in varying shades of gray, and each was carrying a shiny black leather briefcase. An aura of power and privilege swirled around them like a fog.

Wordlessly passing the curved reception desk and the handsome young African-American man answering the phones, they walked briskly to the executive conference room. Coffee and refreshments were already laid out for them, and the room was vacant, as ordered. The men ignored the spread. One of them closed the heavy plate glass double doors. They all sat down at the expansive table.

It was a rare thing for three members of the board of investors to meet alone, and much gossiping had preceded their visit. But, now that they were safely ensconced in the well-appointed conference room, staffers purposely stayed clear of the closed doors.

The oldest of the three, Silas Cabbott, was a man pushing seventy-five, and in failing health, though he still had an air of absolute power about him. He looked at the others gravely.

He was almost completely bald, though a few stray tufts of snow white hair were slicked down in their proper place. His posture was still ramrod straight, though he moved more slowly each day. Liver spots marred his thin skin and his eyes were a cold shade of pale blue. His physical appearance was deceiving. His mind was still as sharp and focused as it was when he was twenty.

People often made the mistake of underestimating Silas Cabbott.

They only did it once.

He pulled out a black leather portfolio from his briefcase. The other two men quickly followed suit, each extracting an identical portfolio from his briefcase.

Silas opened his portfolio with purpose. "Gentlemen, I'd like to make this meeting brief. As you know, sales have been declining this quarter, following the trend of the last *two* quarters." His steely eyes scanned the sheaf of papers that he held in his weathered hands. "Cameron promised an upswing that hasn't materialized."

"I noticed that the Home Arena has showed absolutely remarkable growth," said one of the other men, a spongy looking man with recently implanted hair-plugs named Harrison Howell. He was pointing a well-manicured, stubby finger to a page of paper filled with long columns of numbers. "We have triple digit increases across the board there, and they more than make up for the losses in sportswear and collection."

Silas gritted his teeth, and snapped, "Yes, I'm aware of that!" The force of the statement from the elder gentleman startled the other two men. Not accustomed to letting his true feelings show, the old man took a deep breath and regained his cold demeanor. He would need these men's help. He decided to try another tack. "What about this constant battle with Suzette? If he can't control his household, how can he expect to control his company?"

"Silas, Suzette has always been . . . strong-willed. You can hardly fault Cameron," Dillard Jordan, the third man, reluctantly piped up. He had known Suzette for over twenty-seven years. They had gone to the same college, and had moved in the same circles there. He was also one of Cameron Fuller's oldest friends.

At forty-seven, Dillard was the youngest of the three executives gathered, and much like he did in life, he tried to fade as far into the background as possible. It was almost impossible to do.

Especially in light of his circumstances these days.

Eight months ago, he had kicked his lover of seven-and-a-half years out. In an act of retaliation, his ex-lover was suing him in family court for palimony, claiming Dillard had promised him financial security for life. The lawsuit was being considered a watershed case in the arena of gay rights, and arguments on both sides of the issue had been cropping up in the papers lately. Dillard was mortified to find his previously quiet life splashed about for public consumption, as if it were a soap opera.

A true marketing genius, Dillard had helped propel Cameron Fuller USA to the top by his strong business sense. He had invested in the expanding company early on, and was considered one of the most powerful members of the board. He had championed the internet to Cameron, and had been extremely influential in the design and marketing of the Cameron Fuller website. At first, the website was just an information source. A year ago, it had become interactive, and now they got over three thousand hits a day, with a large percentage of them ordering items. Next to Cameron and Silas, he had invested the most in the company, and he relished the fact that its value kept rising each year.

Dillard had an average-looking face, but he had piercing blue eyes that accurately reflected what he was feeling at any given moment. He had been told more than once that his eyes were mesmerizing. He recently had begun an affair, and his new paramour had told him it was his eyes that cemented the deal. An avid cyclist, Dillard's greatest passion was speeding his black and blue Trek 800 Sport bike through Central Park.

It was the only time he could blot out his relationship woes.

"I *can* fault Cameron," Silas droned on. "And I do. *I* could always control my daughter, disappointment that she is. Cameron has turned out to be a soft man. I am bitterly disappointed in him, as I am in *all* soft men," he spat out, also getting in a dig at Dillard.

Silas Cabbott's displeasure with his son-in-law was well known in the almost incestuous world of fashion retail. What wasn't well known was *why*.

The truth was that Silas had admired the young Cameron when he first met him. Cameron had been a great friend to his beloved son Stanton. After Stanton's untimely and accidental death, Silas had been instantly agreeable to the idea of Suzette marrying the budding entrepreneur.

At the time, Silas thought Cameron was far too good for Suzette. Granted, he had no money, and no real family, and was a *Canadian,* for God's sake!, but he had a fire in his belly to succeed. Silas hoped that fire would rub off on his wayward daughter.

Plus, if his cherished son thought so highly of Cameron, then

Cameron must be a good man. When Cameron and Suzette informed him they were to wed, Silas secretly felt sorry for the struggling designer.

Suzette was no prize.

In Silas's learned opinion, his surviving child was an ugly, spoiled, lazy woman who had few friends. She had a coarse mouth, slatternly manners, and was notoriously promiscuous.

She was nothing like her beautiful, sainted mother. And the only thing she had in common with his beloved son Stanton was the same date of birth.

Silas Stanton Cabbott IV had been outgoing, friendly, and a terrific athlete. He was innately smart, had good common sense, and was the life of any party. He was, without a doubt, the apple of his father's eye. Stanton was everything that Suzette was not. Stanton had often abused his favored child status, but Silas could never stay angry at him for any length of time. The irony that Stanton should die so young, leaving him with his least favorite child as comfort, was not lost on Silas.

At least with Suzette's marriage to Cameron, Silas had looked forward to many grandchildren. Maybe one of them would have resembled Stanton in looks or character.

But the grandchildren never materialized.

Silas had to blame Cameron. His sluttish daughter Suzette was certainly fertile, as she had proved by the four abortions she'd had to have in her college years. His utter frustration at the situation began to color how he viewed his son-in-law.

It wasn't until last year's New Year's Eve party, following a particularly petty argument in which Silas again had felt the need to publicly review his daughter's many shortcomings, that a very drunk Suzette pulled Silas aside and tauntingly told her shocked father her marriage was a sham.

And why.

From that moment on, Silas couldn't stand to be in the same room with Cameron. The very thought that his son-in-law was *queer* infuriated him. *How typical of my idiot daughter to marry a fruit,* he had thought bitterly.

On the rare occasions when he had to be in the presence of the famous designer, such as at board functions or product launches, he endured it stoically in silence. But inwardly, he roiled.

How different things would have been, if only Stanton had lived . . .

Silas had never planned on being in the fashion business. He was an investment banker by trade, from a long line of upper crust investment bankers. The Cabbott family was one of the most respected and admired families in New York society. They were a Mayflower family, and members of the original "Astor 400." Generations of Cabbotts had contributed mightily to the proper charities, supported the correct politicians, and remained scandal-free for decades. In his day, Silas had been heralded as the best and brightest of the Cabbotts, and had performed his duties at the bank exceptionally well.

Cameron valued Silas's acute business acumen, and during a financial crisis ten years ago, when the company was teetering on the very brink of bankruptcy, Cameron had been forced to ask his obscenely wealthy father-in-law for a multimillion dollar loan. In return, he offered Silas a position on the board of investors. Begrudgingly, as a rare favor to his daughter, Silas agreed. He bailed the company out.

Silas had been retired from his vice presidency at First Manhattan Trust for several years and was lonely, and bored. His new figurehead position on the board was supposed to be in name only, but Silas quickly built up a block of investors that kowtowed to him. Soon, he and Cameron were butting heads over how to run the business. As the years passed, Silas's stature on the board grew and grew. Now, he felt it was more his company than Cameron's.

He'd been surprised to find that he actually liked the fashion business. To him, it wasn't really about the ever-changing clothing styles, something Silas just didn't understand (he was a Brooks Brothers man, through and through), but rather, it was about the dollars and cents. That was something Silas understood.

All businesses were basically the same, each one ruled by a common denominator: the bottom line. Over time, Silas's business sense had proved he knew what he was doing, and he cleverly managed to stop many of Cameron's grander ideas. Like the CF/Active sport stores Cameron desperately wanted to open in fifteen high-end malls across the country. Cameron's vision was to create a group of elegant and sleek sport boutiques in each major city. These shops would cater to his more sports-minded customers.

Silas secretly agreed the idea was sound, and would most certainly take off. But he realized that all the extra income these posh stores would generate would make it easier for Cameron to pay back his debt to him, and force him off the board. So, claiming the giant startup costs to open these boutiques would break the company, Silas had managed to squash that idea like a bug.

Silas enjoyed squashing down his son-in-law. Now more than ever.

Before entering the fashion scene, Silas had never before been around any queers, or "gay" men, as he recently learned they *insisted* they be called. In the banking world, homosexuals were deeply closeted, and if he had ever met any, he certainly didn't know it. The few that he *had* met in his life had been quickly forgotten.

There had been an ensign in the Navy during the war who was a nancy boy, but he had been killed pretty quickly during a battle in the South Pacific, so Silas, thankfully, had no real contact with him.

And if he chose to think about it, which he did not, Silas would have been able to recall a real estate tycoon neighbor in Tuxedo who had been involved in a scandalous relationship with the country club's male tennis pro. The tycoon had ended up being ostracized from the club, and eventually left his wife and five children, moving away to Key West with the pro.

The club members had been more upset by the loss of a great tennis pro than the loss of the dues-paying member.

Those two sad examples were the extent of the homosexuals that Silas had known in his life before he entered the world of fashion. And that had suited him just fine.

Silas knew that the rag trade was full of gays, and, regrettably, he now knew some personally, Dillard in particular. He made a point not to be overtly involved with them. And he certainly never socialized with them. With Silas Cabbott, it was definitely a case of "out of sight, out of mind."

However, regardless of his personal feelings about Cameron and his newly revealed homosexuality, he grudgingly admitted, even if only to himself, that Cameron had done the almost impossible: he'd made a national name for himself. National recognition was something that *did* impress Silas. And Cameron's company, despite some recent growing pains, had the potential to be a worldwide conglomerate on the same level with Ralph Lauren or Calvin Klein. Silas simply couldn't walk away from that kind of challenge, or revenue. He enjoyed the game too much. To still be considered a player at his age—well, it was intoxicating.

He would do whatever it took to keep the game going. He was well aware that the way things were going, the debt Cameron owed him would be paid up in a few months. After that, he would be forced out.

He could not allow that to happen.

Luckily, he had a plan.

"Word has it that Cameron and Suzette will separate soon after the launch of the Pacific Coast Highway fragrance line," sighed Harrison.

"Over my dead body!" Silas snorted. "We have spent millions in advertising dollars making those two 'America's Couple.' We will soon have the national rollout of those local Home Arena stores. After that, there will be the outlet store launches. Those will both be huge money drains. Even if the spring line is a complete success, Cameron's options won't be enough to pay me back. He's counting on Pacific Coast Highway to hit big and fill his coffers. We," he said as he looked at each man sternly, "must make sure that PCH is a total failure."

Both men gulped.

"After that happens, Cameron and Suzette *will* stay together as long as I . . . er, we need them to. Once I'm satisfied that I won't be leaving this board, then I'll decide if it's in my insipid daughter's best interests to be rid of Cameron, and how that will be best accomplished. To be honest? I can't decide which one of them will look worse."

The other two men shifted uncomfortably in their seats.

"And since we are on the subject of Cameron," Silas dryly continued, "let us discuss the distasteful chores that need to be done." Last night, in two separate phone calls, he had been forced to take the two board members into his confidence about the true state of his daughter's marriage, when he realized he would need a solidified power base to act from.

Harrison had been shocked. Shocked!

Dillard's reaction had surprised the old man. Dillard hadn't seemed fazed at all. Silas disgustedly chalked that up to one queer recognizing another.

In the phone calls, the old man had insisted it was in all three's best financial interests that Cameron Fuller USA continue on, business as usual, with him in control, and any threat to that had to be dealt with, and dealt with immediately. To do that, they would sabotage their own company. They would have to find a way to purposely ruin the financial success of Pacific Coast Highway.

Now, in the conference room with the elder man, Dillard braced himself. He knew he wasn't included in this small troika for his charming company. The old fossil had made it clear on several occasions that he hated, not only him personally, but also the unwanted publicity Dillard's legal problems had brought upon the company. Dillard knew that the only reason Silas had asked him here today was to ask him to do something. Something dirty.

And, whatever it was, he would have to do it.

"My plan to ruin Pacific Coast Highway has several prongs. First, I've taken the liberty of having it leaked to *Women's Wear Daily* that the focus groups hated it."

"But we got raves," Dillard said.

Silas glared at him. *"They* don't know that. And when the fragrance division gets wind of the bad press and releases the actual, positive results, it will look suspect, and no one will believe them."

Dillard sank down in his seat a little bit.

Silas continued. "Cameron still hasn't found a 'face' for the cologne, and that's good. The longer he dithers, the better. In fact, he may even miss the deadline completely. The packaging teams are screaming for artwork, and until Cameron okays a model, they have to sit on their hands." Silas almost cracked a smile at the thought of everything holding still while his fruitcake son-in-law put off making the monumental decision that could have far-reaching effects on the cologne line.

"Now, it pains me to say this . . ." Silas faltered. He found he actually had to force himself to say the words. "My daughter suspects Cameron is seeing someone on the side." Silas's mouth pursed up into a distasteful sneer. "I want to know who the catamite is. And I want it stopped! He will not humiliate my daughter, me, or our family in this fashion! I can see how life with Suzette would turn any husband to an extramarital affair, and if Cameron were a *normal* man, I would applaud him, but to sleep with another man? I won't have it! In my day, if a fellow was that way—" he looked directly at Dillard—"then he either killed himself to save his family the embarrassment, or he did things very, very discreetly. A lesson you obviously never learned," he said pointedly to Dillard.

The embarrassed investor stared at his hands.

"And so," Silas railed on, "Cameron has apparently decided to flaunt this lifestyle in our faces. Therefore, since it works to our advantage, he should pay the consequences. I want photographs! I want surveillance records! I want to know what Cameron Fuller does every moment of every day. Should matters come to a head, I want to be able to pin him to the wall! Maybe he feels he can risk the ruination of his family with his sinful ways, but I will not stand idly by while he sullies the name Cameron Fuller with his ungodly acts. A name, I might point out, that we have made into a household word, and one that stands for good old-fashioned American values! By God, even our logo is *America!*"

The two other board members sat in silence.

"So, I think this is right up your alley, Dillard. You being one of his kind. You were just in California. I'm sure you know someone there who can help with this."

"I'll take care of it," Dillard quietly assured the rabid old man, knowing instantly who he'd call on.

"See that you do."

"Silas, I do want to thank you for your support in my personal legal problems . . . uh . . . well, you understand. Thank you," Dillard mumbled, almost choking on the false words. In order to save the company from even more embarrassing publicity, Silas had given Dillard carte blanche with the Cameron Fuller USA legal team in order to help quell the horrific lawsuit with his ex-lover.

That Dillard thought Silas did this as a personal favor to him galled the old man, yet he did not correct the error. He simply held up his hand. He didn't want to acknowledge that troublesome subject anymore.

There were some other minor details that Silas wanted to cover and the meeting lasted for another twenty-five minutes. Dillard left the conference room as fast as he could, leaving Silas and Harrison alone.

"Silas, can you trust Dillard? How do you know he won't run straight to Cameron and let him know what you're doing?" Harrison asked, his botoxed forehead creasing in faint worry lines in spite of itself. "They did go to NYU together, you know. They're old friends!"

"Because if Dillard doesn't do as I say, he knows I'll let slip to the authorities the fact that he filed over six million dollars in fraudulent insurance claims last year in that 'mysterious' fire that conveniently burned down his overextended home in Bedford."

Harrison didn't know what to say to that.

The old man's wrinkled brow furrowed, and his face filled with righteous indignation. "I absolutely loathe that he's been in the papers so much with this ridiculous 'palimony' suit. As soon as I get what we need from him, I want him *gone.* I don't want the scandal of his personal legal morass to taint us one day more than necessary."

8

Blake and Chelsea were making last-minute fixes to the large flower arrangements in the foyer of the great entrance when Rafael strolled in. Almost buried in the huge arrangements of pure white lilies artfully spilling out of the exquisite blue and white antique Chinese vases, they were too busy picking out the pollen-laden stems from the giant blossoms to notice him.

Red-eyed and slightly disheveled, Rafael obviously had achieved his goal of an eventful night. Wearing his signature black on black, he was dressed in a pair of too-tight black Montana jeans and a black long-sleeved T-shirt. The visuals team all agreed Rafe stuffed his jeans with a tube sock, because he always had a prominent, and unnatural bulge at his crotch. His hair, already riddled with gray, was too long and brushed back off his face in an odd Prince Valiant sort of way.

Rafe also had developed an odd habit of wearing lots of heavy silver jewelry. Thick, chunky rings adorned several fingers and a massive link bracelet dangled from his left wrist. He also sported a matching link necklace and small silver hoops in his ear lobes. None of these embellishments did much for him. At all.

Rafe was forty-four and looked far older. He had small, beady dark eyes that missed nothing. His face still showed the scarring pockmarks of a horrible bout of childhood chicken pox and teenage acne. At five feet seven inches, he wasn't exactly tall, so he always wore thick-soled biker boots that added two inches to his stature. He was also twenty-five pounds overweight, though each week he promised he'd start a diet and exercise program that never seemed to commence.

Seeing Blake and Chelsea working diligently, he observed that the store was in perfect condition. Everything was where it should be, and the store was immaculately clean. *Blake has done a remarkable job in Spencer's absence,* Rafael hated to admit to himself.

He began to look for a flaw, just so he could point it out, and fix it, thus showing everyone how valuable and necessary his presence was. He scoured the ladies' shirts bins looking for something to bitch about.

He found it.

"These shirts aren't stacked to standards!" he bitched indignantly. "I see eight shirts here, but Cameron Fuller standards clearly state stacks of no more than seven! And this stack is crooked! Blake, come fix this quick before Cameron gets here!" The pompous little man pointed to a perfectly straight and even stack of shirts.

Not wanting to argue, and wanting Rafael to shut up, Blake went to fix the stack. He knew that now that Rafael had found a flaw, he would relax, and leave them alone. As he pulled the shirts out one by one, his mind wandered back to the events of the previous night. He had not slept well, as he was completely confused about Cameron. He was undeniably attracted to him, but how stupid was that? What good could come of it?

Chelsea joined him at the shirts.

"Where *are* you this morning? You seem a million miles away," she asked as she helped restack the shirts.

"Oh, sorry. Just a little tired from the all-nighter. By the way, you didn't tell anyone Cameron was here last night, did you?"

"Not yet," she admitted, privately wishing it was already lunchtime so she could tell everyone.

"Well, don't. He was kinda weird about it. Doesn't want anyone to know he was working in the windows. Please? Just keep it between us?" Blake implored her.

"Dang! It's such a classic story!" she said, dejected. "Fine. What time did you two leave, anyway?"

"God, about four, I think. I'm beat. As soon as this walkthrough is done and they leave, I'm gonna try and slip away and go home and sleep. You can, too. Dusty can keep Rafael company for the afternoon."

Chelsea winked. "Well, you look amazing today. You'd never know you were up almost the entire night."

Blake smiled thinly. He knew that the tight, fitted red CF America V-neck sweater hugged his buffed torso in all the right places, and the black flat front pants showed off his ass to perfection.

He had not chosen these clothes lightly.

Done with Rafael's nonexistent problem, they both turned around just in time to see the black Lincoln limo pull up out front. Blake's face went flush.

"They're here! They're here! Everyone to your stations!" Rafael squealed, clapping his hands together as he scurried out the front doors to greet Cameron and his wife.

Word spread quickly through the store that Cameron Fuller had arrived, and everyone snapped to attention and looked properly busy. Blake and Chelsea occupied themselves fluffing up the thick down throw pillows on the two large pale gray velvet sofas that faced the fireplace in the women's Manhattan Label Collection room.

Looking through the large doorway that separated the room from the grand hall, they saw Cameron and his rail-thin wife sweep in, led by a nervously chattering Rafael. Just before they passed from sight, Cameron happened to glance in their direction, and locked eyes briefly with Blake. An instant, relieved grin appeared on his face, and then he was gone, having passed Blake's line of vision. Blake's heart jumped at the glance, and he realized he was getting sweaty palms; he felt a little queasy.

He also had another physical reaction to seeing Cameron, and the stirring between his legs made standing tall a little difficult. He strategically moved behind one of the sofas to hide the obvious lump in his trousers, and then willed it away.

After a few minutes, Rafael's toadying voice came closer.

"And, as you can see, Cameron, the spring line just arrived and is up. Simply too beautiful, the clothes," he said, gesturing wildly about the large room.

"Did you have them pull my size aside for me?" asked Suzette snidely, already bored to tears with the walkthrough. She instantly started to rifle through the racks of luxurious clothes, signaling her displeasure with the line by a series of snorts.

"Yes, Suzette. Kelly has everything laid out for you in our VIP room," Rafael said, smiling a little too broadly, showing off his newly whitened teeth.

"Then take me there," she said, sighing heavily.

Rafael was on the spot. He didn't want to leave Cameron's side to escort Suzette to the VIP room. He liked to be next to Cameron every second of every day. That constant presence assured his position as Cameron's right-hand man. Flustered, he saw Blake and Chelsea, and thought quickly.

"Of course," he answered smoothly. "Blake? Please show Mrs. Fuller to the VIP room."

"Sure. This way, Mrs. Fuller," Blake said graciously. He started to walk out of the room.

"Rafael?" Cameron stepped in. "Doesn't Blake do the window displays? I'd like to see them. Perhaps this lovely young lady—" he motioned to Chelsea—"could take Suzette over."

Ruffled, Rafael's mouth hung open but nothing came out.

"Of course, Mr. Fuller," Chelsea said cheerfully. "Mrs. Fuller?"

"Christ! I don't care who takes me. Just someone get me out of here," Suzette said, exasperated. She shot a nasty look at Cameron, and followed Chelsea out of the room.

Rafael recovered, and narrowed his eyes. "I hadn't realized you two had met," he said, suspicion in his tone.

"Who else could he be? He's exactly as you described him," Cameron covered smoothly. He held a hand out to Blake.

Stepping close, Blake shook hands with the man he'd virtually given a handjob to the night before. "Blake Jackson. It's a . . . pleasure to meet you, sir."

"No, the pleasure is mine. I really love the windows. I noticed them when we drove up. Very nice." Cameron shook Blake's hand warmly, and gave him a slight wink.

Which Rafael noticed. With great unease.

"Thanks," Blake said simply. He didn't want to let Cam's hand go, but he did.

"Then let's go see these *amazing* windows," Rafael suggested, leading them out.

When all three of them were outside, marching up and down the front of the store peering at the windows, Rafael noticed the apparent comfort Blake displayed around Cameron. It angered him, because, excepting himself, he felt all employees should revere and be slightly afraid of Cameron Fuller. He felt a deep need to put Blake in his place and exert his power.

"Blake?" he asked innocently. "What is that?" He was pointing to the farthest window, the one that Blake and Cameron had originally worked on.

"What is what, Rafael?"

"That color? The fabric on the walls. That's not the color I specified." Rafael was squinting into the window, and stabbing the glass with a stubby finger.

"Um, yes, it is. I ordered it from the same fabric supplier you used for the Warehouse," Blake answered, feeling a familiar sinking feeling in the pit of his stomach. Nothing he did was ever good enough for Rafael.

"No. It's not! I specifically said get 'eggshell.' I believe that's the other color, 'aged cream.' They are not the same!"

"Rafael, I promise you, I ordered exactly what you said. Color number fifty-six," Blake calmly replied, knowing the fabric number by heart. He had learned by now to double check everything he did when it came to Rafael. He knew that number fifty-six was aged cream.

"Fifty-six?! I *know* I said fifty-seven! Jesus, Blake! How hard is it to order fabric? And the positioning of this body is all wrong. Were you asleep when you did this? And I hate the way it's lit. You can't see shit in there," Rafael ranted.

Blake knew exactly what was going on. This was all a big show for Cam. His stomach was now in knots. Rafael was making him look like an incompetent idiot in front of the famous designer.

Typical.

"I'm so sorry, Cameron." Rafael turned to face his boss. "These windows are not up to the standards that I sent Blake, and I'm shocked that he doesn't know this." He shrugged, as if to say, *See? If I'm not around . . .*

"Well, frankly, Rafe, I like the color," Cameron slowly said, squinting deep into the windows.

Blake was not about to be accused of not doing his job correctly in front of Cam, a man he admired so much. "Rafael, I have a copy of the instructions you sent me," he defended himself, trying to keep his tone even. "It clearly states fabric color number fifty-six. I can go dig it up and show you, if you like."

"Don't bother! It's wrong!" Rafael's hands were positioned on his waist in petulance. "Are you telling me *I* don't know color?" His voice was rising in pitch, and his fingers drummed his hips.

"And, Rafe, I think the bodies are fine," Cameron continued, ignoring Rafael's petulance. "What is it you don't like about them?" he asked.

"The positioning is all wrong! Whoever placed those mannequins is an idiot. Whoever placed them knows nothing about visual display and fashion. The attitude is all wrong. Can't you see that, Cam?" Rafael pontificated.

"Really . . . No, I don't see that." Cameron smiled, knowing that he himself had placed the form. "What I *do* see is that Blake and his crew worked very hard to install these windows in time for my visit, and I think they look amazing. I would hope, as their supervisor, you would offer encouragement, not criticisms," he said firmly. After he had finished speaking, he looked sternly at Rafael, who actually seemed to shrink one full size. "And I would also hope that, if these windows were so important to you, you would have been here working late last night with the window crew. Were you?" Cameron raised his eyebrows in question.

"Well, no, I . . . Uh . . ." Rafael stammered.

"Then you don't really have the right to bitch, do you?"

Completely humiliated, Rafael didn't respond. Sweat started to seep out of his pores, as he nervously blinked at Cameron.

Blake wanted to laugh out loud, but controlled the urge.

The three men stood in awkward silence for a full minute. Then Cam walked down the sidewalk to gaze at the other windows.

"I think they're great. I like the positioning, I like the lighting, I like the colors, and I love the graphics on the glass."

"Yes," Rafael hurriedly jumped in, finding something he could take credit for. "I thought you would, when I designed them."

Ignoring him, Cameron walked on. "Your team did a great job, Blake. Kudos."

Blake sheepishly grinned. "Thanks . . . Mr. Fuller."

"Please. Call me Cameron, okay?"

"Cameron."

This was just too much for Rafael. He sensed an unseen threat in the form of Blake Jackson, and he didn't like it. He had to do something. Fast.

"Cameron, we need to go over some models' portfolios for the Pacific Coast Highway campaign. I have them in the manager's office. You have to make a decision on that today. Tomorrow at the latest. And then we need to see the Home Arena." He opened the door, waiting for Cameron to join him.

"That's your area of expertise, too, isn't it? The Home Arena?" Cam asked Blake pleasantly.

"Yes. I have a whole presentation to show you for the spring room change," Blake said eagerly.

"Great. Let's go."

Rafael realized too late that Blake was going to be with them upstairs as well. He wanted to kick himself.

Never worry, he told himself. *I'll take care of Blake.*

He cracked a tight smile as Cam and Blake passed by him, entering the store.

"So we'll change Downtown Retro to Paradise Island," Blake said, pointing at the blueprints rolled out on the large deco cocktail table. He had worked on these blueprints for two weeks, and was proud to show them to the famous designer.

They were standing in the middle of the third-floor Home Arena. The air between Cameron and Rafael was charged with tension. From what Blake could gather, the two men had had what must have been a tense meeting in the store manager's office regarding the new cologne launch. Blake didn't know what the source of conflict was, but as Cameron and Rafael joined him on the third floor, he had heard Rafael saying something about Travis Fimmel being perfect, and Cameron angrily replying No, he wanted a new face.

Quickly, though, they had given Blake and his presentation their full attention. After each point was made, Blake checked to see how it was going over with Cameron. He seemed very pleased. Rafael's face was a mask. Who knew what he was thinking?

Cameron looked up and took an appreciative look around the third level of his store. Each major corner of the space was divided up into rooms. Each room was a different theme, as dictated by the current season's collection. Each room held a stunning arrangement of high-priced but excellent quality Cameron Fuller furniture, accessories, and lamps. The bedding so extravagantly displayed on each of the beds could be found for sale, neatly placed in storage racks, up on the wall behind each bed. Twin, full, queen, and king sheets were sectioned off by size and colors. Additional items such as coordinated throw pillows, comforters, duvets, and the like were also stored neatly and accessible for the customer's convenience.

One of the rooms in front had wide bay windows that looked out over Rodeo Drive. The current group in that room was a fall-themed collection called "Bridgeport Stable." It evoked the relaxed luxury of a Connecticut horse farm. Warm brown masculine plaids and feminine lavender florals were mixed together in the bedding, while a beautiful mahogany carved four-poster and nightstand suite, stained a rich chocolate, anchored the room.

Another area in the store was set aside for "Paris." Gilded bergere chairs, lamps, and mirrors shone gold under the halogen lighting, while a thick black wrought iron bed floated in the middle of the space. Deep red and navy blue bedding and upholstery were the highlights of this room. "Paris" had been a top seller this past season, and the decision had been made to carry over the collection into spring, even if the room was changed to something else.

There was a cottage look in the back right corner called "Newport Summer." Washed blues, pale yellows, and crisp whites were the color scheme here. Whitewashed wicker furniture and a beautiful faux-antique whitewashed iron four-poster complete with ruffled canopy were the furniture offerings for sale.

The three men were standing in the middle of the "Downtown Retro" room. A low slung platform bed of highly polished dark wood with a simple slab headboard was the centerpiece of the collection. Low art-deco-influenced nightstands flanked the bed, and a small sitting area had been made up with two sleek dark wood and chrome chairs, a luxurious tuxedo-style camel colored wool sofa, and an expansive polished cocktail table. The bedding was Manhattan Label, Cameron's highest thread count, and it looked magnificent.

This was the room that was to become a South Pacific beach house bedroom called Paradise Island. The heavy cream wool carpeting would be replaced by sisal area rugs. The walls were to be cladded over with a mixture of seagrass wallpaper and crossed teak woodwork with bamboo accents.

"And over here," Blake said, indicating the space they were standing in, the sitting area, "we'll put the teak daybed. Over it we'll hang mosquito netting to fall down over it. I found some amazingly cool tiki wall sconces for there." He pointed to another wall. "And we'll float the bed in the center."

Cameron studied the blueprints and then surveyed the room. "Sounds perfect. I can't wait to see it. Good job," he said, obviously pleased.

Rafael jumped in excitedly. "Yes, and I think we'll upholster that far wall in that pinkish batik fabric that I found in Bali last year. I knew it would come in handy sometime," he crowed.

Part of Rafael's job duties was to come up with new trends, concepts, and ideas. To do that, he had managed to convince Cameron that he needed to go to the actual places that would inspire future collections. So, twice a year he took a tour of some exotic locale to research ideas. Last year he had gone to Bali to work on an Asian theme that hadn't panned out. But he had brought back some amazing props and fabrics.

"Good idea," Cameron agreed.

"Pinkish?" Blake hesitantly asked.

"Yes. It's a beautiful pink and gold pattern. Really something," Rafael said, already envisioning how it would look on the wall.

Blake gulped. "I don't mean to disagree with you . . ."

"Then *don't*," Rafael warned, his eyes turning into slits.

"Go ahead, Blake. What were you going to say?" Cameron said.

"Well," Blake began. He saw the dagger-filled look coming from Rafael, but he went on, anyway. "I don't think *pink* is right. The colors for this collection are all in the browns and tans and yellows. The Polynesian sheets are a mix of brown and tan, and the upholstery fabrics are yellow and tan. I don't think pink will work. I think any wall fabric should be in the orange family, or maybe the blue, that's all. Or better yet, how about a section of split bamboo?"

You are so fired, thought Rafael.

Cameron stood back and studied the wall, conjuring up the collection in his mind and thinking about the patterns and colors. He envisioned what the wall in question would look like. "Blake, you're right. Rafe, don't you think? I really like the bamboo idea. Let's try that," he said excitedly.

"Yes, it's a much better idea, Cameron," Rafael said in controlled tones.

"Good. Great job, Blake. Everything here looks good, and I'm sure the next room changes will as well." Cameron turned to Rafael. "Do me a favor, Rafe. Go ask Mrs. Fuller what her plans for lunch are. I'm starving."

Now I'm a fucking gofer? Rafael privately fumed. He had to struggle to put on his happy face. "Sure thing, Cameron." He walked briskly away, towards the stairs.

Finally alone with Blake, Cam looked at him with adoration. "You look so handsome this morning," he said.

Blake looked around to make sure they couldn't be overheard. Just hearing Cam speak to him in his rich, deep voice had sent lustful chills up his spine. "Thanks. You, too! I had a hard time getting to sleep when I finally got home."

"Really?" Cameron smiled. "Well, we'll just have to make sure you get to bed early tonight."

Blake laughed nervously. Two salespeople across the floor who were discreetly gawking at Cameron were straining to hear what was so funny.

"I had a hard time sleeping myself. I kept wishing I was next to you," Cameron admitted, eyes now downcast. He reached into his jacket pocket and pulled out an incredibly small cell phone. "I got this for you this morning. My private cell number is already programmed in. Your new number is taped on the back of the phone. Call me whenever you want."

Blake took the phone and studied its cunning design for a brief second before pocketing it. "Thanks. Great idea."

"We're on for dinner tonight, but if I can sneak away from here, let me take you to lunch as well," Cameron urged.

"Is that smart? Tongues would be wagging all over the store."

Cameron slowly expelled a breath of air. "I suppose you're right. I just can't wait to be alone with you. I know this must seem insane to you, but I can't help myself."

Being so close to Cameron, isolated with him, caused Blake's heart rate to shoot up, and he was breathing shallowly. He was unabashedly attracted to the famous designer. Carnal thoughts filled his head.

"Have you seen the storage room over here?" He pointed vaguely to a door cut into a back corner of the wall, behind a large dark armoire. "It's small and quite private. Let me show you."

Cameron hesitated only a second. "Please do."

Cameron slowly followed Blake to the door, and in they went. The second the door was closed behind them, Blake leaned over and passionately kissed Cameron, who responded happily. Their hands crept around each other and held on tightly while they smothered each other in caresses. Blake purposely pressed his hard-on into Cameron's crotch, and was pleased to feel Cameron's hardness as well. They ground their hips together and continued to deep-kiss.

Cameron lowered his hand slowly to Blake's erection and gripped it firmly, eliciting a muffled moan from the younger man. His fingers nimbly undid Blake's belt buckle and quickly popped open the top button of his pants.

Blake knew this was not a wise thing to do with twenty salespeople on the other side of the door, but the sheer excitement and danger of being caught was a definite rush. He did nothing to stop Cameron from his task.

The designer's determined hand dug in and found Blake's immense cock. He pulled it out, and giving Blake a hungry look, dropped to his knees, licking his lips in anticipation. He steadily massaged Blake into his mouth. He took Blake's whole shaft in in one long swallow, and ran his tongue over the head on the return. Blake involuntarily shuddered and dropped a hand behind Cameron's head, tightly gripping his close-cut salt and pepper hair. He gently moved Cameron's head in a natural rhythm.

Cameron allowed himself to slide back and forth, his mouth tightening and loosening as needed. He took Blake all the way in, nearly down into his throat, then letting him slip out, almost letting the head go. His eyes were closed in pleasure and shallow groans came from his busy mouth. His hands had a firm hold of Blake's hard ass and he impatiently quickened the pace.

"Oh, man," Blake whispered.

Cameron continued his job with the dedication of a trouper. By now, Blake's cock was a slippery pole, and Cameron's jaw had relaxed to the point that he slid back and forth on it with a precision and ease that blew Blake's mind.

Cameron Fuller certainly knew how to give good head.

"God, Cam . . . You're gonna make me come . . ." Blake eventually murmured, his fingers tightening in Cameron's hair.

Cameron grunted his approval and redoubled his efforts.

"No, I mean it! . . . I'm gonna shoot! . . . Let go!" Blake whispered hoarsely through gritted teeth.

Cameron shook his head imperceptibly, and kept going, like a well-oiled machine.

"Oh, no! . . . I . . . *Ohhhhh . . . !"* Blake's eyes squeezed shut as he came. Cameron didn't let him loose. Instead, he continued to suck mightily, as Blake shot into his mouth. It was a huge climax, being overdue since the night before, and Cameron almost choked as the hot fluid filled his mouth and throat.

He swallowed.

Blake was breathing so heavily he was afraid the entire store could hear him. He tried to regain control of his senses, but Cameron still had a vapor lock on his dick and was milking every last drop out of him that he could.

"Jesus!" Blake uttered, his heart rate slowly coming back down. He tried to suppress a giggle.

Cameron reluctantly released him, and wiping away a bit of residue from his shiny lips, struggled to his feet. His enormous woody was almost bursting out of the fabric of his suit pants, and there was a tiny visible damp spot from his own pre-cum. "I'm so sorry, Blake. I just couldn't help myself. You were enjoying it so much, I wanted to pay you back for last night," he offered while he straightened his tie and smoothed down his hair.

"Paid in full, I'd say. Damn!" Blake breathed deeply, then began to laugh.

"I'm not ashamed to admit it. I love the way you taste."

"I'm not gonna ask how the fuck you ever learned to do that! I'm just so glad you know how," Blake chuckled, redoing his pants and tucking his sweater back in.

"Like I said, I'll tell you all about it at dinner. We better get back out there. They're gonna think you kidnapped me or something." Cameron adjusted his suit jacket to cover his crotch, and then reached into a pocket and pulled out the small black case of a pack of Jo Mints. He picked one of the small capsules out and popped it into his mouth. He snapped the smartly designed case shut and slipped it back into his pocket. The famous designer then lovingly reached over and stroked Blake's face once. "So beautiful," he muttered to himself.

Blake cautiously opened the door, and seeing no one around, quickly walked out, followed by Cameron.

Rafael, coming up the stairs with the news that Suzette planned on skipping lunch, saw the two men emerge from the back corner of the store.

What in the hell were they looking at there? he wondered. He saw that they were walking around the upper rotunda, away from him, and, unobserved, he quickly sneaked over to where they had been.

There was nothing out of the ordinary in the area. Rafael was stymied. He stamped his foot in frustration.

That's when he noticed the almost hidden door.

Musing to himself, he opened it a crack and peeked in. A closet. What was so exciting about a closet? He was about to shut the door in frustration when he saw something glistening on the dark carpeting.

He crept into the room and leaned over to study the small stain.

Is that what I think it is? he wondered, his curiosity killing him.

He got on all fours and put his nose to the carpet, sniffing it deeply.

If there was one thing Rafael Santiago knew intimately, it was the smell of fresh come.

He sat back on his haunches in amazement. While he had been downstairs with that fucking bitch Suzette, Blake and Cameron had been getting it on in here.

This was huge!

The rumors about Cameron had been right all along! Rafael instantly started scheming as to how this stupendous information could be used to his advantage. That fucking Blake Jackson! How had he slid in under the radar?

Rafael's pride was hurt a tad that he had not been the one Cameron chose to have sex with, but the knowledge that it was at least possible was worth the moon. He decided to hold his cards close to his chest and wait and see how things went during this visit.

Smiling smugly, he sneaked back out of the closet. Acting as though he had been wandering around looking for Cameron, he joined the two men on the other side of the store.

9

Blake swallowed the rich red wine and let the taste linger in his mouth. Not a big wine drinker, he was pleasantly surprised to find that this particular wine, an Opus One, 1995, was quite good. Of course, Cameron had picked it out.

"Well?" Cam asked, eyebrows raised in question.

"Very good. You were right," Blake replied, still savoring the exquisite taste.

They were sitting in a private booth at perennially trendy Kate Mantalini in Beverly Hills, away from the table-hopping regulars. Blake had always meant to try the restaurant, but just hadn't yet. He was very pleased with the choice.

Cameron smiled at Blake. "I'm so glad we're here. Thanks for joining me."

"Thanks for asking."

Ninety minutes earlier, Cameron had come to pick Blake up in his brand new black rental Mercedes-Benz 500 SL, which he drove himself. Wearing a pair of his own khakis and a navy turtleneck, topped off by a beautifully cut camel wool blazer, Cameron, again, looked like one of his own ads. Blake, meeting him at the door dressed head to toe in Cameron Fuller, was equally handsome in his black slacks, black turtleneck, and black fitted leather blazer.

Blake ushered Cam into his small West Hollywood bungalow, and once the door was shut, they gave each other a deep, lingering kiss. When they finally pulled away from each other, Cameron began to take in his surroundings.

Blake had bought the small two bedroom, one bath house two years previously with a down payment provided by an inheritance from his grandmother's estate. While the house was not very big, it had a good-sized backyard and a separate garage with a small studio apartment attached. He rented out the studio to a young man who was working his way through nursing school at UCLA.

The craftsman-style house itself was a rather plain affair, but it was on Spaulding Drive, north of Fountain and south of Sunset, which was a very desirable West Hollywood location. Blake had done wonders to it. The wide front porch was covered by a low pitched roof supported by two thick, squat columns. Painted a rich sage green, with contrasting white trim work, the house gave off the correct impression that it was well tended.

Inside, waxed dark walnut hardwood floors gave a mirror copy of the furniture resting on top, due to the extreme efforts of Blake and a rented floor-sander. Comfortable plush furniture was placed in groups that allowed both conversation and privacy. The scheme of the house was contemporary classic, and following Blake's interior design idol, Barbara Barry, the house was filled with sleek lines and dark woods, with light-colored upholstery. A slight art deco influence was felt, but the whole tone was one of relaxed comfort and elegance.

Cameron was obviously impressed.

"Your house is beautiful," he said genuinely.

"Well, coming from you, that's quite a compliment," a blushing Blake said.

"No, really. It looks like one of my showrooms in New York. Give me the grand tour, please."

They wandered from the living room, through the dining room, and into the compact but functional kitchen. Blake had replaced all of the cabinetry and put in a stunning slate floor. Brushed stainless steel appliances including a Viking stove and a Subzero refrigerator shone brightly against the new natural wood cabinets. Brushed chrome handles and pulls coordinated the looks.

Just as they were about to leave the kitchen, the partially opened back door nudged open and in bounded Joe, Blake's ten-year-old golden retriever. A huge animal at a hundred and five pounds, Joe *was not even remotely aware of his body mass, or age, and when he realized there was a new human in the house, he eagerly jumped up on Cameron to make friends. Huge muddy paws landed squarely on Cameron's lapels and almost knocked him over. Cameron braced himself, and laughingly allowed the dog's huge tongue to lick his face several times.*

Blake, mortified, tried in vain to get the dog down. "Joe! Joe! Get down! No, Joe! Get down!"

Joe, realizing that his master was actually serious, reluctantly settled back on all fours on the floor panting, his tongue hanging out of the side of his mouth.

"God, Cameron! I'm so sorry! He just gets excited when there's someone new around," Blake explained as he held a dishcloth from Pottery Barn under the tap, and then began to dab away the dirt from Cameron's blazer. "He gets sick of only seeing me and Rand."

"Rand? Who's Rand?"

Blake nodded toward the backyard, clearly visible through the large bay window in the breakfast nook. "My tenant. He lives in the studio apartment. He's a student."

"Oh."

Blake continued to wipe away at the jacket, removing most of the stains. Joe, oblivious to the damage he'd caused, sat on the floor near them, his huge tail swishing back and forth on the cool slate.

"Well, I love dogs. I'd have one if I didn't travel so much. You're lucky you have him," Cameron said, smiling at the immense canine. Joe, sensing he was the topic of discussion, perked up his ears comically.

Ultimately getting all of the stain out, Blake relaxed. "There. Good as new."

"And if not, I know where I can get another blazer just like this one," Cameron noted wryly. "On with the tour."

They left the kitchen and wandered down the short hallway to where the bathroom separated the two bedrooms. The bathroom had both a stall shower and a tub, and was tiled in hideous pink. And, defying all logic, there was a purple toilet in an alcove.

"As you can tell, I haven't gotten around to redoing the bathroom yet. I just finished paying for the kitchen and the central air. Bathroom's

on the agenda for this year, though. I can't wait to get rid of the pink tile," Blake clarified, not wanting Cameron to think he approved of the current color scheme.

"Interesting toilet," Cameron joked, nodding toward the ugly fixture.

"Don't ask. You should have seen the place when I bought it. It was purple and pink all over. Pink wallpaper and purple carpeting. It looked like a gay bordello."

"Well, it's a look."

"I kept hoping someone would offer to put me on Trading Spaces, but so far, no luck," Blake quipped.

They backed out of the room and Cameron poked his head into each of the bedrooms. Blake's room was beautifully done with a wonderful platform bed made up of dark wood with a button-tufted headboard of cream ultra-suede. A low framed deco chair covered in the same cream ultra-suede was placed under a large window, next to the bathroom passage door. A large sisal rug covered most of the hardwood floor, and modern Robert Abbey lamps sat on the dark polished nightstands.

"Sexy room," Cameron noted, taking Blake's hand in his own.

The other bedroom was fitted out with a daybed against the far wall, the guest bed. A small dining table used as a desk held Blake's computer, fax, printer, and other office equipment. A LifeCycle on a black rubber mat occupied another corner, next to a set of free weights and other gym products. A twenty-seven-inch Sony TV was hung on the far wall on a wall mount so it could be swiveled around to allow viewing from any spot in the room.

"You seem to have everything you need here. Great place, Blake. I really like it. It's so comfortable. And so you," Cameron noted.

"Yeah, I guess it is. What time is the reservation?"

"Eight," Cameron said, glancing at his thin Cartier tank watch. "We'd better get moving."

Before locking up the house, Blake made sure to fill Joe's water bowl, and turn off a few of the lights. He hesitated at the front door, and in the half-light, the two men again pressed lips together for several minutes.

Now, relaxing in their secluded booth, away from prying eyes, Cameron and Blake had already ordered their appetizers and main courses. They were beginning to learn about each other, and were getting more and more comfortable together.

"So," Blake said, staring Cameron in the eye. "How did you ditch the 'missus' tonight?"

"Yes, I guess it's time I explain all, isn't it?" Cameron winked. He took a sip of his wine and relaxed back into the plush booth. "Let me start at the beginning. It's easier that way."

"Sure."

"I'm originally from a small town outside Toronto, Canada, that you've never heard of. I hated it there. Too damn cold! As long as I can remember, I wanted to live in America. Specifically, New York. I was just obsessed with this country and all things American, which is odd, because being Canadian really isn't all that different."

"Well, Canadians like to use the word 'eh' a lot more than Americans. And they're better ice skaters," Blake cracked.

Cameron smiled. "True. So, my mother wanted to get out of Canada as bad as I did, and when I was twelve, she convinced my father to take over a dead relative's dairy farm in Vermont. I was so excited! I finally got to live in America, though Vermont wasn't exactly the hub of city life I craved. Manning milking machines was *not* for me, I soon discovered." The famous designer smiled at distant childhood memories, and took another sip of wine. "When I grew up and it came time for college, I decided to attend NYU, so I could live in Manhattan. I've *always* loved Manhattan. *That's* where I met my wife. You see, Suzette was the twin sister of my first, and only, boyfriend." Cameron took a deep breath. "She and Stanton were as close as I've ever seen siblings be. It was almost like they were the same person, which I always found odd, because Suzette always came second to Stanton for her father's affection. You'd think she'd resent Stanton, but she didn't. Quite the opposite."

"What about her mother?"

"Ah. Her mother was this famous Newport debutante. Very beautiful. She died giving birth to the twins. Suzette's father never lets her forget how beautiful her mother was. Suzette has always felt like she was this second-class, ugly stepchild."

Blake took another swallow of the extravagant wine. "And Stanton? Was he hot?" He grinned.

"Oh, yeah. President of his prep school student body. Captain of the football team. He *was* Joe America. Everything I ever wanted to be," Cam said wistfully. "We met at NYU freshman orientation, and that's when I got to know Suzette, because she, of course, had to go to the same university as Stanton. In fact, we all ended up living together in this big townhouse they rented near campus. Stanton and Suzette came from old money. Obviously, I didn't. In fact, I worked my way through school to help with my tuition, and that's when I got started in retail. I was also so glad to be open about my sexuality, finally. On the farm, I'd managed to ignore it, but once I moved to New York and met Stanton, well, you know."

Blake grinned again, and nodded.

"Stanton wasn't comfortable at all with his sexuality, and definitely wasn't out to his father. He was afraid he'd be cut off financially if his father knew about us. So we all pretended I was Suzette's boyfriend. She'd do anything for Stanton, so she went along with it. At the time I couldn't understand it, but now I know why."

"Was she in love with you, too?" Blake asked.

The designer thought about that for a second or two. "Yes and no. She was so obsessed with her brother, she wanted whatever he wanted. And that was me," Cameron finally said, shrugging. He took a deep breath. "Stanton had a slight drinking problem, in that he didn't *have* to drink, but when he did, he couldn't stop. The night Stan died, we had gone to a party of a good friend of ours, Dillard Jordan. Do you recognize that name?"

Blake shook his head no.

"He's one of my biggest investors now. But I thought you might recognize his name because he's been in the papers a lot lately. His ex-lover is suing him for palimony."

"Oh, yes! I read about that case. He kicked the boyfriend out after something like eight years, right? Cut the guy off without a dime?"

"That's the one. Dillard says he found out his ex was fucking the gardener. And the cook. *And* the chauffeur. Then the ex got high on T or X or K or L, M, N, O, P—whatever the newest letter drug is—and burned down his house when Dillard kicked him out. Dillard, trying to be a nice guy, covered that up, but now with the lawsuit . . . Anyway, it's a big story in New York right now. It's driving Silas crazy, all the brouhaha." Cameron allowed himself a small smile. "So, anyway, back to my story. Stanton, Suzette, and I went to a couple of parties that night, and Stan got drunk. On the way home, we hit a tree and he was thrown from the car. He was killed instantly." Cameron's violet eyes clouded over with a flash of long-suppressed grief. "Suzette . . . was in the car with us. She didn't get a scratch. I broke my arm, and got this." He pointed to the small scar on his chin, the scar that made him appear so rakish. "His death really affected her. We continued to live together after that to help each other through our grief. When we graduated, I knew I wanted to start a clothing line, but had no cash. And no citizenship. My student visa was up. Suzette had no goals or aspirations, so she suggested we get married, and her father would give us the money for my business as a wedding present. As a bonus, I would get my green card."

The busboy interrupted Cam by placing a basket of fresh-baked breads and a side plate of butter down on the table before discretely disappearing.

Cam ignored the bread. Bad carbs.

"So, it seemed like a good idea at the time, and we got married. I thought we had an understanding that it was a marriage in name only and it would end in a couple of years. At first, it was great fun. We'd party all night. I'd go off with some dude, and she'd hook up with some *other* dude. But, as I got more successful, she got more clingy and needy. She began to see me as some sort of replacement for Stanton. Maybe it had something to do with the respect her father gave me concerning my success. The same kind of respect he had given so freely to Stanton, but never to her. In any event, as I got more successful, she and I started to appear in commercials as a couple. I didn't really date . . . men . . . because I was afraid of the impact it might have on the business. Now, I look back and I think, How stupid of me. But at the time, it made sense." He looked at Blake to see how this was registering. Blake was following every word with interest, and smiled his encouragement. "So, over time I just became immune to my sexual needs and focused entirely on work. And, I have to admit, every once in a blue moon, when I was very drunk, or very stoned, Suzette and I would . . . Well, any port in a storm, as they say." He blushed. "Slowly, I built up the business, which, I have to say, Suzette wanted no part of except when it was time for the commercial shoots. She just wanted to shop and party. She and I began to fight more and more. She wanted a more physical relationship, but that had never really been part of the deal. I finally got my American citizenship about fifteen years ago, but the company was taking off like gangbusters by then, so we stayed together. I don't know how it evolved, but Suzette's become so bitter and mean. She used to be such fun. Then . . . she became pregnant."

Blake's face registered surprise.

"I knew that she had affairs, but I didn't say anything about it. I was too busy to care. When she got pregnant, she claimed it was mine. We'd had sex recently, so I believed her . . ." His voice caught, and he had to clear his throat. "I never had even *thought* about being a father, and we both got so excited. We made plans to fix up the house, to make the most incredible nursery ever created. Then, in her third month . . . ," he faltered.

Blake reached across the table and placed his hand on top of Cam's in support.

"In her third month," Cam continued with difficulty, "she got drunk at a party and fell down a small flight of stairs. No more than four or five steps, practically nothing. But it was enough. She lost the baby. We had been waiting to tell everyone, so we just never mentioned it again. Then the doctors told her she could never have children. She was devastated. You see, she'd had quite a few abortions when she was in college, and I think she felt she had damaged her body and subsequently ruined her chances for having a child. She was never really the same after that. As I got more accomplished in the business, she began to go out of her way to humiliate or embarrass me. She'd cause scenes at the shows. She drank too much. She'd never wear my clothes, and, trust me, *that's* something that gets noticed. She just seemed interested in spending my money. Houses, cars, trips, jewelry, whatever caught her eye. Eventually she started to buy men. She's had a string of lovers over the years, and they get younger and younger as she gets older."

"And you? Have you had a string of lovers as well?" Blake asked lightly, but with interest in his tone.

"Exactly three. One was a married vice president of one of my suppliers; one, a fling in Aspen; and one, a trainer I briefly employed. None lasted more than a couple of weeks. I guess I've always been in love with Stanton, and it's always felt disrespectful to his memory to fuck around. I've just shut that part of me down for so long that I'd almost forgotten it. Until I saw you working in that window." Cameron cast his eyes down in embarrassment. "I can't explain it . . . You . . . *dazzled* me. I knew I had to get to know you better."

"When was the last time you had sex with a man?" Blake asked, both excited by his praise and slightly astonished at the low number of men in Cameron's life. He'd dated three guys in the last month alone. Well, dated was a strong word. *Fucked,* more appropriate.

Not including Brady.

"Four years. Six months. Twenty-seven days. But who's counting?" Cameron grinned.

"Damn, son. You're due!" Blake laughed.

Cameron blushed. "Anyway," he continued, "this past year, Suzette and I have been dancing around the idea of divorcing. It's time. It would be best for her and for me. She needs her own life, and I certainly need mine. Her father, who I had to put on my board of investors years ago, is dead set against us splitting up. He feels it would be bad for business. I frankly don't give a damn anymore what people think of my being gay, and I think it's time for me to see if I can find someone to build a life with. I made the mistake of telling this to Suzette, and she took it as some sort of rejection of *her.* So, now she's gotten all greedy. She's entitled to fifty percent, but she wants the lion's share of our assets. And you know what? I'm almost willing to give it to her. She did me a huge favor when she married me and helped me get started. She gave up a large chunk of her life for me, and she's earned it."

"Well, there's fair, and there's fair," Blake said.

"True. She's been particularly nasty lately. I think she wants to hurt me in some way. Hurt me because I never loved her the way she'd loved me. I think she's taken my desire to live a life without lies to be a big rejection of her, when actually it's something she knew all along. She's always accusing me of sleeping with every man I meet. If only!" He chuckled quietly, leaning forward. "So, when she and I get back to New York this week, we're going to make it official. I'm moving out. Get the lawyers involved. The whole thing. I wanted to wait to announce it until after the new cologne launch, but I suspect Suzette has a different agenda."

"And tonight? How'd you get away tonight?"

"I told her Rafael had set up a dinner with some vendors, could she please be ready at eight. I knew that would make her say no, and so she's out with some of her Beverly Hills friends. I keep hoping she meets someone and falls for him and lets go, but so far, that hasn't happened." Finished, he sat back and exhaled deeply.

"Wow. So when do you think you'll be a free man?"

"God willing, before the end of the year."

"Hmmm." Blake nodded. "Oh, what about your parents? How are they now?"

"My father passed away about twelve years ago. My mother died soon after. They got to see that I was becoming successful, so I'm grateful for that."

"And the dairy?"

"It's now a very exclusive subdivision."

"It's interesting."

Cameron looked up, squarely at Blake. "What is?"

"That your clothes are so identifiably American in their cut and styling. There's no European influence at all."

"You're not the first to notice that. My critics mention it all the time."

"Well," Blake continued, "I guess I see why, now."

"Oh? Why is that?" Cameron smiled.

"Well, not to play armchair psychiatrist, but, you idolized America, so you became more American than most people born here. Even your company logo is America! And you're the great American success story—humble roots, hard work, amazing achievement. I mean, you should be really proud of yourself."

Cameron blushed slightly, and reached a hand under the table to squeeze Blake's thigh. "Thank you for saying that."

Blake looked his handsome dinner date in the eye. "I really mean it."

Their salads arrived, and they spent the rest of the meal eating, laughing, and learning, more about each other. Blake was constantly amazed at how easy it was to talk to Cam. The man was a millionaire a hundred times over, and one of the most recognizable faces in the world, yet here he was.

Having dinner with with me, Blake thought, slightly awed by it all.

Cameron actually listened, and seemed to care about what Blake said to him. He asked intelligent, probing questions, and carefully digested the responses. Blake found himself telling Cameron far more than he had ever told any other quasi-stranger.

"So explain the Brady situation. You keep mentioning him. What does he do?" Cameron asked just before eating a forkful of lobster.

"He's a sheriff's deputy with the West Hollywood Sheriff's Department."

"No kidding? A cop? That must make him sexy."

"Well, he'd be sexy even if he wasn't a cop. He's a great guy. We met when he stopped me for speeding one day. I got a ticket, he got my phone number. He was so handsome in that uniform, damn! I'm not into role playing or anything like that, but sometimes just seeing him with the hat on was enough to . . ."

"So what happened?"

"A lot of things. I think he was the first, and so far, the only man I've ever truly been in love with," Blake answered honestly. "It just didn't work out for us. I don't know why." He ate some of his potato. "No, that's not true. I know why."

"Oh?"

"Yes. I guess our problem was that I wasn't truly *in* the relationship. I loved him, God knows, but I just didn't give him the attention I should have. I mean, he had his issues, too, but I think if I had worked a bit harder, it would have ended differently. Or not ended at all."

"Explain what you mean by you weren't *in* the relationship?"

"Well, I didn't really *listen* to him. I don't think I even tried to meet his needs, not on any deep level. I've always skated through my relationships, and he took it much more seriously. He would get so . . . hurt. He was this big, tough guy and I would make him cry. Finally, we had to agree to split up. It wasn't fair to him. I think I learned so much from that experience, and I hope that in my next relationship I'm able to . . . well, *be there,*" Blake said with difficulty.

"And where is Brady now?"

"I still have him as a friend, thank God. We work out together sometimes, and we fuck sometimes. It seems to work better this way."

Cameron shifted in his seat a bit. "So, he's a fuck buddy now?"

"Exactly. I think he wants more—no, I *know* he wants more, but I think the time has passed for us."

"I see."

There was a pause.

"I *am* single," Blake said, looking deep into Cameron's violet eyes. There was no mistaking his intention.

"Good."

They ate in silence for a few minutes. Cameron was staring at Blake, studying his face closely. Suddenly his face exploded in glee. "Of course! Why didn't I see it before?!"

Blake looked up from his plate. "I'm sorry? Did I just miss something?"

"We're doing this campaign for a new fragrance. Pacific Coast Highway. A very young, very fresh, open-air scent for men," Cameron explained hurriedly. "I've had a problem finding a 'face' for it. Everybody they show me, I hate. You're it."

Blake stopped in mid-bite. "I'm what?"

"You're perfect for it! You have exactly the look that I envisioned when we came up with it. Maybe that's why I'm so attracted to you. I've visualized you in my mind for months."

Blake rolled his eyes at Cameron. "Very funny. Ha. Ha."

"I'm serious! This is perfect! It's brilliant. You're an unknown, you have the total California look. Oh, my God! This is great!" Cameron was excitedly thumping his hand down on the table for emphasis.

"Wait a minute, Cameron. Are you serious? You want me to be a model? I don't know anything about it. I'm flattered, but, get real," Blake said, trying to calm Cameron down.

"No, really! I'm dead serious. I never screw around when it comes to business. Look, let's set up a test shoot. Please? Give me that. You'll see what I mean. I already have the concept down," Cameron excitedly pleaded with him. "You want a new bathroom? Baby, what I'm offering you will pay for the entire house!"

"Just a test shoot? I suppose I could do that. Are you for real? Or is this some gag to get me in the sack, cause, trust me, baby," Blake lowered his voice and put his hand on Cameron's thigh, "that's already gonna happen."

Cameron took hold of Blake's hand with his own, and moved it west, until Blake could feel his stiff erection. "I know that's going to happen, too, and I can barely wait. But, no, it's not about getting you in bed. Hang on a sec," he said, reaching into his breast pocket. He pulled out a cell phone identical to the one he had given Blake, and

punched in a few numbers. "Rafael? Do me a favor," he said quickly
into the phone. "Set up a test shoot for PCH tomorrow. Get whoever
is the hot new photographer in town. I want to shoot tomorrow at the
beach at sunset. Find me a beach. Get a beat-up old jeep. I'll personally go to the store and pull wardrobe. I've found our face!" There
was a pause.

Blake knew the question Rafael was asking.

Who was it?

He shook his head furiously at Cameron. Don't tell him it's me!

Catching the hint, Cameron demurred. "You'll see tomorrow. But
he's perfect . . . Yes, I know it's short notice, but get on it! We'll talk
first thing in the morning." He snapped the phone shut, and returned
to Blake, beaming.

"I guess you're really serious," Blake conceded, allowing himself
to get slightly excited by the idea.

"Oh, man. This is perfect. You're it. You're it," Cameron repeated,
satisfied.

Blake shook his head in amazement. And tightly squeezed Cameron's hard-on.

It was after midnight by the time they got back to Blake's house.
Pulling into the driveway, Blake could see by the lights in the studio
that Rand was home.

Blake unlocked his front door and the two men entered the cozy
house. Joe, instantly awake, rolled off the sofa where he was sleeping, stretched, and trotted over to lick his master's hand, heavy tail
wagging in pleasure.

"Hey, Joe. Let's go outside," Blake said, opening the door wide for
the massive dog. Joe lumbered out of the doorway and down the
brick steps into the grassy front yard.

"I need to use the pink bathroom," Cameron joked as he walked
down the hallway.

Blake nodded and waited patiently at the doorway for his dog to
return.

He didn't pay any attention to the car parked across the street. The
faint clicks emanating from the car's dark interior were muffled by
the evening's soft breeze.

* * *

Blake entered his bedroom to find Cameron sitting on the bed, jacket off, one leg crossed over the other. He had taken it upon himself to turn off the lights and light some of the Manuel Caravas candles that Blake had about the room. The dim, warm glow from the scented candles made him look even more desirable.

He looked up at Blake and smiled. "Joe all taken care of?"

"Yup. The house is locked up, and it's just you and me, baby," Blake said in a low voice, as he started to remove his blazer. "Just remember. You try anything funny, and I've got a big ole baseball bat under the bed, that I'm not afraid to beat ya with."

Cameron held up his hands. "I promise you, my intentions are entirely honorable."

"Damn." Blake fake-frowned.

Cameron stood up. "Hey, let me do that." He walked over to Blake and gently took hold of the leather jacket with his two hands, slowly peeled it down, and off. His face was inches away from Blake's, yet they did not kiss. They both wanted to build the moment. Cameron dropped the jacket to the floor.

Blake reached up and placed his hands on Cam's wide shoulders, and slowly, teasingly, let them drift down his arms, lightly feeling the thick muscles contained by the soft cashmere. Cameron's breathing began to quicken and his lips parted slightly.

"I want to know that you enjoy this," Blake said huskily. "Last night, you didn't make a sound when you came. Tonight,"—he leaned in and put his lips millimeters away from Cam's left ear—"I want to hear you groan. I want to hear you come." He flicked his tongue into Cam's ear, gently at first, then harder as he felt Cameron's reaction.

"Ohhhh," Cam whispered, tilting his head.

"Mmmm . . . you like that? Tell me what you like, baby," Blake barely whispered into his ear.

"Yes! . . . I like that . . ."

Blake reached a hand down, grabbed Cameron's cock, rock hard and straight up in his pants. Cameron shuddered at his touch. "We need to let this out, don't we, baby?" Blake teased, again flicking his tongue into Cameron's ear.

"Oh, God . . ." Cameron turned his face and pressed his lips to Blake's passionately. His arms came up and wrapped around Blake, holding him tightly. He trembled slightly.

Blake, sensing that Cameron was anxious, whispered gently, "Are you okay? Is this all right?"

"God, yes!" Cameron's voice cracked. "I'm just a little nervous. I haven't done this in a long time, and I want you so badly, I just don't want to make any mistakes. I'm afraid I won't be any good," he confessed shyly.

"Baby," Blake looked him in the eye. "That's not *possible*. After what you did this afternoon? I hope I can keep up with you!" he grinned. "We'll go slow, okay? I want you to be comfortable. I want you, too. So badly." Blake smothered Cam in kisses.

They kissed deeply for a minute or two, then Cameron tugged at Blake's turtleneck, and slowly brought it up, carefully pulling it over his head and letting it go to join the blazer on the floor. He let his hands roam freely over Blake's tanned chest, tenderly exploring the cuts and muscle. Blake's breathing turned shallow as he felt the light sensations of Cam's fingers floating on his skin.

Cam bent over slightly and with the very tip of his tongue started to slowly lick Blake's chest. The very act was so completely erotic to Blake that he shuddered in pleasure. Cam's tongue traveled from nipple to nipple, softly flicking each of the hardened nubs with his tongue, causing a sharp intake of breath in Blake. Cam's eager hands slowly unworked Blake's pants and let them fall to his feet, where he stepped out of them, one leg at a time.

Blake had not been wearing underwear, and his engorged erection rubbed up against Cam's chest as he steadily continued his tongue bath. As he got lower down, Cam slowly pulled off his own turtleneck and casually tossed it aside. Standing up, he quickly undid his trousers and in moments was as naked as Blake. Standing tall, the two men visually drank in each other's bodies. Two sets of hands caressed and touched.

Blake was unprepared for Cam's magnificent body. While his own body was in peak form, Cameron's could only be considered a piece of art. Blake wanted to spend days discovering all its wonders. He reached up and pulled Cameron close to him, pressing their two bodies together as one. Stiff cocks rubbed against each other as they ground themselves into one pulsating form.

They fell on the bed, with Cameron, nervous no more, on the bottom. Blake straddled Cam, and gazing at him in total lust, leaned down and began his own explorations. Cameron writhed in ecstasy as Blake ravaged his body with deep, velvety kisses that never seemed to stop. Blake then went down on him with a furor that matched the passion Cam felt. Cam let himself go and enjoyed feeling the soft, pliant tissues of Blake's wondrous mouth as he worked feverishly on his cock. Cam felt like he was in a warm, wet, tight heaven and was afraid he'd come too soon.

"Baby, stop! I don't want to shoot yet," he whispered hoarsely. Blake looked up, dutifully listened, and released him, moving on to other erotic acts.

He eventually kissed and licked every square inch of Cam's magnificent chest, abs, and pubic area. His hard-on ached and he could not ignore the need he felt.

"I want to fuck you, Cameron Fuller. I want to be inside you so bad it hurts." He leaned close into the designer's face, catching the pent-up excitement in Cam's violet eyes. "I want to hear you call out my name as I slide my hot cock . . ." he began to lightly kiss Cam's lips, his voice dropping low, ". . . into your amazing ass."

Cameron gulped. He reached up and took Blake's face in his hands. "I've never been fucked before," he admitted awkwardly. "But, I have to say, I've been thinking about it *all* day. I want you to, but, please . . ." he paused.

Understanding, Blake put a slender finger to Cam's beautiful lips. "Your pace. As slow, or as fast, as you want."

Cameron smiled. "Now. I want it *now,*" he whispered urgently.

Blake reached over to his nightstand, and opening the drawer, pulled out a bottle of lube and a foil-wrapped condom. "Get on top of me. It'll be easier for you that way."

Cam nodded slightly. "I know." They quickly switched positions, Blake resting comfortably on the bed, Cam straddling him, his thick legs braced up on his knees.

"Put this on me," Blake whispered, handing the condom to Cam, who tore open the foil with his perfect teeth. He slid the lubricated latex over Blake's stiff cock, and taking the bottle of lube, squirted some on as well.

Blake took the bottle from him and squeezed a fair amount into his hands, then silently slid his right hand up under Cam's bubble butt. He began to massage the famous designer, smearing the slippery gel around the erogenous area.

Cameron groaned softly and began to shift his ass around in anticipation. "Oh, that feels so good," he uttered as he arched his head back and closed his striking eyes. "Stanton was only a bottom . . . He would never . . . *Ohhhh!* . . . I always wanted him to . . . *Ummmm* . . ."

Blake slowly inserted his index finger up Cam's ass. Cam, relaxed by the massage, accepted him easily.

"Ohhhh! My God," he sucked in. He wiggled his ass around more.

"Yeah, that's it. Just relax and enjoy it," Blake soothed, getting off on Cam's heated reactions. He withdrew his finger, and bunching up three together, entered Cam's ass again. Easily. "Baby, you want it bad, don't you?" he teased.

"Oh, *yeaahhhh* . . ."

After a few moments of this, Blake withdrew his fingers a final time, and shifted his body down, lining up his cock with Cam's ass. Cam reached under, and grabbing Blake's rigid dick, positioned it, and began to push down on it. Grimacing slightly at first, then relaxing and taking him all the way in, he sat still for a moment, Blake fully extended inside him.

"Oh, *maaaaannn,"* Blake sighed.

Cam began to slowly raise himself up, and then lower himself back down, using his massive quad muscles. He stroked his own leaking cock with firm, even strokes. He began to pump his ass faster, and once he got into the rhythm of it, he encouraged Blake to thrust up with each of his downward pushes.

"Oh, God . . . Blake!"

"I know! You're amazing, Cam . . . You're so damn hot." Blake moaned, staring in total arousal at the striking man who was bucking up and down vigorously on him. Cam's tanned skin had a slight film of sweat on it, and his cut abs moved in and out with each deep breath he took. Blake reached up and fondled his square pecs, teasing the nipples. Cam arched his head back again and let out a loud cry of excitement.

"Yeah! Let me hear you, baby! I want to know I'm pleasing you," Blake uttered, suddenly squeezing hard on Cam's nipples.

With a sharp, excited cry, Cam climaxed, shooting a hot spray that kept coming in waves. Blake had never seen a man shoot as much as Cam did. It just seemed to go on forever. The thick white fluid kept pumping out of the engorged head of his beautiful cock. An almost inhuman guttural moan came from Cam's slightly parted lips as he drained himself on Blake's heaving chest.

Completely turned on by this fabulous display of virility, Blake's balls seized up and he knew he was going to shoot.

Now!

"I'm gonna come, baby!" he tried to warn Cameron.

"In me," Cam breathed heavily.

Too excited to pull out, Blake came in the condom, his pulsating cock buried deep up Cameron Fuller's hot ass. His own climax was a pretty close second to Cam's in the draining department.

As soon as he finished, Blake and Cam both burst into gales of laughter.

The two men stayed locked in their respective positions for a couple of minutes, regulating their breathing back to normal, reliving in their minds what had just happened. Cameron remained impaled on Blake's still rock-hard dick.

Then, as if a signal of mutual consent and desire had been passed between them, Cameron began to slowly ride up and down once again.

The next few hours passed like minutes.

10

Silas was sitting at his rococo desk in his home office gazing lovingly at one of his precious leather-bound photo albums, something he often did when he was depressed or lonely. The albums were filled with yellowing pictures of Stanton. Every once in a while a single tear would roll down his lined, craggy face.

The private line of his phone rang. Knowing instantly who it was, he picked it up before it could ring a second time.

"Yes?" he said into the receiver.

"I have some information you might find interesting," said the flat voice on the other end.

"Well, what is it?" Silas asked testily.

"Cameron went to dinner last night with a man from the Rodeo Drive store. A fellow named Blake Jackson. He does the window displays there. Dinner seemed to be very intimate, then they went back to Jackson's house. Cameron didn't leave until five this morning."

Silas rubbed his temples. He could feel a migraine coming on. "Do you have documentation of this?" he sighed.

"Of course. My source is FedExing photos to me today. I'll send them over as soon as I get them. I'm told some of them are pretty raw. They left a window open, and with the night-vision lens . . ."

A low gurgled groan of disgust came from Silas's throat.

"I mean, apparently Cameron loved it. My source says you can see the window dresser just fucking the living daylights out of—"

"Enough!" Silas practically shouted. "I don't want to hear it! Just

. . . just continue to have Cameron watched. Photograph everything. And I want to know if he sees this trash again. Do you understand me?"

"Loud and clear."

"Good. I won't forget your assistance with this, Dillard." Silas hung up the phone.

Well, there it was. Proof.

Silas was practically shaking with rage.

That fucking faggot!

Silas had no personal knowledge of what two men did together sexually, nor did he intend to learn now. When the photographs came in, he knew he wouldn't even look at them; he would just put them in the safe behind the Van Gogh until he needed to use them.

For some reason, thoughts of Cameron merged into thoughts of his dead son Stanton. Stanton had been so close to Cameron when they were in college. Why would his beloved son hang out with a faggot?

As the fire crackled in the large fireplace and his faithful black lab Smoky lay snoring by his feet, Silas began to weep anew for his lost son.

Oh, the dreams he'd had for Stanton!

Silas had planned on Stanton's taking over the bank. Marrying a beautiful debutante, having truckloads of stunning children. Often, when Silas was upset or melancholy, he fantasized about the life his son would have had had he not died that tragic night in that awful car crash. These fantasies always gave the old man much needed comfort.

The fact that his only surviving child was married to one of the most recognizable men in the country, and was a famous woman in her own right, did not impress Silas. Stanton had always been, and would always be, the light of his life, even after he'd been dead for twenty-five years.

But tonight, Silas, for reasons he didn't fully understand, had allowed his mind to wander to areas he had always kept tightly locked down. His strapping son, the best athlete in any game he played, a golden-haired specimen of strong muscle and white teeth, the very picture of machismo, had spent so much time with Cameron, whom Silas now knew was a homosexual.

Why?

Images long forgotten suddenly flooded back, as if a slide show had suddenly flicked to life in his head. Like flashes of bright light, Silas recalled events of the past as if they had just happened yesterday.

—Stanton and Cameron watching TV late one night at the big house in Tuxedo, with no lights on, when they thought the old man had gone to bed, and the quick movements they made to put distance between themselves on the media room floor when Silas had unexpectedly walked in.

—Affectionate hugs between winning sets of doubles tennis matches that seemed to last a beat too long.

—A midnight skinny-dip that Silas had stumbled in on, and their awkward fumbling for clothes as he lectured them on the dangers of swimming in a dark pool so late at night.

—Stanton always insisting that Cameron join him wherever he went.

—Suzette never seeming to be around as her "boyfriend" and her brother romped around together.

The pieces began to fall into place. As Silas slowly realized the truth, his face turned ashen. His breathing quickened and he felt the blood drain from his body.

Stanton and Cameron had been lovers.

How had he not seen this before? Denial? Blind love for an idealized dead child? Stanton's memory was as precious to Silas as his millions sitting in the First Manhattan Trust.

If only there hadn't been that damnable car crash!

Silas knew he had never gotten the full story from Cameron or Suzette about that dreadful night. Suzette had to be sedated for weeks after, so Silas hadn't pressed the point too much at the time, because, he had to admit, he had been too deep in shock over his favorite child's death to ask more questions. Ultimately, he had accepted Cameron's sketchy version as the truth because he'd had no reason not to.

But now the never-answered questions flooded through Silas's brain.

Why had they been on that deserted country road, anyway? Why hadn't stupid Suzette prevented this? Why had Stanton been driving

Cameron's shame pile of a car? Why had Stanton not been wearing his seat belt, even though he had been diligent about that issue every time Silas had driven with him?

In grasping for some sane explanation as to why his own flesh and blood had been taken from him so young, Silas struggled to come up with a reason that would not lay the blame at his deceased son's feet. His precious boy must have been confused. All young men went through a rough period in their formative years, didn't they? He must have been *seduced* by Cameron. There could be no other reason. *He* certainly hadn't raised his son to be homosexual! It had just been a phase Stanton had experimented with, Silas convinced himself.

Somehow Cameron had hypnotized Stanton. Bewitched him. Found some weakness in his sterling character and exploited it.

And Stanton had paid for that sinful weakness with his life.

Why not Suzette? Why not Cameron? Why hadn't Cameron, the instigator of this sordid affair, been the one to die?

As his fury grew, Silas Cochran decided that Cameron would pay. Pay for killing his son. Pay for altering and taking away his precious memories.

In one form or the other, Cameron would know what the pain of extreme loss felt like.

11

Blake was standing in line at the Starbucks when his new cell phone went off, startling him. As the other customers shot him dirty looks, he quickly pulled it out of his pocket and flipped it open.

"Hello?"

"Hey." It was, of course, Cameron. "How are you this morning?" His good mood was clearly evident.

Blake smiled giddily. "I'm good. I'm better than good. Last night was fantastic." He tried to keep his voice down, but he still noted a smirk on the man behind him in line.

"I know. I hated to leave. But, good news! Suzette told me this morning that she's decided to go back to New York today. She's been acting strange all morning. She says she's bored. So I can spend the next two days with you."

"Great!"

"I have a meeting now, then I have a session with the hotel trainer, but I'll be at the store in about two hours. We have to pick out your wardrobe for the shoot later today. So make sure your hot ass is there."

"I'm headed there now. Are you sure about this shoot thing? It just seems so unreal," Blake said, stepping up to the counter.

"I'm sure. Gotta go. See you in a bit, babe." And he was gone.

Blake ordered his usual, then stood back waiting for it to be made. Cameron had been worried about the lateness of the hour when he finally left Blake's house. Blake had urged him to stay over, but Cam said he couldn't. Suzette.

They had made love three times. Cameron, it turned out, was a natural. He couldn't get enough. Blake smiled at the vivid memory of Cameron on his back, legs parted wide, urging him on. It was definitely something Blake looked forward to repeating several times during the next two days.

But this whole model thing! That had Blake a little freaked. He knew he was good looking, and he had used that knowledge for his own benefit on more than one occasion. But he had always resisted this sort of thing. For no real reason other than it seemed like a silly way to earn a buck. But, if Cameron felt he could do it, he would give it a go. He didn't have anything to lose, and if it worked out, the extra money would indeed be nice.

The counterman called out his coffee, and after paying, Blake left the shop, got into his Cherokee, and drove to the store.

"Oh, come out. Let me see."

"All right, but I can't breathe in these damn things!"

The shuttered dressing room door opened and Blake came out wearing a pair of CF America low-rise brown leather jeans. Cameron had picked out a pair that was a size smaller than Blake usually wore. They were uncomfortably snug, but the tight leather accented his elongated quads and his beefy hamstrings. Not to mention the promising bulge between his legs.

Blake stood awkwardly in front of Cameron and Bobby, the men's buyer who was assisting Cameron with the clothes.

The fitted jeans were, without a doubt, the sexiest thing Cameron had ever seen on a man. It took all his self-control not to grab Blake roughly, shove him back into the dressing room and sexually assault him. "Perfect," he said, heartfelt approval on his face.

"I agree!" Bobby concurred. He gave a wistful look at Blake's ass as Blake spun around once. "You have always been a hot man, Blake, but, damn! You *kill* in those!" he gushed.

"They're a little tight," Blake complained lightly.

"They're perfect. Put this shirt on with them," Cameron ordered, handing over a stark white CF/Active tanktop underwear shirt. It, too, was a size smaller than Blake wore. Blake stripped off his T-shirt and pulled on the tanktop.

Bobby stretched his neck, straining to catch a good glimpse of Blake's bare chest in the brief seconds he was shirtless. He decided then and there to ask Blake out. He knew that as an average-bodied, introvertive man of forty-two, he had little to offer this hot stud of a man, but he knew his way around a cock, and he would let Blake fuck him until Blake couldn't keep it up any longer. In fact, they didn't even have to go out; he would be happy to just simply go to Blake's house and give himself to him. And, from what he'd heard about Blake, that would not be an unusual offer for him to receive. Or accept.

With hands on hips, Blake looked at Cameron expectantly. Cameron just nodded.

Cameron could not help thinking of the various sexual acts he would perform on Blake that night. "Put this over that." He tossed over a faded blue denim shirt that, while it looked like an old rag, had a retail price of a hundred and fifteen dollars. Blake slipped into it, and looking like a cover man for GQ, slid his hands into his pockets and struck an unbelievably sexy pose.

Both Bobby and Cameron swooned, Bobby obviously, Cameron less so.

"Okay," Cameron said, clearing his throat. "Bobby, can you have this pile," he waved vaguely at a small mass of clothes resting in an arm chair, "steamed and pressed by two? We'll leave for location then."

"You got it. If you like," Bobby hurriedly added, "I can join you on location and keep track of the wardrobe. It would be no trouble at all."

"Oh, thanks, Bobby, but I think we're covered there. Rafael will swing by and pick them up on his way out to the beach."

Bobby looked crestfallen.

"Can I get out of these now?" Blake said, tugging at his crotch to stretch the leather out.

Cameron laughed. "Sure." Just then Cameron's cell phone rang. "Hello? . . . Oh, Rafe, hello . . . Who? . . . He's good? . . . Oh, him . . . Good! . . . Great! . . . Point Dume? Hang on a sec." Holding the phone away from his mouth, he called out to Blake, who had gone back into the dressing room. "Blake? Do you know where Point Dume is?"

"Sure. North of Malibu. I sometimes take Joe out there," Blake called back as he struggled to pull off the jeans.

Cameron returned to his call. "We know where it is. We'll meet you there . . . Bye."

Bobby picked up the pile of clothes and left the area, heading downstairs to the tailor shop. Cameron was finally alone with Blake for the first time that morning. Looking around quickly, and seeing no one around, he pulled open the dressing room door.

Blake, standing nude, was startled. "What?! Oh, God, you scared me."

Cameron looked at Blake from tousled head to tanned toe. Blake, appreciating the dazzled look Cameron was giving him, stood there, and subtly jutted his hips out.

"You are so beautiful," Cameron said simply.

"What are you going to do about it?" Blake coyly asked.

Like a man possessed, Cameron walked into the dressing room, letting the shuttered door slam shut behind him. He took Blake's naked body in his arms and pulled him close.

They kissed.

"So, who is this photographer again?" Blake asked loudly, straining to be heard over the roar of the wind whipping around them.

"Rafe says he's the next David LaChappelle. He shot that Cosmo layout with Janet Jackson a few months ago that caused all the controversy," Cameron yelled back.

They were in Cameron's black SL, speeding down the Pacific Coast Highway, headed towards Point Dume. They had spent a little too long at lunch at Spago, and now Cameron was racing to make up the lost time. He had not been able to stop staring at Blake during the entire meal.

Cameron knew he had found something special with Blake. Every time he even thought about what they had done the night before, he would start to get aroused. He had to force himself to think about other things.

He had shelved his sexuality for so long, in effect denying who he was, that now he had tasted the apple again, he wanted the whole tree. He felt slightly guilty, as if he were somehow slandering the memory of Stan, but in the rush of excitement that was this new relationship, or whatever it was, he managed to suppress thoughts of his college-years lover.

He had never felt so free, so alive, as he did today, with Blake by his side. All the meetings, all the deals he was in the middle of, the pressures from the manufacturers to raise prices, the infighting with the board, the labor disputes, the disappointing sales of his last women's collection, all of that faded to the background as he completely gave his attention to Pacific Coast Highway and Blake.

His ass was, to be honest, a tad sore, but that didn't stop him from craving the moment when he would again have this gorgeous man inside him.

And that would be tonight.

He almost twitched in anticipation. Now he understood why Stan had always been on the receiving end. He had felt so full and complete with Blake relentlessly ramming into him. The sweet memory gave him a full-blown hard-on, and he had to shift in his seat to give it room to expand.

Blake caught Cam's movements out of the corner of his eye. He looked down and saw the thickened bulge in Cam's jeans. He smiled. He loved to know he caused that reaction in a man, and he reveled in the thought that he was as turned on by Cam as Cam was by him.

This fact actually surprised Blake a bit. Usually, after he'd had sex with a guy, he lost interest pretty quickly. Brady had been different. And so was Cameron. The fifteen-year age difference between them hadn't even crossed Blake's mind until now. He had never found older guys particularly attractive, but then, Cameron Fuller wasn't just any older guy. The man was hot, built like an Olympian, sexy, famous, and rich. What was not to love?

Finding he couldn't resist the temptation, Blake reached over and fondled Cam's crotch. Cam glanced over in surprise, then relaxed, and allowed himself to be felt up.

Life was good.

The black SL followed the dusty dirt road to the beachfront parking area. There was already a red Tahoe SUV parked there with two men sitting inside. At the approach of Cam's car, they got out and waited patiently.

Cam got out of the car first, adjusting his jeans while doing so. He shook hands with Trevor Barbados, fashion's newest and hottest photographer.

"It's *such* a pleasure to meet you, Cameron," Trevor said easily. A good-looking mocha-colored man with a head of tightly curled black ringlets held off his face by a red bandana tied sweatband style, he had intense green eyes that seemed to notice everything.

Born in the Bahamas, and raised in Los Angeles, Trevor had been one of the few successful black male models of the nineties. He had made a smooth transition to photography over the past few years, and had seen his demand rise as his work got more and more good press.

Trevor had reached a stage in his photography career where he didn't do "test" shoots of wannabe models anymore, but the chance to work for Cameron Fuller was a large carrot dangling in front of him. He desperately wanted to parlay this silly shoot into something more solid. Being the photographer of choice for a national designer was like money in the bank.

"Well, it's a pleasure to meet you as well. I really loved the Janet Jackson pictures. Such good work," Cameron replied.

"Thanks. It's hard to take a bad shot of her." Trevor gave Blake a quick onceover, his flat expression revealing nothing.

"Did Rafael explain what I want here?" Cameron led the photographer away from the vehicles and over the dunes.

Trevor looked around, getting his bearings. "Not really. He said you wanted to shoot some tests of a guy for possible use in your new campaign."

"Exactly. No makeup, no hair. Natural. That's him, over there." Cameron and Trevor looked at Blake.

"Cool."

"I want him to be the guy men want to be, and the man women want to fuck."

Trevor focused his attention on Blake again, this time sizing him up. "I think a lot of the men will want to fuck him, too," he observed wryly. "Myself included."

Cameron smiled. "Whatever sells cologne."

"Cool."

Cameron and Trevor then had a long discussion about angles, lighting, and the wardrobe Blake would be wearing. Blake hung out by the convertible, cooling his heels. The other guy who was with Trevor finally walked over and introduced himself.

"Hey, man. I'm Zack. Zack Barnes. I'll be Trevor's assistant today." He held out a strong hand, and the two men shook. Zack had three very expensive cameras hanging around his neck and they bumped together slightly when he moved.

"Hey, Zack. I'm Blake," Blake replied. He was slightly surprised by how good-looking Zack was. Fair-haired and built, and with an inviting smile, the camera assistant could have been a model himself. Blake idly wondered if Zack's relationship with Trevor went beyond "assisting."

"So, what's this all for?" the handsome blond man asked in a friendly way. "Trevor is beside himself that he's working for Cameron Fuller. Full diva mode. I've had to check the cameras four times already, just to satisfy him that everything is going to be perfect." He flashed a broad smile. "I don't want to scare you, but I think it's going to be a looooong shoot," he added good-naturedly.

Blake laughed. "Well, Cameron seems to feel I might be model material. I just hope I don't make an ass of myself."

Zack looked the hot man standing nervously in front of him. If he wasn't already in a committed relationship, he would have definitely hit on the neophyte model. "I don't think you have to worry," he smiled.

Blake laughed. "Trevor looked at me like I was road kill."

"That's just how he is. Trust me, I can tell. He thinks you're hot. He's a great guy, once you get to know him. You'll like him, I promise."

"Sounds like *you* like him," Blake said with a smirk.

"I do," Zack nodded. "He's a great boss. But if you're asking if we're lovers, we're not. Everyone thinks we are, but, nope. I have a boyfriend that I'm crazy about." Zack had recently moved in with Bayne Raddock, the mega-rich heir to the Raddock Communications fortune. "But Trevor is single, if *you're* interested," he winked.

Blake bushed. "Oh, no. I'm . . . I'm seeing someone . . . It's new."

"Well, he's a lucky man, whoever he is."

Blake heard a faint roar and then an older, bright yellow Jeep Wrangler crested the hill and came down to the other two cars. Rafael was at the wheel, and when he made eye contact with Blake, he looked more than surprised. He parked the Jeep, climbed out, and made a beeline straight for Zack and Blake.

"What are you doing here? Who's at the store?" he demanded.

Before Blake could answer, Cameron and Trevor joined them. Zack melted into the background.

"Rafe, this is Trevor Barbados, the photographer."

"Hello."

"Hi."

There was an awkward pause while Rafael tried to determine why Blake was there without having to actually ask again. Finally, he could stand it no more. "Cameron? Why is Blake here? We have a big change in men's sportswear today that I thought he was going to handle."

Cameron put an arm around Blake's shoulder. "Blake's our man, Rafe. He *is* Pacific Coast Highway."

Rafael actually did a double take. *"What?"*

"He's perfect, don't you think? Did you bring all the clothes? Is that the Jeep? Can we take the soft top off and remove the doors? I want it to look as rugged as possible."

Rafael scrambled to keep up with Cameron. "Uh, yes, perfect. I brought everything you requested, and I'll take those doors off now." He gave Blake a last incredulous look, and then took off for the Jeep.

"Zack," Trevor barked. "Go help him take those doors off, then get out the gear and meet me by that bluff." He pointed vaguely to a small dune. "Oh! Don't forget the filters! Let's get busy!"

Zack winked at Blake, and then took off in a fast trot to join Rafe at the Jeep.

Cameron took Blake aside, with Trevor, and told him what they wanted to achieve. Blake asked a couple of questions, but it was all pretty straightforward. He got the gist of it.

"Okay, arch over the hood . . . a little more . . . that's it! Perfect!"
Click. Whir. Click. Whir. Click. Whir.

Trevor shot frame after frame of Blake, who was sprawled on his back over the hood of the now doorless Jeep, his head over the left side, hair falling down, muscular arms outstretched. The tight leather jeans squeaked softly on the smooth surface of the Jeep as he moved. Blake was wearing the too-small wifebeater white underwear tanktop, which Cam had cut off shorter at the bottom, revealing about three inches of his chiseled abs. Trevor had placed his own coconut shell choker-style necklace around Blake's thick neck, and it worked on him perfectly.

Blake's flawless tanned skin glowed in the waning light of the afternoon. Zack held up a gold toned reflector that helped burnish the scene with a golden light.

"Okay. That's enough of that. Blake, get in the Jeep. One foot in, one foot on the side step," Trevor instructed.

Blake struggled back up, and slid off the hood. He plopped down in the driver's seat of the jeep, shook his hair off his face, and stared frankly at the camera.

Trevor quickly began to shoot frame after frame. "I need more glow, Zack!" he shouted frantically, contorting his body to get the best angle. He was surprised at how well Blake took direction, and even more surprised by the fact that he actually looked good doing it. Better than good. Blake had "it," no doubt about it, and Trevor was already thinking ahead.

Zack rushed up, and finding the sun, bounced the rays into Blake's face.

Cameron watched from about twenty feet away. He could visualize this setup as the cologne box photograph. It was exactly the look he wanted for the packaging.

"Perfect, Blake! . . . Perfect! . . . I'm getting so *hard* from this! . . . Give a little more attitude! . . . That's it . . . Perfect . . ." Trevor said as he clicked off the shots.

Rafael stood a few paces behind Cameron, his face a mask. He took everything in and revealed not a trace of how he felt about it.

Which was hatred.

He hated the whole stupid idea. Blake, a model? Please. He had a good body and a handsome face, but that was it. He wasn't model material. For one thing, at thirty-one, he was far too old. And for another, Blake just didn't have "star quality." Sure, you'd want to have sex with him, but have him endorse a product? No way!

And Rafael truly hated that Cameron was so obviously infatuated with him. They were only fooling around, for Christ's sake! Why waste the company's money and time on some cheap hustler? Cameron wanted to impress this piece of trade, that's all. Which was stupid, because Rafael already knew he was having sex with him, so where was the gain for Cameron? He'd already gotten his rocks off.

Why pay for sex already had?

There was no way this was actually going to be the campaign for

Pacific Coast Highway cologne. Rafael already had a great concept in mind. In fact, he had wanted to discuss it with Cameron last night at dinner, but Cameron had begged off, and probably spent the entire night fucking pretty boy.

And not me, he stewed glumly.

After all that Rafael had done for Cameron, after all the long hours, the endless meetings, the constant working, no vacations—after all that, Cameron finally reveals himself to be gay, and falls for the idiot window dresser? How was this possible?

The more Rafael chewed on this, the angrier he got. He would find some way to destroy this little coup of Blake's. Rafe had friends in high places at Cameron Fuller USA, besides Cameron. Blake Jackson would be the Pacific Coast Highway spokesman over his dead body.

"Oh, my God, Blake! . . . You're gorgeous! . . . I want to make love to you for hours! . . . Perfect . . . Chin up! . . . Lean back . . . Perfect!" Trevor was a fiend with the camera. He was moving all around, snapping off shots as fast as the camera would speed-forward the film. He couldn't believe the images he was getting. Each shot seemed perfect, and he prayed that the finished prints contained just half the magic he was witnessing now.

Blake, blinded by the reflector, couldn't see a thing and stared vapidly out to sea. He couldn't breathe, he couldn't move, and he couldn't see. But, deep down, he was having a blast. It was fun to have all these people stare at him, compliment him, watch his every move. Trevor was a trip, telling him how he'd like to sleep with him, while he shot picture after picture.

He caught a brief glimpse of Cameron standing to the left of Trevor, and saw the look of adoration on his face. Erotic images of the night before came flooding back, affecting him so much that he started to get a hard-on.

The growing bulge transfixed Trevor, and he lowered the camera and stared at Blake. "I have an idea."

"What is it?" Cameron asked.

"Trust me."

Trevor motioned Blake out of the Jeep. He hopped in himself, and drove it right to the breaking surf's edge. Everyone watched him as if he were crazy.

"We have just enough light to shoot one roll more. Blake," he grinned evilly as he spoke, "get in the water."

No one said a word. Blake shot a glance to Cam, shrugged, then trotted over to the water's edge. Suddenly feeling free and daring, he pulled off his boots, and then dove into the cold crashing surf, clothes and all. When he surfaced, he walked awkwardly through the low waves back to the Jeep, soaking wet. He shook his head like a dog three times, and as his wet hair whipped around him, he pulled up the waterlogged jeans.

"No! Let them stay low!" Trevor barked. "Stop! Right there!" He ran into the surf himself, the camera held high, away from the lapping shoreline. He aimed at Blake. "Zack! Reflector!"

Zack scrambled to keep up with his boss. He sloshed into the surfline as well. He held the reflective oval high and aimed the echoed sunlight at the model, who was standing tall in the water, seemingly unaffected by the coldness of it.

The reflected light bathed Blake in a warm glow that allowed each glistening water drop to seem kissed by the sun. Blake's hair was tangled, wild, and blowing in the ocean breeze. The tanktop clung to his body in a pasted-on way that revealed each cut muscle of his shoulders, arms, chest, and abs.

But the pièce de la résistance was the leather jeans. Now slippery and slick from the water, they seemed to have become a second skin on Blake. The weight of the water had pulled them low on his hips. So low that the beginnings of his clipped pubic hair could be seen. The taut leather stretched across his crotch, revealing the clear shape and outline of his semi-hard and quite generous cock, which, despite the cold water, was now visible for all the world to see.

It was, without a question, the most erotic sight any of the men present had ever witnessed.

"*Dayum,*" Zack murmured to himself.

"*Fuuuck,*" Trevor uttered to himself.

"My *God,*" Cameron whispered to himself.

"I'll *kill* him," Rafael swore to himself.

12

Blake shivered slightly. Cameron had put the top of the Mercedes up, but after his dip in the January waters, Blake was still chilled to the bone. Or was his chill caused by the chat he'd had with Rafael just before he and Cameron left the beach?

"Can you turn up the heat?" he asked, hugging himself through the sweatshirt he was wearing. "I'm freezing!"

"Sure," Cameron said as he flipped some switches on the car's dash. "I'll turn on the seat warmer, too."

Soon, Blake felt the warmth radiating through the leather upholstery, and that, combined with the heat shooting at him from the vents, did the job. He warmed up.

"You looked amazing, Blake. If the pictures are half as good as I think they'll be, prepare yourself for a whole new career. I knew you were perfect after the first shot this afternoon. I knew it. I was on the phone to New York then and there. I can see the whole campaign in my head now. It's going to be fantastic," Cam enthused.

They were driving back to Blake's small West Hollywood house. It was dark by now, and the convertible snaked through the twists and turns of Sunset Boulevard, its headlights stabbing into the dark.

"You think so? I just felt stupid, but I'll take your word on it."

"Trust me. Trevor told me he'd never seen anyone look as hot as you did. He wants to shoot the whole campaign. Begged me to do it, in fact."

"I liked him."

"Well, he certainly liked you. Maybe a little too much," Cam joked.

"Oh? And that bothers you?" Blake smiled back halfheartedly.

"You bet your ass it does!"

They fell silent as the car continued home to West Hollywood. The impatient driver of the car stuck behind them tried to pass several times. But the road was just too narrow for the car to get by the Mercedes, and Cam wasn't about to speed up on the dangerous road, so they stayed one behind the other for several miles. In Beverly Hills, when the road finally became two lanes in each direction, the dark sedan sped past them.

Blake was too lost in his thoughts to pay any attention to the road drama going on around him. He was thinking about what Rafe had told him not forty-five minutes before.

It had happened by the Mercedes. After they had lost all the light, Trevor called a wrap, and Blake had walked over to the sports car to change out of the wet clothes. He was peeling off the damned wet jeans and tanktop and changing into a pair of sweats when Rafael had casually walked up to him.

"So. Did you have fun?" he asked, forcefully jolly.

"Yeah, I did . . . I didn't think I would, but it was great, though I could have done without the dip," Blake had replied easily, nodding towards the surf.

Rafael leaned in close. "Don't get used to it."

"Excuse me?"

Rafe looked over his shoulder at Cameron and Trevor, who were chatting animatedly by the Tahoe, out of earshot. "I don't know how you did it, you sneaky son of a bitch, but I am here to tell you this is as far as your so-called modeling career at Cameron Fuller is going to go."

Blake looked at Rafe in surprise.

"You may be fucking the boss, and how you managed that, I have no idea, but too many people have invested far too much in this company to watch him," he jerked a thumb in Cameron's direction, "throw it all away on some piece of ass." Rafe's dark eyes were as cold as ice. His unremarkable face had rearranged itself into something ugly as the bile spewed from his lips.

"I have no idea what you're talking about," Blake said shakily. Had Cameron told him? His mind raced trying to think of the possibilities.

"Please. Spare me your protestations. Cameron just told me all about you and him. He said you were a hot fuck, and he would do whatever it took to keep you in his bed. That is what this shoot is all about. You didn't think he was seriously going to make you the new face of PCH, did you?" Rafe took great joy in the hurt expression on Blake's face. "When he gets back to New York, he'll only remember you as some easy piece of cheap ass, and forget this whole stupid idea. And I will be right there to make sure that happens." He stabbed a pointy finger into Blake's chest. "If you're lucky. And I mean very lucky, I may let you keep your job at the store. But, now that I think about it," he got an evil glint in his eye and one lip curled up, "you may have to convince me. I always did wonder what it would be like to fuck you."

"You scummy piece of shit." Blake had finally found his voice.

Rafe snickered. "Maybe so. But I'm still your boss. Best you remember that," he threatened. "So, my advice to you? Enjoy your brief time with Cameron. He's gone in two days. Then you'll have to deal with me." He then leaned in so close to Blake that Blake could feel his hot breath on his face. "And, believe me, you will have to deal with me, pretty boy," he said, lightly stroking Blake's face with a clammy hand.

Blake jerked back, as if shot. "Not in a million fucking years, you psychopath." He was seething.

Rafe laughed again. "We'll see, my boy. We'll see. And if you mention this little chat with Cam? I'll just deny it, and fire your ass. I've been working for the man for seventeen years. He trusts me completely. He's known you, what? A day? Two?" Still laughing, Rafe had walked away and joined Cameron and Trevor.

Blake had looked dully after him, furious, embarrassed, and sad.

"Suzette's gone," Cameron quietly said, breaking the silence. "She flew back to New York this afternoon." There was a tinge of tension in his voice when he spoke about his wife.

"What's wrong?" Blake asked distractedly.

"Oh, we fought again. She says she *knows* I'm fucking someone." He glanced at Blake, who looked surprised. "Don't worry. She's just fishing. She couldn't possibly know about . . ." His face flushed red, and he didn't finish the sentence. "Then she again reminded me that she's taking all the houses," Cameron said, instead. "Like I give a shit about those houses. The only one I really love is the only one she doesn't want. Ironic, huh? If she only knew, she'd probably take that one, too."

"How many houses do you own?"

"Too many. Four."

"How can anyone live in four houses? It seems so . . . greedy." Blake shrugged, staring out the windows.

"I agree."

"Which one is the one you get to keep?"

"The Kauai house. In Hawaii."

"I've never been."

"What? You have to go! It's paradise. I have this house, perched on a cliff over the ocean. There's a secluded beach below it. Amazing views of the Napali coastline. It centers me, when I'm there. As much as I love New York, I always thought I'd retire to the island one day," Cameron said wistfully.

"Sounds beautiful," Blake said offhandedly, his mind a million miles away.

"It is."

Blake returned to staring gloomily out the window.

"You're awfully sullen for a man who's just made the hottest photographer in town drool. What's up?" Cam joked, though his concern could be felt.

Blake focused on Cam. "Can I ask you something?"

"Sure."

"How did you hook up with Rafael? I mean, how did he come to your company?"

Cameron kept his eyes on the curving road as he spoke. "When we opened the first store, on Fifth Avenue, about fifteen years ago, I hired Rafe to do the visual displays. He was this skinny kid from Queens who had so many great ideas about retail. He'd grown up really poor, yet he had this amazing, sophisticated taste. He could pull an outfit or room together faster than anybody I'd ever met. Over time, he was just kinda always there with a good idea at the right time. I've really come to depend on him."

"Huh," Blake grunted.

"What? Why the interest?"

Blake faced Cameron. "He's an asshole. You realize that, don't you? He treats people like crap, and then sucks up to you. I'm surprised you fall for it."

Cameron laughed out loud. "I don't 'fall for it.' I know exactly what he's doing. He's a temperamental queen, and I tolerate him because he's very good at his job. But that doesn't mean I let him get away with murder. Every once in a while, I remind him who's boss."

"Like yesterday? With the windows?"

"Exactly. I saw how he was treating you. He needed to be smacked down a little." Cameron smiled at Blake. "Look, I know he's a bitch to work for, but he just wants what's best for me. He wants the company to be the best it can be." A sudden hard cast overcame his eyes. "I wish everyone that worked for me thought that way."

"But I think everyone does. I know everyone at the store loves you, and bleeds for you."

Cameron's smile grew warmer. "Thanks for that. Just try to get along with him, okay? He *is* a creative genius, if a little unorthodox."

"Have you told him, or anyone, about us? About . . ." Blake let the sentence dangle. "Maybe someone you told said something to your wife."

"No, I haven't told a soul, but, oddly, I want to. I want to shout it to the world. Why do you ask?"

Blake looked at Cam for any trace of deception. Seeing none, he shook his head. How could he have even listened to Rafe? The man was insane and pure evil, and he had Cameron snowed. He smiled in spite of himself. "No reason," he said, warmly taking Cam's free right hand in his own.

They eventually pulled onto Blake's street. As they approached his house, Blake noticed that Rand must have company. There was a large SUV parked in his driveway directly behind his Cherokee.

"Park on the street. Rand must have someone over," Blake said as he gathered up his belongings.

Cameron smiled slyly and parked at the curb. They got out of the Mercedes and walked up the short driveway. The Land Rover Discovery II was brand new. It still had the paper plates from the dealer on it. It was hunter green, and as Blake passed by the windows, he noticed it had a rich light tan leather interior.

It made his Cherokee look very small.

Just as he got to the front of the SUV he saw a large red bow stuck on the hood. Perplexed, he looked at Cameron.

"Congratulations!" Cameron practically shouted.

Completely confused, Blake didn't understand what was going on. He stared dumbly at Cameron, his mouth open.

"A small token from me to my new Pacific Coast Highway spokesman!" Cameron gleefully informed him.

"Are you serious?! No way!"

"I can't have you driving around in that," Cameron waved dissmissively at the Cherokee. "You deserve better."

"Oh, my God! It's beautiful! Cameron, I don't know what to say," Blake was so excited he dropped his stuff, and grabbing Cameron, gave him a big bear hug.

"Say you'll keep it," Cameron laughed, hugging him back.

Just then, the gate cut into the fence that blocked the garage and the back of the house from the front yard, opened. A barefoot man with a spiky blond Weho buzz cut walked out to join them. Young and handsome, he was dressed in khaki shorts and a Britney Spears T-shirt.

"Hey, Rand!" Blake called to him.

"Hi! A guy dropped this off for you." He pointed to the car. "Here's the paperwork and the keys." He handed over a thick packet to Blake. Rand stared at Cameron, realizing who he was. "Ohmigod! You're Cameron Fuller! I love your clothes!" He eagerly stuck out his hand for Cameron to shake. "I'm wearing your shorts now!" He spun around and pulled at the waistband on the shorts, flipping it out, half exposing a pale ass cheek. "See?"

"Yes, I see. Hi, Rand. Nice to meet you."

"So, Blake? What's going on? Did you win this?" Rand asked, motioning towards the luxury SUV.

Not knowing what to say, Blake looked at Cameron.

"Not really," Cameron answered for him. "Blake is going to be the new face of Pacific Coast Highway. My new fragrance. He's going to be on billboards and in commercials all over the world. This is a gift to him from the company."

"No shit! Ohmigod! Blake! That's amazing! Ohmigod!" Rand jumped up and down, and hugged Blake. "Wait until I tell Sam! He'll flip!"

"Sam?" Cameron asked.

"His boyfriend," Blake explained.

"Well, let's go take a ride in your new car," Rand excitedly suggested.

The three of them got in, Blake in the driver's seat. The new car smell was intoxicating to him, and he looked ravenously over the dials and gauges on the dashboard. He flicked on the radio and the dance sounds of Moby came from the surround speakers. Blake cranked the jams up.

He carefully backed out and took the new SUV on a short spin around the block. He loved it. If he had felt even the slightest bit uneasy in accepting it earlier, now that he'd driven it, he had to have it. Using the rear view mirror, he glanced at Cameron sitting in the backseat. They locked eyes and smiled secretly at each other.

Blake's cell phone went off. As he was digging it out from its position on his belt, he saw Cameron's surprised reaction in the rear view mirror. He thought he was the only one who had the new number.

"I gave Brady and Rand the number," Blake explained quickly before answering it.

Cameron settled back into the seat.

"Brady! You are not going to believe this!" Blake said excitedly. He briefly told him about the photo shoot and car. Brady was, of course, suspicious, and not wanting to go into it over the phone, Blake didn't mention his growing romance with Cameron.

Rand pricked up his ears when he heard who Blake was talking to. Blake noticed his tenant's sudden attention to the call, and it confirmed his beliefs that Rand had a not-so-secret crush on the burly police officer.

"Blake," Brady's voice through the phone was grave. "Something doesn't sound right about this. Cameron Fuller just made you a model and he bought you a car?"

"Brady . . ."

The Deputy interrupted him. "Blake, be careful, okay? These big shots, they promise the world, but they always get the better end of any deal. Watch your back, okay? It just sounds too good to be true."

"Brady, I know what I'm doing," Blake said firmly.

"I know you do, but sometimes you're a little naive. I think there's more to this than meets the eye. Just keep your eyes open. If this is legit, then I am so happy for you! But, if it's not . . . I just care what happens to you, that's all."

"I know you do, and I love you for it. Call me tomorrow and I'll give you all the details. Bye."

Blake again looked at Cameron in the rear view.

"Don't sweat it. He's just a good friend, and he's concerned for me." Blake flashed a brilliant smile.

Cameron grinned in spite of himself.

In the flickering candlelight, Blake rolled over and looked at Cameron. His eyes were closed and he had been spooned up next to Blake. Now that they were face-to-face, Cameron woke up, smiled sleepily, and reached a muscular arm over to hug Blake close. He mumbled something dreamy and fell back to sleep.

Blake grinned. Poor Cameron, he thought. He must be wiped out. Vigorous fucking off and on for the past two hours had worn them both out.

They had skipped dinner and hopped into bed as soon as they got back from the quick joy ride. The second their bodies hit the sheets, they were at each other like animals. It had been intense, hard-core man-sex. The kind that Blake had forgotten was possible, and had needed so badly. The pent-up passions of the two men that had been stifled all day were released, and they physically exhausted themselves with their frantic lovemaking.

Blake studied Cameron's relaxed face. It was the first time Blake had seen him completely at ease. His worry lines had smoothed out and he looked so serene in the soft light. Blake gently brushed a stray lock of hair off his brow, smiling. He had never felt this comfortable with a man in such a short amount of time. The only other man he'd ever really cared for was Brady, and he hadn't let Brady sleep over until almost four weeks into the relationship. But he never wanted Cameron to leave. He wouldn't have thought it was possible to feel such strong emotions for this man in the brief time they had known each other.

Blake had always played fast and loose with men. He was acutely

aware of his assets and used them at will. When he seduced his en-
gaged swim coach during an out-of-town swim meet at the age of
seventeen, Blake quickly figured out that his handsome face and
awesome body were a commodity money couldn't buy. He instinctively knew he had something other men coveted. He learned that if
he wanted a guy, he rarely had to do more than look him squarely in
the eye; within the hour they would be fucking. Blake's list of lovers
was shockingly lengthy.

Borderline sluttish. Okay. Forget the borderline. He was flat-out
sluttish.

He was not unfamiliar with party drugs, though he had really cut
that out lately. He also was never one for clinginess. In fact, he usually invented a reason the guy had to leave his house right after sex,
or why he had to go from the guy's house. And once a guy was out of
his sight, he was out of his mind. Names and numbers were never
stored.

Yet, he constantly complained that he couldn't find "true love." He
saw a movie once where one of the characters said that L.A. was a
town full of "tens looking for an eleven." He hadn't gotten the joke.
To Blake Jackson, there would always be someone better on the
horizon, so he was never happy with the man he was with, no matter
how amazing he was.

Blake had a vague sense he treated men badly, and had broken
more than one heart with his cavalier attitude. He would promise to
call, but wouldn't. He would say "I want to see you again," and not
really mean it. He played the game, always planning on changing his
ways "someday."

It wasn't something that he was particularly proud of.

His romance with Brady had tempered the bad behavior some, but
when it hadn't worked out he'd fallen back into his old ways of casual sex.

That's why his strong feelings for Cameron surprised him. He just
wanted to hang out with him, be around him. He hadn't even thought
about another man since he'd met him. Granted, it had only been two
days, but still! And he didn't think it was because of who Cameron
was. It was because of how Cameron made him feel.

Blake was also well aware that their time together was fast running out. Cameron was due back in New York the day after tomorrow, and Blake didn't know when he'd see him again, if ever. He pushed the doubts that Rafe had raised out of his mind. He knew that Cameron was infatuated with him. How else do you explain the photo session and the Discovery II? But he also knew Cameron had serious baggage from his college-days love affair, years before.

Was there a future here? Sadly, Blake knew that was doubtful.

Joe, sensing his master was awake, ambled over to the side of the bed and carefully judged the room available. Deciding there was enough, he leapt up on the bed and settled in next to Blake.

Blake stroked him gently for a few minutes, then felt himself getting drowsy. He felt so safe and content nestled between Joe and his new lover.

He sighed.

I'll just enjoy the hell out of it while it lasts and deal with Rafe later, he told himself, just before he fell asleep.

13

Silas was sitting in the back of his limousine, his lower body kept comfortably warm by the down throw his driver had placed over his thin legs. He was reading that morning's edition of the *New York Times* and paying no attention to the city waking up outside his car's windows.

His cell phone rang four times before he could dig it out of his briefcase and, fumbling with the small buttons, answer it.

"Yes?" he said, patting down the blanket to cover his legs more.

"Cameron has decided to make his new boyfriend the face of Pacific Coast Highway. They did a shoot at the beach yesterday and spent the night together, again, at Jackson's house," Dillard's flat monotone said clearly. His displeasure at having to do this duty for Silas was evident.

"What!?" Silas felt his blood pressure ratchet up.

"From what I'm told, the kid's a natural. He looked good, took direction, and Cameron and the photographer seem to be sold on him."

"This is preposterous! I won't stand for it! Can you imagine? To put some slutty queer boy on billboards all across America?"

Dillard absorbed the crude remark without comment. "There's more," he quietly replied.

"I can hardly wait to hear what else," Silas said dryly.

"Cameron bought him a car. A big Land Rover. I'd say this seems pretty serious. You don't drop forty-five K on a fling." In an odd way, Dillard enjoyed telling the news to Silas. He hated spying on his friend, and if this news hurt the old man, then good. He deserved it.

"Oh, my Lord. Has he gone crazy?"

There was silence on the other end of the phone.

"Thank you for the information," Silas finally said, his face flushed. "Keep me informed of any other new developments."

"Yes, I will." Dillard was about to hang up.

"Wait!" Silas commanded.

"Yes? What is it?"

"I want you to . . . do something about this situation. My God, what if he falls in love with this boy? What if he decides to come out of the cupboard? My family will be humiliated! I don't care how you do it, but keep Cameron away from this man!"

"Well, what do you want me to do? I can't very well walk up to Cam and tell him to stop what he's doing!"

"Think of something, you fool! I don't think you'd like prison very much. Though I suspect you'd enjoy being some con's bitch, I doubt you'd last very long." Silas clicked off the call, and in frustration, threw the phone down onto the floor of the car.

He stared solemnly out the window of the limo, his mind absorbing this news. Cameron was going too far. To be . . . *that way* was one thing, but to risk company time and money on a peccadillo was insane.

One way or another, this affair would have to be stopped.

14

The next morning, while Blake was showering after his morning run, Cameron was drinking a cup of coffee and petting Joe. His cell phone rang.

"Hello?"

"Cameron? Hi, it's Trevor Barbados. I spent the night in the darkroom printing out these shots. You are *not* going to believe them! They're bloody *art,* man! Blake is the hottest male model I have ever worked with. In fact, I have an *Esquire* shoot in a couple of weeks. It's the cover. I want him for it."

"No way." Cameron shook his head. "He's exclusive to us."

"What if he wears Cameron Fuller clothes?"

"Can we make it a tie-in to the cologne?"

"I'll make it happen. Cameron, you are going to *love* these shots! The one in the water? Jesus Christ! You'll have women wetting their pants when they see it. The boys, too."

"Can you send a set to the store? I'll be there in a couple of hours."

"They're already there. Call me when you see them. I want this campaign, Cameron," Trevor said forcefully.

"We'll talk later. Thanks for the good words, Trevor. Bye." Cameron snapped shut the phone, and placed it on the tabletop next to Blake's wallet, keys, and cell.

He was seated in the kitchen breakfast nook and he stared out the bay window into the backyard. The small portable TV on the counter next to the refrigerator was on, and the news anchor was having happy talk with the latest *Amazing Race* castoffs. The welcoming smell of fresh brewed coffee tantalized his nose and the beams of sunlight coming through the windows filtered through the floating dust mites in the air. He couldn't remember the last time he felt so peaceful. So . . . normal.

Through the window, he saw the door to the studio apartment open. Rand, wearing only a tight pair of white undershorts, and a bookish dark-haired young man dressed in khakis, a button-down shirt, and sweater vest came out. They kissed tenderly. Cameron idly watched the dark-haired guy slide his hand under the thin cotton of Rand's shorts and give his round ass a good, firm squeeze. Cameron realized with a start that Rand's underpants were his own label. He watched the two young men continue to kiss deeply. The visitor then sadly turned away and walked down the driveway to the street. Rand had the exact same look on his face that Cameron had on his. One of total bliss.

Apparently, I wasn't the only one getting royally fucked last night, mused Cameron, smiling.

Rand happened to glance at the main house, where he saw Cameron at the table. He waved brightly and threw Cam a huge grin before going back into his apartment.

Cameron returned his attention to Joe when Joe placed a paw on his lap. Blake had explained the night before that that was Joe's signal for "outside." He got up and padded to the back door, opening it for the dog. Joe trotted out. Cameron left the door open and returned to the table.

Cameron liked Blake's house. It was too small, but then, maybe he had just gotten used to the large houses that Suzette had picked out; maybe he had forgotten how real people lived. Blake's house had a lived-in quality, warm and happy, that none of his many houses had.

He had to admit to himself that he was actually jealous of Blake. Surrounded by friends and his dog, he had a good life in a comfortable home.

Cameron also had to admit that he had not slept as well as he had last night in, literally, years. Making love with Blake and falling asleep in his arms was something that Cameron still could scarcely believe he'd done.

He realized, sitting on the cushioned bench in Blake's sunny little kitchen, that he was head over heels in love with the man. The realization that he could actually experience love, after thinking it would never happen again, brought tears to his eyes. He had no clue how Blake felt about him, and it didn't matter. He loved Blake with all his heart. It was as simple as that. The feelings surprised him. He had never gotten over the death of Stanton, and now he was faced with having to completely let that go. He didn't know if he could.

And then he remembered he was scheduled to leave L.A. the next morning.

Blake walked into the creative services office and was immediately attacked by Chelsea and Dusty. They demanded to be clued in to what had happened the day before. Gossip was running rampant around the store and they had to know the truth.

Blake gave them a carefully edited version of the events. He couldn't bring himself to even mention the new car.

"Is it true? You're going to be a model? So are you leaving? Are you moving to New York?" Chelsea pressed.

"I honestly don't know what's going to happen. When I know, I'll let you know, okay? But, I don't think I'm moving anywhere," he said kindly.

"You're going to be famous! You're going to be a star," Dusty said, high-fiving him.

"I doubt that, very seriously." Blake looked over his desk, and saw the stack of display requests there. "Did you guys not do anything yesterday? Jesus! Look at the pile of work we have to do today."

He sat down and sorted through the forms. He handed them off to either Chelsea or Dusty for them to do that day. He made a few phone calls. He lost track of time and was stunned when he looked up and it was after twelve.

He had only had a power bar for breakfast that morning, eaten as he and Cam left the house. Cam had left in his car, Blake in his new Land Rover. They had agreed to meet for lunch, away from the store, at The Grill, a great restaurant hidden down an alley in downtown Beverly Hills.

He was going to be late. Just as he was leaving the store, his new cell phone rang. Knowing it was Cam wondering where he was, he flipped it open and began speaking.

"Cameron, baby! I'm on my way now, you sexy man with the sexy ass that felt so tight when I fucked it last night!" he said in a rapper style accent. "Listen to me. Suddenly, I'm all, Blake Diddy!" He laughed.

There was a pause on the other end. "Hello? Who is this?!" It was a woman's strident voice. *"Blake?* Blake what?!"

Shocked, Blake physically cringed. He looked at the phone, for the first time noticing the initials C.F. on it. He realized, too late, he had picked up Cam's phone by mistake.

"I *said,* Blake what? Cameron's sexy *ass!?* You're fucking my husband?! Wait a minute? You work at the store, don't you! You're that *window dresser!* Where's my husband?!" Suzette was screaming now.

Blake flipped the phone shut. He was panic-struck. What should he do? The phone rang again. He ignored it, staring at it like it was an alien. After ringing four times, the call went into voice mail. The phone rang again.

By the time he got to The Grill, the phone had rung twelve times. Blake was frantic with worry. He didn't know what he was going to say to Cam, but whatever it was, he was sure Cam would be pissed.

The host showed him to Cam's table, at the rear of the restaurant. Cameron was wearing a navy blue V-neck cashmere sweater over a simple white crew-neck tee shirt. The sweater was tucked into a pair of flat front tan slacks. He looked, as usual, amazing.

Cam's face broke out into a huge grin when he saw Blake enter, and he resisted the urge to jump up and kiss him hello. On the table next to him was a large manilla envelope and Blake's cell phone.

"Hi! You look great," Cam said, squeezing Blake's thigh under the table.

"Hi," Blake responded, miserable.

"What's the matter?"

"Oh, Cam, I'm so sorry! I didn't know! I picked up your phone by mistake this morning . . ."

"I know. I figured that out when I didn't get any calls. It was nice actually," Cam interjected.

"Your wife called," Blake said, eyes cast down. "I thought it was you, and I said something I shouldn't have."

Cameron's face was a mask. "What did you say?"

Blake gulped. "I said, 'Hi Cameron, you sexy man with the sexy ass. I sure fucked you good!' Or words to that effect. She freaked out and started screaming. I hung up and didn't say anything else, but it was too late! She knew I was talking about you." He placed the now silent phone on the table. "She's called back, like, ten times. Oh, Cam, I'm so sorry!" Blake looked stricken. Like he was about to cry.

Cameron looked at him, then at the phone. Then he laughed. Hard. "Well, serves me right for getting you the same phone! Blake, sweetheart, don't worry about it." He squeezed Blake's thigh again. "It was an honest mistake. I'll deal with Suzette. She must be thrilled to finally have valid proof. She's thought I've been fucking around for years. This must have made her day," he said through his laughter.

"I'm so sorry," Blake repeated.

Just then, Cameron's phone rang again. Blake almost jumped out of his seat. Cameron reached over and calmly answered it.

"Hello?"

"Cameron? Is that you, you miserable son of a bitch? I caught you! I finally caught you!" Suzette screamed. Her voice was so loud Blake could clearly hear her from where he was sitting.

"And how are you, darling? Did you have a nice flight back?" Cameron replied evenly.

"Fuck you! You're screwing the help? A *window dresser?!* I knew it, I just knew it!"

"Suzette, I'm not going to have this conversation with you. Our so-called marriage is *over.* You know it and I know it. Who I fuck is none of your goddamn business. Just like the parade of men you fuck is none of mine."

"Who *I* fuck! I have no idea what you're talking about!" she hotly retorted.

"Pierre Gleason. Jack Reynolds. Perry Clancy. Do I need to continue?" he said smoothly.

"You son of a bitch! What choice did I have? You wouldn't . . ." she began.

"Shut up and listen to me. I've decided to spend a few more days in L.A. I suggest you get with your attorney and plot whatever you're going to plot. Have him call Hammish Stein, the attorney who'll represent me in the divorce. They can start the proceedings. Just remember, two can play the blame game. I wouldn't push it, if I were you. I think you know what I mean," he said ominously. "So, let's keep this low key, and avoid press, shall we? I'll see you sometime next week. Goodbye, Suzette." Cameron flipped the phone shut and stared at it for a beat. He let out a deep breath.

"Oh, Cam, I'm so embarrassed. I'm so sorry!"

"Sweetheart, forget about it. I know I will. Are you hungry? Let's order."

"Are you really staying a few more days?"

"I am now." He grinned at Blake, completely at ease with his decision.

They perused the menu, and when their server came by, they gave their order. After the server had left, Cam slid the manilla envelope over to Blake.

"Take a look," he said.

Blake opened the flap and pulled out several eight-by-ten shots. They were the photos from yesterday's shoot. Blake looked through them.

They were amazing. The lighting had been perfect, and the reflector Trevor had used gave everything a late summer golden glow. Blake knew he took a good picture, but these were something else. As he flipped through the photographs, he had to admit he looked *good.*

He stopped short when he got to the shot taken in the water. His frankly sexy glare, the way his shirt clung to him, the low-riding leather jeans, it all added up to the most amazing photograph of himself he had ever seen. Then he glanced down at his crotch.

There it was, straining against the leather, semi-hard and ready for action.

"Ohmigod! You can totally see the shape of my dick!" he whispered to Cameron.

"I know. That *alone* is going to sell 50,000 bottles of cologne," Cameron said with a smile.

Blake was shocked. "Jesus! I had no idea those pants did that! You can see my pubes! Cam, you can't use this!"

"I can, and I will. That shot right there is going to be on billboards all across America. Eighty feet tall in Times Square and on Sunset Boulevard. I already told Trevor."

"Oh, my God."

"This displeases you?"

"Well, I just never thought I'd be showing my package to the world, that's all."

"Look at it this way. Imagine it's not you. If you saw this ad, what would you think?" Cameron asked.

Blake forced himself to remove himself from the picture. He looked at it as if it were some other guy. When he did that, he realized the power it had. It was a starkly sexual photograph of a hot man that he would want to not only fuck but marry.

"I see your point," he agreed, reluctantly. "Oh, well. Screw it. Use it." He tossed the picture on the table.

"Thattaboy. Blake, this is going to make you a star," he said, tapping the image.

"Yeah. A porn star," Blake mumbled, shaking his head.

The waiter returned with their drinks, and noticed the photograph lying on the table. His eyes bulged as he tried not to look as though he was staring at it, but stare he did. When he placed Blake's drink in front of him, he realized Blake was the man in the photograph. He gasped audibly.

He almost spilled Cameron's drink he was suddenly so nervous.

After he left, Cameron laughed. "I think that proves exactly what I was saying."

Blake was used to being ogled, but that had been different. He had just been revered.

He liked it.

"I've taken the liberty of calling a friend of mine, Ryne Blackwell. He runs Hunk, the top male modeling agency in New York. I told him all about you, and he wants to take you on as a client," Cameron said, taking a sip of his iced tea.

"I've heard of them! They're, like, the best agency for men around," Blake marveled.

"And you're their newest discovery. They'll handle all your contracts, which should be ready by tomorrow morning. They have an office in Beverly Hills, too. You'll deal exclusively with either Ryne or his L.A. partner, Nelle. In fact, you have to go over to meet her as soon as we're done here. She'll fill you in on the particulars of the financial deal."

"Wow."

"Now, aren't you a tad curious about the money?" Cameron asked coyly.

"Well, yeah, but I didn't want to bug you with it," Blake blushed.

"Well, we're going to use your image on the packaging of the bottles, the gift sets, the promotional items. You'll do TV commercials, print ads, and billboards. There will also probably be in-store appearances and that sort of thing." Cameron went through the items as if he were reading a grocery list.

Blake's eyes got bigger and his heart raced faster as he listened.

"You're going to be under exclusive contract to Cameron Fuller USA, which means you can't do any other competing product. We pay for that right, so don't worry. You're allowed to do other campaigns, but we'll want you to clear them through our people first, to make sure there is absolutely no conflict."

"That sounds fair."

"You'll need to be available to fit our schedule, so all other endeavors have to come second. And for that, we're going to pay you two hundred and fifty thousand dollars a year for the exclusivity, for a minimum of three years, a signing bonus of fifty thousand dollars, and you'll get above market value as your day rates when you shoot ads and do appearances. You'll get the usual residuals from the commercials and that stuff." Cameron eyed him as Blake did the mental math.

"Oh, my God," Blake whistled.

"Get yourself a good accountant. Ask Nelle for a reference. If you plan smartly, in a couple of years you'll be a millionaire."

Blake's mouth opened and closed like a fish. He was having a little trouble wrapping his mind around the information.

"You like?" Cameron asked.

Blake stumbled with his words. "I . . . I . . . like, yes!" He wanted to grab Cameron and hug him for an hour. Instead he squeezed his knee.

"It's going to get crazy for you. It's not all fun and games and having your picture taken. It's hard work and you'll earn every dime you make, trust me."

"I'm prepared."

"Good. Now. I want you to get some some sun this week. I want you bronzed. No tan line. We're going to shoot some more shots next week. I'm thinking up in Big Sur. And I want you to hit the gym hard. You look fanfuckingtastic, but give me that extra that I want, okay?"

"No problem. I'll go right after work tonight."

"No, you better go this afternoon. I have plans for you tonight. I've set up a meeting with Trevor and Nelle and some folks from the ad agency I use. You'll need to be there. I want them to meet, and be charmed by you. Dressy. Go back to the store and get yourself a great outfit, and have them put it on my house charge. Ever had a facial? Get one booked, and do that as well."

"I feel like I should be taking notes," Blake said with a laugh, completely excited by his prospects. "But, I can't just bag work. I have responsibilities there."

"Blake, you're going to be so busy the next few weeks, I think you need to focus on your new job. Rafe will find someone to replace you at the store."

"But, Cam," Blake frowned. "I love my job. Do I have to quit that to do this?"

Cameron was flummoxed. "I'm giving you the world here, Blake. Your 'shopboy' days are over. You're big time now. Get used to it."

"Okay. I guess you're right. Sorry," Blake sighed.

Cameron leaned in close. He took Blake's hand off his knee, and moved it to his crotch. "And, after all the meetings are done, later tonight, we're going to fuck like wild men. Anything you want me to do, I'm going to do." His voice got husky as images of what he desired flashed before his eyes.

"Now, that's the best news yet," Blake replied, also in a husky tone.

15

"But, Daddy! You don't understand!" Suzette wailed. She had been pacing madly about the room, and with an explosive sigh of air, she flung herself on the silk damask sofa, taking care not to wrinkle her powder blue Chanel suit too badly. She also made sure she didn't actually cry. She had a P.E.T.A. luncheon in an hour, and there would be no time for a touchup.

Suzette felt that the worst thing about being a member of the *au courant* and politically correct People for the Ethical Treatment of Animals was having to put all her fabulous furs in storage. She *missed* them. Especially the full-length sable. She was counting the days until she could quit the group and get them back, but for now, it looked good for Suzette Cabbott Fuller to be socially conscious.

Suzette and her formidable father were in the large book-filled study of his Park Avenue apartment, a mere three blocks away from Suzette and Cameron's own penthouse. Her face almost buried in the down cushions of the antique sofa, Suzette sighed loudly once more for emphasis.

Silas watched his daughter's tantrum with wary eyes, studying her performance as he would a ballet at Lincoln Center. His willful girl had always been a handful, not to mention a calculating actress. Through many years of trial and error, he had learned the tools needed to get her to behave rationally.

"I think I do understand. You've known that your husband was queer for years, and have just now faced the hard fact that he's actually getting screwed to the walls by some young buck," he said levelly.

"Daddy! You say it so calmly, like it's an everyday occurrence!"

"Suzette. This whole topic disgusts me. The only way I can even *discuss* it is to remain calm. You told me last year what the truth about your marriage was. You suspected he was seeing other men then. Why are you so stunned now? I've always known you to be charmless, but are you completely dimwitted as well?"

"This is different! I can feel it! I can tell by his tone! It's just like it was when he and . . ." she stopped short, catching herself in the nick of time. Suzette had been drunk when she told her father that her marriage to Cameron was a sham, but she hadn't been so drunk as to tell him the whole story. She had prudently left out the fact that Stanton and Cameron had been lovers.

She knew her father's low opinion of homosexuals, and she was painfully aware of his adoration for his dead son. The news that his own flesh and blood could be gay would rob Silas of his fond and cherished memories. She just couldn't do that to her father. Even though she had always been made to feel like she was fifth runner-up for her father's affections, Suzette actually loved her distant father and craved his approval. Why she felt compelled to constantly seek the good graces of a man who clearly despised her was just another one of the many odd quirks that made up the stylish woman's troubled personality.

"Yes? 'Just like when he and' what?" Silas leaned forward. A new thought briefly flitted through his mind. *Had Suzette known about Stanton and Cameron—and never told me?*

"Nothing," she quickly covered. "I can just tell. He's serious about this one. He wants the divorce now! You haven't seen his fuckboy, Blake Whatshisname. That's who he's screwing. He works at that Godawful Rodeo Drive store. I *met* him! I recognized his voice on Cam's phone! He *bragged* to me that he was fucking my husband! The nerve! This punk is everything that a fag would want! He's very good looking and I think Cameron is just . . . dazzled by him!" Suzette renewed her fake sobs, and feebly punched at the pillow back of the sofa.

"I always suspected that you never could be woman enough to hold on to your husband. This whole unseemly mess is your fault. No one else's."

That stinging statement caused even harder sobbing from Suzette. And more than one real tear.

"And, for the record, the fuckboy, as you so classlessly called him, is named Blake Jackson. He's been an employee of Cameron Fuller USA for just under a year. He owes three hundred fifty-seven thousand dollars on his mortgage and has a small savings account with sixty-three hundred dollars in it, at the West Hollywood branch of US Bank. He was born on September second and owns a dog. A golden retriever, in fact. He has a tenant rent a small studio to help with his house note, and among his many, *many* former lovers is a sheriff's deputy." Silas sat back in his favorite chair and watched with amusement as the shock crept over Suzette's face.

"How . . . how did you know all that?" she asked, incredulous.

"I know everything, Suzette. I make it my business."

"Well, what am I supposed to do?" she wailed, taken slightly aback.

"Divorce Cameron's faggot ass, take a settlement, and live out your days in leisure. What else? You haven't exactly led the virtuous life of a dutiful wife."

Suzette stopped crying and narrowed her now dry eyes. One glance at her father's stern face told her lying would be useless. "That's not fair! I'm a normal, healthy woman with normal, healthy appetites! My pansy husband wasn't meeting my needs. Of course I had to look elsewhere! Don't misunderstand. I want a divorce, too, but don't you see? Once he's rid of me, he'll get rid of you, too! The second he pays off that note, he'll have you dropped from the board." Suzette folded her arms and looked at her father.

"Do I look stupid? Do you think I'm a stupid man, Suzette?"

Suzette didn't know how to respond to this. "Well, no, Daddy, of course not!"

"Don't you think I'm well aware of what your husband's plans are, concerning me?"

Deflated, Suzette nodded. "Yes, Daddy."

Silas almost smiled. "Take my word. *I'm* not going anywhere. You, however, are a different story."

"But I gave that man the best years of my life!" Suzette wailed, her anger returning. "I'm Mrs. Cameron-fucking-Fuller, for God's sake!

I have a position in this town! I'm a goddamn national icon! Women look up to me! How am I supposed to live down the fact that I'm a role model, the 'woman of today,' yet I'm not woman enough to keep my husband from seeking love in the arms of another man?! I'll be the laughingstock of this country!"

"A title you clearly deserve for having married the pervert in the first place," Silas unsympathetically noted. "I suggest, then, you figure out a way to continue living with the lie. Just as you have for the past twenty odd years." Silas crossed his arms and stared at his petulant daughter.

It sickened him to face it, but Silas knew that if Cameron was seeing this young fag in L.A., then there were probably other young fags in other cities that he was seeing as well. Apparently, his son-in-law was finally allowing himself to act like the degenerate that he was. Divorce was imminent. Silas knew he wouldn't be able to stop it. But, with some subtle direction, his idiot daughter would be a useful tool in ruining the life of the man who seduced his cherished son.

Cameron was a weak man, Silas felt, and he deserved all the trouble Suzette could create for him, and more. Cameron wouldn't fight back for fear of losing his company. Things were too delicate right now. The more off-kilter Cameron was, the better it would play for Silas.

The old man stared at his overdressed, over-madeup daughter and waited. Silas wanted her to make the decision.

He didn't have to wait long. His daughter was a predictable creature, and the old man knew what she would say before the words began to form on her lips.

"And let him just *get away* with this?" she hissed, almost on cue. "No way! He needs to pay!" She stood up and resumed her frantic pacing.

Silas actually grinned a toothy, crooked smile. "Oh, I never said don't make him pay."

Suzette, sensing the tide was changing, stopped pacing. "What are you suggesting?"

Silas placed his fingers together like a tent and pretended to muse silently for a moment. "I have some ideas," he said at last. "But nothing I want to completely share at this moment. My suggestion to you is to make your presence known to this Blake character. Let Cameron know you're on to the two of them, and that you aren't going to silently fade away. Put up a fight, then pull back. Keep him off balance. Make outrageous demands for your settlement, then back away from them. Confuse the hell out of him. Then, let's see how this thing plays out. If my hunch is correct, you will walk away from this disastrous marriage smelling like a rose, and your queer husband will be lucky if we allow him to peddle his cheap shirts again."

The tight corners of Suzette's mouth turned upward slightly. It was her version of a smile.

"Oh, and Suzette," Silas said, looking away from his daughter.

"Yes, Daddy?"

"I can't bear to hear it now," he said, rising stiffly from his seat. "But, one day, and *one day soon,* you and I are going to have a long talk about Stanton's death. I've always felt you've held back all you know." He walked to the double doors and turned to face the well-dressed woman with the shocked look on her face. "You *will* come clean with me, young lady, mark my words. I am your father. You *will* do as I say." Having said that, he slowly walked out of the stately room.

Watching her elderly parent leave, Suzette realized she had forgotten to breathe. The very thought of telling Silas the truth about Stanton's death caused the chic woman to need support for a second. Gripping the rolled arm of the sofa tightly, she slowly regained her composure.

Her heart still racing, Suzette was well aware that she could never tell her father the whole story. Who knew what he would do? The uncertainty of how he would handle the shock caused her body to shiver briefly.

Taking a deep breath, Suzette recalled the sacred pact that she had made with Cameron twenty-five years earlier. They had both privately vowed never to waver from the story they had concocted that night.

Even though she had been frustrated, shamed, and hurt by her husband, it was the one vow she would not break. Ever.

16

Blake yawned. "What a long day," he said. "I'm exhausted. This being a supermodel takes it out of you."

"Poor baby." Cameron laughed sarcastically. "I feel your pain. I really do."

"Liar."

Blake was flat on his back in bed, arms stretched over his head. Cameron was laying on top of him, head on his chest. He was stroking Blake's hair with his fingers, idly fanning the long, dark strands out on the pillow.

It was after midnight before they had gotten back to Blake's home from the meeting with the ad people. After locking up the house, they both had stripped down and fallen into Blake's comfortable bed, each fighting to keep his eyes open.

"What did you think of everyone?" Cameron asked, yawning.

"They're all okay. I really liked Nelle. She's a ballbuster. When I met her at her office this afternoon, she'd already seen copies of the photos, and had two other deals working for me. An *Esquire* shoot and a cigarette ad for Japan."

"Yeah, well, nothing until we unveil you. She knows that," Cameron said.

"The ad people were cool. That one guy, what was his name, Johnny something? He slipped me his phone number as he left. As did the waiter at lunch today. Things are picking up for me," Blake joked lamely.

"I do believe my tender feelings are hurt."

"Please. I can't even think of anyone but you. I'm smitten. I'm a smitten kitten."

Cameron smiled warmly and nuzzled up against Blake's hard chest. "Me too, baby. Me, too."

Blake yawned again. "Sorry. I worked chest and back so hard today. I'm kinda sore. Sore and tired. A full hour on the treadmill. I *hate* the treadmill."

"Just fall asleep then. Drift off." Cameron kissed his chest lightly. " 'Night, sweetheart."

"G'night . . . Cam . . . I . . ." Blake slid into a deep sleep, safe and happy under Cameron's weight.

"I love you, Blake," Cameron said faintly, closing his eyes. He soon was asleep as well, his head gently rising and falling with each of Blake's deep breaths.

Blake woke up about four A.M. He sleepily watched Cameron breathing in the moonlight. He had shifted to his back, one meaty leg still laying across Blake's thighs.

He must be having a good dream, thought Blake. Cameron had a full boner going on.

Blake became mesmerized by it, and slid down the bed gently, so as not to wake Cameron.

Yet.

He gently took the hard-on into his mouth. He slid his mouth up and down with slow, deep movements that soon elicited moans from Cameron, who was waking up to the wondrous sight of Blake going down on him.

"Oh, baby," he breathed, relaxing his body. He placed his hand on the back of Blake's head. The gentle tickling of Blake's long hair brushing against his belly added to the pleasure of the act.

"I'm sorry . . . I wanted it . . . it looked so good," Blake whispered between movements. Cam shuddered. Blake had Cam's cock in his hand and was stroking it up and down as he licked the underside of his balls.

Cam spread his legs wide in anticipation. "Fuck me . . . fuck me now," he managed to demand through desire-clenched teeth.

"No. Tonight," Blake said thickly, "you're going to fuck *me*."

"Oh, God."

Blake reached up and pulled Cameron over on top of him.

Within a matter of minutes, Blake felt his lover enter him slowly. It had been a while since Blake had been penetrated, and while he was slightly apprehensive, his need was stronger. Surprisingly, he felt no pain. Cameron fit him perfectly.

He looked up at Cameron's beautiful chest hovering over him, the hard ab muscles flexing as he thrust, and felt a wave of hunger like he had not felt in years. He never wanted Cameron to stop. He relished the feeling of Cam's hard cock inside him, the thick head teasing the inside walls of his rectum with its constant motion.

Cameron looked down at the beautiful man writhing beneath him. Blake had opened his muscular legs wide, and was stroking himself with his right hand. The look of rapture on his face told Cam that he was doing him well. Even through the condom, Blake felt warm and tight and soft and hard around his dick and Cam hoped he wouldn't come too soon.

"Damn, baby! You feel . . . *Mmmm!* . . . So good in me! . . . *Ohhh!*" Blake gasped.

"God, I love you, Blake! . . . *Mmmm* . . . I love you," Cam blurted, without even realizing that he'd said it out loud.

"*Ohhhh!* . . . What? . . . *Uhhhh!* . . . What was that?"

"I'm gonna . . . come," Cameron panted, shutting his eyes tightly.

"What . . . did . . . *Mmmm!* . . . you . . . *Ohhhh!* . . . say?!" Blake insisted, getting dangerously close himself.

"Oh, *maaaan!* I'm . . . I love you! I'm sorry . . . *Ohhhh!* . . ." He was trying so hard to hold his release back, he couldn't think straight.

"I love you, too! . . . Oh, *God!*"

With a gurgled cry, Cameron came, and wave after wave of delectation coursed through his twitching body. He had never felt a climax as intense as this one.

Blake came at the exact same moment, a tidal wave of peace overcoming him as he shot.

Afterwards, as they lay side-by-side tenderly touching each other's face, they repeated those three important words over and over until they fell back asleep.

*   *   *

Cameron felt a warm, wet tongue on his face. "Mercy! I beg mercy," he croaked, not wanting to open his eyes. When Blake didn't reply, but kept licking him, he opened one eye and was startled to see that the tongue was connected to Joe. He rolled away and felt for Blake.

He wasn't there.

Cameron sat upright in the bed and looked around the room. The sun was well up in the sky, and when he glanced at the bedside clock, he was surprised to see it was after eight. Even though it was buried in his pants, which had been tossed on the floor, he could hear his cell phone chiming, letting him know that he had messages waiting.

Joe began to lick his feet.

"Joe! Stop . . . that tickles!"

The sound of Cameron's deep voice excited Joe, who then leapt up into the bed and lay down on top of him, his big furry paws resting on his shoulders. He began to lick Cam's face vigorously. Cam laughed. Resigned, he gave in and let Joe give him a tongue bath.

Blake walked into the room and smiled at the sight of Joe almost covering Cam, licking away. Blake was dressed in old running shorts, a new Hammer microfiber T-shirt with the sleeves cut off, and slip-on running shoes. His hair was hidden underneath a *Survivor 7* black-colored buff, a gift from a friend who worked for CBS.

"I leave you two alone for one hour, and look what happens!" he said in mock anger, hands on hips.

"It's true," Cameron struggled to say as he twisted his face about to get away from the massive pink tongue. "Joe and I are in love. We were planning on telling you today."

"I'm shocked."

"I thought you saw it coming. All the dog treats in my pocket? The knowing glances when I let him out? We've been very indiscreet," Cam laughed.

"You, I expected something like this from. But, Joe! How *could* you? Well! We'll just see about that!" He ran across the room and flung himself on the bed, exciting Joe even more. The three of them ended up wrestling around, Joe's excited barking egging them on. The fun ended when Joe stepped on Blake's crotch.

"Ooww! Joe, ya big doofus!" he said, rubbing the crushed area.

Joe, oblivious, retreated to the side of the bed and flopped down, panting happily.

"Hey, baby," Cameron said, moving in for a kiss.

"Hey."

They kissed briefly and Blake sat up. "I need a shower. I just ran six miles. I smell."

"I like the way you smell," Cameron said, gently stroking Blake's arm.

Blake stood up and stripped off the buff and his shirt. "What's on your agenda today? Your phone's beeping, by the way." He kicked off his shoes.

"I need to call New York, do a conference call with a manufacturer in China, work out, approve some designs for Montana Rough Wear, and wrap up a few loose ends," he said, gazing at Blake's sweaty body.

"You moguls. Busy all the time." The younger man pulled the waistband of his shorts down and, completely nude, stepped out of them.

"And you?" Cam could not take his eyes off his lover. He watched him as if his every movement was a matter of life or death.

"First, shower. Then gym. I have to sign some papers at Hunk. Then that facial. By the way, Rafe was less than happy when I told him I wouldn't be back to work."

That was an understatement. The string of obscenities that had flown from Rafe's lips would have made even Madonna blush.

"Don't sweat it. He'll live."

"I'm serious. He has some severe issues with me and this whole PCH thing."

"Like I said, don't worry about it. Want some company in the shower?"

"Normally, yes, but I need to get my butt in gear, and if you joined me, one of us would end up ass against the tile. How about a rain check?"

"You got it."

Blake headed for the bathroom. At the doorway, he turned and looked back at Cameron. "Hey," he called.

"Yeah?"

"I love you."

Said simply, without the urgency and hunger of sex behind it, the beauty of those words almost made Cameron cry. "I love you, too," he replied, with difficulty.

Blake smiled and went to his shower.

Cameron allowed himself to flop back on the bed, luxuriating in the activity of doing nothing. He was in love and was loved back. That's all that mattered to him right now. What a great world! He wanted to spend as much time as possible with Blake this week. He was supposed to go back to New York on Sunday. He had meetings scheduled all next week that could not be delayed. He sighed.

Then, an idea began to form in his head.

17

Blake pulled up to his house at half past noon, still bothered by his near-death experience. He stopped the big car and turned off the engine. He sat in his new SUV and took a moment to think about what had just happened . . .

After kissing Cameron goodbye earlier in the morning, he had left the house and headed straight to the gym. He had really pushed himself on his workout. Today had been arm day, and his arms still felt like rubber. He had curled, pressed, extended, and dipped until he thought he was going to pass out. He also did another hour on the treadmill.

He had then run by his agent's office (would he ever get used to saying that? "My agent?") to sign countless contract pages, and to pick up his first check, the signing bonus. Nervous about having such a large check in his hands, he wanted to deposit it in the bank as soon as possible. A branch of his bank was across the street from the Hunk agency, and Blake waited at the crosswalk of Beverly and Little Santa Monica until it flashed "walk."

He was crossing the street when he heard the deep throttle roar of a car picking up speed. He looked over his right shoulder just in time to see a dark-colored sedan barreling towards him. In the split second he had to gape, he noticed the automobile's windows were heavily tinted, so he couldn't see who was driving.

Blake was shocked to realize that the sedan was swerving, heading straight for him. Instinctively, he leaped back to the sidewalk.

Landing wrong, he fell down. He rolled over once and came to a rest against one of the cement trash cans provided by the city.

The car picked up even more speed and roared down the street. At the next intersection, a block down the busy thoroughfare, the car cut the corner too short and jumped up on the right-side curb. It slightly clipped a light pole as pedestrians scrambled to get out of its way. In an instant, it was back on the road, then gone from sight.

Blake was breathing heavily, and he knew that if he hadn't jumped back up on the sidewalk when he did, he would have been flattened. The near accident caused some panicked screams among the other pedestrians, and several people came to Blake's side to make sure he was okay.

He was shaken, but otherwise fine. He had ripped his favorite pair of jeans and had a jammed thumb, but other than that, he was grateful to be alive.

"Crazy driver! This corner is so bad! There's always someone trying to run that light," an elderly woman said soothingly while Blake dusted himself off.

It had all happened so fast that Blake hadn't even seen what make car it was. He assured the passersby he was fine, and then carefully crossed the street to deposit the check. That chore done, he headed straight home.

Now that he was in the safety of his own driveway, he hoped to have thirty minutes before Cameron got back. He wanted to take a nap and lose the uneasy feeling he was trying unsuccessfully to ignore.

The earlier call from Cameron had been rather mysterious. He had asked Blake to be home by one, for a surprise. Not really sure if he could handle any more surprises, Blake was nonetheless curious as to what was going on.

He was still sitting in the luxury SUV, thinking, when Rand emerged from the gate. "Hey, Blake," he said cheerfully as Blake got out of the Rover.

Reaching over the SUV's console, Blake grabbed his gym bag. He was surprised by the sudden snap in the air. A cold front must be moving in quickly. Even though L.A.'s winters were mild, to say the least, every once in a while the air could turn downright chilly. It hadn't been this cold when he'd almost been run over, not an hour before.

Lost in his thoughts, Blake hadn't seen Rand, or even heard him call out to him.

"I said, 'Hey,'" Rand repeated, laughing. "Earth to Blake . . ." Rand was wearing worn cargos and an old Los Angeles Sporting Club sweatshirt that Blake had given him. A backwards *Queer as Folk* cap was pulled low on his towhead.

Startled, Blake jumped, and looked over at his tenant. "Oh, Rand! Jesus! You scared me," he chuckled, catching his breath.

"Sorry."

Blake shook his head. "No, no problem." He felt his heart rate start to come down. "What's up? How's school?" He shouldered his gym bag and walked toward the front door.

Rand winked. "Good. I'm getting an A in bedside manner."

"Well, that's what happens when you date the professor," Blake joked.

"Sam's the professor's assistant! Not the actual professor. Him, I wouldn't touch," Rand sassed back. "Where's Brady been?" he suddenly asked, eyes downcast. A spreading blush began overtaking his face. "I haven't seen him around much lately."

Blake smiled. Rand's minor infatuation with the deputy was a running joke between Brady and him. "Well, you know we aren't dating each other anymore. He's still a friend, but he won't be around like he used to. He's single now, you know." Blake winked.

Rand blushed even more. "Um, some packages from the store came for you today. I put them in the living room."

"Thanks, buddy," he said, unlocking the front door.

Did Rafe have his desk cleaned out already? What an asshole!

Blake tossed the keys on the hall console and marched to the living room, where two large Cameron Fuller logo shopping bags were placed. His anger building, he ripped one bag open, expecting to find his personal effects.

Instead it was a tan vinyl CF America duffle with brown leather handles and trim. Blake had always loved the handsome duffles, but even with his employee discount, they had just been too pricey for him. He unzipped the duffle, and found it was well packed with clothes. Specially, CF/Active sports gear. Shorts, swim trunks and Speedo-style bathing suits, tanktops, T-shirts, and underwear. A crisp white pair of CF/Active running shoes was buried at the bottom.

Confused now, Blake opened the other shopping bag. It held a matching, larger CF America duffle. In this bag was an assortment of dressy resort wear including shirts, slacks, a couple of thin merino V-neck sweaters, and two pairs of dress shoes.

Blake sat on his sofa, stumped. Everything was his size, even the shoes. It was bizarre. Just then, his cell phone rang.

"Hello?" He was cautious when he answered it now.

"Hey, baby. You home?" It was Cameron.

"Yeah. Where are you?"

"About two blocks away."

"Oh, cool. I've had the weirdest day."

"Why's that?"

"I almost got run over this morning in Beverly Hills," Blake said.

"What? Are you okay?" Concern instantly colored Cam's voice.

"Yeah, I'm fine. Just an idiot driver not paying attention, I guess. I'm more shook up than anything. And, get this: I got two bags of stuff from the store delivered here. Clothes, shoes, underwear. I'm baffled."

"Don't be. All will be explained shortly. Do me a favor. Be ready to leave the house the minute I get there. I'm taking you somewhere special for dinner."

"Dinner? Cam, it's not even one," Blake protested slightly.

"Just be ready, sweetheart. Oh, I can see your house now. See you in two secs." Cameron was gone.

Blake stood up and walked to the front door. He watched in mild curiosity as a black Lincoln limousine pulled up to his curb. Before it had completely stopped, Cameron leaped out of the back and ran up to Blake.

"Get inside!" he urged.

Stunned, Blake backed up and let Cameron in. Cameron quickly shut the door, grabbed Blake by the shoulders, and pushed him back up against the wall.

He then leaned in and began to kiss Blake warmly. Blake relaxed and responded in kind.

"Hey, you," Cameron whispered when they finally broke apart.

"Hey, you." Blake rested his head on Cameron's shoulder.

"You sure you're okay?"

"I am now. So, what is going on with all the cloak and dagger stuff?"

"Where are the bags?" Cameron looked around.

"In the living room. Are they yours?"

"No, sweetie, they're yours."

"But how did you know all my sizes?"

"I didn't. I asked Bobby at the store to get everything together. He knew your sizes and exactly what to pick out for you. Is Rand here?"

"He's in his apartment. Why?"

"Nothing. I'll be back in a few. Go grab your toothbrush and dopp kit. I'm taking you on a little trip," Cameron called back as he raced to the kitchen door.

"What? What are you talking about?" Blake called after him, but Cam was already out the door.

Feeling flustered and not knowing why, Blake went to his bathroom. He quickly filled his dock kit with the essentials. Before he was done, Cameron was by his side.

"Hurry up! Let's go!" he chided Blake.

Laughing, Blake pushed him away. "What the hell is going on?"

"You'll see . . . come on, anything you forgot, we'll buy. Let's get out of here!" He pulled Blake out of the bathroom and they walked through the house.

"Rand is going to watch Joe and the house for you while we're gone, so don't worry about that," Cameron said as they picked up the duffles and headed out the front door. The limo driver had the trunk open and took the two bags from them, placing them next to an identical set in green vinyl, already in place.

It wasn't until they had settled back in the comfortable leather upholstery that Blake finally had a chance to exhale.

"This had better be good," he warned playfully. "I feel like I've been kidnapped."

"You have," Cameron said, sliding a hand in between Blake's knees.

Blake leaned his head back on the seat and closed his eyes. "Well, wake me when we get there."

                                    *   *   *

The limo driver took Laurel Canyon, and fought the early afternoon traffic all the way over the hill into the San Fernando Valley. In Burbank they passed several movie studios and ultimately turned down Hollywood Way.

Blake didn't actually sleep; he just relaxed and let the motion of the moving car lull him into a vegetative state. Cameron was on the cell phone the entire ride, dealing with small fires in the New York office. His hand never left Blake's knee.

The car stopped and the driver opened the passenger door. Blake blinked a few times as he adjusted to the bright light flooding the car. Getting out with Cameron, he was surprised to find they were at the Burbank airport. He and Cameron each grabbed one of the bags, while the driver took the other two.

The pass through security was actually quick, and they were soon strolling down the long concourse. Cameron hadn't gotten any tickets, so Blake assumed they'd check in at the gate.

The chauffeur led them to a secluded side door, and out they went, back into the daylight. A sleek white and blue Gulfstream IV jet was parked about thirty feet away. A crew member was walking around the underside, doing a preflight check. The stairwell door-gate was down, and Cameron smartly walked up the stairs as if he owned the plane.

Which, actually, he did.

The cabin attendant was chatting intimately with the pilot, a muscular, cocky-looking man. When the steward noticed Cameron coming up the stairs, he quickly ran over and took Cameron and Blake's bags and walked aft with them, storing them in a small cargo compartment. The driver dropped off the two bags he'd been carrying, and with a friendly wave, he was off the plane.

Blake had never been in a private jet before, and he allowed himself a little "gee whiz" time. Beautifully decorated in soft beiges and creams, it was a flying conference room. All along one cabin bulkhead was a long benchlike seat in plush, button-tufted leather, with seat belts placed every three feet. A highly polished table was split and could swing in front of the bench or be stowed back. Regular first-class type seats that matched the leather bench seat were spaced one after the other on the opposite bulkhead. Aft was a small galley kitchen and a bathroom. The carpeting was plush pile, the curtains a soft silk damask, and the wall paneling a mixture of polished burl wood and off-white high-grade plastic.

Blake was impressed, to say the least.

"Mr. Fuller, we'll be taking off in about ten minutes," the cabin attendant said pleasantly, a slight southern drawl giving away his origins. He was a handsome though thin man, with lively brown eyes and a large mouth with full lips. His hair was neatly cut in the standard "boy cut," and he had gelled the front bangs to spike up slightly. He had long, thin fingers and a slightly effeminate air about him. His uniform was a matching ecru button-down shirt and tie set, and brown flat front slacks. He wore brown monkstrap shoes. His name tag said "Dan."

"Thank you, Dan," Cameron said as he settled himself down in one of the large single chairs. "Blake, come sit down." He motioned to the chair directly behind him. Hitting a switch under the seat, he swiveled completely around to face Blake's seat.

"Would you or your guest care for something to drink before we taxi?" asked Dan.

"I'd like an orange juice. Blake?"

"The same, thanks." Blake sat down and fastened his seat belt. Dan walked briskly to the rear of the plane to fetch the drinks. "This plane is amazing! It's just amazing," he gushed.

"Something I bought for myself last year. Just made sense. It's one of my favorite toys. Wildly expensive, but, fuck it. That's what the money is for."

"Now, can you please tell me where we are going?"

"Nope. I want to surprise you. But settle in. It's a long flight." Cameron gave a cheshire grin and pulled out his cell phone to finish off his calls.

Blake gave up and let himself go. Whatever happened would be fun, so just enjoy the surprise, he decided. He caught Cameron's eye and silently moved his lips. "I love you."

Cameron stopped talking for a beat, reached out a hand and pressed it on Blake's. "Me, too," he mouthed back.

Dan interrupted them with the drinks. He expertly pulled out the small table between the seats and placed them down. Noticing Cameron's hand on Blake's, his eyebrows raised slightly, but he said nothing.

18

Three hours, one delicious meal, two snacks, and three bottles of water later, Blake put down the *People* magazine. Cameron was on the other side of the plane, pecking away at an iBook laptop. He was obviously lost in his work, and Blake got up to stretch his legs. He peeked out the window, again, to see where they were, but the heavy cloud cover beneath them still completely obscured the terrain below. He wandered to the back of the plane where Dan was sitting on a wide jump seat reading a Ben Tyler novel. Seeing him approach, he quickly put down the book.

"Can I get you something, Blake?" he asked, rising.

"Please, don't get up . . . and no, thanks. I'm well hydrated." He pointed at the book Dan was holding. "I read that one."

"Good ending?"

"Yes. All will end well, I assure you," he smiled. "I don't suppose you can tell me where the hell Cameron's taking me?"

"My lips are sealed. But I think you'll like it," he said, grinning broadly. "I understand congratulations are in order. You're the new Pacific Coast Highway guy, aren't you? That must be very exciting for you."

"Thanks, it is." He leaned against the bulkhead. "You know, Dan, I got the first check today. I'd never seen so many zeroes in my life! I still can't believe this is all happening."

"Well, you're very handsome. And Cameron has an eye for talent. He only hires the best."

"I see that. You're here, right?" Blake said, flashing the flight attendant a toothy smile.

Dan blushed, then laughed. "Smooth talker." He looked over at Cameron, who was still typing furiously away. He lowered his voice. "Okay. I have to ask. And I know it's none of my business, so tell me to fuck off if you want, but . . ."

Blake looked at him quizzically.

"How long have you been screwin' the boss?" From anyone else it would have been an impossibly rude question. But from Dan, it had no bite.

Blake thought for a moment. "That obvious?"

"Honey, I half-expected to see him go down on you in the aisle! And the way he looks at you? That ain't lust, sweetie. That man's in love."

Blake blushed. "I know." He then broke into a goofy grin.

"Ooohhh. It's a mutual thing, is it? Well, good! The little missus is a . . . handful. Mr. Fuller deserves to be happy." He gave Blake an appreciative look, all the way from his feet to his handsome face. "And honey, I'm sure you make him very happy."

"I try."

"Oh, my. That must just be a sight to see, the two of you!"

"Honey," Blake said, imitating Dan's accent, "you have *no* idea."

Dan waved a hand in front of himself like a fan. "Oh, my! Ah do believe Ah'm gettin' tha vapors! Well, don't worry. I'm the very soul of discretion. Y'all's little secret is safe with me."

Blake winked at him and passed on to the small lavatory. After finishing up in there, he came back out and sauntered over to Cameron, sitting next to him on the bench seat.

"Hey," he said playfully.

"Hey. Sorry I'm not so much fun right now. But, if I take care of this work now, I'll have more time for play later," Cameron said, not looking up from the small screen.

"Oh? So this is a fun trip?" Blake fished.

"Well, fun, and maybe a little work. You'll see," Cameron said mysteriously. He looked up at Blake, saw how close he was sitting, and shot a quick glance to Dan.

"Oh, the cat's out of the bag with that one," Blake whispered, nodding his head toward the rear of the cabin. "She was on to us the second we got on board. Seems we look and act like a pair of horny teenagers in love."

Cameron chuckled. "Well, then. Since the secret's out, come here." He reached over and put his arm around Blake's shoulder, pulling him even closer. Cam closed his eyes and kissed the man he loved.

When they separated, Blake repositioned himself so that he was lying on the bench, his head resting on Cam's lap. Cam gently stroked his hair and continued to work on the laptop, now typing slowly, with only one hand.

An hour later, when Dan strolled by taking drink requests, they were still in that position.

"Sweetheart, wake up. We're landing." Cameron gently nudged Blake awake. He had fallen asleep resting on his lover's lap, and as he slowly sat up, he stretched.

"What time is it?" he asked, yawning.

"Umm," Cam looked at his stainless steel Baume & Mercier watch. "Let's see . . . with the time change, it's only five o'clock in the afternoon."

"Seems later."

"Well, that's seven to us. Look out the window," Cam pointed to the small oval opposite them.

Blake got to his feet and walked across the aisle to peer out the window. He looked down and was instantly thrilled to see dazzling blue water topped by slight whitecaps. He looked to the right and saw the beginning of a land mass. He could see wide open white sandy beaches nestled between coves of craggy rock. Here and there a tall palm tree swayed in the late afternoon trade winds. He looked back at Cameron, excited, but puzzled.

"Welcome to Kauai," Cam said as he came over to look out the window with Blake. "This whole side of the island is the east coast. They filmed a lot of movies here. All of the *Jurassic Parks, Raider's of the Lost Ark,* and a bunch of others. My house is near Kilauea, on the north shore." He put his arm around Blake.

A broad grassy plain came into view and Blake could see the beginning of the airport's landing strip.

"Gentlemen, please take your seats for landing," Dan said politely as he ushered them to comfortable chairs. They buckled in, and Dan had barely strapped himself into his own jump seat when the plane touched down smoothly. After a brief taxi to the airport terminal, they stopped.

They were escorted from the plane to the terminal by an exotic young airport security woman whose name tag read "Leilani." Her long, dark hair fluttered prettily in the breeze. She was wearing a brightly colored floral shirt known everywhere as an "aloha" shirt. This riot of color was neatly tucked into a pair of black Bermuda shorts.

Dan followed them into the terminal, helping carry the bags. Leilani had placed fragrant plumeria leis around each man's neck upon greeting them.

"Mr. Fuller, your car is parked at the curb out front. It's a green Explorer. I'll show you to it," Leilani said in a singsong voice.

They strolled through the terminal, past baggage claim and out into the incredibly sweet smelling air. The Explorer was there, right where Leilani said it would be, and they quickly loaded the baggage in. Leilani waved goodbye and went back into the terminal.

"This is where I leave you two," Dan said, smiling. "The flight crew and I are staying at the Hyatt in Poipu, and we have you scheduled for a late Sunday evening departure. Please call me if I can be of any assistance."

Cameron shook the flight attendant's hand. "Thank you, Dan."

"Bye, Dan. See you soon," Blake said happily.

"I'll be poolside for the next two days working on my tan. Come over anytime." He winked at Blake, and quickly walked back into the terminal to join the other crew members.

"Oh, my God, Cam! It's so fucking beautiful here!" Blake said, twisting his head around left and right, not wanting to miss a thing. His hair, tucked behind his ears, flew loose and whipped around his head as the warm, slightly humid air washed over both men through the open windows of the Explorer. Blake could barely contain his excitement at finally making it to one of the Hawaiian Islands, a dream of his since childhood.

The drive to Cam's house was like traveling through a postcard. They passed several small towns, each with an intriguing name. Lihue. Kapaa. Anahola. There were towering mountains on the left and glorious beaches on the right. As the two-lane Kuhio highway wound through the island, cutting back from water's edge to deep valleys of tropical vegetation, Blake drank it all in. Every once in a while he would bring his flower lei to his nose and inhale the power-fully sweet aroma.

Cameron was chuckling at Blake's enthusiasm, but he also re-called his own first visit to the island many years before. He, too, had been that excited, and truth be told, he felt an elation at his return that surprised him. He pointed out various landmarks to Blake, giving him a semi-tour. Blake was amazed at the deep red color of the earth, and eagerly asked question after question. Cameron answered the ones he could.

The sun, though still bright, was settling down into the west. As the shadows lengthened, Cameron felt the weight of his responsibili-ties fall off him like unwanted stones. Then his phone rang.

Not a man to let his phone go unanswered, Cameron answered the call.

"Hello?" he said, slightly irked at the intrusion.

"Cameron? Rafe here. We have a crisis. Where are you? I stopped by the hotel today and they said you had left for a few days."

"Where I'm at is none of your business. What's the problem?"

"Cameron Diaz's gown didn't get delivered in time. She's a nomi-nee and a presenter this weekend at the Golden Globes!"

"Jesus Christ! That was supposed to be sent out from New York last week! You find out who dropped the ball on this and kick their ass! Find out where it is, and get it to her!"

"It's not that easy. It seems to have been lost in transit. Her stylist is having a cow, and her back-up is Armani."

Armani!?

Fuck *that!*

"Then you get your ass on the phone with New York, have them stitch up another dress and get it out to L.A.! Have someone fly it out personally if need be, but get it there!" Cameron yelled into the phone. Blake gave him a surprised glance.

"That's what I thought . . . I just wanted to get your okay on that."

"Well, good. Don't let me down on this, Rafe."

"I won't! Oh, Trevor called. He wants to shoot some more pictures of Blake tomorrow, but I can't seem to locate him. Should I get another model? I know for a fact that Travis Fimmel is in town." Rafe's tone was one of hope.

"Tell Trevor that Blake is here with me, and no, he's not to use a different model. Blake's the one. Trevor knows that." Cameron gave Blake a loving look.

There was a slight delay on the other end. "Blake's . . . with you?"

"Yes."

"Oh. Is this something I should be involved in? I could join you two wherever you are."

"No!" Cameron said, a touch too forcefully. "You stay there and hold down the fort. Get that goddamn dress to L.A. I'm counting on you, Rafe," Cameron pacified him.

"Okay. Oh, Suzette is looking for you, too. She called the store five times."

"Thank you, Rafe. Anything else?"

"No. But I have to ask. There's so much riding on Pacific Coast Highway. Are you sure that using an unknown, untested model is the right way to go? Cam, I really think—" Rafe was saying as Cameron snapped shut the phone. He then hit the switch and turned it off.

"Well. I don't think Rafe is wild about my new position," Blake said, pulling his hair into a low ponytail with an elastic he had dug out of his pocket.

"Well, fuck Rafe."

"No, thanks."

There was silence for a full ten seconds, then both men broke out into raucous laughter.

The Kuhio highway dipped down a steep grade, and as it picked back up again, Cameron slowed the Explorer and turned right onto a tree-covered lane called Kalihiwai Road. Blake tried to repeat the street name phonetically, but gave up after a few tries. As they passed a red-dirt road, Cameron pointed down its dusty length.

"Secret beach is located down there. It's one of my favorite beaches here," he said.

"I can't wait to see it!"

The SUV continued down the winding road for about a mile, and then came to a slow stop.

"Here we are," Cameron sighed happily. He turned the wheel and drove up to the gate. Punching a code into the security box, he waited until the slow-moving gate swung all the way open, before driving in.

The truck's tires crunched over a carefully tended crushed gravel drive. The driveway was long and quite beautiful. Exotic native bushes and trees lined it, with strange and unfamiliar blossoms weighing down the branches. Through these enchanting trees, great vistas of rolling meadows could be seen.

Off to the right of the drive, the property rolled down a steep hill, terracing once with a large flat pad of cut grass, then sharply dropping into craggy rocks soaked by the crashing surf. On the grassy area, several benches had been placed to offer a tranquil spot to read, think, or stare at the view. The rough, dangerous-looking boulders below this haven were called lava rocks. Cameron explained to Blake that these boulders were formed from spewing lava when the island was created eons ago.

At the end of the slightly curving driveway was the house. A large structure with an enormous covered lanai, or porch, wrapping around it from front to back, it bespoke an age gone by. Prominently placed on a slight rise in the land, and between swaying palm trees too numerous to count, it was in the typical Hawaiian plantation style, with simple, clean lines that showed little frivolity.

A slatted tin roof, occasionally broken by a tall dormer window, rested on top of clapboard walls that held simple wide-louvered windows. The louvers were open and the gentle billowing of the curtains inside could be seen through the unobstructed panes of glass.

Painted a pleasing khaki-tan with bright white trim work and hugged by luxurious vegetation, the home looked like a movie set. The driveway circled in front of the wide lanai, and when Cameron parked the Explorer there, Blake hopped out so fast he almost tripped on the loose gravel.

He dashed up the short flight of stairs to the teak decking of the lanai and looked at the view from there. He could hear the crashing and booming of the surf somewhere behind the house, and he was wildly impatient for Cam to unlock the door.

Before Cam could join him, Blake was surprised by the crowing of a rooster that had ambled into the grassy lawn beside the house. The rooster was soon joined by two hens and several small chicks.

"You got chickens?" he asked, quite mystified.

Cameron laughed. "No. There's roosters and chickens loose all over the island. I think they went wild after a hurricane wiped out all the chicken coops. They've bred, and now they're just free to roam wherever they want. You'll get used to them."

"Why does the house seem open already? Does someone live here?"

"No, I have a local couple who take care of it. I called them this morning and told them I was coming. They prepped the whole thing. Down to food in the fridge," he said, joining Blake on the lanai. He was about to open the carved teak door when Blake put a warm hand on his arm.

"Hey."

"Yes?"

"I just wanted to say thanks for this. It's beautiful. And I love you." He leaned in slowly and kissed Cameron with deeply felt gratitude.

Cameron literally thought his heart would burst. "I love you, too. I'm just so glad we're here." He unlocked the door, and in they went.

The downstairs hall was tall, wide, and cool. It went from the front of the house to the open rear. Various doorways and rooms all led off this main roomy corridor. A large bright sitting room, complete with lava rock fireplace, was to the right. Decorated with comfortable linen slipcovered furniture, it was a calm retreat. Directly across the hall from this room was a spacious dining room with the most gorgeous wooden dining table Blake had ever seen.

"It's made of koa wood, and it used to be in one of King Kamahamaha's houses. I bought it three years ago in Oahu. It was a *bitch* to ship here," Cameron explained, taking in his house as well.

"Wow." Blake walked to it and let his fingers lightly glide across its glossy and highly polished surface. The slipcovered Parsons chairs were a Cameron Fuller design called Parfect, and covered in a local tapa-style print of brown and tan. An enormous Barbara Barry-designed server filled up one wall, while a giant china cabinet occupied another. The floor here, as well as throughout the house, was highly waxed and stained a deep, almost black brown, covered every so often in natural sisal rugs.

Blake wandered out of the dining room and down the hall which opened into the gigantic main living room. He walked in, and had his breath taken away.

He had never seen such a gorgeous and inviting room before. It was a vast space filled with a wonderful mix of antique Hawaiiana and modern furniture. Large, comfortable-looking, natural-colored sofas and chairs were placed smartly around the floor, accented by heavy teak tables and lamps. Huge, natural sisal area rugs covered the dark plank flooring.

To the right, there was the obligatory lava rock wall that took up the entire east side of the room. Anchored by a massive fireplace almost five feet high, the rock wall was the dramatic focal point of the room. A simple koa wood mantle ran the entire length of its rough texture, with stunning black and white signed original Herb Ritts photographs of various beach themes hung carefully above.

As Blake wandered drop-jawed further into the space, he turned slowly around and saw the free-form koa wood staircase with sisal carpet runner that hugged the south wall and led to the upstairs bedrooms. Hawaiian hieroglyphs depicting ancient scenes of hunting, worship, and dance had been intricately carved into the native wood, adding yet another custom touch to the overwhelming room.

Completing his circle, Blake found himself looking out at the absolutely staggering view from the large plate glass windows. It was a view that allowed the eye to see miles up one side of the Napali coast and back down the other. From the house's vantage point on the bluff, Blake could see expansive, lush beaches stretching out before the sparkling surf and little colorful dots that represented the sunbathers soaking up the last fleeting rays of the day on them. The sun was falling fast in the west, and the trade winds tossed the palm fronds outside about merrily.

The ocean was crashing onto the rocks a few hundred feet below the wraparound lanai, and the potted palms strategically placed every few feet on the teak flooring danced in the strong gusts. There was a pool and Jacuzzi built into the lanai off to the left, overlooking a beachy cove, protected from the wind by a four foot glass wall that enclosed the whole area. This glass corral allowed sunbathers to lay on the roomy Brown Jordan chaises and be spared from the upwind blasts that raced up the jagged cliffs.

"Here. Let me show you how to open these doors," Cameron suggested, flicking a hidden latch beside one of the large glass windows. He easily pushed the heavy glass door back on its track in front of the next window. A strong blast of wind raced into the room and ruffled the flowers artfully arranged on the huge square teak cocktail table. "There are screen doors in here." He reached into a pocket built next to the windows and pulled out a screen door that slid on the same grooves and replaced the glass door. "There's a gate by the pool, where you can take a path down to the beach. It's pretty private, though all the beaches in Hawaii are open to anyone."

"So amazing," Blake marveled. He opened the screen door and walked out onto the lanai. He placed his hands on the railing and gazed out onto the beauty of the view, his clothes and a big section of his pulled-back hair whipped around by the zephyr winds.

His senses were on high alert. He smelled, and almost tasted, exotic fragrances he never knew existed. He saw indescribably beautiful vistas spread out before him. He heard the gentle, almost delicate, rustling of palm fronds rippling in the breeze and the soothing roar of the surf below. Cameron came up behind him and crossed his arms around him, enfolding him, so he felt the warmth of his lover's body.

Blake smiled contentedly.

Cameron kissed the back of his neck, slowing running his tongue from the hairline down to his shoulders. Blake sighed, and leaned back into Cameron, his eyes closing. Cameron's hands began to roam, and cupped Blake's big pecs and gently squeezed. Blake reached backwards with his own hands and took hold of Cam's thighs, gently kneading the corded muscles. Blake could feel Cam's arousal against his ass, and he teasingly ground back into it, getting a murmured moan as a reward.

"Wanna fuck?" Cameron breathed softly into Blake's ear.

"*Mmmm,* oh, yeah. But first, how about a drink? Something fruity and tropical."

"You got it. Then, let's just sit and watch the sun set."

"You're reading my mind."

Cam reluctantly broke free and disappeared into the house. A few moments later, soft island music wafted out through the hidden ceiling speakers, enveloping the house with a tranquil vibe. When Cam returned holding two mai tais a few minutes after that, Blake hadn't moved.

"Let's sit over here." Cam motioned toward the pool, where the groupings of Brown Jordan outdoor furniture were. They settled into two armchairs facing the ocean.

The designer reached over and took Blake's hand in his own, and held it tightly. They said nothing, just enjoying the view, each other, and the fact that they were there.

19

Dillard Jordan strained to see Silas through the hissing, swirling fog. Dillard hated, absolutely hated steam rooms, and he hated this steam room most of all.

It was the steam room at Silas's club. A club that was located in a beautiful Beaux Arts building in the mid-Seventies. A club that had the best Cobb salad in town. A club that pampered its extremely exclusive membership to such an extent that some members had to be gently ushered out the doors every night at eleven when it was closed. A club that three generations of Dillard's family had been proud members of. A club that had rejected Dillard's membership bid some six years before. Dillard always thought that Silas had thrown in the black ball that kept him out, and he resented the fact that Silas loved to hold meetings here.

Just to rub my nose in it, Dillard suspected. "Silas?" he called out into the mist.

"Over here."

Dillard followed the sound of Silas's voice, and found him sitting on a raised marble platform bench on the far wall. A thick white Egyptian cotton towel was wrapped loosely around Silas's waist, revealing the sagging and loose wrinkled skin of a seventy-five-year-old man. His head was hanging down and he was sweating profusely. His normally plastered-down tufts of hair were now wildly standing on end. Oddly enough, he had a thick honest-to-God Cuban cigar in his right hand.

"I didn't think smoking was allowed in the club," Dillard said, eyeing the stogie.

Silas brought the cigar to his lips and inhaled deeply. "It isn't." He exhaled the thick, acrid smoke in Dillard's direction.

"Well," Dillard said, resisting the urge to shoo away the stinking fumes. "I have another Cameron update." He wiped his brow with the palm of his hand. He was perspiring up a storm, and his own white towel threatened to come undone at any second and drop to the floor. He had to hold it at the knot to keep it on.

"And, what now?" Silas took another long drag on the Cuban.

Dillard looked around and was glad to discover that they were the only two men in the steam room. He would have been uncomfortable discussing Cameron in front of others, but now he felt able to talk freely. "Cameron's taken his boy to Hawaii. I'm sure they're staying at his beach house in Kauai. I checked, and he has a lot of meetings early next week, here in New York, so he can't be away long. The flight crew is registered at the Hyatt until Sunday, so I'm betting that's when they'll return."

"Well. Isn't that romantic? A weekend getaway," Silas snorted in disgust.

"And I think you should know that Cameron rushed a set of contracts through. Blake Jackson is now officially the new face of Pacific Coast Highway. Your son-in-law was more than generous on the financial end. He paid for exclusivity and the kid's got a pay-or-play clause." In a spiteful way, he was actually glad that Cameron had pushed through the contracts so quickly. It obviously upset Silas, and that in itself was reward enough.

Silas snorted again.

Cameron's pulled a fast one, the old man thought. His son-in-law knew an untested and unknown model would be a tough sell to the board, and the pay-or-play clause meant that his boy toy Blake would get paid in full whether he did the campaign or not. So, if the Board wanted to fire Blake, for any reason, he would still be paid just as if he fulfilled his contract. It was a masterful move on Cameron's part, Silas had to admit.

In effect, it assured his plaything an income without Cameron's having to personally foot the bill. It was just the sort of thing that Silas himself would have done.

He cursed out loud.

"But it's not all bad," Dillard interjected. "I saw the photos from the shoot the other day. The kid *is* hot. Exactly what Cameron was screaming for all last month. I think he'll actually be okay in the gig."

"He's having . . . *sexual relations* with my son-in-law!" Silas growled.

"Well, there is that. But I'm telling you, Silas, Cameron may just pull this off. I think he picked a winner."

That was the last thing Silas wanted to hear. "So this kid is perfect for the job, huh?"

"Yeah. I think he is. He's got 'pinup' written all over him. His new agents have already booked several extra jobs for him as a tie-in to PCH. The photographer that took the shots is putting him on the cover of *Esquire,* and there's talk of a poster. He's got what they call 'buzz.' "

Silas cursed again.

"I've sent a set of the pictures to your home. Judge for yourself."

Silas didn't reply.

"Well, I'm about ready to pass out from this heat. I'll keep you posted on any new developments," Dillard said. He turned around and walked toward the exit. "Have a good night, Silas."

Silas waved him away.

Dillard is a weak man, just like Cameron, Silas thought. A petty, swindling homo who couldn't even take a little steam heat. A tight smile crossed Silas's face when he recalled blackballing Dillard that time, years before, when he had tried to join the club. Silas couldn't even *imagine* having a queer as a fellow member here.

Silas would have disposed of Dillard long ago, but Dillard had the rare cachet of having known Stanton from their days at NYU together. Silas had a soft spot for anyone who had known his son. Therefore, he allowed Dillard to continue at Cameron Fuller USA.

But Dillard's personal life was just too public now. The unseemly lawsuit, the tabloids. As soon as Silas got the information he needed to "handle" Cameron, he would take great pleasure in destroying Dillard. He would let the authorities know about the insurance scam, anyway. It was too good an opportunity to pass up.

Leaning back against the warm, wet tile wall, more pressing matters soon overtook Silas's thoughts. He sat and stewed for a few minutes, and realized he was a man in distress. On one hand, it would be good for his master plan if Cameron's boy toy was a total flop and

PCH tanked. That would make it so much easier to control Cameron if he continued his losing streak.

On the other hand, what if Dillard was right and this Blake joker did actually hit, and the cologne was a huge success? Blake Jackson would become a highly visible member of the Cameron Fuller team whether Silas liked it or not. And Silas didn't like it. At all.

He couldn't bear the thought of two men being together. Sodomy and fellatio and God knows what else! Good lord!

And worse than that, Silas would have to stand there at the cologne launch party and smile as if nothing were wrong. He'd have to meet Cameron's catamite! With his certain knowledge that Stanton and Cameron were once intimate, how could he control his rage against Cameron and his new lover?

An idea began to form in his feverish mind.

He reached for the cell phone hidden from view under his towel. It was against the rules to have cell phones on club property, but Silas wasn't much for rules. He punched in his daughter's number.

When he heard Suzette answer, he jumped right in. "Hello, Suzette. I have some interesting news for you."

20

The occasional breeze caused the palm-leaf-printed sheers to balloon out, then float gently back flush to the windows. The two white ceiling fans whirred silently, helping stir the air of the large bedroom. Blake was on his side, gazing out the opened sliding glass doors at the palm frond silhouettes waving beyond the lanai. Cameron sighed and spooned closer to him, holding him tight with his left arm.

They were deep in the soft cocoon of the feather bed. The actual bed frame was a bamboo four-poster, complete with mosquito netting swagged dramatically along the canopy, headboard, and sides. The polished teak nightstands held two strikingly modern black urn lamps with a subtle Polynesian-print motif on the shades. A pair of chaise loungers were separated by a round, sleek table and positioned near the sliding doors. The upstairs lanai ran the length of the room and also held a pair of the same Brown Jordan chaises that were down by the pool.

Earlier, after watching the sun set, the two lovers had changed into fresh clothes and driven in to Kapaa, stopping to have dinner at Coconuts, a wonderful restaurant that Cam had always wanted to try. Blake had Mahimahi, and Cameron, the seared Ono. The food and the wine had been superb, and the meal put the two men into a relaxed mood that carried over upon their return to the cliffside estate.

Climbing the stairs to the bedroom, they had held hands, knowing that another night of sexual pleasure was before them. Their lovemaking this night had an added layer to it, one that their previous couplings didn't have. A layer of silent commitment.

Afterwards, breathing deeply, Cam had drifted off to sleep while Blake stared out the doors into the fragrant night. He felt so safe, so protected here with Cameron, and it bothered him. He had been on his own for so long that the thought that he needed someone else was slightly scary. Even when he was with Brady, he had never really felt like he needed him.

He knew that when he told Cameron "I love you" that he wasn't just saying words. For once, the words had true depth and meaning to him. The knowledge that he could love another man thrilled him, but also filled him with despair. Cameron would soon leave, and he would not be going with him.

If the modeling thing worked out well, he imagined he would be going to New York a lot, and could see Cameron then, but his home was in L.A. He had lived there for ten years, owned a home, and had a circle of friends that he didn't want to abandon.

Would they try the long distance thing? Blake knew of other guys who had that sort of arrangement. One or the other would fly out on alternate weekends to have a rushed two or three days alone with his lover, then part sadly again on a Sunday night. Phone sex replaced real sex, and whenever they thought about the lover, it was always tainted by longing.

Did he want that with Cameron?

Would he be able to remain faithful to a man three thousand miles away? He had never been very good in the monogamy field and wasn't sure he would be able to commit to it. He knew he would expect Cameron to, so it stood to reason that he would have to as well.

His usual "go with the flow" attitude wasn't going to work anymore, he realized. He was in love with this man sleeping beside him, and hard decisions were soon going to have to be made.

"What are you thinking about?" Cameron's soft voice came from behind him.

"Nothing. Go back to sleep."

"Nothing, my ass. You've been staring out the window for almost an hour. What's wrong?" Cameron propped himself up on his elbow.

Blake rolled over and faced his lover. "You. You're what's wrong."

Cameron's face clouded over with confusion.

"Christ. I've only known you a few days, yet here I am, trying to figure out how I can keep you in my life from now on. I'm in love with you, and that scares me. It's all been so fast. There's so much against us, and I don't know what to do," Blake whispered.

"Oh, babe," Cam said, pulling Blake close to him. "You don't know how badly I wanted to hear that. We'll figure something out. I don't want to lose you, either."

"How? How is this going to work? It's got disaster written all over it."

"No, it doesn't. What do you want to happen, Blake?" Cam asked.

"I want us to end up happily ever after. You. Me. Joe. It's *how* that happens I can't seem to figure out. You live in New York. I live in L.A. You're married, at least for now, and you know that's going to get messy. You're . . . *you,* for Christ's sake! I'm not sure I know how to deal with all that you have. I sorta feel out of my league when I'm with you," Blake honestly said.

"Blake, I don't think you realize how your life is going to change in the next few months. You are going to be huge. And, yeah, I have a lot. But I *earned* it. Every damn thing. You'll earn yours as well. Don't sweat that stuff." He squeezed Blake hard for emphasis. "Do you love me?" he directly asked.

"Yes." Blake's eyes did not lie.

"And I love you. That's all that matters now. The rest of it will sort itself out. You'll come to New York. I'll go to L.A. We'll meet halfway in Kansas if we have to. Just don't worry about it, okay?" Cam stroked his face tenderly.

"Okay." Blake half-smiled.

"What time is it, anyway?" Cameron strained to see the clock on the night stand beside Blake.

"Mmm . . . it's four twenty-five."

"Let's get some sleep, okay? We have a very full day of loafing tomorrow." Cam hugged him tightly a last time, then settled back down. Within minutes he was fast asleep.

Sleep came a little harder for Blake.

He was on a farm somewhere in the heartland, the strong breeze flattening the fields of wheat as it passed by. Blake gazed out over the horizon, but sensed something was off-kilter. The rooster in the barn crowed again. And again. And again.

What the hell am I doing in Kansas? Where is everyone? Why is that fucking rooster crowing so goddamn much?

He opened a sleepy eye and focused on the clock beside him. 8:45 A.M. He heard the rooster crowing again, and realized that was not part of his dream. That was real.

And apparently nonstop.

"Stop. By all things holy, please, God, make it stop," he mumbled. He reached back with his free hand and felt for Cam. He felt only touseled sheets. Cam wasn't there.

The rooster outside was joined by a friend who felt the need to answer back. The crowing became constant.

"Cam! Cam? Get me a gun. Please," he called out, half-rising.

"What was that?" Cam said, entering the room. He was towel drying his hair, standing in the doorway in a wet black speedo.

"Ohmigod. Those fucking chickens! Be a good man and chase them off, will you?" He pulled a pillow over his head, and flopped back down.

Cam laughed. "That, I'd like to see. You'll get used to them. Get up, you lazy bum. Let's go take a run. Then we'll drive up to the Princeville resort and hit the gym there."

"Sadist." Blake pushed the pillow off, and truly noticed Cam for the first time. "Did you go swimming? Without me?" He feigned hurt.

"The early bird, my love."

"Well, you're looking mighty fine there, Mr. Fuller. Wanna fool around?" Blake not so casually threw back the covers, exposing his taut naked body—and morning wood.

"As tempting as that is, no. Come on. It's a beautiful day in paradise. Get up."

"I'm up. I'm up." Giving in, Blake got out of bed and padded over to the bathroom. "Just give me five minutes."

Four hours later, Blake was lying on a chaise in the hot sun by the house's pool. He was wearing a bright yellow bikini bathing suit, and had slathered himself up with baby oil to get as dark as he could, as fast as he could. His skin was radiating back the heat it was absorbing, and Blake was drifting in that delicious state between consciousness and unconsciousness.

Cameron had explained during their run along the exquisite

beauty of Secret Beach that he wanted Blake to work out like a fiend, tan himself silly, and watch what he ate. Cam wanted Blake to be in top form for the photo shoot scheduled for the following week with Trevor.

They had run three miles, then driven over to the Princeville Resort Athletic Center, situated at the entrance of the Princeville Golf Course. They had pushed each other on the gym equipment until their muscles ached and burned. They had quickly eaten a light breakfast at the clubhouse dining room and then returned to the beach house.

From the far reaches of his mind, Blake heard a distant clinking. Waking up fully, he rolled over to his stomach. "Cam? Whatcha doing?" he called into the house.

Cam sauntered out carrying a tray with a fruit plate and two tall iced teas. "At your service, master."

Blake looked over at him and nudged down his Tag Hauer sunglasses to get a better view. Cam was wearing his black Speedo again. And that's all. He looked so good in it, it was awe-inspiring. His crotch, full and tempting, filled out the front of the shiny lycra suit, while his rock hard ass brought up the rear.

Literally.

"Hey. What do you think you're doing?" Cam asked mock-seriously.

"What do you mean?"

"The bathing suit? Uh, I want no tan lines, Mr. Jackson. Take it off," Cam instructed firmly, a twinkle in his eye.

"I'm gonna burn my ass, but, whatever you say, Mr. Fuller." He reached back with his hands, and sticking his thumbs into the waistband, began to slide the small swimsuit off. Never taking his eyes off Cameron, he heaved up his gorgeous buttocks, and slowly pulled the suit down, exposing his pale ass cheeks, hard and firm. "A little help, please?" he asked with a suggestive leer.

Cam was entranced, but snapped out of it. He casually walked over, set the tray on the side table, and reached down, taking the stretchy fabric of his lover's yellow swimsuit in his hands. He slowly worked it down the rest of the way off Blake's oil-slicked legs.

"Uh, could you put some of this sun block on?" Blake had grabbed a bottle of Banana Boat lotion and handed it to Cam. Cam squeezed a good size dab of the lotion into his hands and began to massage it onto Blake's ass.

"Mmmm," Blake moaned, slowing pushing his hips up and down. Cam "accidentally" allowed his fingers to stray into delicate territory, causing Blake to buck up and gasp twice.

Cam put the lotion down and picked up the baby oil. He began to massage it into Blake's back, squeezing, kneading, and pressing hard into the dense muscles. Blake was breathing deeply, his hands loose at his side. The erotic nature of the rubdown had totally turned Cam on. He stood up and tugged at the drawstring of his own swimsuit. After adjusting his stone-hard erection, he pulled the brief Speedo off.

He went back to his job, rubbing Blake down. Everywhere he touched on Blake seemed to be an erogenous zone. Blake began to groan loudly and writhe under Cam's steady, probing hands. Cam enjoyed the sensations of the wind blowing around his naked body, his hard-on slapping up against his stomach, and Blake undulating beneath him on the chaise.

Cam spread Blake's legs apart, threw one of his own huge legs over, and then sidled up between his lover's parted legs. He gently began to push his cock between Blake's buttocks, causing a heated reaction in the man he loved.

"Oh, maaaan . . . you feel so good . . ." Blake sighed.

"You too, babe . . . *Mmmm . . .*"

The combination of the sun, the scents of the island, the breeze coming up his backside, the touch of Cam, and his own desire had a profound effect on Blake. He literally felt he was going to swoon, an effect he'd caused in other men but had never experienced himself. He was short of breath and begged Cam to stop, but Cam wouldn't. He kept rubbing him, sliding his body up and down against Blake's back, pressing his gorgeous cock up against Blake's ass, every nerve ending alive and tingling. Blake's hair was falling into his eyes, and his vision blurred and came back into focus. His dick had never been as hard as it was now. With a mighty burst of power, he spun around under Cam, and the two men were face-to-face.

Cam continued rubbing his body up and down the greasy and slick form of his beloved. He could feel the heat generated from

Blake's skin, and had never felt Blake's cock as erect and elongated as it was now. He kissed his lover with a passion that had no equal. They could not stop pressing lips to salty lips.

"Oh, my God . . ." Cam murmured when he finally moved away from Blake's beautifully hungry face. He leaned back and balanced his knees on the side rails of the chaise. He grabbed Blake's oil-slickened dick, and with a firm, solid movement, guided it into his ass, pushing down and taking the entire length in one eager downward thrust.

"Ohhhh!" Blake cried out, not expecting the velvet sensation of entering Cam unsheathed.

"Fuuuuuck!" Cam panted. He pumped his ass on Blake with a need and insatiable hunger that surprised them both. He shifted his body weight to his feet, and lifting himself up slightly, slammed his ass up and down like a machine.

Blake, for his part, could hardly breathe for the great cries coming out of his mouth. He heard Cam telling him that he loved it, that he couldn't stop. The vision of the man he was completely in love with, riding him, his big chest coated with sweat and oil, glistening in the sun, his nipples hard and erect, excited him beyond reason.

He saw Cam throw his head back in great shouts of joy over and over.

He saw Cam's hand stroking himself hard, with purpose and intent.

He saw the great gush of seminal fluid as Cam exploded a tsunami onto his chest.

He saw Cam shift slightly and let him slide out, and in seconds Blake added his own seed to the mess pooling on his chest. The howl that came from his throat as he shot was almost inhuman in its intensity.

"I'm bored."

"What?" Cameron was on his stomach, half asleep. The sun felt so good on his nude body, and he still had the lover's high going from the world class fuck he'd gotten just an hour before.

"I'm getting antsy. I never was a good tanner. I always have to be moving around." Blake sighed deeply. "All this inaction drives me crazy."

Cameron looked over at Blake's naked body and was stunned at the deep color he had already gotten. Must be that Indian blood. "So what do you want to do?" he asked, as one would ask a child.

"Let's go exploring! Show me the island. I've been laying out for three hours. That's enough. I'll hike around without a shirt. Trust me, I'll be black before this weekend is over." He rolled over on his side and looked imploringly at Cameron.

Cam laughed out loud. "Okay, okay. Let's go walk around Hanalei. You'll love that."

"Thank God!" Blake got up out of the chair and was collecting his things when Cam crept up behind him. With a hard shove, and a loud shout, he pushed Blake into the pool, jumping in right after him. Blake came up sputtering and started to splash big waves at Cam, who returned the favor. The water fight lasted a few minutes, and then the laughing men got out of the pool, toweled off, and went into the house to change.

21

Hanalei was a quaint little village nestled in a lush valley on Kauai's north shore. Local legend had it that the song "Puff the Magic Dragon" was written about the enchanted town.

To get there, Cam and Blake drove down the most spectacular road Blake had ever seen. Blake drank in the sweeping panoramic vistas to the right of the sloping road: the valley with its carefully tended taro fields that resembled a giant patchwork quilt. This lush, green quilt was framed by a mountain range that was so picture perfect as to defy description. Distant waterfalls cutting through the mountains glistened on their way down as they caught reflected beams of sunlight.

The sun above was occasionally blocked by giant puffy clouds that sailed lazily across the sky. Over the multicolored mountain range, the cloud cover was more dense, and darker. Somewhere over there it was raining hard. A slow-moving, languid river threaded its way through the taro fields and out to sea.

After crossing a seemingly ancient one-lane suspension bridge, the road flattened out and went into the town proper. Old plantation houses from Kauai's sugar cane days lined the side of the dusty road. More than one had been converted into a shop of some sort. Entering the downtown area of Hanalei, which filled both sides of the two-lane road, they found a collection of small shopping centers and ramshackle structures.

Cam parked the Explorer and they hopped out and meandered through the town. Well-maintained old buildings housed an odd assortment of gift shops, art galleries, and shave ice stands, the Hawaiian variation of the mainland's sno cone carts. Restaurants were at every corner and the vegetation was lush green. Wild chickens crossed the road at will, oblivious to any reason why. The pace of the town was sleepy and relaxed.

Blake loved it.

Before they left the beach house, they had each pulled on a pair of faux-faded CF/Active surfer jams, Blake's in yellow, Cam's in red. Blake had on a loose tanktop, while Cam wore an aloha shirt, casually buttoned only once, so it opened often in the wind, exposing his muscular pecs and cut abs. They each were wearing flip-flops, though socks and sneakers had been tossed into the back of the SUV, just in case. CF/Active yellow-tinted sunglasses guarded their eyes and Blake had slung a toggle-covered messenger bag over his shoulder.

He pulled Cameron into shop after shop to see what was being offered for sale. Blake was unabashedly a world class shopper. Not that he *had* to buy anything, he just loved to browse.

They bought some T-shirts at the Kai Kana surf shop, got two Diet Cokes at Bubba's Burgers (and while Blake also wanted a hamburger, he resisted), and were wandering through an art gallery when Blake stopped short, causing Cam to bump into him.

"Wow! Look at that," he said, pointing to a unique lithograph framed in koa wood hanging among a small display. All of the lithographs were by the same artist, Michael Cassidy, and were fanciful retrostyle travel posters of Hawaii. Very stylized and brightly colored, they were fun and vibrant, and they caught and held the shopper's attention.

One in particular had Blake spellbound. A sleek dark-haired young beauty in a 1940s style bright red one-piece swimsuit was leaning up against a wooden surfboard. Her tan was golden, and she exuded life. Written in fifties style block lettering at the top of the picture were the words "Surfer Girl 1948." Blake could not take his eyes off of it.

"That would look so amazing hanging over my mantle back home," he said. He asked the price from the proprietor of the shop and was shocked at the total.

"Let's get it, if you like it," Cam said. "I find that if art moves you, you should have it." He reached into the velcroed pocket of his jams and pulled out his platinum card.

"What are you doing? I'm a man of means now." Blake fished out his own credit card, plain, not platinum, and placed it proudly on the counter. "I'll take it."

After settling up with store, giving the shipping address and such, they left and continued their walkabout.

They discovered a small store full of vintage Hawaiiana located at the back of the shopping complex, where Cam bought an impressive amount for use at the beach house and the new London store. While he was dealing with the shipping information, Blake got to talking with a local. They were deep in conversation when Cam joined them.

"Cameron, this is Keali'i. He was telling me about this amazing trail at the end of the highway," Blake explained.

Keali'i, recognizing Cameron, shook his hand heartily. "Yeah, Brah, the Kalalau Trail. It takes you to Hanakapi'ai Beach. It's a hike, but really worth it. You bruddahs should check it out." He smiled, the strange sounding words easily flying out of his mouth.

"Let's do it! Let's go," urged Blake, practically jumping up and down.

"Sure. I've heard of it, but never hiked it. I'm game."

Blake got directions from Keali'i, and a few words of wisdom about the trail, and they were off.

The drive to the end of the highway was simply too beautiful for words. Blake's head was spinning from all the craning he had done in trying to soak all the scenery in. Everywhere he looked, he saw a postcard worthy view. By the time they parked alongside the road and grabbed their water bottles and bandanas, Blake was beside himself with excitement.

The beginning of the trail started at Ke'e Beach, one of the prettiest beaches Blake had ever seen. Rounding the western corner, behind some other ridges, was the famous pointed Bali Hai mountain. It was notable for its prominent use in the 1950s movie *South Pacific,* which had been shot on location on the island.

As they tied on bandanas do-rag style, Cam led Blake to the trail start, and up they began to climb. It was a steep haul, over slippery rocks, and exposed tree roots. Within minutes both men were panting from the exertion, and soon they were sweating up a storm. As they hiked deeper into the jungle, they passed other hikers coming back down from their own excursions. Blake always called out a cheery "hello!"

About an hour later, they arrived at a bluff above the beach. The two sweaty men stopped and gazed down at the overwhelming seascape. It was as spectacular as described. Completely hidden from prying eyes, it was a long expanse of soft cream-colored sand. A trickling brook ran from it, and it was surrounded on all three sides by steep palm tree–covered mountains that stood guard over the sand. On the far side of the beach, sea caves were cut into the rock walls. They had been formed ages before when hot lava had spilled into the ocean from steaming vents cracked open into fissures in the rock surface. The violent surf crashed into these caves, sending up great flumes of spraying water.

There was no one else around this eden. Cam and Blake had this enormous playground all to themselves.

The second Blake's feet hit the sand, he whipped off his damp tanktop, pulled his muddy sneakers and socks off, and ran to the water's edge. He dove into the rough water and cooled himself off. Sticking very close to the shoreline, he allowed himself to be dunked by the rough waves. Cam stood on the beach laughing at his antics.

Blake could feel that the surf was extremely turbulent, so he left the water reluctantly, and walked back onto the beach. He had seen the warning signs posted on the way down to the beach telling of the people who had drowned at this very spot, and he didn't want to add his name to the memorial list.

He playfully walked up to Cam and shook his entire body, sending a spray of water in Cam's direction. Cam yelped and jumped back.

Blake snickered while Cam recovered. Cam had to crack a smile as he got a good look at Blake. His head was tilted back, water bottle pressed to lips as he drank. The sea water was slowly running down his body in rivulets and dripping off where it could. His surfer jams, already loose to begin with, had sunk so low on his hips that fully two inches of his trimmed pubic hair could be seen. His tan had gotten darker as the day had worn on, and he was so brown now that he looked like a native. His hair, tangled, wild, and blowing in the humid breeze, was drying quickly into loose ringlets.

"Good Lord," Cam whispered to himself, constantly amazed at Blake's handsomeness and his own good fortune in finding him.

"You ever see this movie called *From Here to Eternity?*" Blake asked, throwing the now empty water bottle next to his bag, a lascivious grin on his face.

"Sure."

"Well," Blake said, suddenly leaping at Cam, grabbing him around the waist and wrestling him to the sand. "I'm Burt Lancaster, and you're Deborah Kerr!" He laughed as Cam fake-struggled to get free. They held each other tight and kissed deeply as the waves crashed against them, soaking them both.

"You know," Cam said dreamily, "there's no way I'm Deborah Kerr. I am so Burt Lancaster, it's not funny."

Dinner that night was at Duke's Canoe Club overlooking Kalapaki Beach, in Lihue. Both men were starving by the time they got seated at their covered-lanai table looking out over the wide beach. They had a glorious view of Kalapaki Bay and idly watched the distant airliners come in sporadically to land at the airport, four miles away. Blake resisted the temptation to devour the bread basket placed in front of them, and after they had ordered their meals, they sat back, relaxed, and sipped their delicious mai tais.

Just another perfect evening in paradise, thought Blake.

When they had arrived back to the beach house after their incredible hike to Hanakapi'ai Beach and back, they both jumped in the large glassed-in shower stall and spent many minutes scrubbing each other down, trying to get all of that damn sand out of their asses.

Blake made a mental note never to make out in the surf line again.

Now seated at the table, both in vibrant aloha shirts and khaki shorts, all courtesy of the CF/Active line, they gave in to the simple luxury of vegging out.

"My legs are so sore. They feel like rubber," confessed Cam, rubbing his quads gently.

"Mine too. I didn't think that hike was that strenuous, but I guess it was. I feel like I have polio!"

"I think we'll do the whole spa and massage thing tomorrow. There's a great spa at the Hyatt in Poipu. We'll go there." He took out his cell and punched in a few digits. "Dan? Hello, it's Cameron here . . . Oh, fine, thanks for asking . . ." He glanced up and looked at Blake, smiling. "Yes, he is, isn't he? . . . Listen, will you please book Blake and me a day at Anara? The whole treatment . . . .Oh, about one. I don't want to have to get up too early, you know . . . Thank you, Dan."

The server brought them their salads, and peppered each one.

"We're getting rubbed and wrapped and aromasized tomorrow," Cam joked.

"Good deal."

They ate hungrily and in silence for a few minutes.

"So, Cameron. Tell me. How did you get started in the business? I mean, you're huge now. Did you know it would go the way it did?"

Cam looked up from his salad. "Not like this, no. I wanted to be successful, but I never dreamed it would go this far. When Suzette and I started, I just wanted to corner the dress shirt market." He grinned. "But they sold really well, and then I got a sweet deal on some abandoned blazer fabric, and I started making jackets. It all grew from that."

"You must be so proud of yourself. You're an institution. Does it ever get too much for you?"

"All the time. Sometimes I think I just want to walk away from it. Move here and raise orchids, or something. But I have people who depend on me. People whose families depend on me for their livelihood. So I can't."

"You're always yelling into the phone. Can't be all fun and games, huh?"

Cameron laughed. "No. Not always." He looked out to sea for a moment. "I don't get along with my father-in-law, and because he invested heavily in my company, he's on the board of investors. Now he has a block of people who listen to him, and not me. I have to fight for everything I feel is right."

"But you built up the company. Don't they know that?"

"We've had a few bad quarters lately. That's why PCH has to be a hit, right out of the box. Not only do I need the cash flow, I need it to be successful for credibility. Once that happens, I can settle some old . . . obligations. Once Suzette is out of my life, I can maneuver the old man out as well."

At that moment a good-looking, built young man of about twenty-three walked up to their table, a slip of paper and pen in his hand. "Excuse me, Mr. Fuller, but can I have your autograph?" He smiled shyly and stuck out the pen and paper.

"Sure. What's your name?" Cam asked, graciously.

"Justin."

Cam scribbled on the paper, and as he handed it back, Justin quickly handed him another folded piece of paper. He blushed deep red and mumbled thanks as he walked away.

"What was that?" Blake asked.

Cam unfolded the paper and grinned. "His hotel phone number."

"Jesus! That was fucking ballsy. You're sitting here with me, for Christ's sake!" Blake was pissed.

"It happens all the time. You'll see. You'll have guys coming on to you like never before. Brace yourself."

Another man came up to their table, followed by an older couple with a camera. Justin's request apparently opened the floodgates, and everyone else now felt comfortable approaching Cameron.

It took fifteen minutes for Cameron to sign all the autographs and pose for all the pictures. He did it with grace and good humor. Blake was perturbed by the intrusion on their romantic dinner and couldn't wait for all the people to go away.

"Man. *That* was annoying," Blake said, after the last autograph-seeker left the table.

"Can't be helped. It happens. It'll happen to you too, sooner than you think," Cameron warned.

"Oh, great."

"So where was I? Oh, yes. The business just kept growing. We went multinational. Who knew I'd be huge in Bolivia?" he cracked.

Their fish dinners arrived, and they ate with gusto. Blake's good humor quickly returned and they enjoyed the rest of their meal.

22

The drive home was under the bright light of a full moon. The stars were so plentiful and clear, Blake was transfixed by them. After living in L.A. for so long, he'd forgotten what a real starry night was.

He and Cam were holding hands, gently stroking each other's fingers, and both of them had never felt so content in their lives. They were two men in love with each other, away from the rest of the world, and alone together in a dream house by the beach.

What could be more perfect than this? they both wondered.

Cam stopped to punch in the code at the gate to the estate, and as the gate swung open, he leaned over and kissed Blake.

"I love you, Blake. So damn much it's frightening."

"I know *exactly* what you mean. I love you back. And I can't wait to show you how much. I'm gonna make you come so hard it's gonna blow your mind," Blake whispered in reply.

Cam felt himself get stiff just from the anticipation.

As the Explorer crunched down the gravel drive to the house, Cam and Blake were surprised to see a car, a red Mustang convertible, parked in front of the house.

"Who's that?" Blake asked.

"I have no idea." Cameron was perplexed. He could see slight movements and shadows in the house.

Someone was actually inside the house!

Cameron parked behind the convertible and got his cell phone out, his finger resting on the emergency button. He briskly walked up to the front door, and before Blake could stop him, he burst into the home.

"Hello? Who's here?" he called out loudly.

Blake rushed up the stairs and followed Cam into the house. Both men stopped short when they saw the trespasser.

Suzette.

She was standing in the center of the living room, a cocktail in one hand. She was dressed in a perfectly pressed pair of khaki slacks and a white button-down shirt tied around her midriff Mary-Ann style. Her hair, as always, was perfectly in place.

"Hello, Cam darling," she said sweetly. She shot a look at Blake. "I remember you. You're Blake, the fag whore who's been screwing my husband." She took a long sip of her drink.

Blake was speechless.

This was bad. This was *really* bad.

"Suzette! What the hell are you doing here?" Cam bellowed, enraged by Suzette's condescending demeanor.

"It's my house. I can come here if I want to. And I wanted to."

"You *loathe* this house!"

"Well. I've suddenly grown very fond of it." She smirked, looking directly at Blake. "Though we may have to have it exterminated now. It seems to be infested with vermin."

"How did you even know we were here? I told no one!" he said, trying to control his anger.

"Oh, Cameron. You don't make a move without me knowing about it. Did you really think you could sneak off to paradise with your gay lover and I wouldn't care?"

Blake didn't know what to do. Stay or leave?

"Well, you're not staying here. I hope you booked a hotel suite somewhere," Cameron countered, crossing his arms across his chest defiantly.

"Don't be ridiculous, darling. This is our house. I'm staying here, with you, my husband." She looked at Blake, hatred blazing in her eyes. "Slut boy can go sleep somewhere else. I couldn't care less where. But I want him gone. Now."

"Cam, maybe I should—" Blake started to say. Cameron held up a hand to stop him.

"Suzette. I always knew you could be a bitch. But really, this tops them all! Blake isn't going anywhere. He and I are staying right here. You need to go fuck yourself, and leave."

"Sure, darling. I'll leave." She sashayed up to Cameron. "But I'm going to run right to the papers. I'll tell Liz Smith how my husband's fucking a man! Boo hoo! And not just any man! The man he's picked to launch a thirty million dollar fragrance! How could he do this to me, I'll say!" She smiled evilly. "I wonder what *that* will do to sales?"

"You cunt," Cameron seethed.

"Why, Cameron. I didn't think you knew I had one. You do care," she laughed.

"Cam, I'll go. Let me go pack my bags and I'll leave," Blake said quietly.

"Don't bother. I threw all the clothes your size into that bag there. Take it and go." Suzette waved vaguely at an unzipped duffle bag next to the sofa.

Blake went to pick it up and noticed that all of his belongings were stuffed in haphazardly, and covered with a film of sticky liquid. He looked up at Suzette, perplexed.

"Oh, yes. I'm so sorry. I found your bottle of fucking lubricant, and somehow the top came off when I was packing your clothes. It got over everything. So sorry." She turned her back on him and stared out toward the lanai.

Blake picked up the bag of ruined clothes and looked helplessly at Cameron.

"Wait for me. I'm leaving with you," Cameron said, his voice hard as steel.

"Oh, no you're not!" Suzette uttered, her tone steely. "I didn't fly ten thousand miles, *commercial,* to have you leave with your trashy man-whore. You're staying right here with me, sweetheart." She took another long swig of her drink, draining it. "Now, say goodbye to your fuck-boy, Cameron."

Blake gritted his teeth and walked out of the room, Cameron following close behind.

"Blake! Wait!" Cameron called after him.

"What?" Blake stopped.

"I'm sorry! She's crazy! I'm so sorry . . . Go check yourself into the Princeville . . . I'll be there in a few minutes," Cam said, digging into his pockets. He pulled out the car keys and handed them to Blake. "Take the Explorer. I'll see you in a few, okay?"

"Promise? This is awful, Cam! I feel like we got caught doing something wrong." Blake was angry and scared at the same time. He didn't like it.

"We're not doing anything wrong, sweetheart. I'm so sorry!" Cam repeated.

"All right. I'll go check in. But I'm getting the biggest fucking suite they have, and it's going on your credit card." Blake half-smiled. "Hand it over."

Cameron pulled out his wallet and gave him the plastic. "Deal. See you in a few. I love you, Blake."

"I love you back."

Blake walked out of the house and to the truck. He hopped in and started it up and drove the few miles to the Princeville Resort.

A huge structure built on, and into, a cliff overlooking picturesque Hanalei Bay, the Princeville was the north shore's premiere resort. Blake left the truck with the valet, and strolled through the immense lobby to the front desk.

"Aloha, and welcome to the Princeville," said the front desk concierge.

"I'd like a suite, please," Blake said affably to the man.

"What name is your reservation under, sir?"

"I don't have one."

A slight crease appeared on the concierge's brow. "Oh, I'm terribly sorry, sir, but we are completely booked up. There is not one spare room in the entire hotel."

"It doesn't have to be a suite then. Just a regular room will be fine."

"No, you don't understand, sir. I'm sorry, but we are completely full. There are two conventions and four weddings this weekend. I simply don't have anything for you."

Could this night get any worse? Blake wondered. "If I told you the room is for Cameron Fuller, would that make a difference?" he finally asked.

"I thought Mr. Fuller owned a home here."

"He does, but there's been . . . a situation. He'd like to stay here tonight."

"I'm so sorry, sir, but I just don't have a room available. Would you mind waiting while I check other area hotels?"

"Oh, yes. That would be great, thank you," Blake said, relieved.

"Just wait over there, Mr. uh . . . I'm sorry. What is your name?"

"Jackson. Blake Jackson."

"Very good, Mr. Jackson. I'll just be a moment."

The dapper concierge disappeared into his office and sat down at the phone. Blake wandered over to an enormous plush sofa and sat down. The minutes ticked by like hours.

Finally, the concierge came out of his office, a grim look on his face. "I'm so sorry Mr. Jackson, but I can't find a single available room on the island. This is one of our busiest times of year here on Kauai. I even tried as far south as the Hyatt. Nothing is available." He truly looked saddened.

"Oh, man," Blake moaned dejectedly. "What am I going to do? I don't have a place to stay now."

"Do you have any friends on the island? Someone you could bunk with for tonight?"

"No, I . . . Wait. I think I do know someone. Thanks for your help."

As the concierge walked away, Blake was dialing a number on his cell phone.

"Hello, yes. Can you please get me the number of the Hyatt in Poipu, Kauai, Hawaii? Thank you . . ."

Cameron grunted in exasperation and stormed out onto the lanai. He stared down at the dark surf line and scowled.

"I'm fixing another," Suzette called out from inside. "Do you want one, too?"

"Fuck off!" he snarled.

He heard her heels clacking across the polished wood floor, then there was the soft whoosh of the screen panel sliding open, then closed.

"Cameron. Don't be an ass."

He turned around and faced his wife. "What the hell do you want, Suzette? Why are you doing this? I . . . I just don't understand you."

Smiling a cheshire cat grin, Suzette joined him at the railing. "Lovely evening tonight, don't you think?" she asked, ignoring his question.

"It was. Until you showed up."

She play-pouted at him.

"Suzette, this isn't going to work. Whatever you're trying to pull,

I'm still going to leave you. It's over. Don't you get it?" Cameron tried to keep his voice even and calm, but his anger still crept through.

Suzette faced him. "You said you'd *always* love Stanton, Cameron. It was the one thing I truly believed in."

That threw the designer. "Wha . . . what?"

"The two of you. You were in love. It was sweet and pure, and it was something I always wanted. Just to see it, to be near it, was enough for me. How can you forget him like this?"

"What are you talking about?"

To Cameron's surprise, Suzette's eyes filled up with tears. "You're breaking your promise . . . for that window dresser?"

"Oh my God," Cameron uttered, stunned as the realization of what she was talking about hit home. "That was twenty-five years ago! We were kids."

"You promised. You swore an oath to me that Stanton was the only man you'd ever truly love! Now I find you here, on a romantic getaway with that . . . that *trick*. I see the way you look at him. It's the same way you used to look at Stanny."

Cameron sighed. "Suzette, it's time to move on, don't you think? We only get one shot at life, and I intend to make the most of what time I have left on this earth. Don't you want that? Don't you want to find a man who can be with you, cherish you, love you the way you deserve?"

Suzette stared out to sea, but her face softened.

"You're an amazing woman, Suzette," he said kindly. "You're gonna meet a great guy, I know it. In time, you'll wonder why we waited so long to end this, I promise you."

Tears began to slowly seep from the corners of her eyes. "Who's going to want me? I have nothing to offer," she said, sniffing.

Cameron felt his heart break for his wife. She actually believed that. He moved toward her, wrapped his strong arms around her trembling form and pulled her close. She was vulnerable and sweet now, the woman he used to know. "That's not true. You've listened to your father for too long. You are one of the most dynamic women I know. You're smart, dedicated, driven . . ."

"I'm a spoiled bitch, and you know it."

Cam smiled slightly. "Well, there is that." Suzette chuckled softly. "But you're also passionate, strong, and involved," he continued, now stroking her silken hair. "I do love you, Suzette, just not in the way you want me to. And I'm sorry about that, I truly am."

Suzette reached her thin arms around him and squeezed her husband tightly. "I know . . . I know. And I love you, too. I suppose I always knew this would never work, but, God, Cameron, I *love* being your wife. The respect it gives me. People finally look up to me. Me. Not Stanton, not Silas. Me." She glanced up and gazed into his handsome, compassionate face. Instinctively, she reached a tiny hand up to gently brush aside a stray lock of hair that had fallen over his forehead. "You're a good man, my darling. You really are." She smiled. "How is it that you always know exactly what to say to calm me down? Besides Stanny, you were the only person who could do that." The small woman sighed. "The truth is, I'm just so scared. I don't know what I'm going to do. I've never been on my own before, and I'm petrified."

Cameron arranged his face into one of mock surprise. "You? Afraid? What has the world come to?" He grinned gently. "You're going to be fine, I know it."

The thin woman nestled against her strong husband. She breathed in his scent and felt safe again. "I wish Daddy thought that."

Cameron took his wife by the shoulders. "Suzette, look at me," he directed. She complied. "Your father is a very bitter man. He has no heart, no soul. I've stood by and watched him degrade you, criticize you for so long that it's like white noise now. He's wrong, Suzette. He's never given you the credit you deserve. Don't let him beat you down. You need to separate yourself from him. He's toxic for you."

Suzette stiffened. "Don't talk about my father that way," she warned. "After all he's done for you? For us?"

Cameron was amazed. She was still defending her father. "Suzette, he has done nothing but run you into the ground since I met you! He clings to the memory of his dead son and berates you constantly, don't you find that pathetic?"

Suzette's eyes narrowed and a churlish cast came over her. "Pathetic? I'll tell you what's pathetic. You! You fucking some low class kid in *my* home. That's pathetic!" Her body was now tensed again, her small hands balling up into fists. She pushed herself away from Cameron.

Cameron closed his eyes and breathed in deeply. For a brief moment he'd seen the Suzette he'd always cherished; the calm, under-standing woman that she used to be. But it was only a tease, a glimpse into a personality she no longer let out. He reopened his eyes and turned to leave. "I'm going over to the Princeville now."

"Oh no you're not!" she screamed.

Cameron turned back around and faced her, grim determination on his face. "Yes. Yes, I am. I want to be with Blake, Suzette. Please, for all our sakes, get used to that idea."

Suzette couldn't believe what she was hearing. "Never!" she spat out. "That little fuckfest is over! As of this minute! I won't allow it!"

Cameron laughed. He actually laughed. "I really don't see what you can do about it."

Like a cat stalking its prey, Suzette moved toward Cameron. "Oh? You think I'm *joking* when I say I'll go public with this? You try me! I'll publicly come out against you and your rotten Pacific Coast High-way. I'll personally see to it that sales are flatter than a pancake! You'll never be able to pay Daddy off this year! Or the next! Or the one after that!"

Cameron shook his head in disgust.

In the dim light of the lanai, Suzette's features took on an ugly shape, old, withered, and spiteful. "Of course, I'll become known as the idiot wife whose husband went faggot on her, but fuck it! It's a small price to pay to see you still under Daddy's thumb for years to come!"

"Suzette—"

"Shut up! I don't want to hear it! How *could* you? How could you bring that muscle-bound slut into our home? I hate him! I *loathe* him! I will see him destroyed! He will never replace Stanton! Never!" The bile spewed forth from Suzette's crimson lips like acrid poison. She had lost all sense of composure, and her true tormented rage was on full display. "He's trash! Cheap trash! It disgusts me that you even touch him! The same lips that kissed my Stanny, kiss him?! It's pu-trid! And you want him to be a model for us? Ha! *That* will never happen, either!"

Cameron couldn't hear anymore. White spots blurred his vision as his rage boiled over. "Don't you *ever* speak about him that way again!" he bellowed, so loud that Suzette actually shrank back a few feet. For a brief instant, he wanted to strike her, to physically beat some sense into her, but he wisely restrained himself. "I made sure he's got a contract," the designer yelled, his voice thunderous. "So fuck you, and fuck your threats!"

Suzette suddenly became calm. She even half-smiled. "Contracts are merely words. They were made to be broken, darling. And you, of all people, should know about breaking your word." She arrogantly sailed past him, and went into the house. "I'm going to bed. I suggest you join me. You won't be seeing the fuck-boy tonight, my sweet."

Cameron, seething with rage, walked to the lanai railing and gripped it tightly. Gulping in huge amounts of the slightly sweet night air, he forced deep breaths into his body.

Slowly, the physical stress this confrontation had caused ebbed away from his body. The mental anguish, however, refused to vacate.

He was a man torn.

23

Poipu, Kauai, Hawaii

"Honey, come on in!" Dan held the door open wide and let Blake pass through. "Just drop that anywhere."

Blake dropped the bag just inside the door. He looked about the spacious room. There was a king-size bed, a comfy-looking chair and ottoman, a round table that acted as a desk, and a low armoire that housed the TV and mini bar. The colors of the room were pale green and peach. Tasteful lithograph prints depicting the fruits and flora of Hawaii hung on the walls, and the bed coverlet was a quilt with a Polynesian design.

The view out the large sliding glass doors was spectacular. Just beyond the lush grounds and pools of the hotel, the ocean crashed onto a coarse sandy beach that ran the width of the property.

"Nice digs," he said wearily.

"Cameron always has us stay at great hotels. We're very lucky to work for him. You don't mind sharing the bed?" He was wearing a pair of cut-off sweatpants and a navy blue T-shirt with the word "Catcher" imprinted on it in white letters, obviously his sleeping attire.

"Not at all. You're safe with me."

"Dang."

"Is there a laundry service here? My clothes are . . . they need to be cleaned."

"No problem. I'll take care of it."

There was an awkward silence.

"Do you want to tell me about it, or should I just not concern myself with why you're staying here with me and not at the beach house?" the flight attendant asked gently.

Blake flopped on the bed. "You won't believe it. Suzette's here."

"What? She hates the islands. Complains every time he brings her!"

"Apparently, she found out we were here. Together. She sure hates me, the fucking bitch. You should have seen how she treated me."

"Oh, I can imagine." Dan smiled. "I've seen her cut down CEOs before. She's a piece of work, that one." Dan sat down beside Blake. Cameron's new lover looked so miserable, and he felt sorry for him.

"Cam was so weird on the phone when I told him about the hotel situation. He actually sounded relieved when I said I was coming over here to bunk with you," Blake complained, closing his eyes tightly. "He was, all, like, 'good, *whatever.*' Like it didn't fucking matter that I was on the other side of the fucking island and had to spend the night with another guy."

"Oh, honey, I'm so sorry."

"We were having such a good time, Dan! It was perfect. I love that house, I love the island, and I love him. Now I'm all pissed and don't know who I should be pissed at."

"I vote for Suzette."

"Yeah, well, I didn't see him racing after me, or even leaving with me. She's such a bitch! He doesn't need to put up with her crap!"

"Well, honey, sadly, he does," Dan said. "It's really delicate for him right now. She can claim half of his assets. That includes the company. Sales are soft this year, and he's banking on this new fragrance to pull the company up. He can't afford any scandal that might affect that."

"Fuck!"

"Yeah, well, looks like neither of us is gonna be doing *that* tonight," Dan said with a sigh, flopping back on the bed.

Blake looked at him oddly. Huh?

"I'm kind of screwing Rick, the pilot. He's in a relationship, and it's stupid and has no future, but a girl's got needs." Dan blushed. "He's sharing a room with the copilot, and now that I have a roomie . . ."

"Damn. Sorry. We make a great pair, don't we?"

* * *

"I want another mai tai. Where's the waitress?" Blake asked crossly, looking about. He'd already had one and a half, and wanted to enjoy the buzz. He wasn't.

Dan looked over the rims of his sunglasses at the frustrated model. "Honey, I believe they're called 'servers' . . . and she'll be back soon. Relax."

They were lying on identical sun loungers, side by side, in a small secluded nook of the gigantic pool area. Several pools were terraced through acres of the property, with meandering streams that went from one large body of water to another. Along this "river" were caves and grottos that welcomed swimmers for intimate encounters. Waterfalls were liberally flowing all over the grounds, and soft Hawaiian music came through discreetly hidden speakers.

Blake was on his stomach, wearing his tiniest Speedo, and had pulled the sides up into his butt crack to help minimize any tan line. He correctly assumed that nude sunbathing was not allowed at the family-friendly Hyatt.

Dan actually had a good body, though he was too thin for Blake's taste. He had a swimmer's build, and there was not an ounce of fat on his slight frame. He was wearing a pair of box-cut swimming trunks in lime green lycra. He had on oversized black Gucci sunglasses and was reading a new book by William Mann, having apparently finished the Ben Tyler he'd been reading on the plane.

"Sorry, Dan. I'm just in a foul mood. He hasn't even called!" Blake sputtered, his words laced with petulance. "What am I supposed to do? Hang around? We were supposed to leave tomorrow morning. Is that still on? What the fuck!"

"Well, I haven't heard differently, and he can't go without his flight crew, so . . ."

"Yeah, well, fuck him."

"Oh, you are in a bad mood," the flight attendant snickered.

Blake leaned up on his elbows. "You know what we're going to do today, Dan?"

"No telling."

"You and I are going to have a day of beauty. We're going to use that Anara Spa *up*. Whatever we want. And we're going to charge it to his credit card. Fuck him!" Blake decided petulantly.

"Could you please not get me fired? I like my job," Dan chided him.

"Don't worry. I'll take full responsibility. So, soak up the sun. We exfoliate in an hour."

Blake was lying in the late afternoon sun by the secluded pool at the center of the spa. Dan was still getting his massage, and Blake had wandered out to the pool area to wait for him. Half asleep, he was completely relaxed from his own eighty-minute massage. His skin still tingled from the seaweed wrap, and his face felt renewed from the facial. Not a bad way to while away a Sunday afternoon.

He felt a shadow shade the hot sun from his body, and he cracked open an eye to see who was blocking his rays.

"Hi." It was Cameron, wearing the same clothes he had on the day before. He hadn't shaved and he looked like he hadn't slept. He sat down in the empty chaise next to Blake and began to fidget with his hands.

Blake sat up. "Hi."

Cameron looked uncomfortable and it was almost a full minute before he spoke. "I'm so sorry about last night, Blake. I had no idea she would come here. I don't know what else to say."

"How about, 'I kicked the bitch out'?"

"I wish I could. But I just can't right now, Blake. Please try to understand. She is *freaking* over you and me. I had no idea it would be this bad."

"She's freaking? How about *I'm* freaking! What am I supposed to do, Cam? I came here with you. I want to be with *you.* And, as much as I like Dan, he's not the bed partner I want. You are." Blake knew he was being slightly unreasonable, but he couldn't help himself.

"Blake, I'm sorry! But, I have to tell you something, and it's not going to make you happy."

"I can't wait to hear this," Blake said sarcastically.

Cameron took a deep breath. "I . . . Suzette is flying back to L.A. with me tomorrow on the jet. I'm going to have to fly you home commercial."

"You're kidding me!" Blake was stunned.

"I know, and I'm sorry . . ."

Blake shook his head. "Whatever, Cam."

Cameron couldn't have looked more miserable if he tried. "Blake, I don't have a choice. She's threatened to go public with this . . . with us. I have to go along for a while. I love you. Please understand that this isn't what I wanted. But I just have to appease her for now. We can have plenty of trips in the plane later," he said.

"The *plane?!* Cam, this isn't about the plane! I don't give a fuck if I fly home strapped to the wing of a FedEx cargo jet. I just want to be with *you.* That was the point of this. And do you know how I feel now? Like I'm some trick that you have to shoo away now that the little woman has come home." Even though he was trying to keep his voice down, Blake's anger was getting the best of him. Several of the other guests started to look over and watch them. He stared at Cam, and saw something else was bothering him.

In an instant, he knew what it was.

"Am I out of a job as well?"

Cameron looked down at the ground and didn't say a word.

"I am, aren't I? She doesn't want you to use me as the spokesman, does she? Tell me."

"Blake . . ." Cameron couldn't even finish the sentence.

"That's just great, Cam. I fucking quit my job over this! I signed contracts with your company! I put your check in the bank! Now I have to give that back?" Incredulous, Blake struggled to get out of his chaise lounger.

"Of course not! You can keep the money you've received. And maybe later, when she and I have, well, later . . ."

"Later my ass, you son of a bitch! I didn't even want to be a fuck-ing model until you planted that seed in my head." Blake was stand-ing over Cam, his nostrils flaring in rage. "And it's not even that I want it so bad *now,* you know. I just liked the way *you* made me feel about myself. Like I was worth something. Something other than a hot piece of ass, which is how everyone else makes me feel. That I had something to offer. You screwed with my head! Fuck you!" He was struggling to keep his voice down, and losing the battle. "You used me, just like Rafe said you would, and now you run home to momma. Tell you what, Cam. You let me know when you grow a pair of balls!"

Cameron, not having been spoken to like this in years, was speechless, his mouth hanging open in a small "O."

Blake started to walk away, but stopped and looked back at Cameron. "I don't think I have ever been so disappointed in another human being as I am right now in you." He turned away, tears stinging his eyes, and left Cameron sitting on the chaise, crushed.

24

In seat 2-B on Nui Loa Airlines flight #8, Blake sat glumly staring ahead. He was on his third cocktail, feeling no pain and pissed off.

Even though it was two o'clock in the morning, and almost every other passenger on the redeye flight was asleep, Blake could not close his eyes for more than ten seconds without seeing the hurt look on Cameron's face as he walked away. He wasn't watching the movie, a flick starring Travis Church that he'd seen before. He found himself just simply staring at nothing. He downed the remains of his drink and put the glass down.

"Can I get you another, Mr. Jackson?"

Pulled from his funk, Blake faced the flight attendant. He was a handsome man, obviously Hawaiian. Probably about twenty-eight, he had dark skin and the whitest teeth Blake had ever seen. His somewhat blockish face was softened by a wide, straight nose and merry hazel eyes. Thick black hair was slicked back neatly. He was built, and looked good in the floral aloha shirt and loose pleated pants that were his uniform. He'd been especially attentive to Blake since he boarded the plane.

"Oh, I better not." Blake squinted at his name tag. "Luka. That's a cool name."

Luka managed to smile even broader, and he squatted down to Blake's eye level. "Anything else, then?" He placed his hand on the seat back cushion, lightly grazing Blake's neck.

Blake wasn't too tipsy to recognize interest when he saw it. *What the fuck?* he thought. *He's cute.* "Well, I can't think of anything at the moment, Luka. But I'll let you know when I do," he answered seductively.

"Well, you make sure you do that." Luka winked. "It's pretty quiet tonight. Everyone's asleep. That's why I like the redeye. Once we feed everyone, they pass out."

Blake smiled. He looked around but didn't see any of the other flight attendants. "Where's the rest of the crew?"

"Oh, they're all in the back, talking," Luka said. "Did you have a good time in Kauai? I noticed on the computer that you booked your ticket this afternoon. Have to leave early for business?"

"Something like that."

Actually, the second Blake got back to Dan's room, he picked up the phone and booked a return ticket. He didn't want to stay on the island any longer than he had to. He was even able to get a seat in first class, and after leaving a note for Dan to explain the situation, he took off for the airport. He returned Cam's Explorer to the rental place and caught the next flight to Honolulu, where he then switched planes and boarded flight 8.

"That's too bad. A trip to Hawaii should be extended, not shortened. Do you ever spend any time on Oahu?"

"No. Tonight at the airport, when I switched planes, was my first time there. I'm sure it's beautiful."

"It is. You should come back sometime." His voice dropped low. "I'd be glad to show you around."

"Really? Well, that's good to know, Luka. But, right now, I have to use the restroom," Blake said, unbuckling his seat belt.

"Certainly. There, right up front," the Hawaiian said, pointing to the cockpit area, by the first class galley. "Be sure to lock the door. If it was . . ." (he glanced around conspiratorially) ". . . *unlocked,* then *anyone* could just walk in on you . . . Just so you know." Luka stood up, and Blake couldn't help but notice his erection.

"Words to live by," he smiled, sliding past Luka. As he passed him, he let his hand casually brush across Luka's hardened crotch, and gave it a quick squeeze. Luka sucked in a breath of air and watched Blake walk to the front of the plane.

Blake entered the small lavatory and purposely left the door unlocked. He actually used the facilities and was washing his hands when the small door creaked open. Luka popped in and quickly shut and locked the door behind him. The wasn't really enough room for two full grown men, and headroom was at a premium.

"Just thought I'd see if you need . . . anything else," Luka said, licking his lips nervously.

"I can think of a few things," Blake replied. He reached down and gripped Luka's rock hard cock through his thin poly-cotton uniform pants.

It was big, he realized.

Luka gasped and leaned forward. They kissed hard and often. This wasn't about love and passion, it was about pure animal lust. Blake let himself go and savagely went after the Hawaiian's mouth and lips.

Before he knew it, Luka had dropped to his knees, undone Blake's pants, and was blowing him.

Blake grabbed Luka's head and tightened his grip through the slick hair. He forced Luka's head back and forth, thrusting his hips forward, jamming his cock deep into the flight attendant's enthusiastic mouth. Luka, not having a problem with this at all, undid his pants and was soon stroking himself furiously.

Blake glanced down and was stunned by the size of Luka. It was the biggest dick he had ever seen. Absolutely mammoth.

I'd never be able to get that in my mouth, he thought.

Or, maybe he could . . .

Always one for a challenge, he grabbed Luka by the shoulders and indicated a position switch. He dropped down and came face-to-face with the monster. He gulped, then went to work. Luka looked down at this incredibly hot man preparing to suck him off, and it drove him crazy. He was absolutely apoplectic when Blake started to work him into his mouth.

Blake knew he himself was well-hung, and now he understood what some guys had gone through to take him. He could barely get his lips around it, and as the head finally slid in his ever-widening mouth, Luka shuddered. Blake tried mightily to take it as far as he could, but found he could only go down halfway. He bobbed back and forth, covering it with slippery saliva.

"Fuck! You're . . . I'm gonna fuckin' shoot, Brah!" the hot flight attendant gasped, his hands frantically pushing Blake away from his dick.

Blake reached up, and with solid, hard strokes, jerked off the slick cock. Luka gasped again, and Blake knew what was coming. He aimed it away from himself, and watched in awe as Luka shot an enormous load all over the wall of the lavatory.

Luka shuddered a few times and then let out a deep breath. "Damn!" he said.

He then refocused on Blake's hard-on. He pulled Blake up and assumed his original position. He furiously worked on Blake, but to Blake's surprise, the thrill of the illicit union was gone. He began to feel guilty about what he was doing. He tried to push all thoughts of Cam from his mind, but couldn't. Finally, he gently pulled Luka's head away from his work. "Hey. Look, I'm sorry, I don't think it's gonna happen for me."

"Why? What am I doing wrong? I want to make you shoot," Luka said intensely. "Tell me what you like."

"No, really. Seeing you come was enough for me."

Luka looked confused, but came to his feet. The two men awkwardly zipped and buttoned up their pants.

Ever the flight attendant, Luka took a couple of paper towels and cleaned up the wall. He kissed Blake softly on the lips, then opened the door carefully, looked around, and quickly left.

Blake stared at his reflection in the mirror for a full five minutes.

I can't believe I just did that, he kept saying to himself.

He felt a gentle shaking, and opened his eyes to see a smiling Luka at his side.

"We're landing in a few minutes, Mr. Jackson," he said formally.

"Oh. Thank you, Luka."

"No, thank *you*, Mr. Jackson." He leaned in close to Blake's ear. "I have a two-day layover in L.A. I'd like to see you. We have some unfinished business, I think." He slipped a folded piece of paper into Blake's hand. "My hotel number. Call me." He looked around and lowered his voice even more. "I want you to fuck me so bad I can taste it." He stood upright, and then continued his rounds in the cabin.

"Blake! Blake! Over here!"

The puffy-faced model with the bloodshot eyes looked over and saw Brady standing by the exit doors of the terminal. He waved back at him.

"Hey! You got my message," he said, giving Brady a big hug. "Thanks so much for picking me up. I didn't know if you'd be here or not. Sorry for the late notice."

Brady took one of the bags from Blake. "No problem. So I'm a little late reporting for duty today. Fuck 'em." He was dressed for work, his brown and khaki uniform sharply pressed. "You're so tan! Jesus!" he said, looking Blake up and down.

They started to walk across the street toward the parking structure.

"So, what the hell were you doing in Hawaii?" Brady asked.

"It's a long story. And one I don't want to go into right now. It's just good to be home. I am so tired!" Blake glanced at his watch and still couldn't believe it was six-thirty in the morning. He had only slept for about two hours during the last part of the flight, and he was a little loopy from jet lag.

"What time do you have to be at the store today?" Brady asked, opening the trunk of his car, a late model navy blue Ford Taurus.

"I don't. I don't think I have a job there anymore."

Brady gave Blake a surprised look, but said nothing. He tossed both bags into the trunk, and slammed it shut. "Well, let's get you home and in bed, then."

Forty minutes later, when they pulled up to Blake's house, Brady noticed the Discovery II immediately.

"So that's the new car, huh?" Brady said, nonjudgmental.

"Yes."

"It's nice." He stewed for a minute. He turned to face Blake with hurt eyes. "You're fucking him, aren't you? My God, Blake. You'll never change, will you?"

"Jesus, Brady . . ."

"Why can't you just admit you're fucking him?" Brady pressed. Then he held up his hand. "Never mind. I really don't want to know. Forget I asked." Brady threw open his door and practically leapt out of the Taurus. "I'll get your bags," he called back harshly to Blake. "You go on in."

*   *   *

Blake flopped onto his bed, grateful to be home. His sadness about the incidents in Hawaii was a constant buzz in his head, but now that he was on his own turf, he knew he could handle it. Joe, happy that his master was back, jumped up on the bed, vigorously licked him for a minute and then laid down beside him.

"You need anything else before I go to work?" Brady asked gently from the doorway.

"Nope. Thanks again for the ride. Can I call you later on? I'm just so sleepy." Blake didn't even raise his head to speak.

"Sure you can." Brady walked into the room and went to his ex-lover's side. He placed a warm hand on Blake's back, and slowly rubbed it in circles.

"You want me to stay? I will, you know. And I'm sorry about what just happened outside. I have no right to quiz you about your life."

"Brady, it's okay. Forget it. And I'm fine. You don't need to stay." Blake raised his head a little and allowed Brady to kiss him goodbye gently.

"So call me later. Maybe we can do dinner tonight?"

"Mmmm . . . Okay . . . Bye . . ." Blake drifted off to sleep.

After wistfully watching him sleep for a few minutes, Brady let himself out as quietly as possible.

25

When the doorbell rang, Joe barked loudly. The huge animal excitedly jumped off the bed, and with huge paws thudding on the wood floor, ran to the front door.

Blake woke up with a start, his face puffy on one side from his sleeping position. The doorbell rang again, and he forced himself to get up and go answer it.

"Joe! Get back," he said as he tried to shove the dog away from the door. He opened it to face the largest bouquet of red roses he'd ever seen. He let the delivery guy into the house to set the flowers down on the sofa table. "Where do I sign?" he asked, ignoring the gift card attached.

"Oh, I have more of these in the truck. I'll be back," the driver said flatly. He raced out the front door, and made five trips back and forth, bringing into Blake's house the most wondrous arrangements of flowers. Roses, tulips, orchids, all spilling down the sides of heavy glass vases. The house was filled with flowers and the mixed scents were intoxicating.

Blake fumbled through his wallet to find some bills and found he only had two twenties and several hundreds left over from Hawaii. He gave the driver one of the twenties and shut the door.

He went to each arrangement and snapped off the card, making a small white pile on the sofa. He wandered to the kitchen, got a bottle of water, and came back to the living room to sit down and read the cards.

He knew who they were from.

Each plain white card was handwritten in Cameron's bold script, and said the same thing:

> *Blake,*
>
> *I'm so sorry! <u>Please</u> forgive me!*
> *I'll fix everything, I promise you . . .*
>
> *I love you,*
> *Cameron.*

Joe barked again and sat by the door. There was another ring on the door bell. Blake stood up and went to open the door.

Another delivery guy, this one holding a small Cartier shopping bag.

"Mr. Blake Jackson?" he asked officially.

"Yes," Blake answered as he signed for the bag.

When he was back in the house, he reached in the bag to find two small wrapped boxes, which he opened. After tearing off the wrapping paper of the first box, his breath was literally taken away by the gleaming silver tank watch. He noticed there was a tiny inscription on the back of the casing, "To BJ, All My Love, CF."

"Oh, Cam," he said aloud.

In the second small box, he found a dazzling monogrammed set of sterling silver cufflinks and shirt studs.

Twenty minutes later the doorbell rang again.

This time the delivery was a luxurious padded garment bag from the Rodeo Drive store. Inside, Blake found a beautifully cut narrow-lapeled Cameron Fuller Manhattan tuxedo complete with shirt and tie. A separate box contained a sleek pair of dress shoes. Everything was in his exact size.

Bobby never forgets a detail, Blake marveled.

In ten minutes, again the door bell rang.

It was a messenger holding a simple envelope which he handed over wordlessly, then left. Blake opened the note and found another handwritten card from Cameron.

Blake,

*Please do me the great honor of joining me
for dinner tonight. I'll pick you up at eight.*

I love you,
Cameron.

P.S.—Wear the tux!

Blake stared at the neat penmanship, as if to glean more insight into the man who wrote it.

Sighing heavily, he knew he'd be ready at eight.

Blake was brushing his hair for the last time when he heard the knock. Roused, Joe barked and ran to the door. By the time Blake got there, Cam had already let himself in and was standing in the foyer. He, too, was in a tuxedo, and was quite possibly the most handsome creature Blake had ever seen. The two men stared at each other for almost a full minute before Cam broke the silence.

"I'm so sorry, Blake. I handled that situation completely wrong, and I don't blame you for leaving." He moved toward Blake, not entirely sure of his welcome.

"I felt like I was some trick. You just bailed on me," Blake said flatly, not moving.

"I know. I know! I didn't know what to do. I was caught off guard, and I . . . I . . ." Tears started to fall from his violet eyes, leaving tiny dark stains on the satin lapel of his tuxedo jacket.

His anger suddenly evaporated, Blake took a step forward and the two lovers hugged tightly. Kisses quickly followed, at first tentative, then building in passion. Whispered phrases of love were said and lost in the moment.

"When did you get back?" Blake asked, finally ending the make-up session.

"Around one this afternoon. I missed you so damn much," Cam answered, straightening Blake's tie.

"Me, too. Where we going?"

"It's a surprise."

"I don't know if I can take another surprise."

"You'll like this one. I hope."

Blake took his tuxedo jacket from the hall closet, and was about to usher Cameron out when Rand walked in from the rear of the house.

"Wow! Look at you two. It looks like gay prom night!" he joked.

"Only no corsages," Blake countered.

Rand chuckled. "Listen, I'm sorry to intrude. My TV's busted. Can I watch in here? Do you mind? There's a couple of movies on Showtime I wanted to watch."

"Sure. No problem, we're going out. Just let Joe outside a couple times, and clean up after yourself," Blake replied.

"Okay if Sam comes over?"

"Sure. No sex on the sofa, though. I just had it steam cleaned."

"Damn! How about the floor?" Rand grinned.

"Have at it. Bye, Rand." Blake and Cam left the house.

There was another limo parked out front, this one an actual stretch job that was so long, it almost embarrassed Blake. The driver opened the door for them, and after they clambered into the roomy interior, he shut it and walked to the front. The screen separating the driver from the rear was down and Cam reached over subtly to press the button that caused it to rise up, giving them complete privacy.

"Ever fuck a man in a limo before?" Cam asked Blake suggestively as he wrapped his arms around him.

Blake hesitated. "Well, actually, yes."

Cam leaned back in surprise. "Oh? Do tell."

"It was a million years ago . . . I was dating this actor. Major closet case. One night, after the Academy Awards, which he won, by the way, he stopped by my old apartment and picked me up and we drove around for two hours screwing our brains out in the back of the limo. It was okay, but not spectacular. I kept thinking people could see us, which, oddly, seemed to turn him on more." Blake chuckled at the memory. "I'll never forget seeing his Oscar laying on the seat next to his pants."

"Well, I don't want to follow in someone else's footsteps," Cam teased. "So I'll hold my passion in check. Who was the actor?"

Blake told him, and they both laughed.

Blake had a thousand questions for Cameron, but knew it wasn't the right time. He would wait, but he did want some answers, and he would get them before the evening was through. They fell into silence as the car threaded it way through traffic and headed up into Beverly Hills.

Blake lost his sense of direction after one too many looping turns and soon had no idea where they were. At a massive stone gate, the car stopped briefly while the driver punched in some numbers at the security box. Then they drove along a winding drive that seemed to go on forever. Blake was astonished that anyone could own so much property in Beverly Hills. Wherever they were, this estate was huge.

A monstrous stone mansion was situated firmly on top of the hill. The limo pulled up to the expansive porte cochere, and stopped. When the driver opened the door to let the occupants out, Blake could not get over the scale of the house. Everything was oversized. Huge high multi-paned windows went up twelve feet in the front rooms, while the massive stone blocks that made up the facade on the house balanced out the scale.

The enormous and heavy front door opened and a butler ushered the two men inside the house. The great hall entry was easily thirty feet tall. Hanging high above them was the biggest chandelier Blake had ever seen, aglow with the light of over a hundred dimmed bulbs.

"Good God!" Blake whistled as they were led through one astounding room to the next. "Whose place is this?"

"A friend who was kind enough to loan it to me tonight," Cam replied, enjoying Blake's reaction to the impressive home.

"Some friend! Who? The queen?"

"Well, not the kind you mean," Cam laughed.

After walking through endless rooms, each one more dazzling than the previous, the butler led them out to a terrace. Exquisitely cut Italian marble was the flooring, and it was walled in on the opposite side with a low stone balustrade. The terrace was as long as the house was wide. Small groupings of expensive outdoor furniture were carefully placed, and exactly every eight feet, there was a well-tended potted palm.

At the far side of the terrace, Blake noticed a table had been set up with only two chairs. As they moved closer he saw it was elaborately laid out for a dinner for two. Sterling silver candelabras filled with ivory tapers burning softly were centered on the table, while stunningly beautiful china was set out with matching silver flatware. The crystal was obviously Baccarat, and the floral arrangement perfection.

That's when Blake looked over the stone railing and noticed the view. It was as if they were up in the clouds. The house was on top of the hill, and the grounds gracefully sloped downward. The entire city of Los Angeles was laid out before them, as if a gift. Lights twinkled and blinked, and the gentle breeze coming offshore gently rustled the trees and bushes that dotted the grounds. There was a space heater glowing warmly next to the table, so that the diners wouldn't catch a hint of the late January chill.

"My God, Cam. It beautiful," Blake said, gawking.

"This estate belongs to a very good friend of mine who happens to be out of the country right now. Every time I'm in L.A. I always try to make a visit up here. It makes me feel like I'm the king of the world."

"You did not just say that!" Blake laughed. "Does that make me Rose? Is this house going to sink?"

"Well, it had better not until *after* dinner." He walked to a chair and pulled it out for Blake. "Please, be seated."

Blake did as he was asked. Conscious of the butler, he sat down stiffly. Cameron leaned over and planted a lingering kiss on his lips as he sat.

I guess we're not worried about appearances, Blake mused.

The butler smiled sweetly and held out Cam's chair. Cam sat and watched as the wine was poured.

Seemingly from out of nowhere, a trio of musicians, also clad in tuxedos, began to play music from a balcony one terrace below them.

Blake half-expected to see angels flying overhead any minute.

"Thank you for joining me tonight," Cameron said. "I just felt the need to do something really nice to make it up to you."

"Well, this'll do until you figure out what that is," Blake said dryly.

Cam smiled. "I spent a lot of time with Suzette yesterday and today, obviously, and I showed her the photos from the shoot."

"That must have made her day."

"Actually, she appreciated their value. It would have killed her to admit it, but I think she saw your potential. We went back and forth on it, but I managed to sweet talk her. You're the right man for PCH, and whether she likes it or not, it's tough shit. Of course, I didn't put it that way to her. The point is, she's agreed to let you stay on as the PCH spokesman." Cam smiled from ear to ear.

"Bully for her," Blake blandly responded.

"I've had to make a few concessions to keep her in happy, but, overall, it will all work out."

"Really."

"I thought you'd be pleased by this." Cam was confused. "Don't you understand? You still have the contract!"

"Yeah, I understand, Cam, and that's great. But don't expect me to sing the praises of your wife. She was a complete bitch to me, and I never want to be in that position again." Blake was firm.

The designer nodded vigorously. "I hear you. But you have to give a little. It's going to take her a while to get used to you and me . . . well, us as us. Blake, I love you. I don't want to lose you over this. It's so minor. We'll get through this, I promise."

"*I* have to give? Can I just remind you that I was whisked three thousand miles away by the man I happened to have fallen in love with, only to be thrown aside as soon as it became inconvenient. Do we have to ask her permission every time we want to spend time to-gether?"

"You're being unreasonable. I already explained . . ."

"I don't think I *am* being unreasonable. Tell me how you see this *arrangement* working out?"

"We'll keep a low profile until my divorce is final. After that, I want to tell the world about us. It's just delicate right now with Suzette. If she weren't around or if we were already divorced, it'd be a different story," Cam calmly explained.

"Define 'low profile'," Blake countered, crossing his arms across his chest.

"We'll just have to be discreet. No going out any place public. That'd piss her off. We can't be photographed together, except in our official capacities at PCH functions that she also attends. Nothing major."

Blake could not believe what he was hearing. It must have regis-tered on his face.

"Look, it's not that big a deal. Just try to see it my way—" Cam began.

Blake held up a hand to stop him. "Everything seems to be your way." He rose to his feet and tossed his napkin on the table. "I'm really not very hungry. I'd like to go home."

"Wait a minute!" Cam almost shouted. "I was supposed to be in New York today! But I wanted to see you, so I delayed my return. As it is, I am going to catch fourteen shades of hell for missing as much work as I have for you! I wanted tonight to be about *us!*"

"Hey, Chief, I didn't *ask* you to do all this! And if this is about *us,* why do I feel the ghost of Suzette standing here? Cameron, be your own man. Tell her to fuck off! Tell her to get her own life, I don't care, but there is one thing that I *do* know."

"Oh? And what's that?"

"I am not Stanton, Cameron. I never will be. I'm just . . . me. I will not hide how I feel about the man I love. I won't do it for her, and I won't do it for you. I love you. I wish I didn't, but I do. You say you love me, too. Prove it."

He walked away from the table and started for the house.

"How dare you mention Stanton's name in that way! You know nothing about it!" Cam thundered. "Blake Jackson, I swear to God! Don't walk out on me again! I won't put up with it! Who the fuck do you think you are, anyway? Some nobody that I'm offering the world to. Don't screw that up!" His eyes blazed with an intensity that Blake, stopped dead in his tracks, hadn't seen before.

Blake, shaking, faced his lover. "Some *nobody?* This 'nobody' loves you! This 'nobody' made you feel alive again for the first time in twenty years! This 'nobody' gave you the hottest sex you've ever had! And this 'nobody' has a fucking ironclad contract with Cameron Fuller USA! I called my agent today and it turns out I have a pay-or-play clause. You don't want to use me in the ads, fine. But you still have to *pay* me."

Sensing that the scene was getting horribly out of control, Cameron tried to bring the tension back down. "Blake, I don't want to fight with you."

"Then don't. Stand up for me."

Cameron sighed. "I can't. Not right now."

"Can't? Or won't?"

Cameron's silence signaled his response.

"Goodbye, Cameron." Blake turned and went into the house.

Halfway home, sitting alone in the back of the immense limo, Blake wanted to cry. And scream. And yell. And punch someone.

Namely Suzette.

Fuck Cameron Fuller, he thought, irate beyond belief. This is exactly what I deserve for getting mixed up with an American icon.

His fury and outrage at being helpless fed his need to lash out somehow. His cell phone rang. Thinking it was Cameron, and feeling the need to yell some more, he answered the call.

"What?!" he shouted into the mouthpiece.

"Blake? Blake Jackson?" asked a familiar sounding voice, but Blake couldn't place it.

"Yeah. Who's this?"

"It's Luka. Luke Kapaka, from the flight last night?"

"Riiight. Hey, Luka. What's up?"

"I am," he snickered. "I can't stop thinking about you. I'm sorry to call you. I lifted your number from the flight records. Don't have me fired," he joked.

"Don't sweat it."

"So," Luka said, then hesitated. "Can I come over? I can get a car."

Blake sat in the sumptuous leather of the limousine Cameron paid for. He thought for a second. "Okay, sure."

"Great! What's your address? I'll be there in thirty minutes."

26

It was after one in the morning when the dark car slowly cruised by Blake's house. The driver studied the scene. There were some subdued lights on, so Blake was probably still up. The thin washed linen curtains were drawn and a flickering blue-gray tint to the living room windows showed that the TV was still on.

With the push of a button, the driver's side tinted window silently rolled down, allowing the cold night air into the cabin of the car. The automobile went to the end of Blake's block and U-turned. The car's headlights turned off. The driver could see the silhouette of Blake moving around the living room. Now there was another. He had someone with him, and from the look of their commingled shadows, they were having sex.

The fucking slut!

The gloved hand of the driver reached over to the passenger seat and picked up the gun. German, and lethal looking, it had a stumpy silencer attached to the barrel. The driver pointed the gun out the window and lined up a shot at the window of the small house.

The car rolled to a stop and the driver squinted. Blake's shadow could clearly be seen fucking another. Wrathful fury boiled up in the driver, and the finger on the trigger twitched. Blake's shadow stood upright, giving a clear shot line, and the driver quickly knocked off two rounds. The muffled puffs kicked the gun ever so slightly, but the shooter had achieved the goal of a direct hit.

The bullets pierced through the glass windows, and found their mark. A crashing sound came from the house as the intended target fell to the floor.

The dark car jerked away from the curb and sped off into the night.

27

The taxicab got as close as was possible, but due to the large crowd gathered and the policewoman directing traffic away, it wasn't that close. The passenger was confused as to the activity, and hurriedly dug into his tuxedo pants pocket to find some money. He tossed the bills to the driver, and ever more frightened, scrambled out. As he noticed where the activity was centered, he quickly broke out into a run. The policewoman guarding the street stopped him.

"I'm sorry, sir, but this street is closed temporarily. No one is allowed near the crime scene," she said officiously, holding up both hands.

"Crime scene?! My God! What happened!" asked the now panic-struck man.

"A man's been shot. Now, please sir, I'll need you to stand back."

"But . . . but . . ." the man sputtered, trying to comprehend what was going on.

"Blake? Blake!"

Blake turned away from the policewoman, and saw Brady, in full deputy garb, advancing toward him. He saw a quick look of surprise, then intense relief spread across Brady's face.

"Brady! What the hell's going on! What happened?"

Brady reached Blake and gave him a long hug. "Thank God you're all right!"

"Brady, tell me what's going on! This officer won't let me in!" The words rushed out of Blake's mouth in a torrent.

Brady turned to the puzzled policewoman. "Officer Canter, this man is okay to enter. The shooting took place at his residence. I'll take full responsibility for his presence here."

Officer Canter grudgingly let Blake through.

"Brady! What happened?!" Blake insisted.

"Someone shot up your house. They shot right through the living room window." Brady gingerly led Blake through the maze of police cars and equipment scattered in the street. The red and blue flashes from the emergency vehicles filled the night with an eerie hue.

"My God," Blake said, dazed. "She said someone was hurt?"

"Rand . . ." Brady started to say.

"Oh, my God! No! Not Rand!" Blake was paralyzed by fear, borderline hysterical.

"No, no! Rand's all right. His boyfriend, Sam. He's been taken to Cedar Sinai Hospital. Rand's with him. He's in surgery now. I don't know how extensive his injuries are."

"Oh, my God. When did this happen?"

"About an hour ago. Rand called 911 as soon as it happened. The EMTs got here within minutes and took him to the hospital."

Blake just shook his head in disbelief. He suddenly looked about wildly. "Where's Joe?"

"He's fine. He's in Rand's place."

Blake's shoulders slumped in minor relief.

"Why were Rand and Sam in your house?"

"Uh . . . ," Blake faltered, trying to focus. "Rand's TV is broken. They wanted to watch movies. I was . . . out for the evening, so I said they could watch on mine."

"Did anyone know they were going to be there?"

"I don't know. I doubt it. Who would care?"

For the first time Brady noticed Blake's clothing. "Nice tux. Were you at a ball or something?"

"What? Oh, no." Blake was flustered and confused. He looked at his front door just in time to see two policemen leave with two small clear plastic bags marked "Evidence." Each bag seemed to have a small lump.

Brady saw Blake staring and he explained. "They've dug the spent bullets out of the walls."

Blake nodded dully, his eyes wide.

"Blake, I need for you to calm down, because I have to explain something to you. Okay? Can you focus? Do you understand what I'm saying to you?" Brady gently prodded.

"Yes . . . I'm okay . . . ," Blake responded, looking away from the cops.

"Blake, someone shot up your home. It stands to reason that they were shooting at who they thought was *you*. Do you understand what I'm telling you? Someone tried to kill you tonight."

Blake looked at Brady as if he were insane. "No. There has to be some other reason."

"Blake. Someone deliberately shot into your house. Your neighbor across the street, Mrs. Tudor, was letting her dog in and saw a car deliberately slow down, shoot, then speed off. This was no accident."

"Jesus," Blake wailed. He covered his face with the palms of his hands and began to cry. Brady, oblivious to the crowd of officers around the scene, took his ex-lover into his arms and held on to him, gently rocking back and forth, as Blake cried.

A tough-looking man with pure white hair and a rumpled suit walked up to the pair. He hesitated about interrupting, but finally he had to. He coughed.

Brady noticed him, silently nodded, and pulled Blake away from him. "Blake? This man is Detective Ed Cooper from the homicide division. He's going to be in charge of this case."

Blake blindly shook hands with the man.

"This is Blake Jackson, the owner of the property, Ed," Brady explained.

"Mr. Jackson, I'm sorry to have to do this now, but I do have a few questions for you."

"It's okay. I'll answer anything you want." Blake wiped his tears away with his jacket sleeve.

"The two men that were in your house. Did they have your permission to be there?"

"Yes."

"Did you know they would be engaging in . . . sexual activity?" he asked gruffly, one eyebrow arched high.

"No . . . Yes . . . I mean, I didn't think about it. I didn't . . . I don't . . . care." Blake was flustered.

"Do you have any reason to believe someone would want to harm either of them?"

"God, no! They are two of the nicest people I've ever met. Rand's been my tenant for almost two years. He's like my little brother. Everyone loves him," Blake answered, eyeing the policemen tramping through his flower beds to measure something.

"And the other fellow? Samuel Scolari? Anyone want to hurt him?"

"I have no idea. I doubt it seriously."

"Was it usual for these two . . . men to frequent your house for sexual purposes?"

"What?" Blake asked, startled by the question. "No! It just so happened that tonight I wasn't home and they wanted to watch my TV."

"I see. Where were you tonight when this crime was committed?"

Blake blushed slightly, but answered. "I was at the Hilton near the airport. In room number 1512." Blake saw Brady stiffen.

"Were you alone? Or, can this be verified?" the detective asked, scribbling some notes down in a small pad.

"No, I was not alone, I was with someone. He can verify that." Blake avoided looking at Brady, who was studying the ground with intense interest. "Oh, my God!" Blake suddenly exclaimed.

"What?" asked the detective.

"I just realized! He was going to come over here, but I changed my mind and went to his hotel instead. If I had been here, maybe this wouldn't have happened," Blake said miserably.

"And who was this other party?"

"A flight attendant I met on a plane yesterday. He flies for Nui Loa Air . . . His name is Luka . . . um . . . something Hawaiian . . . Kalala or Kalapaka . . . something like that."

The detective looked up at the strapping man in front of him, and smirked. *Was everybody in this fuckin' town queer?* he wondered. "And how long were you with this Luka fellow?"

"From about ten o'clock until about an hour ago. I took a cab back from the hotel, and came home to find *this.*" He waved helplessly at the scene.

"So this was a romantic, or sexual, interlude?" the detective pried, his distaste evident on his face.

"Why do you need to know that?"

"I don't see how that's relevant," Brady spoke up.

Ed Cooper looked hard at Brady. "Deputy, everything in an attempted murder case is relevant." He returned his gaze to Blake. "Was it of a romantic or sexual nature, this visit?" he repeated.

Blake looked the detective square in the eye. "Yes. Yes, it was. Would you like to know exactly how many times I fucked him? How many times we came? Will that info help you find a suspect?" he said evenly, his eyes blazing.

"Blake!" Brady admonished.

"I don't think that information is required right now, son. And I'd advise you not to adopt that tone with me. I'm guessing this has all the markings of a passion hit. Who else you screwing, boy? Any of your other boyfriends jealous enough to want to take you out?"

"You're out of your fucking mind! Someone just shot up my house and may have killed someone I know! All you seem to be interested in is our sex lives! Excuse me. Make that our *gay* sex lives!" Blake shouted at the man. "Why do I get the feeling that if I was straight you wouldn't care about any of this shit!"

"Blake! That's enough!" Brady warned, grabbing his arm hard.

"Mr. Jackson, I've seen enough murders in West Hollywood to know that ninety percent of the time it has to do with a romance gone sour. You people are so emotional! Somebody wanted you dead. This was no accidental shooting. We have a witness who saw the car, saw the bullets hit the window, but heard no shots. That means a silencer was used, and that means someone was serious about taking you out. Think about that!"

Blake stared dully at the man, breathing hard.

"I'm going to check this Luka fellow out. It's easy enough to verify. I'm going to want to talk to you again. Soon." The detective gave Blake a last mean look, and walked away.

"What the fuck!? He's acting like I'm the criminal here!" Blake seethed at Brady.

"You shouldn't have lost your temper. He's a good cop. Old fashioned, but good. You want him on your side," Brady said slowly.

"On my side? I didn't do anything wrong!"

Brady looked down at the ground again.

"What?" Blake asked him hotly. "What!?"

The tough deputy looked miserable, and his hands were shoved deep into his pockets. "Jesus Christ, Blake. A flight attendant you just met? Can't you keep your dick in your pants for just one day?" *Or in me,* he silently added.

"Please, Brady. Don't you give me shit, too. You have no idea what I've just been through the last few days. *No* idea. And now this!"

"You're right. I don't have an idea, because you never really talk to me. You never did. Not about stuff that's important to you."

"Oh, Brady. Not again! This just isn't the time for that. You wanna know? *Was* I whoring around tonight? Yes. I was. I admit it! Lock me up! Fuck!" Blake was as enraged as Brady had ever seen him. "And you just stood there while that asshole called me 'you people'! I'd like to point out that you're 'you people,' too!"

Brady said nothing. Blake stormed around the area for a few minutes then began to calm down.

He took several deep breaths. "Brady, look. I'm sorry. This is just too much for me to take right now. I didn't mean it," he said, reaching out for Brady again. His eyes once again filled up with tears, and he felt very alone, very lost.

Brady allowed himself to be hugged, and slowly began to hug back. "Do you want to stay at my house tonight?" he asked gently.

"Yes. Thank you."

Brady walked Blake over to his Taurus, and left him there while he went back to make sure it was okay for them to leave. After filling in the officer in charge on where they were going to be, he got Joe from Rand's apartment. He put the dog in the backseat and drove Blake to his apartment on Westmount Drive.

Blake was snuggled up in Brady's bed, but he had a hard time closing his eyes. He kept seeing the policemen tramping about his yard and house. Joe snored lightly on the floor next to him. Brady flicked off the bathroom light and, nude, quietly padded to his bed. He gingerly lifted the covers back and slipped in.

"It's okay. I'm awake," Blake whispered.

"Trouble sleeping?" Brady spooned up next to Blake and wrapped his massive arm around him, pulling him close.

Blake was grateful for the human contact, and allowed himself to be comforted and held. "Yeah. I'm so sorry I yelled at you. It wasn't fair, and I feel bad about it," he apologized.

"Don't sweat it. I'm used to your moods," Brady said graciously. "I'm just so damn glad you were out tonight and not home, even if you were fucking some guy. If you had been killed, I don't know what I would have done."

"I keep thinking that same thing. If I had been there, they wouldn't have. Sam would be okay now," Blake pondered.

"But you might be dead! I know it's hard, but you can't change it, so let it go, baby. Besides, Sam did fine in surgery. The doctors are confident he'll make a full recovery." Brady squeezed his ex a little harder. He had called the hospital as soon as they'd gotten to his apartment, and had received the optimistic report from the nurse on duty.

Blake had to admit, it felt good to be held. Brady was a big strong man, and Blake felt so secure with him. He hazily remembered Brady telling him stories about his early days in the Sheriff's Department as a deputy at the county jail. That's where all deputies started out before being promoted to the precincts. Brady'd had to stop more than one jail house fight, and always came out on top, while the rioting detainees usually ended up in the hospital.

Oddly, this brief thought had the effect of relaxing Blake totally. He was safe with Brady. No one could touch him here.

Thoughts of Cameron then flitted into his head, but he pushed them out, deciding, like Scarlett O'Hara, he would think about that tomorrow.

"It's so nice to have you here in my bed again. I've missed this," Brady ventured quietly.

Blake felt himself slipping away. "Ummm . . . ," he mumbled.

"Go to sleep, Blake, go to sleep. I'm here, and nothing's going to happen to you while I'm on watch," Brady whispered into Blake's ear.

Blake woke up to gentle kisses. He fluttered open his eyes to find Brady on top of him, straddling him, cupping his sleepy face in his large hands. Brady was murmuring indistinguishable words and methodically kissing Blake's face, lips, neck, shoulders.

"Brady," Blake whispered, reaching his arms around Brady's back.

"*Mmm* . . . Good morning," the deputy replied between feather-light kisses.

"Brady, stop . . ."

"I'm sorry . . . It's just so nice to have you here . . . I just wanna make you feel better . . . Let me make you feel better . . ."

Blake could feel Brady's thick hard-on pressing into his stomach as Brady ground himself into him. *I don't think I'm the only one you want to make feel better,* Blake thought.

He gave Brady a few sweet kisses back, but was unprepared for the lip assault he got for his trouble. Brady mashed his mouth down on Blake's with a ferocity that surprised Blake. To his amazement, Blake found himself responding in kind.

"*Mmmm* . . . You taste so good . . ." Brady sighed. He reached down between his legs, and tugging on Blake's now erect cock, pulled it up between his own ass cheeks and teased himself with it, pressing it hard into his skin. "I want you inside me, baby! Give it to me, please? Oh, man, I gotta have this . . ." He thwacked himself against the ass with Blake's dick, and to be fair, Blake found he was completely turned on by the act.

But a flash of Cameron saying those exact same words passed in front of his eyes. Like a scene out of a bad movie, Brady suddenly transformed into Cameron, and Blake wanted to make love to him for hours. He wanted his touch, his smell. He wanted to see the look on his face when he slid inside him. He wanted to love him.

"Can I, baby? Can I sit on your beautiful dick? Please?" Brady begged, lifting and lowering his ass, rubbing it against Blake's throbbing cock.

Blake snapped back to the here and now.

"Brady, no. I can't . . . I'm sorry . . . My head's not . . . I . . ." Blake fumbled at the words.

"You want to, I can tell. Let me do this for you . . . for me . . ." He bent over and began kissing him again.

Blake had to physically push his face away. "Brady, I said *no!*"

Brady's passion-filled eyes clouded over. "So, you can fuck some stewardess for hours, but you can't fuck *me?*"

"Brady . . ."

"Screw you, Blake." Brady let go of Blake and rolled off to the side, breathing heavily. "I guess I see where I stand."

"Hey! That's not fair! I care for you, Brady, I do, and you know that. This isn't what I plan . . . I don't think . . ."

Joe poked his head over the side of the bed, deciding if it was a good time for him to jump up on the bed. He sensed the mood, and dropped back to the floor with a grunt.

Brady turned to look at his ex-lover and sighed. "There's someone else, isn't there? And it's not the flight attendant, is it?" The pain it caused him to say these words was evident.

"Not him, no. I just . . ." Blake tried to explain. "Oh, fuck it. I just had sex with him to get back at someone else. Yes, Brady, I think I have fallen for someone. I'm so sorry. I didn't plan on it, but it's happened. It's way fucked up, no future at all, but it's there, and I have to deal with it."

Brady's worst fears were realized. "Who is he? May I ask that? Or, do I already know?"

"Cameron Fuller."

"Fuck!" Brady said forcefully. He actually bolted upright at the news.

"Yeah. And there's more."

Blake then told Brady everything from the first meeting to the shoot to the trip to Hawaii. He left nothing out, and when he was finished talking, he actually felt better.

Brady was strangely silent.

"Brady?" Blake asked.

"What?"

"I know this hurts you, but you and I, we never . . . we aren't . . ."

"I know. I know." Brady nodded sadly. "I hoped that would happen again, though, I won't lie to you. You see, Blake," he faced him, "I'm still in love with you. I can't seem to shake you, and trust me, I've tried. You're selfish and thoughtless and you don't think how your actions affect others, but I love you anyway." He shrugged helplessly.

"No, really. Don't hold anything back." Blake half-smiled. "I didn't realize I was such a burden."

"Blake. Come on. You know you're high maintenance. I just didn't mind maintaining you." He sighed deeply. "So you think Cameron Fuller is the one for you, huh?"

Blake nodded silently.

"Then what are you going to do about it? Pee and moan about how you think he wronged you? Jesus, Blake. Look at things through someone else's eyes for a change."

"What do you mean?"

"Did it ever occur to you to go along with the low-profile thing for a while? Give it a chance? If you love this man, then you should be willing to sacrifice anything to be with him. *Do* anything for him." *How the fuck did I end up giving Blake advice on how to make it work with another guy?* Brady wondered.

"But he let her . . ." Blake began to protest.

"Oh, shut up! Please. What did you expect him to do? Kick his wife out? It was a bad situation, but he didn't plan it. It just happened. You fool around with a married man, and you get what you get. Stop being such a baby!"

Nonplussed, Blake didn't know how to respond.

Brady got up out of the bed. "Face it, Blake. You create your own problems, and you get angry when it gets messy, and then you blame everyone else. Isn't it time you grew up?" He walked into the bathroom, and shut the door.

By the time Brady came out of the bathroom, Blake was dressed in a pair of his sweats and an old West Hollywood Sheriff's Department T-shirt.

"I didn't think you'd mind if I borrowed some of your clothes. I don't think the tux is appropriate for daytime."

"No problem."

"I've been thinking about what you said. You're right, of course. I do get myself into these situations, and then I bitch about it. I'll get myself out. And I'm sorry if I hurt you."

Brady shrugged. "I'll live, I suppose. I guess I don't have a choice. And I'm sorry if I was a little harsh. But a good friend is someone who tells you the truth, whether you want to hear it or not."

Blake digested this for a minute. "So. Will I be able to get into my house?"

"I think so. I'll drive you. But I think it's best if you don't stay there. Why don't you stay here? That way I can keep an eye on you, and if you're with a cop, well, that's a big kind of protection."

"I don't want to put you out."

"Don't be silly." Brady tried to smile. "I promise you, I won't throw myself at you again."

Blake reluctantly agreed.

28

"What is it, Dillard? I don't have time for this right now," Silas snapped. He was with Tina Hawkins, Cameron Fuller USA's lead tax attorney, and they were going over employee records to determine the validity of a worker's compensation claim from the Soho store.

"Someone took a few shots at Blake Jackson last night."

"What are you talking about?" Silas said into the phone.

"Someone fired off a couple of rounds at the kid's house last night," Dillard calmly explained. "There was a serious injury."

Silas dropped his Mont Blanc pen to his immaculate desktop. "Was this Jackson fellow hurt?" he asked hopefully.

"No. He apparently wasn't at home at the time."

"I see." Silas digested this news. "That's too bad."

"Silas!"

"Just a minute, hold on, please." Silas put his hand over the receiver and looked at Tina. "Tina, can you please excuse me for a minute. I have to take this call."

Tina looked up from her paperwork, saw Silas's mood, and quickly got to her feet. "Of course. I'll be right outside." She left the room. Fast.

Once she was gone, Silas returned to the call. "Did you have anything to do with this, Dillard? I know I asked you to do something about this . . . situation. I would have hoped you would do a better job than to miss!"

Dillard's tone was one of disbelief. "Are you insane? Of course I had nothing to do with this!"

"Are you sure? I would hate to have to distance myself from you.

If you were caught doing anything of this nature, I would of course, have to disavow any knowledge of it. Not that I would be upset, mind you, if something terrible happened to that . . . young man."

"My God, Silas. What are you saying?"

"What I'm saying, you idiot," Silas spoke forcefully, "is, next time, don't miss."

29

Blake wanted to avoid walking into his living room, but he found it was the first place he went upon his arrival home. After putting Joe in the backyard, he took a deep breath and entered the room. The coffee table had been knocked over, and there was a large bloodstain on the sisal rug. The air smelled sticky sweet from the blood, and for a second, Blake thought he would throw up. Grabbing onto one of his bookshelves, he steadied himself and focused on the job at hand.

He moved all the spilled coffee table tchotchkes aside. Then, lifting furniture here and there, he rolled up the rug and dragged it outside. He dumped it behind the small garage, away from where Rand might see it. He took a mop and bucket and began to mop down the wood living room floor. By the time he was done, he was crying.

He felt violated and mad and hurt and guilty and he felt bad for Sam. He didn't know the guy very well, but what little interaction they'd had had been pleasant, and he knew that Rand liked him.

Blake had called the hospital first thing that morning and had spoken to his distraught tenant. Rand told him that Sam was stable and the prognosis was good.

Sam had been shot in the neck and left arm. The bullet that entered his neck had missed his jugular vein by only millimeters. Sam was sedated now and couldn't speak. Blake planned on going down to Cedars later in the afternoon to see him.

After he had put the room back into some kind of order, he took a breather. That's when he noticed the two bullet holes in the wall. They were jagged ugly scars where the police had dug out the spent slugs. Sighing, he looked out the windows only to find a TV news crew aiming a video camera at the house. Realizing he was in full view by standing in the bullet-riddled window, he jumped back, and quickly closed the sheer drapes. There were tiny holes in those as well, he noted.

When he heard the persistent knocking at his door, he ignored it. Damn reporters.

But the knocking kept on, and fed up, Blake came up with a plan. He opened the kitchen door, letting Joe in. Hearing the knocking on the door, Joe went ballistic and started growling his deep bark. He thundered to the door, and threw himself on it, still barking excitedly.

The knocking stopped.

Satisfied that they were going to leave him alone, Blake returned to the kitchen and spied his answering machine blinking furiously at him. He had twenty-three messages.

The vast majority were hang-ups.

Cameron.

There were two from Trevor asking him to call as soon as he could. Three from his new agent. Various friends calling to offer condolences.

As he was erasing the machine, he heard his cell phone go off. It was on the counter nearby so he grabbed it and glanced at the caller ID screen. The number seemed familiar, so he answered.

"Hello?" he cautiously said.

"Blake? Is that you?"

"Yes. Who's this?"

"Thank God. It's Trevor Barbados. You didn't return my calls!"

"I'm sorry, Trevor. Things have been a little . . . crazy around here."

"I know. I saw the news. Are you all right?" There was genuine concern in his tone.

"Yes, I'm fine. I wasn't home when it happened."

"Well, thank God for that! This town! You can't even be in your own home anymore without the crazies trying to shoot you!"

"I know," Blake glumly replied.

"Do you need a place to stay? You can stay with me. I have plenty of room here."

"Thanks, but I'm covered. I'm going to stay with a . . . friend, for a while."

"Good. Friends are important at a time like this. Anyway, I just wanted to give you a heads up. I need to shoot some stuff of you in the mountains tomorrow. I think we'll drive up to Big Bear. Plus we have to go to Big Sur over the weekend to shoot some backup shots. Cameron has stepped up the deadline and I have to get all the shots in by next week."

"But . . . I thought I wasn't . . . when did you speak to Cameron?" Blake sat down, slightly stunned by this news.

"Just now. About five minutes ago. He was in the plane heading back to New York. Actually it was a little weird. He said he'd been trying to get you, but couldn't, and would I please not stop trying until I spoke with you personally. He's very worried about you. He hadn't heard about the shooting until I told him just now. He was quite upset."

Blake's head was swimming. He wasn't fired. He still had the job. What the fuck was going on? "Well, that's thoughtful of him to think about me."

"He likes you. He's concerned about you."

"Uh huh."

"So, I'm going to figure out the schedule today and I'll call Nelle at Hunk and give her the details," Trevor said, wrapping up.

"Okay. Great. I'll be ready. Bye, Trevor. And thanks for the kind words."

"See you later, Blake," the photographer said just before he ended the call. Blake had no sooner closed the phone when it rang again.

"Hello?"

"Blake? Are you all right? I just heard!" Cameron's voice had a tinge of panic in it, and Blake immediately felt a warmth spread over him as he listened. "Trevor just told me!"

"I'm okay, Cam. I'm fine. Rand's boyfriend was shot, though. Here! In my house . . ." Suddenly, Blake burst into tears and started to sob again.

"Babe, don't cry . . . please! I'm so sorry I'm not there for you right now. I didn't know, or I would never have gotten on the plane. Do you want me to have them turn it around? Do you want to see me?" The tentative inflections in his voice gave away his fear that Blake would tell him no.

"Of course I want to see you! What kind of stupid question is that?" Blake cried.

"I acted so badly last night! The things I said to you . . . I'm so ashamed of myself. I don't think that way about you, Blake, you know that. I love you! I'm so sorry . . . I was just so mad and frustrated . . ."

"I know. I know," Blake said quietly, wiping away the tears with the back of his hand. "Oh, Cam! Someone was trying to kill me! That's what the police think! Who would want to shoot me?"

"What?!"

"They say it was like a 'hit.' That someone purposely tried to kill me, but shot poor Sam instead!"

"That's crazy!"

"They want to know who hates me enough to do this. I don't have any enemies!" he said forcefully. ". . . That I know of."

"Goddammit! Blake, I want to come back. I'll come back . . ."

"No. Don't. You have enough shit to deal with in New York. Trevor wants to do a shoot tomorrow, and we'll be gone over the weekend, so I'm not even going to be around."

Twenty-seven thousand feet above Denver, Colorado, Cam sighed hard. His first thought was of the conversation he'd had last week with Suzette while he was in the shower.

"If I ever find out who you're screwing," she had threatened, *"I'll be up for murder one."*

Was it possible? Could she have done this? He looked at her dozing softly in one of the lounge chairs, a new copy of *Vogue* open in her lap. They had barely said two words to each other since their return to L.A. from Kauai. She had taken a bungalow at the Beverly Hills Hotel, and he a separate suite. He had no idea where she'd gone in their brief stopover in L.A.

"Cam? Cam, are you there?" Blake asked through the airphone.

"Yeah, sorry. I'm here. Okay. But I don't want you to be alone . . . How's Rand? Will he stay with you?"

"He's at the hospital with Sam. I'm headed over there as soon as I get off the phone with you."

"Oh, Blake . . ." Cam didn't know what else to say.

There was a pause. Cam saw Dan in the cockpit doorway, chatting with Rick, the pilot. Blake had mentioned that the two men were having an affair. Seeing them talk intimately, Cam realized Blake had been right.

"Cam? I love you. I *miss* you. I wish you were here," Blake started to cry again.

"Oh, stop, babe . . . don't cry! I'll come back out as soon as I can! I promise. I'll call you later, when I get to the office."

"Okay."

Suzette snorted, and woke herself up. She stretched and noticed Cam was lost in a phone conversation. She strained to listen.

"I love you, babe. This is all going to work out, I promise. I love you," Cam repeated soothingly into the mouthpiece.

"What!? You *love* him?! Is that the fucking model?!" Suzette shrieked. She tried to get out of her chair, but forgot the seat belt was buckled. It caught her hard in the midsection and she scrambled frantically for the release latch.

"I'm hanging up now, Blake. I'll call you later!" Cam hurriedly said, disconnecting the call almost as soon as the words came out of his mouth.

Suzette successfully got the latch unbuckled, and she flew at Cameron, grabbing for the phone. She wrestled it from his hands, and screamed into the receiver.

"You fucking gayboy! Leave my husband alone!"

She realized there was nothing but dead air on the phone and she angrily threw it down to the cabin floor, shattering the phone into many jagged pieces. Dan pretended not to notice. Suzette drew back her hand and slapped Cameron across the face as hard as she could. While it didn't hurt him, it did surprise him.

"You fucking faggot!" she hissed at Cameron. "In front of me? In front of your wife you tell that scum 'I love you'?!"

"But I do love him, Suzette," Cam calmly replied.

"Fuck you!" she screamed at the top of her lungs. The shrill sound reverberated around the cabin. She slapped him again.

Dan prudently chose this moment to have to visit the lavatory.

"How can you say that to me?! You bastard! You again flaunt your fag lover in my face?! We just made a deal, and already you're breaking it?!" She was standing over him, pointing at him angrily with her thin, bony finger. "I'll fucking ruin you! You *will* lose it all!"

Something snapped inside Cam. He was tired of the screaming. He was tired of the name calling. Tired of hiding how he felt. And, most important, tired of the seesaw emotional ride with Suzette. He stood up quickly and grabbed her by the shoulders and threw her roughly back down into her seat. She was stunned into silence, and her expression was one of shock.

"Listen to me, you fucking harpy," he snarled at her. "I've had a bellyful of your histrionics! Enough! Just shut the fuck up!"

"Cameron! I have never . . ." she started to say, her eyes wide, indignation creeping into her voice.

Cam leaned in so his face was only an inch from hers. "Shut up! You knew what, and who, I was when you married me. I *am* leaving you, you bitch. I don't give a fuck who you tell, or what you tell them. You want to take me on? Let's go, girlie. We'll see who wins in the end. I built this company. You think you can tear me down? Try it. Trust me, I'll fucking bury *you!* Don't forget, sweetheart, you and I have a dirty little secret that daddy dearest would love to know!"

Suzette shrank back from him, her mouth hanging open in shock. "You . . . you wouldn't! You promised me we'd never, *never* talk about that!"

"And you promised me you'd never stand in my way if I wanted out. So here it is: yes, I'm in love with Blake. That's his name. Blake. You ever call him anything else in my presence, and I swear I'll knock you on your bony ass so fast it will make your bleached head spin! Now, you sit there, and don't say another fucking word to me for the rest of this flight." His violet eyes had deepened to almost purple with fury. He was actually shaking, struggling to control his temper. He stood up stiffly and walked back to his seat. He sat down, and stared out the window for the remainder of the flight.

The plane landed in the twilight of the day. After the short taxi to the terminal, Dan carefully opened the door, and lowered the metal stairs. Not bothering to wait for Suzette, Cameron snatched up his flight bag and dashed off the plane, practically vaulting into the waiting limo. He slammed the door shut and told the driver to go.

Suzette walked serenely down the stairs and was perturbed to find there was no other waiting car. She watched Cameron's limo speed off and disappear into traffic.

Cameron checked into the exclusive Stanhope hotel, and the first thing he did after the bellman had ushered him to his suite was call Blake at home. There was no answer, so he left a brief message. He then punched in Blake's cell phone number.

"Hello?" Blake answered, the sound of rushing air in the background.

Cameron sat on the edge of the bed, and sighed in relief. "Hey, sweetheart. It's me. Where are you?"

"In the car."

"How are you?"

"I'm okay. Long day. I'm so tired."

"I'm sure. You're not staying at your house tonight are you?" Cam asked, anxiously.

"No, I'm going to stay at Brady's."

That caught Cam by surprise. "Your *ex, Brady?*" he asked, the suspicion not hidden.

"Yeah." There was a pause on the other end of the phone. "Why?"

Cameron shook his head to clear it. "No reason. I just had a flash of jealousy. Sorry."

"Don't be. I'm all about you. Even if you aren't here for me to prove it."

"You do say the sweetest things," Cam smiled.

"I'm going to Big Bear tomorrow with Trevor to shoot some mountain stuff. Then we're going to Big Sur on Thursday for the weekend," Blake added.

"Good. I talked to him this morning and told what I wanted. I have some ideas that I want to go over with you, after I get some mockups made. I'm going to try to get back out there next week."

"Good," Blake sighed. "I miss you. We haven't really had any time alone since Hawaii . . ." Blake started to say.

"Well, there was a big dinner, but *that* didn't go quite as planned," Cam gently chided him.

"Uh, let's not go there," Blake said with a laugh.

Blake's laugh was like medicine to Cam. He instantly felt better.

"I checked into a hotel. The Stanhope. But you can always get me on the cell."

"So, you left her." There was silence as Blake absorbed this. "For good?"

"For good. I don't care what she does. I'll be fine. And I'm so sorry that I put all that in our way. I promise you this: I am going to be there for you, Blake."

"Back at you. Oh. I'm here at Brady's now. Let me go, and I'll call you later, okay?"

"You bet. Bye, sweetheart. Love you."

"Love you back."

Cam snapped shut his phone and sat on the bed thinking. He hated being so far away from Blake, but he had things he had to do here in New York that demanded his full attention. He had a clear vision of what he wanted the Pacific Coast Highway campaign to be, and he had a scant few days to pull it off.

But, as exciting as the prospect was of creating a new line, and a new source of income for Cameron Fuller USA, he felt alone and lonely. Finding Blake had forced him to reevaluate his life, and he wasn't happy with the path he'd been on. He now knew he couldn't ignore the core basics of who he was. He had shut down his heart for so long, and now it was time to open it up again. The idea excited him greatly.

He looked around his sumptuous one-bedroom suite and realized sadly that this was going to be his home for a while. He would contact a real estate agent in the morning and start looking at apartments. Something nice that he could share with Blake when he was in town. Those thoughts made him think more about the man he loved, and before he knew it, sensual images flooded his mind.

Images of him and Blake making love.

His physical reaction to this was painfully obvious, and he reached his hand down into his pants and shifted his erection around to give it room. Enjoying the feel of skin on skin, he pulled out his hand, unzipped his fly and took his cock out. Leaning back on the bed, he conjured up more erotic images of Blake that completely turned him on.

For far too long, his sexual fantasies had been of faceless bodies, and vague acts recalled from memory. Now that he'd met, and was in love with Blake, he had a face to attach to the body. And Blake's body was so much better than anything he'd ever dreamt up.

His stroking became more intense as he allowed his mind to wander over the sexual acts they had performed. He imagined the way Blake's face looked as he climaxed, and the knowledge that he had been responsible for that reaction caused him to grunt. His left hand was now cupping his balls, squeezing gently, and his right hand was a blur of up and down motion. Breathing heavily, he unconsciously pushed his legs up and down, digging his heels into the bedding, his very being responding to the pleasure. Every muscle in his body contracted, then relaxed, as he gave himself over to the sensual waves he was causing himself.

Sensing he was close, he used his left hand to pull up his shirt, exposing his ripped and tensed abs. He then snaked his hand under the mussed shirt, and found his right nipple. He alternated between gently rubbing and pinching hard on it.

When he imagined Blake penetrating him, whispering "I love you" as he fucked him, his beautiful tanned chest moving with the rhythm of his pumping, Cam felt his balls seize up. He exhaled loudly as he came, shooting the hot fluid all over his stomach.

He lay there for a while in that wondrous and calming state of relaxation that comes after an intense climax. He allowed himself to unwind and drift away. His thoughts were of Blake on the chaise by the pool in Kauai.

He fell asleep, content, his pants still open.

30

Blake was freezing his ass off.

He was perched precariously on an outcropping of craggy rocks, a pair of extremely tight, extremely worn Montana Rough Wear jeans and a fleece-lined tan corduroy jacket his only protection from the thirty-four-degree weather. He was shirtless and had a red bandana tied haphazardly around his neck. The jacket was unbuttoned, so each time a gust of freezing cold wind charged up the mountains, it cut into him like a knife.

"Blake, turn a little to the left . . . that's it! Don't move!" Trevor called out from the warmth of his down-filled parka. He leaned over and looked through the viewfinder again. Blake was positioned about twenty feet above him on a ledge, and behind him the entire sweeping vista of the Big Bear mountains could be seen. It was a spectacular sight. Snow covered the trees and ground, giving it a slight alpine feel, but it was still unmistakably California. The light was perfect and everything was bathed in a late afternoon glow.

Blake's ledge, while easily accessible from a stone-ladened trail on one side, jutted out a good hundred and fifty feet above the next area of level ground. Small scrub brush and brambles littered the area, and everything was coated in a fine layer of snow. The ledge was only about five feet wide by three feet long. One wrong move and he would be pitched over and fall to a certain death.

Blake concentrated on stopping the chattering of his teeth and leaned back, arching his back more.

"Perfect!" cried Trevor. Zack was standing slightly behind him, holding a prepped and readied second camera. A few yards away from them was a small cluster of hair, makeup, and wardrobe people huddled together to stay warm by the van.

Even though he had on some loosely laced lug-soled boots, his feet were frozen. Blake felt like a human Popsicle.

"Sasha? I'm getting a shine on his forehead! Touch him up . . . and oil his chest a little more," Trevor ordered.

A small, heavyset woman grabbed her makeup box and scrambled nimbly up to Blake. She dabbed an unspeakably cold and wet sponge on his face, and smeared more baby oil on his chest, working it in so he had a smooth, dull shine.

"How ya doin there, sweet cakes?" she asked jovially, as she basically played with his chest.

"I think I have frostbite on my ass."

She leered. "Hmm. Want me to rub that too?"

"I wouldn't complain."

"Well, you look amazing, so keep it up." She was done, and left him alone again.

"Blake, I want you to lean back more. Can you do that?" Trevor called up to him.

"If I lean over anymore, I'm going to fall off!"

"Well, try, will you? I have this great line with you and the mountains and I need to mirror that. Try, will you?"

"Okay," Blake sighed, and arched his back more. *"Idiot Model Killed By Stupidity,"* the headlines would scream, he thought as he tried to balance himself.

"Perfect! Absolutely perfect! You're looking so hot, Blake, I want you now!" Trevor whooped, snapping off frame after frame.

Blake sighed, looking off into the distance. They had been at this since ten o'clock in the morning. It was now three, and there was no end in sight. And tomorrow it would start all over again up in Big Sur. He was cold, tired, hungry and now, thanks to the acrobatics he'd had to perform to get the look right, sore.

Everywhere.

Still, he wasn't going to complain. Well, not much. He knew he was the luckiest man alive, and he was determined to give them everything they needed. He was a professional, even if he was a little green at this. Looking past the photographer, he caught Zack's eye. Zack pressed his thumb and first finger together to form the "okay" sign with his right hand, and smiled broadly.

Trevor snapped a few more pictures, then stopped. "Okay, stud. Come on down. I want to get some of you by those trees over there." He handed off the camera to Zack and walked over to a small grove of scrub pines, lost in thought as he planned his next shot.

Blake gingerly picked his way down from the ledge, his body sore and stiff. The wardrobe stylist guy was instantly ready with a long down coat and quickly wrapped Blake up in it. The hair guy handed him a fresh cup of hot coffee and went to work detangling his hair.

Just as he had warmed up and was feeling human again, it was time to pose. The comforting coat was whisked away and Blake was once again half naked in the elements.

Two hours later, snuggled up under the toasty warm coat in the back of the passenger van they had used to bring the crew up to the mountain, Blake thawed out again.

Trevor was on his cell phone, chatting away.

The hair, makeup, and wardrobe people were dozing against each other in the middle row of seats.

"Yes . . . I got some amazing shots, exactly what you asked for . . . No . . . Yes . . ." Trevor was droning on while Zack steered the long van down the narrow mountain road.

Blake tried to tune him out.

"Yes . . . He's right here. Hold on." Trevor turned around and looked at Blake. "Hey, Blake!" he called to him. "It's Cameron." He tossed the phone back to Blake who caught it gracefully.

"Hello?"

"Hey, babe! I hear you did a fantastic job!" Cameron's excited voice filtered through the tiny phone.

"I guess. Mostly I just froze. I've decided that's what modeling is all about. Being cold."

"Well, I wish I was there. I'd know how to warm you up . . ."

"Damn, Cam," Blake lowered his voice. "I wish you were here too. I miss you."

"I know. Me, too. But I have an idea. What don't you come to New York next week? I'll send the jet. You need to meet the marketing people anyway. We can get a lot of work done, and as a bonus we can see each other."

"Okay."

"Good. I'll have Bette, my assistant, take care of the details," Cam's voice drifted off into silence.

"Cam? You there?" Blake asked, shaking the phone.

"I'm here. I just wish I was wherever you are. I feel kinda alone right now. A little sad. It's weird."

"I know what you mean. I'd like to really get away from L.A. I had to check in with the homophobic cop who's investigating Sam's shooting before I left town today! Can you believe that?"

"Any news on that front?"

"They've determined the caliber of the gun from the bullets. Other than that, they're at a standstill. I did see Rand yesterday evening for a few hours. He's really shook up. They were . . . well, Sam was screwing him when he was shot. Rand totally freaked out. He thought Sam had had a heart attack at first, but then he saw the blood and called 911."

"My God."

"I know. Can you imagine? Sam's going to be okay, but he has to stay in the hospital for a week or so. Rand's going to stay at his mom's in Santa Monica for a few days. He may move out. He doesn't know if he can stand to be near where . . . well, who can blame him?" Blake shifted his weight around and stretched out on the wide bench seat. He pulled the jacket up like it was a blanket. "How'd Suzette take the fact that you didn't go home?"

"Who cares? I suppose I'll see her tonight. I'm going home to get some more of my clothes and stuff. By the way, any particular part of Manhattan that you'd like me to live in? I'm supposed to look at a few places tomorrow. I saw one today at Park and Eighty-second, but ground floor."

"I just adore a penthouse view . . ." Blake sang, affecting a bad Hungarian accent.

"That's a given."

"I really don't know anything about Manhattan, but you should live somewhere great. Lots of room and light."

"I'll keep that in mind. Listen, I'd better get moving. Call me later, okay? I miss you, babe."

"Me, too."

They hung up and Blake tossed the phone back to Trevor, who instantly started dialing someone else on it.

Blake settled back down under the warm coat and tried to go to sleep.

It wasn't hard.

Cam sat in back of the town car in a bad mood. He hoped he would only be a few minutes. In and out. And he hoped Suzette wouldn't be there when he got his clothes. He could have let a subordinate do this unpleasant task, but it was part of Cameron's character to tackle unpleasant tasks himself, head on.

His driver pulled into his apartment building's garage and stopped at the garage elevator door.

"I'll be out in twenty minutes, Oscar."

"I'll be right here, Mr. Fuller," Oscar replied. A fifty-two-year-old Bronx-born man with mild arthritis and a gruff demeanor, Oscar had worked for Cameron for the past seventeen years. He had heard and seen more secret goings-on in the past few years than most people see in a lifetime; yet he had never told anyone. He took his job responsibilities seriously.

He had seen the end of the Fuller marriage coming for years. Suzette was a bitch, and Cameron was obviously a closet case—not that Oscar ever saw him do anything about it.

Oscar wished he would. Cameron deserved a life.

He watched the famous designer stride confidently to the elevator bank. He settled back into his seat and picked up his book. He was halfway through a good novel, and was looking forward to finishing the next chapter.

Cam walked into the elevator, and punched the button for Penthouse 8-A. After a swift ride to the top of the eight-story building, Cameron was deposited into the lobby of his apartment.

Exquisitely decorated by a team from the creative services staff under Rafael's supervision, the elevator vestibule was beautifully done in warm browns and blacks. Cut Italian marble was underfoot, while a small pair of Bavarian leaded glass chandeliers hung overhead. A hundred-year-old antique bombe chest was against one wall, an elaborate arrangement of fresh flowers placed carefully on top. A graceful pair of gilded bergere chairs covered with a rich gold damask anchored the opposite wall. Cam pulled out his key, and silently opened the door to his and Suzette's apartment.

He walked into the spacious foyer and gazed up at the antique chandelier glowing softly above him. It had once hung in a manor house in London, and had been bought at auction for over two hundred thousand dollars. Suzette had seen it in a catalog and had to have it.

Cam noticed soft music was playing from the built-in stereo system speakers discreetly hidden behind the thick crown moldings. He walked through the apartment toward the long, wide hallway that led to the bedrooms. As he passed the enormous living room with its gilded moldings, antique furniture, grand piano, and stunning view of Central Park, he saw two martini glasses resting on the Venetian mirror cocktail table. The condensation from the crystal stemware had formed small pools of water around the bases of the glasses.

"Suzette?" he called out. "Are you home?"

He got no response, and continued to the bedroom. He passed the formal dining room with the long formal table that could easily accommodate twelve. A rare Baccarat chandelier and eight matching sconces provided flattering light in this regally appointed room. He passed his study with its walls covered by oak bookcases filled with books that he had actually read. The fireplace was roaring in there, and that struck him as odd. It was normally lit only when he was in residence.

He was walking down the wide hallway to the bedroom suites, when he heard the muffled cry. He stopped short. He tried to figure out where it had come from. He heard another cry, and realized it was coming from behind the closed door to the master bedroom. He quickened his stride and threw open the door.

"You've been a bad boy, and I'm going to have to punish you again!" Suzette was saying, as Cam entered the spacious bedroom.

The sudden movement caught Suzette unawares. She looked over at the door and yelped out a shriek of surprise.

Cameron's initial shock quickly turned to hilarity.

Suzette was holding a small riding crop in her outstretched hand. She had on a leather bustier, with cutouts where her breasts were. The straps crossed in front and in back, and it was covered in metal studs. Hooked to the bustier by tiny little clips were red fishnet stockings. Her feet were clad in the trashiest pair of shiny black lace-up thigh-high boots Cameron had ever seen.

She was also wearing red crotchless panties, which didn't seem to bother the muscular man under her, who was wearing full leather gear, including chaps and armbands. His hands were actually hand-cuffed to the headboard's bedpost and he was propped up on a sea of pillows. A leather daddy's cap was on his head, but it had fallen over his eyes, so he was unaware that Cam was in the room.

"Oh, Mistress Suzette, I'm going to come!" he said thrusting his hips up and down. "May I? May I please come? . . . *Ohhhh!"* he called out urgently.

Suzette scrambled to get off the man, but because he was deep inside her, it was difficult. Her frantic movements caused her partner to start bucking.

"Oh! Mistress Suzette! I'm gonna come! Tell me I can! Tell me quick! I can't hold it!" he shouted, his hands straining at the hand-cuffs.

"You idiot! No!" Suzette barked. She covered her breasts with her small hands and slid off him sideways. Her movements were just too much for the poor sap under her, and just as she disengaged herself from him, he climaxed in a high arc.

Cameron laughed. "Don't fret, my dear," he called out to his wife. "They say it's good for the skin."

Suzette frantically wiped her face, disgust her only reaction.

"Who's there?" the man asked, instantly alarmed. He shook his head furiously, and knocked the daddy cap off. He focused on Cam and shock registered on his face.

"Well. Rick. Putting in a little overtime, aren't you?" Cameron said, amused. "I hope you're getting hazard pay for this."

Rick, the pilot, *Dan's pilot,* struggled to get off the bed, but since his hands were still cuffed to the bedpost, he got nowhere.

"Mr. Fuller! I . . . uh . . . we . . ." he stumbled.

"What the fuck are you doing here?" Suzette screamed, vainly trying to get under the covers to hide herself.

"I came to pick up some of my stuff. Please. Don't let me stop you two. Carry on." He laughed again at the sight of Suzette in her dom-inatrix get-up.

"Get out of here!" she screamed.

"I'm trying!" Rick cried. "But I'm still tied up! Get the key!"

"Not you, you idiot!" she hissed at the frantically struggling man. "Him!" She pointed at Cameron.

"Oh, God! Please don't fire me, Mr. Fuller! I support my mother!" Rick pleaded, panic-stricken.

"Shut up!" Suzette said to Rick, snapping him with the riding crop.

"Ow! Oh, God," he whimpered.

Cam couldn't tell if Suzette's smack had shut Rick up or turned him on.

He just shook his head and walked into his closet. He grabbed some of his favorite things and crammed them into a pair of duffles he found on the top shelf. He was almost through when Suzette walked into the closet. She had thrown a sheer pink chiffon and marabou feather peignoir on over her outfit, but the ridiculous contrast only made Cam laugh more.

"Well, I hope you're happy," she said frankly. Her hands were on her hips, and she had a defiant attitude. "This must have made your day."

"I'm overjoyed. I always knew you were a ballbuster, but to see living proof . . ." He chuckled.

"You bastard!" she hissed, defeat in her voice. "Who are you going to tell? Huh? My father? Are you going to spread this all over town? Tell everyone that Suzette likes it a little rough sometimes?"

"Sweetheart," he said, putting the last of his things into one of the bags, "I don't care what you do, or who you do it to. I just want out. And I'm not going to tell anyone about this. Unless you make me. Understand?" He looked at her, his meaning clear.

"Yes."

"Good. Then I think the lawyers can handle it from here. I'll need you to put in a few appearances at some events this month, but after those, I don't care if I never see your thin face again."

With that, he picked up the two bags and walked out of the closet. *In more ways than one,* he smirked to himself.

"Goodbye, Rick," he said to the leather-clad man still struggling to get free from the bed.

"Goodbye, Mr. Fuller," Rick said meekly.

Suzette also came out of the closet and sighed heavily.

"Oh, Suzette, by the way," Cameron said on his way out the door, "Rick here is also sleeping with Dan, our flight attendant."

"What?!" she shrieked, looking at the humiliated man.

"Yet again, you've picked a man who fucks men. Your record is perfect." Cam shut the door behind him.

Suzette sputtered a string of obscenities.

"Uh . . . I—" Rick tried to interject.

"You said I was the only one besides your *girlfriend!*" she screamed at him, grabbing the crop from the bed. "I guess you meant to say boyfriend, huh?!"

As Cameron left the room, he heard the stinging sounds of the crop hitting flesh. Rick's cries of pain quickly faded into shouted requests for more.

31

Dan brought Blake a chilled orange juice and a slice of wheat toast. No butter. No jam.

"Anything else for now?" he asked, smoothing out his uniform shirt.

"No, thanks. Sit down. All this bobbing around you're doing, it's making me dizzy. Take a load off," Blake answered. He indicated the empty cabin of the Gulfstream. "Don't think anyone else needs anything, so . . . ," he joked.

Dan shot a quick glance to the closed cockpit door, then sat in the seat in front of Blake. He hit the release handle underneath and swiveled around so they were facing each other.

Blake was comfortably dressed in a pair of tight Montana Rough Wear jeans, worn black cowboy boots, and a thick drab green turtleneck sweater that he'd owned since college. It fit better now than it did then.

"Listen. I never got a chance to say thanks for letting me crash with you in Hawaii. I left so quickly to catch the flight back to L.A. that I didn't even get to say good bye," Blake apologized.

"Please. Don't sweat it. You were pretty stressed out. I completely understood."

"Did you get a chance to have a little quiet time with your pilot?" he nodded towards the cockpit door.

"Actually, yes. The night you left. You would have been proud of me. I couldn't walk for two days."

"You tramp."

"Guilty as charged," Dan smiled. "But he's left the company.

Resigned. I haven't heard from him. Oh, well. Not like it was going to go anywhere." He sighed. "So. How's the big modeling career going?" He changed the subject, with genuine interest.

"The shoot this past weekend was fun. We did it in Carmel. I'd never been there, and it was so . . . what's the word? Quaint. Slow, but quaint," Blake offered as he took a sip of the fresh squeezed juice. "We shot stuff everyday. They brought in the Cameron Fuller girl, Sharique, and they had us splash around in the water in our underwear. So fucking cold!" He shivered involuntarily, remembering the shock of the water against his skin.

"Sounds like fun!"

"It is, I agree. But it's also a lot of work. Who knew? Stand here. Move that. Put your arm up. Bring it down . . . on and on . . ."

"Oh, please. Remember what you said about never seeing so many zeroes, when you got that first check? It's really hard for me to get worked up about your misery when you're getting paid so well," Dan said, poking him in the ribs.

"I know," he agreed. "I feel like I'm stealing. I'm really not complaining at all, but between the workouts and the shoots, I'm beat. I just want to sit down with a pizza and a bowl of ice cream and watch soap operas so bad I can't stand it."

"Interesting."

Blake looked at Dan, puzzled. "Why?"

"Well," he drawled. "I happen to have a pint of Ben and Jerry's Phish Food in the freezer on board."

"You bitch!" Blake feigned shock.

"Aren't I just awful?" he smiled devilishly.

"And yet you dare to give me this weedy piece of toast? With all due respect, get your tight ass up and bring me that ice cream!"

"So demanding. Just like a supermodel." He got up and walked back to the galley. He spent a minute rummaging for a spoon and a napkin. "You want it in the carton, or fancy, in a bowl?" he called out to him.

"Whatever's easier!" Blake bellowed back.

Dan brought him the ice cream and mock curtseyed.

"Oh . . . my . . . God." Blake sighed, happily, as he tasted the forbidden desert. "Marry me. Raise my children."

"Only if we get a nanny. I can barely take care of myself. By the way . . . speaking of marriages . . ."

Blake grinned. He had wondered how long it would take Dan to ask.

"What's the 411 on you and Cameron? On? Off? What?"

"I'm on the plane going to see him, aren't I?" Blake slyly said. "He left her. Moved out. I'm sure it's not over yet, but he's making the effort, and that's all I can ask for."

"Good for you. You should have seen the blowout they had here on the flight back to New York last week. She slapped him! Twice! Can you imagine? I left, and didn't see what happened after that, but when I came back to the cabin, they were seated far apart from each other and didn't say another word until we landed. I've never seen Mrs. Fuller so quiet."

"Wow."

"And, as further proof he's crazy about you, he sent the plane all the way to California to pick you up, so . . ."

"I know. How silly is this? I could have flown in on United. I don't care."

"Oh, honey. It's a whole other world when you're part of the Fuller inner circle. You'll find out."

"Oh, really?"

"Really."

They fell into silence.

"Have you been to Manhattan before?" Dan asked.

"Once. A long, long time ago, on a high school field trip. I just remember that it seemed like a great town to visit, but I didn't think I could ever live there."

"Oh, you'll change that tune in a hurry. I love it! So much to see and do."

"So they say. Where do you live?" Blake was almost halfway through the ice cream, and not stopping.

"Chelsea. I lucked into a sub-sublet. Actually reasonable. Say! You'll have to go out with me and my friends one night while you're there. It's a great crowd—straight, gay, and everything in between. You'd fit right in."

"Deal. I don't even know how long I'm going to be here. Cam said at least through the week. He has meetings set up with all these execs for them to meet me and fill me in on the campaign. It's all very exciting. I do know that I have to be back in L.A. next week to do an *Esquire* cover shoot."

"My, my. Well, I had better get back to work. I'm gonna go make a snack for the flight crew. I'll talk to you in a few." Dan rose and headed towards the front of the plane. Blake turned and looked out the windows at the slow-moving clouds below. He tried to guess where they were, but he had no idea.

The plane landed about four o'clock New York time. There was a black Lincoln Town Car waiting for Blake upon his arrival. After hugging Dan goodbye, Blake hopped in and the coarse-looking chauffeur began the drive to the city. Blake allowed himself the "gee whiz" time to gawk out the windows at the passing scenery. He felt an exhilarated rush from being here that surprised him, but he couldn't tell if it was being in a new place, or the anticipation of being with Cameron.

The drive to Soho took just over an hour, and soon they were pulling up to a very tall black glass building a few blocks up from where Blake knew the Warehouse store was. Oscar, the driver, opened the passenger door and Blake got out. He played the typical rube, looking up at all the tall buildings. He was ushered into the building by Oscar, and soon found himself standing in an elevator racing up to the fourteenth floor.

When the doors parted, he stepped out into a huge vestibule, and once through the oversized double doors, found himself staring, in a moment of surreal realization, at . . . *himself.*

There was a giant blowup—ten feet tall by twelve feet wide—of the shot of him with the low-riding wet leather jeans in the surf. Tinted a light shade of sepia, it was spellbinding. Superimposed over the photo in a masculine-looking font at the bottom were the words:

PACIFIC COAST HIGHWAY. A PLACE. AN ATTITUDE. A NEW SCENT.

CAMERON FULLER USA

Blake realized it was a mockup of a billboard.
He was thrilled.

The prominent bulge of his dick was two feet long.

The receptionist, a handsome, built African-American man of twenty-five, almost dropped the power bar he was eating when he realized Blake was the actual person from the photograph he had been fondly gazing at for the past two days.

"Mr. Jackson! We've been expecting you! Please, let me take your bag," he gushed as he reached for the CF America duffle in Blake's hand. He gave Blake a dazzling smile and ushered him into the reception lobby. "My name is Darrell, and everyone here is so glad that you'll be spending some time with us this week. I'll call Bette, Mr. Fuller's assistant, to come fetch you. Please have a seat. Can I get you anything?" he earnestly asked, secretly hoping against hope that Blake would ask for his phone number.

"No, I'm fine. Thanks." Blake sat down in one of six black leather Barcelona chairs and waited.

Darrell zipped back to his desk, a circular steel and polished wood partition, and called Bette.

It took only two minutes for her to arrive to pick Blake up. A sharply dressed Hispanic woman, she was in her middle forties, and had worked for Cameron from the beginning. She was a stylish woman who carried herself with grace and ease. Tall and thin, she was wearing a rose-colored sweater dress with a plunging V-neck that showed off her ample bosom. Her salt and pepper hair was cut short in a boy's style that flattered her angular features. Lively brown eyes welcomed Blake.

"Hello, Blake. I'm Bette, Mr. Fuller's assistant. Please come this way." She indicated that he was to follow her, and he did.

As Blake passed from view, Darrell leaned out from his cubicle and watched his jeans clad ass until it made the final corner and disappeared from view. "Damn!" he whispered to himself. He'd been staring at the crotch on the poster almost nonstop since it had been placed in the lobby. He had teased himself with fantasies of a close encounter with the amazing dick captured in the photograph. Having just met Blake personally, he was determined he'd have the real thing in his hands, mouth, and ass before the week was through.

"Did you have a nice flight?" Bette asked sweetly.

"Yes, it was fine. No bumps."

"We like that."

She was leading him down a long corridor off of which dozens of doors opened. There was a rush of frantic activity as impeccably well-dressed staffers came and went from office to office, an air of urgency about them. After making another turn, Blake noticed the office doors got further and further apart.

That meant the offices were getting bigger.

She came to a set of open double doors and walked him into her outer office, a large room complete with sitting area. She indicated a closed door. "Right in there, Blake. Welcome to Cameron Fuller USA."

Blake went through the heavy wooden door and entered the largest office he had ever seen. Easily sixty feet long, it was covered in beautiful maple-colored paneling. A large, glossy conference table surrounded by black leather ergonomic chairs held court in front of the floor-to-ceiling windows. A comfortable seating area was made up of a black leather George Smith standard sofa with two gray flannel club chairs situated on either side of it. The cocktail table was a Cameron Fuller design of polished teak. A fully stocked upright bar was towards the back of the room, and Cameron's desk was a monstrous oak block set opposite the seating area. One whole wall was covered in cork with hundreds of flyers, sample drawings, and swatches tacked onto it. Multiple doors that led to who knows where were spaced along the walls. Everything else about the office faded away as he saw Cameron coming towards him, hand outstretched. He was dressed nattily in a pair of Manhattan gray pinstripe trousers and a crisp white shirt with a sedate gray tie. His shirtsleeves were rolled up and the tie had been loosened from his collar.

"Blake! You made it! So glad you could join us," he said, shaking Blake's hand energetically. Blake then noticed the two other men in the room: Rafael, and a man he'd never seen before.

Cameron, as always, looked so wonderful that Blake had a hard time acknowledging the other gentlemen.

"Hello, Blake," Rafael said quietly.

"Hi! I'm Ted Dawson, Creative Director, BBHL & O Advertising. Damn glad to meet you!" The unfamiliar man shook Blake's hand furiously and smiled broadly. "We have been looking at your pictures for days now, and it's a pleasure to meet the real you. You take a great photograph. Cameron sure can pick 'em!" He smiled easily. A short, compact man, he exuded personality.

Blake disliked him immediately.

"So how was your flight? Good weather?" Cameron asked, his eyes drinking in every square inch of his lover.

"Yes, it was fine. Smooth sailing all the way."

"Good, good." Cameron moved to his massive oak desk and buzzed Bette. "Bette, get the marketing people in here so we can fill Blake in on the next few weeks, okay? . . . Thanks. And see if Silas is in the building. I'd like him to meet Blake as well." He returned his attention to Blake. He was practically beaming with joy at seeing his lover, and it showed.

Blake had the same look on his face.

Rafael thought he might throw up. "Well, you're looking good, Blake. Nice tan," the pockmarked man said flatly while studying his immaculate fingernails. "I think you might want to lay off the desserts for a few days, though. You need to drop another five pounds, I think."

Blake, afraid of Rafael no more, stared numbly at him. "Thanks for the tip, Rafe. But I'm a thirty-one-inch waist now. When was the last time you were a thirty-one waist?" He knew it was a bitchy remark, but he didn't care.

Rafe, in the process of popping a few M&Ms in his mouth, blushed red. "Well, I'm not a highly paid fashion model, though, am I?" he countered.

Blake let his eyes run up and down the overweight form of Rafe. "So true."

Rafael put the candy back in the dish.

Blake felt better. He knew he'd scored a direct hit.

Cameron stepped in, sensing the tension building. "So, Blake, what I want to show you is the marketing plan for the next six months. You're going to do print, commercial, and personal appearances. You'll do a tour of our leading department stores. A meet and greet thing that we'll pump up through TV and radio advertising," Cameron said, getting things back to the business at hand.

He could have been talking in Sanskrit for all the attention Blake was paying to what he said. He was mesmerized by his lover's eyes, his face, the way he moved in his office, the king of his domain. Blake found himself nodding absently to words he wasn't hearing.

"And to kick it off, I've decided to hold the launch party at the Rodeo Drive store. It'll be huge. My promotions department had a cow when I told them to switch it from the Warehouse to Rodeo Drive, but I think it's a smart move."

"That's great."

"We're shooting a TV spot tomorrow with you in the studio," Ted interjected. "So get some sleep tonight. We want you to look your best. The setup is easy. We'll mix in still shots of you, and the new stuff of you in bed."

"Excuse me? In bed?" Blake was confused.

"Yes, we had a beach house set built at the studios over in Chelsea. I'll give you a packet of materials before you leave for dinner and it will have everything in it you need to know."

"Okay." Blake looked at Cam for reassurance, and got it.

"The ads we shoot tomorrow will start hitting the air in the next two weeks. There's going to be tremendous interest in you, so brace yourself. I understand there was a little trouble at your house last week?"

He slipped that in slyly, Blake thought. "More than a little trouble. Someone shot, and wounded, a friend at my house. The police are still investigating."

"Any suspects? Can we hope for a quick resolution?" Ted pressed.

"You'd have to talk to the police about that. I have no idea."

Ted frowned. "Well, we'll work around it."

There was a strong knock at the door, and soon the room was filled with suits all trying to get some face time with Blake and Cameron.

The marketing team.

After a few minutes of mindless chit chat, Blake noticed a solemn figure enter the room silently. The tall, old, and extremely thin man hung back from the crowd of executives and studied Blake from head to toe. Cameron caught sight of the older gentleman as well, and hurried to his side.

"Silas," he said to the formal looking man. "This is Blake Jackson. The new face of Pacific Coast Highway. Isn't he perfect? He's going to make PCH huge!" Cameron's pride was painfully obvious.

Silas gave a curt nod. "Yes. He seems to be everything you want."

Blake thought that was a curious choice of words, and instantly felt the deep animosity running between Cameron and his father-in-law. He walked boldly up to the old man and held out his hand to shake. He smiled brilliantly. For some reason it seemed very important to make a good impression with the old fart.

Silas took Blake's surprisingly firm handshake and introduced himself. They indulged in brief small talk before Cameron took hold of Blake's shoulder and led him to the conference table.

Silas watched them together, hating the young man with a passion he hadn't felt in years.

The attraction Cameron felt toward the model was almost palpable. It was as clear as day, and Silas was embarrassed for them. Surely every person in the room had to know that this kid was fucking Cameron. It was that obvious. Silas had to bite his tongue in order not to let out a string of obscenities condemning both men to hell and back.

Silas would never be voted father of the year, and he was completely comfortable with the fact that he had little affection for his only surviving child. Still, even though she had gone into this ridiculous marriage with her eyes wide open, and deserved what she got for marrying a queer, Silas felt that the Cabbott name had taken a hit. Or was it more than that? Besides doing the unforgivable, seducing his innocent son, Cameron had, after all, hurt his daughter with his queer love for the model. Silas would not, and so far had not hesitated to hurt Cameron back.

The elderly man joined the group settling down at the table.

For the next two hours Blake endured a litany of items about him, for him, and with him. He was sitting next to Cameron at the long conference table as the execs droned on and on about his participation in the advertising campaign. Every once in a while Cameron would slide his foot over and rub it up against Blake's. Each time he did this, Blake got slightly aroused.

Mockups of posters, shopping bags, and billboards were presented for Cameron's review. It was a little unnerving for Blake to be in a room with so many images of himself. Everywhere he looked he saw a picture of himself, half-naked, pouting. He was amazed that shots from the weekend trip to Big Sur were already being used in proposed ads. The ones in the water with Sharique were especially good.

The whole thing turned even more surreal when he was presented with a mockup of a cologne gift set box with his face on it.

"What? No thermos?" he cracked, studying the box.

"Not yet," Cameron played along. "We're working on that."

"Well, I think that's all to show you today, Cameron, Blake. If you have any questions don't hesitate to ask them," Ted said. He pulled out a thick legal-sized manila envelope and slid it across the slick table surface to Blake. "All the info you need for the shoot tomorrow is in that. Your call time is eight A.M. There will be a car and driver waiting for you at the Stanhope at seven-thirty. My phone numbers are in there, and please call if you need anything." He looked around the table at the tired faces. Clearly, everyone wanted to go home. "I think that's it."

"Yes, everybody go home. Thanks for everything," Cameron agreed, standing.

The meeting broke up and the people trickled out of the office one by one. Silas was the first to leave. Soon only Blake, Cameron, and Rafael remained.

Cameron smiled. "Rafe, you go home, too. I have a few things I want to go over with Blake personally." It wasn't a request.

Rafael bowed his head slightly, gave a stiff look to Blake, and left without saying a word.

"Man, that guy is a trip," Blake said, after the door had shut behind Rafe.

"Oh, forget it," Cameron said, moving in close. "Finally. Alone at last with my supermodel boyfriend!" He took Blake into his arms and they kissed hungrily. Their hands roamed freely over each other's body, and soft groans of pleasure bubbled up between them.

"Hey, ever do it on your conference table?" Blake asked while nibbling at Cam's neck.

"Not yet."

"Then maybe we should explore the possibilities." He dropped his hand down and rubbed it against Cameron's crotch, feeling the hardness within. *"Mmm . . . I missed this,"* he said.

"Ohhh . . . ," Cam breathed, "me, too . . ."

The buzzer on Cam's desk rang, startling them both. Cam disentangled himself from Blake, and answered the phone. "Yes, Bette? . . . Oh, no, go home. Thank you . . . Goodbye." He hung up the phone. He looked across the room at Blake, and noticed his thick hard-on pulling at the denim of his tight jeans.

Blake watched Cam confidently walk over to the door, and turning a knob, lock it. He turned and came back toward Blake removing his tie.

"You were saying?" he asked as he slowly unbuttoned his shirt, one button at a time, lust in his eyes.

Blake gulped. "I . . . I was saying we should explore the possibilities of a joint merger on your conference table." He was mesmerized by the sight of Cam moving toward him, shedding his clothes.

"That proposal has merit," Cam said, dropping his shirt to the floor. He paused briefly as he stepped out of his shoes, undid his belt, and unbuttoned his fly. He let the pants fall and quickly stepped out of them. He was only five feet away from Blake. "I think I'm ready to move on that acquisition."

Blake literally ached to touch him. To feel him. To kiss him.

Cam stuck his fingers into the waistband of his briefs and pulled them down, bending over slightly to remove them, along with his socks. Completely nude, he stood up straight and stared candidly at Blake, his stiff cock jutting up and out.

"Damn," Blake whistled. He pulled off his sweater and quickly undid his jeans, all while Cam stood still, watching him.

Within seconds, Blake, too, was naked.

His body had never been in better shape. He had stair-stepped and run off every extra ounce of fat, and his all-over tan gave the shredded muscles a depth that caused Cameron to breathe heavily. The erect python between his legs was swaying gently with each exhale, and had the effect of hypnotizing Cam. They allowed themselves the small luxury of studying each other from head to toe.

"Come here," Blake whispered.

His spell broken, Cam did as he was asked.

Darrell was the last one in the office, and he had watched each departing employee, but he had not seen the hot model, or, for that matter, Cameron Fuller, leave.

They must still be in the designer's office, he thought.

He switched the phone to night calls, and shut down his work station. Deciding he should check to make sure they didn't need anything, and hoping for a chance to be alone with the model to ask him out, he walked down the deserted halls to Cameron's office.

When he got to Bette's office, he saw that it was dark, the double glass doors shut and locked. He could see a thin line of light coming from under the doors to Cameron's office, so he knew they must still be in there. He continued down the hall, and into a small service pantry. There was a back door to Cameron's office located here and he reached for the knob. Just before his hand touched the cool metal he heard a noise.

Not just a noise, but a shout.

Not knowing if it meant trouble, he put his ear to the thick wood door and strained to hear what was happening inside.

He got an earful.

The deep sound of Cameron's voice was saying something urgent, and the model, Blake, was responding.

What is going on in there? Darrell wondered.

Gritting his teeth, he carefully, and very slowly, turned the knob, and gently pulled the door open a half inch.

It was enough.

"Ohmigod!" he excitedly whispered to himself, stunned by what he saw.

Through the little crack, he could clearly see the conference table and chairs. But that wasn't what he found so compelling. It was the sight of Cameron Fuller, President and CEO of Cameron Fuller USA, buck naked and flat on his back, his beefy legs parted wide and high, the hot model nestled snugly in between, fucking the bejesus out of him.

Darrell thought he'd seen hot sex in his life, but nothing he had ever witnessed, or participated in, came close to the frenetic thrashing happening on the polished surface of the twenty-three-thousand-dollar table.

He instantly popped wood watching the two hot men ravage each other. Cameron kept urging Blake on, telling him harder, deeper, faster! He would throw his head back to let out a cry of ecstasy every once in a while that was so raw in its emotion that Darrell felt it in his gut.

Blake, for his part, was pumping like a stallion and would slow down or speed up as he sensed was needed. Cameron would clutch at Blake's back as he raised himself off of the table surface, spasming in pleasure. They would kiss so deeply and with such love that Darrell wished he would one day find that for himself.

And, try as he could to resist it, he began to rub his own hard-on through his trousers.

He noticed that Blake began to completely withdraw from Cameron's ass, then glide back in. Each time he did this, Cam jerked his head back and shouted out "Yes!"

Suddenly, Darrell was acutely aware that what he was watching was something so intimate and private, he could no longer spy. Breathing hard, he slowly closed the door, and after adjusting himself so he could walk, he quietly left the service pantry.

Standing alone in the elevator, Darrell broke out into a huge smile.

"I always *knew* Cameron Fuller was gay!" he said to no one.

32

"So, Blake, you'll get out of the bed, *here,* and walk over to the window, *there,* and gaze out to sea. Got it?" the short-tempered director quizzed him.

"Seems easy enough," Blake replied, mentally going through the paces of the shot.

"Good. Where's Sharique? We need her for this setup!" the director yelled out.

"She's in makeup right now. She'll be on the studio floor in three minutes, Lou," said the competent-looking assistant director.

Everyone was standing inside the beach house set trying to get ready for the next shot. It was hour three into the shoot, and Lou Swartz, the notoriously temperamental but award-winning director of the commercial, was already in a foul mood.

Blake walked over to the director's chair with his name stenciled on the back, and sat down. He was dressed in a pair of pale blue oxford cloth CF America pajama bottoms with no shirt and bare feet. The light blue color set off his total tan wonderfully, and his hair had been carefully arranged to look like it hadn't been arranged. It was hot on the set, so being half naked actually made him comfortable.

So far this morning they had gotten one shot. A shot of him in bed sleeping, then slowly waking up. Blake had climbed into the bed, made of polished steel tubes welded together in a very stark and contemporary style, and a flock of stylists had descended on him.

One stylist was there to make sure the Cameron Fuller Malibu sheets he was sprawled on looked good and didn't wrinkle too much. Another stylist was there to make sure that Blake's pj pants looked their best and didn't reveal too much. The third stylist was there for Blake's hair, and she spent far too much time fanning it out carefully across the pillow, so it would look like Blake had casually fallen asleep.

The actual set for the shoot was the interior of an ultra-contemporary beach house. It had been built in only four days, and in some places the paint was still wet. The three-walled set was smack in the middle of Stage 12 at the Chelsea Studios. The walls of the set went up twelve feet, and there was, of course, no ceiling, so that the studio lights gridded overhead could be directed down as needed. From the outside, or backside, it was just a mass of two-by-fours and plywood with bracing holding it up.

The inside was another story.

The house was supposed to give the feeling of luxury and style, but had touches of whimsy, as if the owner was someone who appreciated the best things in life, but wasn't ruled by them. Placed here and there on the set were telling accessories, such as an antique bubble gum dispenser by the front door, an ancient Coca-Cola machine in a nook by the kitchen, and a large vintage Coco Palms Hotel sign hung on the wall over the bed.

The set was built as one giant room that had been carefully divided into smaller spaces. A kitchen area, a dining area, a living room area. Even an open bathroom with an enormous chrome shower nozzle coming straight down out of the "ceiling."

Tall, wide windows situated along all three walls of the set were treated with thin bamboo roman shades under sheer draperies. Blown-up photographs of the California coastline were positioned outside the windows, so that if you stood inside, it looked like that was the view.

The house was decorated in a very modern hip style, with low flat furniture in shades of blue and green. These colors had been chosen to replicate the shades of the ocean. Large sisal rugs covered the hand rubbed cement floors. Photography was the artwork of choice on the sparse walls, and it was all black and white shots of beach scenes. Palm trees, sandy beaches, shells, that sort of thing. The kitchen was completely white. White counters, white barstools, white appliances, and white floors.

In the raised bedroom area, the steel bed was up against a faux-cement wall, and two low steel nightstands had been placed next to it.

To Blake, the set was completely opposite of the comfortable, relaxed style he had experienced at the beach house in Kauai, so he wasn't wild about it. But the decor wasn't his responsibility, and this was the look they were going for.

He sensed the heavy hand of Rafael in the sets' design.

Rafael was hovering off stage watching everything. Every once in a while he would scurry out of the shadows to plump up a pillow or tell a stylist how to move a fold of fabric around Blake, or where to place a flower arrangement. He never said a direct word to Blake, always referring to him as "the model."

Whatever, Blake thought.

Sharique made her appearance. As one of Manhattan's darlings, she was the last of the great supermodels. She was twenty-six, five feet ten inches, a hundred and seventeen pounds, smoked like a maniac, and was heartstoppingly beautiful. She was constantly in the gossip columns and tabloids for her exploits about town, and was known to have no gag reflex. Willowy blonde with a chopped up shoulder-length hairstyle that was currently all the rage, she carried herself with an attitude of superiority. She had exclusive contracts with Revlon, Norwegian Cruise Lines, Bally's Health Clubs and Cameron Fuller. She was the face of Cameron's Silk Damask makeup and fragrance line, and she had been pressed into duty on Pacific Coast Highway to help give it that extra *umph.*

She languidly crossed the stage floor in a pair of CF/Active men's jockey shorts and tanktop, and hopped into the bed. A bevy of stylists attacked her at once.

Blake was soon asked to join her in bed.

"Hey there, PCH man," she cooed at him as a makeup artist plucked out a stray eyebrow hair that had dared to grow in the wrong direction.

"Hey, Sharique," Blake answered amiably as he crawled under the sheets. "Are there always this many people in bed with you?"

"God, I fuckin' wish! I haven't been laid in weeks!" she hooted. She pulled down the thin cotton fabric of her tanktop and exposed her perfect right breast, flashing Blake. "You wanna have a go?" she kidded him.

Blake laughed out loud. "I thought you had a boyfriend. That movie star."

"He's in Belgium filming some dumb war movie." She leaned in close to Blake's ear. "And my girlfriend is out in L.A. doing the hair on a J-Lo video. So you see, my boyfriend and my girlfriend are *both* gone. I've got no one!"

Nonplussed, Blake smiled. "That must make for interesting Friday nights."

"Oh, you have no idea!" she laughed. "Thank God they like each other."

"I saw the stuff from Big Sur. It all turned out really great. You look so good," Blake said, allowing himself to be face powdered once again by the preening makeup artist.

"I'm sure I do," she said without a trace of conceit. "I always look good wet."

"Okay, Blake, Sharique. Here's the setup . . ." Lou told them what he wanted them to do, and then he went back to his place beside the camera.

It was after seven at night, and Blake was starving. He'd barely had time to wolf down a couple of chicken breasts at lunch and now could feel his stomach grumbling.

He was still on the set, doing the last of the pickup shots needed. Sharique had left hours ago, and the work had stopped being fun. All he had to do in this shot was turn slightly to the camera, the lighting streaming in from "outside," highlighting his chiseled face.

So far it had taken fifteen takes. And counting.

Cameron walked quietly onto the stage floor, staying in the background, behind the camera. He just observed the action. He didn't want Blake to see him or be distracted by him, so he simply hung back.

Rafael spied him, and wasted no time in getting to his side.

"Hello, Cameron. Did you approve those batik patterns for 'Bali'?" he asked.

"Yes, Rafe, I did. I made a slight change on the color charts. I'd like a hint more magenta. Other than that, they're fine. How's this going?" he indicated the madness on the stage floor.

"It's . . . all right. We're running late. Blake isn't quite up to this, but I think we'll be able to cut together bits and pieces and get . . . something," Rafe said, slamming Blake again.

"Really?" Cameron was surprised. Blake looked good on set, and when Cameron had talked to the director earlier in the day on the phone, Lou had said that Blake was doing a terrific job.

"Well, I know you were sold on him, but he's a non-pro. That's always going to cost us if we continue to use him. It's not too late to bring in a big gun like Travis Fimmel, you know."

Cameron turned to face Rafael, his face hard, his voice steel. "I'm only going to say this one more time, Rafael. Blake is PCH. Get used to it. If you can't get behind this and support it fully, then we need to seriously think about your future here."

Rafe's eyes grew bigger as the impact of what Cameron was saying to him registered. He began to feel as if his legs might give out beneath him. "But, Cameron, I—" he feebly tried to say.

Cameron cut him off. "I'm sick of you whispering in my ear your thoughts on this subject. As far as I'm concerned, it's closed. Blake is here to stay. *Embrace it.*" He walked out from behind the camera and gave a small wave to Blake.

Rafael's face had turned ashen. He wanted to run after Cameron and somehow smooth it over, but he knew he better not. In all the years he had worked for Cameron he had never been spoken to like that. The wind was changing, and Rafe realized he had better get on board with Blake. The little hustler had done it.

The window dresser had won.

Blake had just been told he was wrapped for that night when he saw Cameron walk onto the set. Instantly flooded with happiness, he caught his eye. They communicated their happiness at seeing each other silently. Cameron had to walk through the gauntlet of crew to get to Blake, and when he finally appeared at his side, Blake had been snagged by Lou, who was giving him some ideas for the stills shoot scheduled for the next day.

"Hello, Lou. Hi, Blake," Cameron said, a twinkle in his eye, as he shook Lou's hand.

"Hi, Cameron. We're wrapped for tonight. Blake did a fantastic job. I wish all the talent I use was as professional."

Blake was glad to hear the words. He had felt like the delays might have been his fault, even though he had done exactly what they had told him to do.

"Well, Blake's a great guy!" Cameron said happily, throwing his arm around Blake's shoulders and giving him a friendly squeeze.

Thirty minutes later they were in Cameron's limo driving to the hotel.

"While I was being puffed and fluffed, what did you do today?" Blake asked Cameron.

"Nothing that would interest you. Lots of meetings. I did see two apartments at lunch, and one of them I really like. I want you to see it, too. We'll go over tomorrow at lunch, okay?"

"Sure. I think I'm not needed until, like, three, for some meeting at your office."

"Oh, right. Your publicity tour meeting."

Blake laughed. *My publicity tour meeting!* he thought. It was all so surreal.

"So what are your thoughts about dinner? What do you want to do?" Cameron asked, rubbing his hand up and down Blake's thigh lovingly.

"Actually, I am hungry, but for what, I don't know. Something light. I still need to go to the gym. I want to try the Chelsea Piers. I hear it's really cool there."

"We'll just order something up then. Suits me fine. I'm bushed. But I'll hit the gym with you, if you want."

"That'd be great!" Blake looked at Cam, and couldn't help himself. He leaned in and gave him a soft kiss on the lips. He half expected Cam to shy away from it, what with the driver and all, but he was surprised to find that Cam accepted it warmly.

Oscar happened to pick that exact moment to glance in the rear view mirror. He saw the two men kiss tenderly, and quickly returned his gaze to the road ahead.

Cameron unlocked the hotel suite door and let Blake enter before him. Cam's good humor was slightly tarnished. He had gotten a stack of messages at the front desk, and he now had to return over fifteen calls. He told Blake to go on to the gym without him.

Blake changed his clothes quickly and was out the door in under twenty minutes. He hopped into the waiting car and Oscar sped off, heading crosstown to take him to the gym at Chelsea Piers, which Blake was eager to try out.

"Are you enjoying New York, Mr. Jackson?" Oscar asked, looking at Blake through the rear view mirror.

"Yes, I am, thanks. I'm sorry, but I didn't get your name yesterday."

"I'm Oscar. I've worked for the Fullers for years."

"Well, Cameron only hires the best, or so I've been told."

"He's a kind man. A pleasure to work for," Oscar said, maneuvering the big sedan through the crowded traffic like a ballet dancer. "I look out for him, you know what I mean?"

Blake looked at the back of Oscar's thick neck. "No. What do you mean?"

"Well, I've seen all kinds of guys try to shimmy up to Mr. Fuller. He's never bitten the fruit before. But he's got a big heart. He likes everyone. Sometimes he don't know trouble when he sees it, is all."

"Do you think I'm trouble, Oscar?" Blake asked.

Oscar eyed him through the mirror. "I don't know yet. I know Mr. Fuller likes you a lot, and that's okay by me. He deserves a little fun and romance in his life. I just don't want to see him get hurt. Or used. Cause if that happened," he said, his voice getting slightly ominous, "then maybe I'd have to step in and protect him, if you know what I mean."

"Yes, I think I do."

"I thought you might."

Blake sat in silence for a moment. "I think I like you, Oscar," he finally said.

Oscar didn't say anything back, he just kept driving, a slight smile appearing on his lips.

Even though it was a little far to travel, the Chelsea Piers gym was spectacular. Blake felt like he was at a sports-themed Disneyland. He wandered through the facility with a dazed look on his face, trying to absorb all the activities going on.

The Chelsea Piers sports complex had been built on an actual pier in lower Manhattan. The pier had originally been used to dock the magnificent transatlantic ocean liners of yore, but as the airplane overtook steamship travel, the piers became unused, then rundown. A few years ago, the piers were bought and transformed into the sports complex. Golf, rock climbing, basketball, swimming, weights, exercise classes, you name it, they had it there.

Blake attacked the weight room equipment with gusto and soon had worked up a good sweat. The gym floor was elevated over the complex, and you could look down on basketball games taking place on the multiple courts. A spin class was in progress in one corner of the workout floor, and Blake was anxious to join the next one.

"Hey. Can I work in?"

Blake focused on the man standing nearby. He was of average height, but that was the only thing average about him. He had a lean and compact muscular body that was barely contained by the thin cotton/lycra shirt and shorts he was wearing. His short dreads were edged with sweat, and he had on worn workout gloves that covered large hands. His face was cheerful, with dark brown eyes that were protected by the thickest set of lashes Blake had ever seen.

"Sure. Sorry, I was just vegging out for a bit," Blake said, getting up off the seat of the chest press.

"Oh, no problem. Did you have a good day at the shoot?" the stranger asked, settling into the seat, adjusting it slightly for his height.

"Sorry?" Blake asked, confused.

"I'm Darrell. I work at Cameron Fuller." Noticing Blake's blank stare, he added, "I work the front desk?"

"Oh! Oh, yes! Of course . . . Sorry! I thought you looked familiar, but I'm so bad with names." Blake blushed, as he apologized.

How had he not noticed this hot man at Cameron's office? He *must* be in love.

"Oh, no problem. I tend to disappear behind the desk," Darrell said through gritted teeth as he pushed out a set of ten.

"It went fine. They tell me it'll look great."

Darrell got up and wiped down the seat with his workout towel. "I'm sure it will. You're a hot man. How could it be otherwise?" He grinned at Blake, and subtly pushed his pelvis out a bit, brushing his crotch against Blake as Blake took the seat. "Sorry. Tight quarters here," he said impishly.

"No problem." Blake did his set, effortlessly.

"Damn, son. You did that like that was nothing. Let me add some real weight," Darrell offered, slapping another twenty-five pounds onto each side of the machine. Blake shrugged, and did a second set.

It was a little harder to do.

Darrell never took his eyes off the hot model doing the presses. He studied his body and his muscles as they strained against the resistance, burning them into his memory for later perusal. He had been stunned when he recognized Blake working out. His fantasy man was right in front of him, and even though he had been doing triceps, Darrell quickly changed his workout to chest so as to "accidentally" need to use the same chest equipment as Blake.

"Good set," Darrell said, trying to sound as butch as possible. He could not get the mental picture of Blake, on the conference table, fucking the hell out of Cameron, out of his mind.

He had jerked off to thoughts of Blake twice in the past twenty-four hours, and had to figure out a way to experience the ride for himself.

"Thanks."

"So where are you staying?"

"The Stanhope." Blake had a small suite there, but had really only stopped by it once, when he first checked in. He had spent all his time in Cameron's suite. He couldn't even remember the number of his own room.

"Wow. Nice place. I've never been there." Darrell dropped down to do another set. "I always hoped I'd meet someone staying there and they'd invite me up for a drink, so I could see what it looked like . . ." He let the sentence hang.

"Oh, sure. Come on over anytime. Look around. It's pretty nice," Blake said absently.

"Oh, yeah? How about tonight? I've got nothing planned after this." Darrell popped up out of the seat and stood inches from Blake. There was no mistaking his intentions. He reached out a hand and brazenly let it travel up Blake's thigh, just missing his package.

"Hey," Blake said, stepping back to break contact. "I hardly know you," he lamely joked.

"Then, let's change that." Just touching Blake's body had excited Darrell to an extent that surprised him. "My roommate's out of town this week, and my place is only sixteen blocks from here. We can walk it."

"Walk it? Sixteen blocks?" Blake's Los Angeles sensibility was more shocked by the notion of walking that long distance than he was by the come on.

"It's not far. And I promise you it'll be worth it," Darrell whispered into Blake's ear. He wanted to stick his tongue deep into that ear, but he barely restrained himself.

"Darrell, look. I'm sure you're a great guy, but I'm . . . I'm seeing someone."

Yeah, and I know who, Darrell thought. "So? You never party and play?" He again leaned in close to Blake's ear. "I'm just saying that I find you so incredibly hot, and I want you to ride me like a cowboy. What's the harm? Who'll know?"

"I'll know," Blake replied honestly.

Darrell realized he wasn't going to get what he wanted. His shoulders slumped a little, and he started to get embarrassed. "Okay. Sorry."

"Hey, I'm flattered, honest. You're an incredible man yourself. If I wasn't seeing . . . this guy, I'd be all over you. But . . ."

"Yeah, sure. Well, keep it in mind. Things change," Darrell said hopefully.

Oscar was sitting in the car, waiting patiently in front of the complex for Blake. It was freezing cold. Blake ran to the car and hopped in before Oscar could get out and open his door.

"Back to the Stanhope, Mr. Jackson?"

"Yes, and please call me Blake, Oscar. Mr. Jackson is my father," Blake said, rubbing his arms to warm up.

Oscar eased into traffic and began the journey back to the hotel. Blake allowed himself to stare idly out the windows at the city moving past him. He thought back to his response to Darrell: *"I'll know."*

Blake felt he'd grown in some way. He would be the first to admit that monogamy wasn't his strong-suit, and if he was forced to testify under oath, even when he was with Brady he'd messed around on the side. His fling with Luka, the flight attendant didn't count, because as far as he was concerned, like Ross and Rachel on *Friends,* he and Cameron had been "on a break."

He was attracted to Darrell, obviously. But he was so happy to be with Cameron that the thought of sleeping with anyone else was just foreign to him now.

He smiled contentedly as he realized that this was the kind of love that everyone had always talked about.

*   *   *

Cameron hugged Blake close and snuggled his head in the crook of Blake's neck. "Mmm. You smell good," he murmured.

"Whatever the soap was in your shower, that's what I used."

Cameron sighed. "I like it."

Blake reached an arm back and laid his hand on Cameron's leg, gently stroking it.

"I set up an appointment to see that apartment I told you about, tomorrow. I really like it and I want your opinion," Cameron whispered.

"Sure."

Both men soon drifted off to sleep.

"Well?" Cameron asked, holding his arms out wide and doing a slow spin in the living room of the empty apartment.

"Wow," was all Blake could muster. The place was huge. Fourteen foot ceilings soared above them and crown molding at least a foot thick surrounded the room. The floor was a masterful mix of woods laid out in a diamond pattern that seemed to stretch forever across the apartment. The walls were thick and looked solid, as if they had stood for a century, and could stand for another one.

"I felt at home here the second I walked in the doors," Cameron said, opening one of the numerous tall windows.

"It's pretty amazing. It suits you."

"I'll have the creative services team do it over. I want it to be a mix of modern and traditional. I have a thousand ideas for the space!" Cameron was almost giddy. This would be his first real home. One that would be all his, and he was excited by the freedom.

"Show me the rest of it," Blake said, taking Cam's hand in his own. They wandered through the rooms, making comments and trying to figure out furniture placements. The master bedroom suite was enormous, with a huge fireplace centered on the longest wall. Cameron imagined the room as a lush bedroom where he and Blake would make love for hours in front of a roaring fire.

Blake caught sight of his watch and noticed the time. "Hey, we gotta go. We're gonna be late for the meeting." He tugged at Cam, trying to pull him out of the empty bedroom.

"They can't start it without me," said Cam. He smirked and pulled Blake into a hug.

"True, but I want the people to know I'm a professional. One who is on time. I don't want to be seen as your 'boy,' " Blake said earnestly.

Cam looked at him, and realized he was right. "Okay. Let's go. I'll tell the agent to put in an offer today."

33

Blake arrived back in L.A. a week later.

His schedule had rapidly filled up, so Nelle at Hunk insisted he get back home. He had to shoot the *Esquire* cover with Trevor, and there were wardrobe fittings he had to be at. As much as Blake hated to leave Cam in New York, he was glad to be back in his own house with Joe.

There had been an awfully touching and teary scene in the Towncar, and one on the tarmac, by the jet. Cam had insisted on going with Blake to the airport and, oblivious to Oscar up front, the two men hugged and kissed the entire way there. Neither wanted to let the other go.

The week in New York had been filled with more shoots, more meetings, and lots of working out. The two had spent every night in Cam's suite at the Stanhope, beginning to take on the routine of an old married couple.

Blake was completely in love with Cameron. He had no problems with it anymore. He knew Cam loved him back, and the two men had formed a bond that Blake could not see breaking. He no longer looked at things in a sense of "I." He saw them in the way of "we."

Even though he was relieved to be home in his small house, he missed Cam terribly. They spoke on the phone at least three times a day, and Blake couldn't wait for Cam to come to L.A., for the cologne launch.

The days passed quickly.

When he woke up each morning, Blake would call Cam. They

would talk for half an hour or so, then Blake would head out to the gym. If he had business to attend to or a shoot to do, he did that. If not, he would tan, then call his agents for the latest news and offers. He would go for a late afternoon run around Lake Holly-wood, call Cam again, then eat a light dinner and settle down in his comfortable living room and watch TV. Just before bed, he would again call Cameron, and the two men usually ended up having heated phone sex. It allowed each to climax, but the physical intimacy was sorely missed. Life seemed almost normal, except for the longing Blake had for his distant lover.

Preparations for the launch party were going full tilt, and Blake was kept in the loop through his agents and his friends at the Rodeo Drive store. He was scheduled to do a round of media interviews the day after the launch, and then, when the commercials started to air, he would do another round. He was also to be the star of the massive party being scheduled at the store.

Chelsea had told him that Rafael was killing himself to make the launch the PR event of the year. He had been in L.A. for days now, driving Spence and the whole creative services team crazy with his demands. Several hundred A-list guests had been invited, and so far, it looked like there would be a record turnout. Buzz had been building about Blake for weeks now, and everyone was interested in him.

Nelle called him several times a day to explain the new offers that were coming in. It all amazed Blake. He was nobody. All these people wanted him because he was the "it" boy of the moment, and he hadn't even done anything yet. He discussed the offers with Cam during their nightly calls, and Cam helped him weed out the bogus ones from the good ones. He signed to be a spokesman for Bally's Fitness and Finlanda Vodka.

A few days before the launch party, Blake drove by the store to check on the progress of the party preparations. He was amazed to see bleachers built up on the sidewalk and a wide red carpet stretching from the front of the store all the way down the block. It looked as if the Academy Awards were going to be held there. Huge banners touting Pacific Coast Highway were hanging on the front of the store building, and Blake knew these would be changed the night of the event to show the picture of him coming out from the water.

It was almost overwhelming. The display windows were hidden behind large scrims announcing the launch date of PCH. Blake was aware that displays of Pacific Coast Highway accompanied by shots of him would be revealed on launch night. He was actually going to be the focus of the windows! The very same windows he used to design. He had to grin at the irony.

There happened to be a rare parking space right in front of the store, and on a whim, Blake heaved the Land Rover over and parked in it. He hopped out, dropped a few coins in the meter, and entered his old place of employment.

The front entryway had been redone as a reception area. Display cases, and most of the furniture, had been removed to open up the space so there was more room for people to mill about. The night of the party, there would be over three hundred people passing through here, and now that the space was empty of fixtures, the traffic flow would be greatly increased.

Chelsea came around the corner carrying a large black-framed poster of the PCH bottle done in brightly colored quadrants à la Andy Warhol. Chelsea was wearing a denim jumpsuit from the Manhattan Collection and had tied a hot pink silk scarf around her hair in do-rag style.

"Blake!" she squealed when she caught sight of him standing in the foyer. "Our very own celebrity!"

"Hey, baby," he said as they hugged warmly. "How are things here? The whole setup outside is insane!"

"I know! They've been building the bleachers for two days. They expect a crowd in the hundreds to watch the celebs arrive. We all have to wear ID badges."

"That's right! I was supposed to get mine done this week," Blake suddenly remembered.

Every person who was a member of the store, or event staff, had to have a photo ID badge made before they would be allowed into the building the night of the party. Blake's agent, Nelle, had told him to stop by the store anytime this week and have it made, but Blake kept forgetting to do it.

"Well, the people that make them are here. They're set up in the lunchroom. Why not go get it done now? I have to hang this." She indicated the framed poster.

"I think I will. Are you free for lunch today? Let me take you out to eat. Dusty, too."

"Well, Rafe has us running our asses off. He will freak if half the visuals team is off site actually eating a normal meal. But, if *you* ask him, he *might* let us go together."

"Where is Rafe?"

"Upstairs. Home Arena. He and Spence are doing the Spring install. The place is a mess. But Rafe wants it done before Friday, launch night."

"I'll go talk to him. See you in a few." Blake gave her another hug and walked further into the store. He climbed up the stairs, saying hello to the sales associates he knew passing him along the way.

They all reacted differently to him now, he noticed. He had worked with these people for almost a year, yet now they hung back, allowing him a wide berth. Just like he had used to do whenever a known celebrity wandered through the store.

As he hit the second floor, he almost ran right into a handsome blond man with a scruffy beard who was casually clutching a buff-colored vinyl blazer bag over his left shoulder. The man was just starting down the stairs, and he quickly stepped aside to let Blake pass.

"Excuse me," Blake said, without really looking at him.

"Blake?"

Blake looked over at the grinning man, and broke out into a wide smile. "Jesus! Clay! I didn't even realize that was you!" Blake whooped as the two men hugged.

"I know. I had to grow this for a movie I'm about to start shooting," Clay Beasley said, rubbing his right hand over the rough beard. His hair was cut short and choppy, and it was expertly styled and sticking up every which way with carefully arranged haphazardness. The sandy colored beard added a roguish look to his geometrically perfect face. He looked rugged and raffish, and every inch the movie star.

"How are you getting away from your soap role to make a movie?"

Clay was an Emmy-winning contract player on the daytime drama *The Insiders*. It was the number-two-rated soap opera on the air, and those stellar ratings were due in large part to Clay's compassionate portrayal of lawyer Trent Blackwell. "I'll be in a coma for a few weeks, what else?" He grinned easily. "So. Congratulations! I haven't seen you since all this happened for you. What's it like to be a world famous model? When do we get to see you naked on a billboard?"

"No naked ads, thank you, but something almost as bad. Let's just say the mystery about my physical attributes will soon be over."

"Hmm. As I recall," Clay said, grinning impishly, "it's quite an impressive attribute."

Blake blushed slightly. He and Clay had had a brief fling a couple of years ago, right after Clay had been left by his cheating ex-boyfriend, and before he hooked up with his current lover, Travis Church. "I think we were equally matched in that department," he said. Both men broke out into laughter.

"Do you still laugh like this when you come?" Clay teased.

"Christ! I can't believe you remember that! Yes, I do, only now I'm with a man who does the same thing, so we laugh together."

"Well, that *is* good news. Who's the lucky fella?"

Blake looked around and lowered his voice. "Cameron Fuller." He knew he could trust Clay. After all, Clay had a live-in relationship with Travis, a prime-time TV star himself, so he knew how to be discreet.

Clay's eyes grew large and his mouth formed a big "O."

Blake nodded. "Yep. It's true."

"Damn! That's a mental picture! I had no idea he was . . ." The handsome actor didn't finish the sentence. He didn't have to.

"He is, and I got him. I love him, Clay. He's leaving the wife. I think it's gonna work out for us."

"Well, congrats! Can I tell Travis? He'll bust when he hears this! He used to do underwear ads for Cameron, you know."

"I remember. I had them pasted up on the fridge for years. Just tell Travis I said hi, too."

"You'll have to come over sometime soon. We'll do the barbecue thing or something."

"That would be great!"

"I just popped in to pick up a new blazer. I have to go to a soap fans' convention and dinner tonight at the Four Seasons. Five hundred rabid fans and ten stars. It can get scary," Clay grinned.

"I'm sure you'll survive it."

"I will." He leaned in like he was about to share a huge secret. "I actually kinda like it. Soap fans are the *best*. They love you no matter what."

"I wouldn't know."

"Oh, you'll find out about fans soon enough. Brace yourself. Your life will never be the same. I was so not prepared for it at all," Clay admitted.

"You're coming to the launch party, aren't you?"

Clay winked. "We wouldn't miss it for the world."

The friends hugged once more, then Clay said goodbye and continued down the stairs. Blake looked around the sales floor, saw nothing interesting, and then went up one more floor to the Home Arena.

As he crested the top of the stairs he saw the floor overhaul was in full force. All the furniture from the previous season had been sold off and the new pieces were lined up in neat rows along the far side of the store. Construction teams were building new faux walls and adding appropriate trim to existing walls. There was a thin film of sawdust over everything, and in the middle of all this was a haggard looking Rafael, who was screaming at poor Spencer.

It was the first chance Blake had had to see Spencer since his liposuction, and while Spence was still clearly wearing the elastic compression garment used to contain the swelling, a change could clearly be seen. He looked pretty good.

"No! No! No! Are you stupid? I said bring the Bali bed here to the store, not to the warehouse! What good does it do us at the warehouse?" Rafe was ranting.

"Rafe," Spence answered wearily, "you changed your mind. You said you wanted to use the Clarington bed instead. That's what I had brought over."

"I changed my mind back, and I know I told you!" Rafe angrily retorted.

"You didn't. I'm sorry, but you didn't." Spence quietly stood his ground.

"Well, stop standing there contradicting me and get on the phone and have it brought over! Or do I have to do everything?"

Spence turned away from the maniac, saw Blake, gave him a tight nod, and walked off to find a phone.

The whole scene he'd just witnessed disgusted Blake. How long could this asshole get away with bullying his employees? Wasn't it time someone called him on it? Blake felt his ire begin to build. Ire at having to see such abuse. Ire at having to have endured it when he worked for the man. And a resolution to see that it stopped.

Blake sauntered up to Rafael. "Still spreading your special brand of charm around, I see," he said pointedly.

Rafe, sweating from his labors, looked startled to see Blake. "What are *you* doing here?"

"Getting my ID for the gala event. You know, the party to celebrate PCH? And *me.*"

Rafe's eyes narrowed and he put his hands on his hips. "Oh, I see. You think you're hot shit now. Please," Rafe snorted. "You're just some lucky idiot who got a good break. It won't last. You'll be yesterday's news before you know it."

"Maybe. Maybe not. The fame thing isn't what excites me about this whole deal, though."

Rafe took the bait. "I can't wait to hear what *does* excite you."

"Well," Blake said, giving him a toothy smile. "For one thing, being with Cameron excites me." Blake took delight in the way Rafe's eyebrows shot up. "It's the hottest sex I've ever had. The man is an animal. He can't get enough." Blake could see the color rising in Rafe's face. "And that must just *kill* you. Everyone knows you're in love with him. But, you miserable psychopath, you'll never have him. So I guess what makes me feel all warm and tingly inside is knowing that each time I fuck him, I'm also fucking you *over.*"

Rafe's mouth opened and closed but no sounds came out. His face turned beet red and he clenched and unclenched his fists.

"Now, you once told me, not so long ago, that when this was all over, I'd have to deal with you. Do you remember that?" Blake's gaze had turned hard. "It was just after you told me I'd have to sleep with you in order to keep my job, remember?"

"I remember," Rafe said through bared teeth.

"I'm glad. Because you're going to eat those words. Your days of terrorizing and intimidating the people here are *over.* I will see to that." Blake turned to leave. "I'd start brushing up my resume skills," he said offhandedly, "if I were you, because I am going to make it my mission to see you out on your ass as soon as possible."

Blake didn't even wait to hear a reply from the shaking man he left behind. He calmly started to walk back down the stairs, then stopped.

"Oh, and by the way," he called back up to Rafe, "I'm taking Dusty and Chelsea out to lunch. We'll be back in an hour or so. If you have a problem with that, go fuck yourself."

34

West Hollywood, California

"Blake! Hurry up! We have to get to the store by seven for the pre-party!" Cameron shouted down the hallway. He fidgeted with his black merino wool turtleneck, and, finally satisfied that it was turned down correctly, tore himself away from the hall mirror.

"I'm coming. Hold your water," Blake called back. "My hair is doing some weird flip thing! I can't fix it!"

"There're hair and makeup people at the store. Let them deal with it. Let's go!"

Blake emerged from his bedroom and walked down the hallway. He was dressed in his usual tight jeans, a fitted strategically distressed denim shirt open halfway down his chest, giving a good glimpse of his sexy pecs, and a beautiful buttery soft tan leather blazer. A coconut shell necklace he had bought in Kauai was roped around his neck, and even though he didn't like it, his hair was down and flowing perfectly.

"Dayum," Cameron said in appreciation.

"Back at you. You look amazing," Blake said leaning in for a quick kiss. Cam did look good. Along with the black turtleneck, he was wearing black flat front pants and a black broadcloth coat that was expertly tailored to his size. "I thought you were going to wear the navy suit."

"I am. I'll change after the pre-party. Keep 'em guessing," he grinned.

"Slick, you are. Okay. Let's go."

They kissed again, this time with more passion and feeling.

Cam had arrived the night before, delayed one day due to an emergency meeting with his attorney regarding the divorce. Suzette had thrown another wrench into the works, and the negotiations had ground to a halt.

After landing at Burbank Airport, Cameron had gone straight to Blake's little bungalow. After a rousing session of hot sex, the two men had lain in each other's sweaty arms catching up with each other.

Blake told Cameron about his week—the shoots he'd done, who he'd seen—and went over the details of the party. Cameron clued Blake in on his divorce proceedings and announced he'd gone into a short escrow on the apartment they had liked.

Blake didn't tell him about his blowup with Rafe.

"Did you talk to Suzette today?" Blake asked as they left the house and headed toward the waiting limousine. Oscar had come out with Cameron and was their driver this evening.

"No, but she'll be at the party. So will her father. Oh, joy."

"Is she going to be civil to me? I won't put up with her shit on my night, Cameron. I'm warning you now," Blake said forcefully.

"She promised. And with Silas there, he'll help keep her in line," Cameron said soothingly.

"Where is she, anyway? What hotel is she staying at?"

"You know what? I have no idea."

Oscar opened the door, and Cameron slid in first. Blake grinned at the crusty driver who surprised him by winking back at him. Once inside the car, Blake took Cam's hand in his own, and tried to relax.

Oscar pulled away from the curb and they were on their way.

"Hey, Oscar! How you doing? You digging the easy L.A. traffic?" Blake affably called up to the driver.

"I like it here okay, but I still prefer New York. Something about the air here messes up my sinuses," Oscar replied, carefully merging with traffic.

"Come on, Oscar, admit it. Swimming pools. Movie stars. You love L.A.," Cam joked, giving Blake's hand a good squeeze.

"I love New York." The driver watched the two men in the rear view mirror. Cameron was so happy and in love with this kid that he actually glowed. Oscar sighed. "Mr. Fuller? I ever tell you about my older brother, Hank?" he questioned.

"Hank?" Cameron thought for a second. "I don't think so. What about him?"

"Well, Hank's this big guy, like me. He's a fireman over in Brooklyn. Toughest hombre you'd ever want to meet. Always getting into fist fights. Always won. Always stood up for me when we was kids. Anyone I wanted taken care of, he took care of, if you know what I mean." Oscar was staring at Blake.

Blake was beginning to feel a little uncomfortable.

"I think I get your drift," Cam replied, wondering where the story was going.

"Well, my big bad-ass brother, it turns out, went gay. He and another fella from the station, Joey, fell in love, then moved in together. I visit them every Sunday night for dinner. I love Joey like he was a member of the family."

"Uh, that's nice, Oscar," Cam said.

"The point is, Mr. Fuller, I'm glad my brother found his soul mate. Love shouldn't be a matter of gender, but a matter of the heart."

Cam looked at Blake.

"I'm happy for you two, that's all," Oscar said gruffly, but the underlying tenderness was clear.

Cameron was clearly touched. "Thanks, Oscar. That's probably the nicest thing anyone's said to me in a long while."

"I just say it as I see it," the driver replied, again turning his attention to the road.

It took a while for Blake to realize that the car was heading in the opposite direction of the store in Beverly Hills.

"Hey! Oscar's going the wrong way!" he protested.

"No, he's not. I want to show you something." Cam grinned mysteriously. The black car pulled out into Sunset traffic and headed west. Just past Crescent Heights Boulevard, Blake felt the car pull over to the curb. Cam popped open his door and hopped out so fast that Blake was concerned.

"Get out! Come take a look!" Cam called to him.

Blake, confused as to what was going on, carefully opened his door and got out. He saw Cameron looking up toward the western sky. Blake followed his gaze, and it took a second before he realized what he was seeing.

It was the biggest billboard he had ever seen. It was on the site of the famous old Marlboro Man billboard at the curve of Sunset, by the Chateau Marmont. The entire space had been leased by Cameron Fuller USA, and there Blake saw a fifty-foot-tall reproduction of himself. It was the wet leather pants shot, and the tagline letters were six feet tall. Blake stared at it, mesmerized. He looked good, and he knew it. It was such a rush to see himself hovering over the traffic. He could see people in cars straining to look up at the giant, handsome man staring back at them.

A red Miata pulled over a bit further down the road, and a couple of men hopped out. One of them was carrying a digital camera. The other leaped up to a slight ledge under the billboard. The man with the camera took several pictures while his partner clowned at the base of the billboard, screaming up to the erotic visage "I love you! Marry me!"

"I told you. This is going to be huge," Cameron whispered to him.

"How huge do you think it is, anyway?" Blake said, intently staring at his prominent bulge.

"Easily six feet."

"Damn. I'm hung, huh?"

"No complaints here," Cameron laughed. "Come on. Let's go."

Reluctantly Blake got back into the limo. As they pulled away and drove down the street, he could not take his eyes off the enormous billboard.

Several hundred feet away, and sixty feet up, Dillard walked around his spacious suite at the Chateau Marmont. He stopped at a large framed mirror and adjusted his tie. He was dressed in a chocolate brown Manhattan Label suit, and looked quite dandy.

"Babe? Are you almost ready? We're supposed to be there already!" he called out.

"Just two minutes," came a voice from the bathroom. "I just need to fix my hair. I can't get it right."

"Jesus. You're worse than that idiot I kicked out! It would take him forever to get ready. I thought you would be different." Dillard sank down on the edge of the mussed bed and let out a sigh.

"That idiot you kicked out burned down your house! You hide money in bank accounts all over the world so he can't get a hold of it, you spy on one of your closest friends. And you have the balls to bitch about *my* behavior?" the voice from the bathroom archly asked.

"Look, I've done some things I'm not proud of, but I did all those things to protect what I've earned. What I want to share with you. To be honest, I never knew sex could be so . . . amazing. And I love you for that. But, if you don't get your hot ass in gear, we're going to be late!" Impatient, Dillard looked at his watch.

"I'm just adjusting my earring . . . hold your horses."

"I know *you* hate him, but I think Blake is going to be huge. I really think Cameron made a wise choice. The buzz on him—" Dillard started to say.

"A good choice?!" shrieked the voice. "Are you for real? He's a two-bit slut! His being a model is the worst decision Cameron Fuller ever made! He will *ruin* Cameron Fuller USA, you'll see!"

"Oh, I don't think it's all that bad. You're just too close to the situation to see the logic of it all."

"Fuck logic! I'll never forgive him, never! And I'll never accept this relationship with Cameron as real!" The voice was getting a little frantic now. "I just wish I'd run him over when I had the chance."

Dillard looked up sharply. "What are you talking about?"

"A few weeks ago, I saw the fuckhead crossing the street. I wanted to spook him, so I aimed the car right at him, and at the last minute I swerved away. You should have seen him jump!" the voice hooted. "It was classic!" Haunted laughter flowed from the bathroom.

"What? Are you crazy? Why would you do that?"

Dillard's new lover stepped out from the bathroom, still adjusting the troublesome earring. "Don't lecture me, Mister 'Oh, Officer, my house burned down accidentally!' Please. You're no Snow White. So don't pretend to be high and mighty!"

Dillard looked uncomfortably at the floor, taken aback by the ferocity of the attack.

His lover continued. "Not only do I wish I had run him over, I wish I'd fuckin' killed him! No one deserves it more!"

"Calm down—" Dillard tried to say, but his hot-tempered boyfriend cut him off.

"Calm down? *You* calm down! I'll admit it, I have an ax to grind. But, believe me, before this night is through, Blake Jackson will be history. Cameron Fuller will see him for what he truly is. Worthless.

I will see to that personally." Steel determination came through, and Dillard actually felt a small stab of fear.

Dillard was shocked to discover he saw a complete stranger in front of him. "I've never seen this side of you before. I'm not sure I like it."

"Who gives a shit what you like? Let's go. We're late."

"You ready?"

Blake looked from Cameron to the hundreds of people clogging the bleachers and roped-off areas. He looked back at Cameron. "I think so. I'm excited, but kinda scared. I still can't believe this is happening to me."

"Well, it is. Enjoy it. Moments like this only come along once or twice in a lifetime." Cameron put his hand on top of Blake's and squeezed it gently.

"Well," Blake sighed. "If that's true, than I can't tell you how happy I am that you're here to share it with me. I love you, Cam. Thanks for everything."

"Oh, babe, don't. You'll get me crying."

Blake leaned over and the two men hugged hard.

"Okay," Cam said. "Let's do it." He nodded at Oscar, who got out of his door, walked to the back of the car, and opened Cameron's door. Cameron stepped out of the limo, and was greeted with a tornado of flashes. The crowd's dull roar became a crescendo and Cameron waved happily to the multitudes gathered for this event.

Blake emerged next. He glanced up at the new banners hanging from the store's front. They were images of him from the Big Bear shoot, and again, he looked *good.* He was temporarily blinded by the hundreds of camera flashes going off in his face, and Cameron actually had to reach out and grab his arm to lead him away from the car.

As the crowd realized he was the man from the thirty-foot banners, the screaming began. People thrust autograph books and pens at him and hands were shoved out for a brief shake. The wave of adulation was overwhelming and Blake found himself too stunned to speak. Cameron was a few paces in front of him and he focused on his back. They finally entered the store and a whole new round of photographers' flashes went off. There was a round of applause, but Blake couldn't tell if it was for Cameron or for him.

The PR people quickly ushered Blake and Cam into the ladies' Manhattan Label room, which also had been cleared of furniture. Smartly outfitted servers wafted through the throng of people offering up Wolfgang Puck delicacies from silver platters.

They were headlong into the pre-party.

Blake blinked a few times and tried to find a familiar face in the room. He could see Rafael standing by the fireplace, highball in hand, talking heatedly with Dillard, the corporate suit. He then saw Suzette on the far side of the room. She was chatting blandly with Faye Dunaway.

Suzette was beautifully dressed in a black sequined minidress and slick gold heels. She was wearing the most stunning diamond necklace and earring set. She caught his eye and he watched in fascination as her expression changed from one of utter boredom to one of extreme hatred.

Past Suzette, Blake saw Rand and Brady talking to each other. Blake had made sure they were both invited to the shindig, and he wanted to go talk to them, but the crowd was too thick. He waved at them, but they didn't see him.

"Blake! Congratulations! This is so cool!" Clay Beasley said loudly. He had walked up behind Blake, and now shook his hand mightily.

"Thank God! A friendly face!" Blake exhaled happily. "I hardly know anyone here."

Clay held up his gift bag and indicated the free bottle of Pacific Coast Highway cologne inside. "I like this scent! It really stinks good," he cracked.

"Yeah, it does, doesn't it?" Blake agreed.

Clay smiled, and turned behind him. "Trav? Trav, come say hello to Blake."

Travis Church, quite possibly the best looking man Blake had ever seen, with the exception of Cameron, came over and gave him a bear hug. "Congratulations! I don't think we've ever met, but Clay's told me all about you. You enjoying your night?"

"It's a little scary. All these people to see me? I hope to Christ I don't trip or anything."

"Ah, you'll be fine, don't sweat it. The trick is to act like it doesn't impress you." Travis winked.

Cameron interrupted them at that moment. "Blake? How you

doing? Everything okay?" He then noticed Travis standing next to Blake. "Travis! Hey, buddy! How are you?"

The two men hugged fondly.

"I'm good, I'm good," Travis laughed.

Cameron turned to Blake and indicated the handsome television star. "You know, I gave him his start. He filled out a pair of jockey shorts better than anybody I'd ever seen." He then leaned over to his lover. "Until you," he whispered into Blake's ear.

Blake smiled broadly. "I sure as shit hope so, or you ain't getting any tonight," he whispered back.

As Suzette witnessed the intimate exchange from across the room, her blood boiled.

Cameron excused Blake and himself, and they went to the VIP room for a quick breather. The VIP room had been closed for the event so that Cameron and his private party could have a place to go and get away from the madness of the crowds.

A security guard at the door checked their yellow security badges and let them in. Cameron carefully closed the door behind them. The VIP room was really nothing more than a small sitting room filled with comfortable chairs and sofas. It had been created so that important clients or celebrities could shop in the store without having to wander around being annoyed by fans. Sales staff would bring suggestions to them in here, while the celeb would munch on snacks or enjoy a cool drink from the fully equipped bar.

"Hey," Cameron said, slipping his arms around Blake.

"Hey," Blake replied, pulling in close for a deep kiss.

"You're a sensation," Cameron murmured between kisses.

"Everyone's told me they like the smell of the cologne, so I think that's the sensation."

The two men resumed their heavy petting, and didn't even hear the door open.

"Good God!" Silas thundered as he saw the intensity between the two lovers. He had never personally witnessed two grown men kissing passionately, and he was shocked to his core.

"Jesus Christ!" Suzette shrieked. She had walked in a second after her father, but still had a clear view of her husband locked in the arms of his male lover.

Blake tried to pull away from Cameron, feeling like he was caught in the act of doing something wrong, but Cameron had a firm hold on his arms, and held him close.

"Hello, Silas. Suzette," Cameron calmly said, nodding his head slightly at them. "PCH seems to be a big hit, don't you think?"

"Mother of God! You dare to speak to me while you hold your . . . your . . ." Silas sputtered, not able to bring himself to say the word "lover."

"And what would you have me do with the man I love?" Cameron asked, genuinely curious.

"You bastard! How can you say that in front of my father? In front of me?!" Suzette screamed. The security guard stuck his head into the room to see what the fuss was, but Suzette spun around and slammed the door shut, barely missing his face.

"Suzette, please control yourself," Cameron warned.

"Control myself?! I walk in here and find you with him? That fucking whore you've plastered all over our building?! I'm supposed to calm down? We had a deal! Get him out of here, now!" She shook with rage. The veins in her neck were standing out and she was clutching her highball glass so tightly that her knuckles were white.

"No," Cameron calmly said.

"I said get that piece of scum out of my sight! You can fuck his white trash ass on your own time, but not here!"

"Okay, that's it! I will not stand here and be put down by this fucking bitch anymore," Blake said, his voice shaking with anger. He left Cameron's arms and took a step toward Suzette.

"What did you call me?" Mrs. Cameron Fuller was shocked to her core that this faggot would dare speak about her in such a way.

"I called you a fucking bitch," Blake said evenly, staring her dead in the eye. "But, let me repeat it slowly, so you'll understand each word. You. Are. A. Fucking. *Bitch!* Did you hear that?" he asked, his eyebrows raising.

The look of stunned surprise on Suzette's face was priceless. Even Silas was taken aback by the ferocity of Blake's cold rage.

Cameron just had to laugh.

"You *faggot,*" Suzette hissed, her eyes narrowing into slits. "How dare you speak to me that way! You're nothing! A piece of trash that my husband is pity-fucking. And you have no idea who you're messing with, boy."

"Yeah, I do. A lunatic cunt. Now, why don't you get your pampered ass out of here and leave us alone?" Blake retorted.

Silas finally found his voice and took a step forward. "You shut your mouth, young man. That's my daughter you're speaking to, and I've heard enough!"

"Suzette, I warned you not to do this. You just don't listen, do you?" Cameron said slowly.

"I don't need you to defend me against this faggot, Daddy," Suzette snarled out, ignoring Cam. "You're such an idiot," she said to Blake.

"Oh, really? How's that?"

"He'll never love you completely!" She jerked a thumb in Cameron's direction. "He's already had the love of his life, and it ain't you, boy! You'll never be able to overcome what he felt for my brother! *They* were in love! They were meant to be together, not you two! You fool! You'll never truly own his heart!" she crowed. Only too late did she realize that she had made this pronouncement in front of her father.

"What?" Silas took a step back, as if hit.

"Oh, Daddy, wake up! Cameron and Stanton were *lovers!* They lived together in college for Christ's sake! Stanton loved him more than he ever loved you, or me."

"No! No, I won't hear this." Silas shook his head back and forth in denial. "Cameron *tricked* him! He seduced him! Stanton didn't love him . . . He couldn't!"

Cameron turned his back to Suzette and Silas. He walked a few steps away, over to the bar, and gripped the counter with both hands.

"Oh, Daddy! Stanton, your fair-haired golden boy, was a fruit! They used to fuck in your bed at the house in Bedford for kicks! And you never knew! All this time, you never knew. You never loved me the way you loved Stanton, and he's been dead for twenty-five years. Why couldn't you love me, Daddy? Why?" Suzette was pleading with her father now.

"Suzette, for God's sake, shut up!" Cameron shouted from his position at the bar.

"Fuck you, Cameron! It's time Daddy faced the facts. Tell him. Tell Daddy that you and his son were in love. Tell him! He never believes anything I say." Suzette threw up her hands in disgust. She crossed over to Cameron's side and began to make herself a fresh drink.

"Is this true, Cameron? Is it?" There was a faint trace of hope in the old man's voice that he would not hear what he knew he would. What he had only recently begun to believe.

Cameron sighed, then shrugged his shoulders. "Yes. It's true. We were both so devastated by Stan's death that we came together. We thought we'd never be able to love anyone like we loved Stanton. We got married to share our pain. It made sense then. It doesn't make any sense now," he whispered, hot tears threatening to fall from his eyes.

"And you got your green card, you fucking *Canadian!*" Suzette pointed out spitefully.

"How . . . How is this possible . . . *My* son?" Silas babbled. He rubbed his forehead with his liver-spotted hands and tried to blot out the words.

"Suzette and I promised each other we'd never tell you the real reason we married. That was wrong, and I'm sorry. But, since we're all being so candid tonight, Silas, there's something else you should know. Something about the night Stan died," Cameron said quietly, walking back to Blake's side. He put his arm around his lover's waist and squeezed.

Suzette perked up, and wheeled around. "No! No, don't!"

"I warned you, Suzette. I begged you not to cause a scene tonight, but you wouldn't listen. Fine. You pay the price, then."

She flew at Cameron, arms upraised, her right hand still clutching her glass, the fluid inside spilling all over the place. "No!" she screamed. She swung at Cameron in her wrath.

Cameron easily deflected her feeble blows. He shoved her gently, but firmly, away from him. She tripped on her high heels, and stumbled backwards and sat down hard in an easy chair that was positioned behind her.

"Silas, Suzette and I also made a pact never to tell you what really happened the night Stan died, but I can't see that keeping it has done any good. I think you deserve to know the truth."

Silas, fearing the unknown, but also knowing he had to hear what had actually happened that night, nodded solemnly.

Suzette, starting to cry, buried her face in her hands.

"We had gone to a party that night," Cameron began. "Stanton and I had been fighting all day. We'd been fighting about telling you about us. I wanted to, to get it out in the open, but he was afraid if we did, you'd cut him off. We'd been back and forth about it all afternoon . . ."

35

"Why not? Give me a better reason why not," Cameron said, his face flushed with annoyance. He threw his copy of The Deep down on the floor and faced his boyfriend, hands on hips. They were in Stanton's bedroom, which was actually their bedroom, only they never let Silas Cabbott know that. As far as Silas knew, his son's friend slept in the downstairs suite.

"Because he won't be able to handle it! How many times do I have to say it? Fuck, Cam, grow up! In the real world, what we are is not normal! He'd never understand, and I'd be left without a dime! Can you really see me flipping burgers at McDonald's? Because I can't. Just forget it, okay?" Stanton argued. He ran his fingers through his feathered sandy blond hair and turned his back on his boyfriend.

"You don't love me. That's what this is really about, isn't it?" Cam pouted. He crossed his arms across his chest and picked at his silver Timex Twist-O-Flex watch.

Stan sighed heavily and turned back to face his boyfriend again. "Cam, stop acting like a twelve-year-old girl! Of course I love you. My God, why do you think this is so hard on me? I never knew I could love anyone the way I love you. We'll be together forever."

"I just hate the sneaking around and lying to your father, that's all," Cam sighed. He flopped down on the water bed, ripples radiating out to the sideboards and back. His cut-off blue jean shorts were riding up, so he reached down and tugged them back into place.

"How do you think I feel? Jeez, you act like I like all this." Stanton *reached out and picked up his puka shell necklace from the bureau. Reaching behind his neck, he screwed the small clasp together. "Listen, Suzette wants to go to the party at Dillard and Michael's tonight with us. I said she could. I hope you don't mind."*

"I kinda hoped we'd be able to spend some time away from her. She's always around, Stan. I don't think she likes me very much. I think she's in love with you!" Cam teased.

"Yuck! That's gross! She's my twin sister. We have a bond. You don't understand it because you don't have a twin. And she likes you fine." He pulled himself away from the mirror and held out his hands. "Well? How do I look?" he asked. His faded chinos fit his slim waist perfectly, and the pale yellow Izod polo shirt showed off his tan wonderfully.

"Mmm, good enough to eat!" Cam yelped, jumping to his feet and sweeping his boyfriend into his arms and kissing him repeatedly.

"Down, boy. I have to leave. Is that what you're wearing?"

Cam looked down at his green rugby shirt and the tight cutoff shorts. "Yup."

"I hate it when you show off your ass like that," Stan admonished. "All the boys will be staring at it."

"That's the plan. Keeps you on your toes." Cam pulled on a worn pair of Topsiders. "So, you're going to stop by campus and pick up your sister and head over to the party, right?"

"Yup. How late are you working?"

"Only till nine. I'm only going in to lock up. I told Sal I needed the night off." Cam worked part-time at a small men's store in the Village. He knew he wanted to be involved in the fashion industry as a career, but he hadn't yet decided how. So he was a retail slut for now, and he liked it. "I'll meet up with you guys at the party."

"Okay. I'll see you later, turkey," Stanton leaned in for a kiss and then was gone, off to fetch his sister.

"Stan, you're not driving in this condition," Cam insisted, holding up his inebriated boyfriend.

"I've driven lots of times higher and way more drunk than this . . . I'll be fine," Stan slurred.

"Jesus, Stanton. Don't be so pigheaded. Let Cam drive and let's

get the fuck out of here. How I let you talk me into coming out to Long-fucking-Island, I'll never know!" Suzette stamped her Jacques Cohen white canvas espadrille in the soft dirt, and was instantly annoyed. The soft cloth shoes were impossible to clean once they got dirty. "Now, hand me the doobie," she ordered. Stanton passed the joint to her and she inhaled deeply. She passed it to Cameron. Cameron also took a long hit.

Suzette exhaled slowly and let her head fall forward. Her shoulder-length dark hair was held back off her face by a lime green grosgrain ribbon which contrasted perfectly with her pink Lily Pulitzer sundress.

The party in the city at Dillard and Michael's had been a bust, and by the time Cam had joined them, Stan had heard word of a better bash way out on Long Island, and he insisted they drive out there. Suzette bitched about the long drive, of course, but, as usual, she deferred to her brother's decision.

Stan's silver Mercedes-Benz 280 SL had been blocked in by other guests' cars, so they all hopped into Cam's four-year-old blue Ford Maverick and took off for the parkway.

The party on Long Island was only marginally better, and after three drinks Stan was ready to bolt. But he insisted on driving, and he was in no shape to do it.

Cam and Stan got into an argument, each insisting that the other wasn't going to drive. It started to get heated, and Suzette, anxious to get the hell out of Long Island, grabbed Cam's keys and said she was going to drive.

The wind was blowing through the open windows, making all three passengers' hair fly about wildly. Cam's air conditioner had broken down weeks before and he hadn't bothered to get it fixed. It was a warm spring night and Suzette found she was actually enjoying the drive. The doobie was gone now, and Cam and Stan were in the backseat nestled up against each other, eyes closed.

"Hey, guys? I think I'm lost. Where's the turnpike?" Suzette strained to see ahead of her headlights. She was on a residential street and couldn't seem to find her way to the highway.

"Just look for the signs. You'll see one soon," Stan called out from the back.

"Look for the sign! Look for the sign!" Cam joked. Stanton thought this was hilarious and began to laugh uproariously.

"Oh, shut up, both of you. Fat lot of help you all are!" Suzette huffed, turning down another road. "I have no idea where the fuck we are."

"Mmm, who cares? I got all I need right here. I got my hot boyfriend." Stan grabbed at Cam's crotch and squeezed it hard. Cam liked the touch and spread his legs a bit wider. Stan took that opportunity to slide two fingers up one of the short legs, grazing Cam's balls. "And my best friend in the world, my sister! I don't give a fuck if we're lost!"

Stan didn't let go of Cam. He continued to squeeze, tease, and play with Cam's balls. He was immensely enjoying the fact that he could feel his boyfriend getting hard under his touch.

"Mmm, Stan, stop . . . ," Cam protested meekly, as he opened his legs even wider.

"I don't want to stop, baby," Stan murmured, reaching up with his free hand and pulling Cam's face to his. He kissed him hard, and repeatedly. Cam's soft grunts turned to loud groans as he felt his boyfriend unbutton the fly of his shorts and dig in to pull out his rock-hard cock.

Suzette glanced in the rearview mirror and watched the goings on in the backseat with bemused detachment.

Stan was stroking Cam's dick and Cam thought he was going to go out of his mind. He was so turned on by the naughtiness of what they were doing, out in the open, right behind Stan's sister. He climbed on top of Stanton, not an easy task in the small backseat. He dug in himself, and freed Stan's erection. Soon the men were rubbing their dicks together, each writhing in pleasure.

"Oh, baby," Stan whispered. "I want you to fuck me right now! I want it, right here. I want to feel you inside me! Give it to me, please, baby. Please."

"Stan! We can't . . . your sister's right there!"

"Fuck her! She can find her own dick! I want this one, and I want it now," he panted softly. He reached down and clumsily pulled off his pants and spread his legs so that Cam was situated between them, his hard cock pressing right up against his ass. "Mmm, that's it, just slip it in now, baby. Give it to me," he urged.

"Stan, I can't." Cam nervously glanced up and saw Suzette looking back at him through the rear view mirror.

"Do it, baby," Stan commanded. *"She watches us all the time. There's a hole in the wall at home that she watches us through. She doesn't care. Fuck, I watch her get it all the time, too. It's no big deal."*

Cam stopped his gentle pushing. *"What?"*

"Isn't that right, Suz? You watch Cam fuck me all the time, don't you? You get off on it. Admit it," Stan called up to his sister.

Cameron watched Suzette glance from him to Stan, then back to the road.

"Yes," she admitted quietly. *"I watch."*

"And I bet you touch yourself while you're watching, huh?" Stan laughed, as he reached down, grabbed Cam's cock, and lined it up against his opening. He brought his hand back up close to his mouth, and hawked up a large wad of spit into it. He reached back down and slathered Cam's cock with the spittle. He then pushed his weight down a bit and felt the first sensations of being penetrated.

"Sometimes," she agreed.

Stan groaned loudly, then he pushed down more to take Cam deeper in. *"Mmmm, yeah, baby! . . . Oh, I jerk off watching her get fucked all the time, don't I, Suz! . . . Yeah . . . This is what I want!"*

"Stan, I don't . . . I can't do this . . ." Cameron was so confused. He was high and had drunk too much, and was completely turned on. He wanted to please his lover, but at the same time he was mortified that he had been spied on during those most intimate moments, and that Stan knew about it. Not to mention Suzette checking them out constantly in the mirror as she drove ever more erratically down the empty road.

"Yeah, fuck me, baby . . . Fuck me good!"

"Yes, Cam. Fuck him! Give it to him!" Suzette said, a strange lilt in her tone.

Stan kept moving under him, inching him deeper inside, and soon Cam picked up the motion and began to thrust back and forth. Something came over him, and the rawness of what he was doing, the newness of exhibitionism, the exquisite sensations he was feeling, all turned him on so much that he began to pump harder. He loved to *hear Stan beg for it, and Stan was in fine form tonight. Stanton was a wild man, begging, groaning, and squirming around under him, clawing at his back in ecstasy, yelling for more.*

Suzette by now had given up on the mirror and was turning around to stare blatantly. When she felt the car swerve, she'd whip around and correct the steering, then turn around and watch some more.

"Come on, Cameron! Fuck him! Fuck him good! It's what he wants! Oh, Stan, you look so happy!" she cried out, giddy.

"On top! I want to sit on top!" Stan suddenly decided. There was a moment of awkward fumbling as the two large men shifted positions in the small space.

But where there's a will, there's a way.

Stan was soon impaled on Cam and moving his ass up and down. His hands were braced on the headliner of the car and his weight was all in his knees.

"Yeah, baby! Ride him like a bronco," Suzette laughed, turning around again to watch the show.

"Oh, man! This is so wild! I love it! I love you, Cam . . . Oh, man . . . You feel so hard inside me!" Stan was tilting his head back and enjoying the fucking. He looked over and saw his sister watching him, a glazed look in her eyes. He smiled at her, and leaned over. She stood up as best she could in the confines of the seat, absently pressing her right foot harder on the accelerator, and leaned back.

Cameron watched in amazement as Stanton kissed his sister with a passion that he had only seen reserved for him.

Suzette slipped in her seat, and broke the kiss. The sudden end to it made Stan open his eyes. From the depths of the backseat, Cam witnessed a change come over Stan's face. From a look of passion to a look of terror.

"Suzette! Look out!" Stan yelled, moving his hands down.

Startled by the shout, Suzette glanced to the front of the speeding car, and saw the tree she was headed for. There was no time to react, and the front right side of the small car hit the large oak with a crashing sound that seemed to come from hell itself.

Cam felt himself sliding forward in slow motion, and he watched in detached wonder as his lover was pulled off him and pitched forth toward the cracking windshield. He tried to cry out a warning, but he was smashed into the back of the front passenger seat. He felt a searing pain shoot through his right arm. Stars exploded in his eyes and the last thing he saw before blacking out was Stan's feet flying past him and over Suzette's head.

36

Suzette was staring at her hands, nervously rubbing them over each other. "You promised me . . . You bastard, you promised me," she moaned over and over.

"You!" Silas stared at his daughter as if he'd never seen her before. "You did this awful thing? You were driving? Not Stanton. You?"

Suzette looked up and locked eyes with her father. "Yes."

"You killed him. You did, as surely as though you held a gun to his head! Such depravity! What were you thinking?" His voice began to rise as he got more upset. He was ashen faced, standing directly over his surviving child. "You allowed him to do these . . . perverse acts in your presence? My God! You killed him! You killed my boy!"

Tears started to flow as Suzette shook her head back and forth. "No! It was an accident! I was young! We were *all* so young and irresponsible! I didn't know . . . I'm so sorry, Daddy! I'm so sorry . . ."

"Irresponsible? That's an understatement!" Silas thundered. "You killed your own brother with your slatternly ways! I have always been dissatisfied with you, Suzette. You never had your mother's style or grace or beauty. Your strongest character traits are selfishness and pettiness. I had at least hoped you had inherited my brains, but you lack even those. You are a waste of human tissue. I cannot stand the sight of you. Get out of here! Leave me alone." The old man walked stiffly to the bar and hung his head. "I don't ever want to see you again."

Suzette stood up and boldly faced her father's back. "You're disappointed in *me?* That's a laugh! When you have done *nothing* but disappoint me every day of my life? When have you *ever* been there for me? When? I'm speaking to you, *old man!* I have spent my life trying to be everything you wanted. But no matter how hard I tried, no matter what I did, it was *never* enough!" The tears ran down her cheeks and she shook in her fury. "All you ever cared about was a faggot who died years ago!"

Silas spun around and raged, "Shut your filthy mouth, you bitch!" He slapped Suzette across the face. Hard. "Don't you speak about your brother like that!"

Suzette's head snapped to the right, but she absorbed the blow. She slowly faced her father again, defiant. "We were young and we made a mistake and Stanton died. Deal with it! Get over it. You have never even given me a chance to be anything *but* a disappointment to you! Well, fuck you, you bitter, sad, pathetic excuse for a man. Fuck you!" She spun around and marched out the door.

Blake and Cameron stood silently watching Silas. When they saw his shoulders start to convulse in racking sobs, they moved to leave the room.

"Not yet. Cameron, you stay. I . . . want to speak with you. Alone," Silas sputtered between sobs.

Blake looked at Cameron, who gently took his arm and led him to the door.

"I'll be right out. I'm so sorry you had to witness the Fuller dirty laundry," he said, eyes downcast.

"And I thought *my* family was fucked up," Blake joked weakly. "You and I should talk about this later, okay? Are you all right?"

"I'm better now. I'm just glad it's out." He leaned forward and kissed Blake tenderly. "See you in a few."

After Blake left there was a strained silence between Silas and Cameron. Finally, Silas turned around and faced his son's lover.

"What have you got to say for yourself?"

"I don't follow."

"You . . . you lead my son into a life of depravity and you don't accept responsibility?"

"Silas," Cam sighed. "It's not a life of depravity. It's just . . . life. And I'm not going to apologize for being who I am. And, no matter how you feel about it, your son *was* gay. I wasn't responsible for that. No one was! What I am responsible for is not being truthful with you about this sorry mess years ago. Suzette was so afraid you'd disown her, shut her out, that I agreed never to speak about it. We were wrong to do that, and I am deeply sorry."

Silas stared at him, his eyes dead.

"Silas, I know it's hard for you to hear, but Stanton and I loved each other very much, and I grieve for him still. I think that's why I was with Suzette for so long. She was a part of him that I could hold on to. But now I've met Blake and I've realized I can love again. It's time for me to bury Stanton as well."

Silas shook his head back and forth.

Cameron actually felt sorry for the old man. He softened his tone. "He's dead, Silas. He lived, and he was loved, and he died. In the long run, who can ask for more than that?"

"I can!" Silas pounded his fist on the bar top. "I want my son back! The two of you . . . you took him from me! I will never accept that!"

"You don't have a choice. He's gone. My God, Silas! It's been twenty-five years! Let him go . . . it's time. You have a daughter that you've practically ignored her entire life! You still have time to build a relationship with her."

"I don't have a daughter!" Silas shouted. "Not anymore!" He started to cry fresh tears. They fell down to his jacket lapel unabashed. "And *you*. You tricked him. You seduced my boy! I don't know how you did it, or why, but you will pay for this. So will Suzette. Mark my words!" His face distorted by the fury he could barely stand, Silas stormed out of the VIP room and was soon lost in the crowd.

Cameron stood rooted in place.

The pre-party went on for another hour and then the rest of the guests began to arrive. The lower floor of the store started to fill up, and soon people began to drift upstairs. A DJ was spinning in a specially built booth in the back of men's sportswear, so hip dance music kept the mood upbeat and lively. Blake wandered about saying hello to seemingly everyone. The PR flack assigned to him whispered in his ear the name of each reporter he came across, so it appeared that he knew them all on sight.

Everywhere he looked he saw another celebrity. The place was crawling with them. When he saw Cameron again, he had changed into his suit. He was listening intently as his investor, Dillard, was speaking into his ear. Cameron's face seemed drawn and tired, and Blake knew whatever had transpired between Silas and him had not been pleasant. He wanted to go and just be near him and show support, but he couldn't get away from the persistent photographers. There was always some new celebrity to be photographed with.

Dillard walked away, and Cameron spied Blake across the rotunda. He desperately wanted to join him. Blake looked a little uncomfortable with all the attention he was getting, and Cam wanted to stand beside his man. It was time for him to completely support the man he loved, and he couldn't get to his side fast enough.

Oprah Winfrey and Drew Barrymore stepped up to Cameron to congratulate him again on his latest accomplishment. They chatted together briefly. As he was listening to Oprah tell how nervous she had been during the opening of her first restaurant, he saw Silas standing back from the crowd. He was with Dillard Jordon and Harrison Howell. Cam caught his eye, and gave him a tight smile, but the old man ignored him.

Cam nodded at something Drew said, and again caught sight of Blake. They locked eyes and Cam winked at him. He had never wanted to be next to his lover more than he did now. "Excuse me. I see someone I have to say hello to," he apologized, turning away from Oprah and the actress.

He felt a tug on his sleeve.

Rafael had been circling the clump of people around Cam, looking for an opportune moment to get in and suck up to his boss. He was frankly worried that Blake would get him fired. He knew now, belatedly, that he had underestimated Blake and his trick pelvis. But, if there was one thing Rafe could do, it was to adapt. He would figure a way to get back in Cam's good graces, and Blake's, too. Perhaps a really good present for Blake might do the trick.

He saw Cam excuse himself from Oprah and realized it was his chance. He briskly tried to cut through the milling people, but by the time he could get close enough, Suzette had already approached Cam and they were having a "discussion." Suzette was obviously drunk.

Nothing new there, Rafe thought.

Cameron looked very unhappy to have to deal with his soon-to-be ex-wife. Seeing an opportunity, Rafe stepped up to the bickering couple.

"Is everything okay, Cameron?" he asked, putting on a concerned face.

Silas was also watching Cameron and Suzette. Privately seething, disgusted with the both of them, he nonetheless knew they were on the brink of causing a scene. Suzette was obviously drunk.

So the rumors about her drinking are true, he realized. She was a failure in every way. It amazed him that this sullen, stupid creature was the fruit of his loins. Why had he been burdened with her, and robbed of the boy he loved so much?

Not wanting the two people he despised most in the world to bring more attention to their dysfunction, Silas stepped up behind Cameron. Suzette was struggling to shake Cam's grip on her arm. She stumbled on her own feet.

Good God. She was such an embarrassment to him. "Suzette! For God's sake! Sober up!" the old man hissed at her.

Suzette had had enough of her distant father telling her what to do. She tried to flip him off, but couldn't get her fingers to form the right signal. It came off as a weak wave.

As Silas watched his sad excuse for a child stumble off, he was filled anew with a rage so deep he thought he would explode.

Cameron decided Suzette couldn't be left alone. She was too unsteady on her feet. He followed her closely as she picked her way to the staircase. She took a light hold of the banister and was about to descend when she stumbled because of her shoes. Quick as lightning, Cameron reached down and grabbed her arm, pulling her back up to level ground.

"Jesus, Suzette! Be careful," he said, his heart racing from the close call.

"Let me go, you bastard!" she barked at him, and she whipped her arm out of his grasp. "I can take care of myself. Fuck off!" She again attempted to go down the stairs.

"Suzette, here. Let me help you."

Cameron sighed in relief as Silas stepped in and took his daughter's arm.

"Easy now, Suzette. You've had too much to drink," Silas said soothingly as he and Suzette stepped down the stairs.

"Oh, Daddy, thank you," she said in heartfelt gratitude. Her daddy had come to rescue her. Just like she had always dreamed of him doing.

Silas stopped for a moment, which caused Suzette to stop as well. She looked at him expectantly. "What is it, Daddy?" she asked.

"You killed my boy. I can never forgive you for that," he whispered to her, tightening his grip on her arm.

"Daddy, you're hurting me," she groaned, trying to pull her arm away. She was surprised by the strength in his grip.

"I'll see you in hell, you bitch!"

Suzette's eyes opened wide as Silas jerked her arm forward, causing her to lose her balance. She screamed, and Silas whipped her around and let go. She teetered on the edge of a step, but her forward motion carried her weight over. She lost her footing and fell.

At first, Cameron was frozen in place. But, as he watched Suzette bounce down the hard stone steps, he came to his senses. "Suzette! My God!" he shouted, and he took off down the steep staircase after her.

He passed Silas, who was rooted in place, dully staring at his daughter's tumbling form. Halfway down the staircase, Cam slipped on a slick dark red patch. His stomach turned when it registered that it was blood. He righted himself and continued down after his wife. He wasn't even aware of the flashes from the multitudes of cameras now pointing his way.

By the time he got to Suzette's lifeless form, there was nothing he could do. He lifted her upper body and hugged her to him. Her head lolled back and her unseeing eyes stared blankly out into nothingness.

"Call 911! Someone, please! 911!" Cameron cried out. Just then, he glanced up and saw Blake, and he focused on his lover's shocked face.

37

"Cam? Do you want some coffee or anything?" Blake asked, placing a warm hand on his lover's shoulder.

"No, I'm fine. Thanks, babe." He smiled weakly, his eyes red.

"So, Brady, what happens now?" Blake asked. They sat on the sofa in the VIP room while the coroner removed Suzette's body. Brady had switched into work mode and volunteered to coordinate efforts between the Beverly Hills police and Cameron. The guests and event staff had all been ordered to leave the store hours ago, and now Cameron and Blake were waiting to be told they could leave.

"Well, Mr. Cabbott has been taken into custody and is being booked now. I don't think he'll be getting bail anytime soon. We have over a hundred witnesses who saw him deliberately shove his daughter down the stairs, not to mention all the photographers who captured it on film."

"Oh, my God. I just can't believe this," Cameron moaned. He was in borderline shock, and Blake was deeply worried about him.

"I think you two can leave now. The B.H.P.D. have your statements. They'll contact you if they have more questions. I'd just go home and try to get some sleep."

"Thanks, Brady," Blake said. He stood up and hugged his ex-boyfriend warmly.

"I should let you two know that there are paparazzi all over the place outside. Is there a way out of here through the basement?"

Cameron shrugged, but Blake spoke up. "Yes. I know how to get out. I just need a car in the garage below us."

"I got mine back from the valet when they were shutting down. It's already parked on level two." Brady dug into his pockets and handed his keys over to Blake.

"How will you get home?"

Brady nodded toward Rand, who was standing alone in the far corner. "Rand'll take me. Don't worry about me. Just get out of here. I'll get the car from you tomorrow."

"Thanks, Brady. I appreciate everything you've done for us to-night." Cameron stood up as well, and also hugged the officer.

Brady stiffened, but then relaxed and accepted the hug. "Go on. Get out of here."

Blake took Cam's arm and led him out of the VIP room and to the elevator bank. In minutes they were safely ensconced in Brady's sensible, but nondescript Taurus, and speeding out of the garage past startled photographers who realized too late that Cameron Fuller and Blake Jackson had gotten away.

"Damn! I'm so glad to be away from there," Blake said, steering Brady's car down Santa Monica Boulevard.

Cam stared out the window in silence.

"Hey," Blake said, glancing at him. "Cam, I'm so sorry about Suzette. I truly am." He reached his hand across and placed it on Cam's knee. He gently rubbed it back and forth. "Talk to me, Cam. Tell me what you're feeling."

Cam shook his head.

"Okay, okay. I'm sorry."

Cam sniffed and Blake noticed the tears falling from his cheeks.

"Oh, baby." Blake shot a quick look behind him, and seeing the lane was clear, pulled over to the curb. He flicked on his hazards and leaned across the center console. He wrapped his strong arms around his beloved. Cam buried his head in Blake's chest, great sobs racking his body.

"Shh . . . shhh, it's okay . . . it's okay," Blake soothed.

"I just can't believe this . . . She's really dead . . . Oh, my God!" Cam sobbed.

"I know, honey . . . I know . . ."

"How could Silas do that? To his own child? I don't under-stand . . ."

Not having any answers, Blake just held his lover tightly and gently rocked him. Eventually Cam's sobs subsided. He looked up at Blake. "I'm all right. I'm all right. Let's go home. I'll deal with this tomorrow. Let's just go home."

"You got it." Blake pulled back into traffic and continued on their way home.

"Do you have any Kleenex? I'm pretty messed up here," Cam said, patting his suit pockets down for a nonexistent handkerchief.

"I don't, but Brady usually has one of those travel pack things in the glove box. Look there."

Cameron popped open the glove box and rummaged through the debris it contained. He pulled out a stubby object.

"What's this?" he asked, holding up the gunmetal gray cylinder.

Blake glanced over and recognized it instantly. "It's a silencer. Brady took me shooting one time, and he had that thing attached to his gun."

"Kinda creepy to keep it in the car, isn't it?" Cam noted, putting it back and finding the small package of tissues. He pulled two out of the pack and then closed the glove box door.

"Well, he is a cop, you know. I'm sure there're firearms all over this vehicle."

"Great. Now I feel safe."

Twenty minutes later they pulled up to Blake's house. He parked the car on the street and quickly hopped out to open Cam's door for him. As he was rounding the front of the car he noticed a cracked blinker light lens cover and scraped fender on the right side. His first thought was that he somehow did it while driving home, but he knew that was silly. He hadn't hit anything.

"What are you staring at?" Cam asked, letting himself out of the car.

"Oh, nothing. Brady must've had an accident. The car's dented. Anyway, are you hungry? I don't know that I have anything in the fridge, but we can always order something in."

It was one in the morning, and Blake and Cam still hadn't fallen asleep. They were spooned up against each other, staring into the dark. Every so often one of them would softly speak about what he was feeling and the other would listen carefully.

Cam actually did most of the talking, and Blake learned more about his difficult relationship with Suzette. As Cam talked about his former wife, it was obvious that he had once cared for her deeply, but had become so disenchanted with her that he had lost sight of her good qualities. That was what he was grieving for, the woman she had been so long ago, and her unused potential.

Cam was stroking Blake's back, and telling him about the hilarious time Suzette insulted Princess Margaret, when they heard voices in the backyard. Blake leaned over, and parted the soft linen curtain on the opened window. He saw Rand stumbling toward his door, another man close behind him, cupping Rand's ass cheeks in his hands.

"Shhh! You'll wake them up," Rand said in a loud whisper.

"I don't care," came the slightly slurred response. "Fuck 'em . . . Fuck Blake! And speaking of fucking, I'm gonna fuck you like you've never had it before, baby."

Blake's eyes grew large.

It was Brady.

"Oh, man!" Rand said, grabbing Brady's lapels and pulling him close. They kissed in a very sloppy, drunken way. When they broke apart, Rand fumbled at his door, trying to open it. "I can't believe I'm doing this! I've had a thing for you for, like, forever. I'm so drunk! I hope I don't pass out too soon."

Blake was shocked. What the hell was this about? Rand and Brady?! Had the world gone crazy? Even though he used to joke mildly about Rand's obvious crush on him, Brady had never given Rand a second look. It was all so weird.

"What's going on out there? Who's with Rand? Is Sam out of the hospital?" Cam asked, pulling Blake back down into the warm confines of the bed.

"No. It's Brady! He's with Brady! What the fuck?"

"What do you care?" Cam asked pointedly. "Are you jealous?"

That took Blake aback.

Was he?

"No, I . . . Okay. A little, I guess. I shouldn't be, I know. I have you now, and I wanted him to find somebody . . . but . . . Rand? Brady hasn't dated anyone else since me, so I guess he's due. But, *Rand?* It's just so weird, that's all."

The noises from outside subsided as Rand and Brady went inside the tiny studio apartment.

"Well, I wouldn't worry about Brady. And you're wrong about him not seeing anyone," Cam said nonchalantly. "Though his sleeping with your tenant tonight doesn't bode well for Dillard."

Blake rolled over and faced Cam. "What are you talking about?"

"I meant to tell you this earlier, but then Suzette . . ." the unspoken words hung in the air. Cam took a deep breath and continued speaking. "Remember I told you I have an old college buddy on the board? Dillard Jordan?"

Blake remembered. The lover-lawsuit guy. He nodded.

Cameron continued, pulling Blake closer. "Did I mention that his ex burned his house down to the ground as an act of revenge?" Blake nodded again. "Well, whatever he used to torch the house was undetectable. The fire investigators couldn't say whether it was arson or not. Dillard convinced the insurance company that a candle had fallen over and started the fire. You see, he didn't want his ex to go to *jail,* he just wanted him out of his life. But, in his deposition for the lawsuit, his ex states it *was* arson, only he says Dillard planned it. He's threatening to reveal how it was done. If the palimony case goes to trial, Dillard will most likely lose the six million dollar insurance claim, and he could be charged not only with arson but also with insurance fraud. Somehow, Silas found out about the deposition and used it against Dillard."

"Good God. I need a scorecard to keep up with this," Blake joked weakly.

"It gets even more interesting. Brace yourself. Dillard was out here a few months ago, meeting some vendors. He's an avid cyclist. He was biking along Sunset, or Santa Monica, one of those streets, and got clipped by a car. He wasn't hurt, but your Officer Brady happened to come upon the accident. They started to date right after that, but on the sly, because Dillard couldn't appear to be fucking around, the very thing he was accusing his lover of doing."

"What?" Startled, Blake sat upright.

"Like I said, Silas somehow found out about the torch job on the house and threatened to go to the authorities about the insurance fraud. He basically blackmailed Dillard into spying on us."

"You knew this? Why didn't you tell me?" Blake was stunned.

"Because I only found out tonight. Dillard pointed out Brady at the party and told me the whole story."

"Oh, my God! This is crazy . . ." Blake's head was swimming. "Why would Dillard come clean with you about this tonight?"

"He wanted to warn me about Silas. He told me Silas was planning something against me, and he begged forgiveness for informing on us. He said Brady had been his little spy."

"Oh, please. I don't believe that for a minute!"

"That's what he says. I know you don't like to hear this, but it makes sense."

"It's just not possible. Brady is my friend. He would *never* do that to me. Dillard is lying." Blake rolled over on his side and hugged his pillow tightly.

It couldn't be true. It just couldn't!

"Look, babe, let's just forget about it. Forget about Brady. It doesn't matter anymore." He took a deep sigh. "And, as for Rand and him, well, it doesn't affect you or me, *either,* does it? It actually takes a load off my mind. I don't feel the need to be jealous over . . ." he pointed out the window, ". . . that."

Blake sat in the dark, his mind swirling. He tried to sort out all this new information. He had thought that Brady was pining away for him, yet he was dating someone else all the time.

How stupid am I? he thought.

Loud moans and groans soon wafted through the window. Rand was apparently getting it, but good. Cam and Blake could do nothing but listen to the sounds of hot fucking.

"Oh, God! Yes!" Rand shouted out, clearly audible.

"You like that, baby? Is this what you want?" from Brady.

"Yeah! . . . Oh, yeah . . . Fuck me!" Rand again.

"All right. This is too much!" Blake snapped. He sat up and shut the open window.

"Hey, relax. We've made more noise than that before," Cam said, chuckling.

"I'm sorry, but this is all so bizarre! Something just isn't right. I can't put my finger on it, but there's something odd about *all* this."

"Baby, forget about them. Come back to bed. I want to hold you some more, okay? Please?"

Gazing at Cam in the bed, the covers half pulled off his body, reminded Blake of what he had. Observing the look of love and need on Cam's face was exactly what Blake needed to see. He gratefully got back into bed, snuggled up against his partner. Thoughts about Brady were soon forgotten and both men fell asleep.

38

Blake woke up with a start. Something was wrong. When his eyes adjusted to the dark, he saw the form of a powerful man leaning over the bed, his arm outstretched toward Cameron's still form.

"Wake up, Blake," the man said. Blake instantly recognized his voice.

"Brady? What are you doing in here? Get out!"

"Not quite yet." He reached over and turned on the bedside lamp. Blake blinked at the sudden bright light, but when his eyes focused he saw that in Brady's rubber-gloved hand was a revolver. It was pressed hard into Cam's left temple. Cam was awake, and traces of fear were easily readable on his face.

"What are you doing?" Blake's voice rose in confusion and dread.

"Blake, calm down," Cam said evenly.

"Yeah, Blake. Listen to your new boyfriend. Calm down." Brady sneered. He was dressed in his shirt and pants from the party, only the shirt was unbuttoned. "You *had* to go and fuck it up, didn't you? We had it all, you know. I *loved* you! I didn't care that you fucked other men, because you always came back to me. Hell, you think I didn't sneak around a bit? We're men, Blake. It's what we *do*. We fuck around. But you had to go and meet this asshole." He pushed the barrel of the gun hard into Cam's head, causing Cam to groan in pain. "You lost sight of us because of him. I can't accept that."

"Brady, please don't do this," Blake said mechanically, desperately trying to think of some way to defuse this situation.

"Shut up!" Brady snapped. He grabbed Cam's hair with his free hand and pulled him up to a sitting position. "Get up off the bed—

slowly," he said to the frightened designer. "You move one muscle, Blake, and I swear to God, I'll blow him away right here."

Blake helplessly watched the man he loved being herded over to the side chair by the bathroom door.

"Okay, Blake. Come here. Very slowly," Brady directed, carefully watching Blake approach him. He kept the gun pressed hard against Cam's temple. "Now. Take the handcuffs out of my back pocket."

Blake did as he was told, all the while looking for some way to snatch the gun away, but knowing that Brady had been the sharp shooting champion of the Sheriff's Department four years in a row made him reconsider doing anything rash.

"Good. Now, cuff one of your boyfriend's wrists."

Blake looked sorrowfully into Cam's eyes and snapped the cuffs on.

"Now, pull his other arm behind him." Brady intently watched Blake perform this chore. "Perfect. Now cuff that wrist."

Blake did this, too.

"Good boy. See how easy that was? You'd of made a good cop." Brady was still smirking.

Cam was now standing awkwardly, wrists connected behind his back. Brady shoved him down roughly and Cam fell into the chair. He cried out as shooting pain emanated from his bound wrists.

Blake instinctively started to move when he saw his lover's agony, but Brady swung around and pointed the gun directly at him, stopping him in his tracks.

"I wouldn't, if I were you," Brady said serenely. He backed up a few paces and pointed the gun at one and then the other of them. "Now, Blake, get the second pair of cuffs from my other pocket. Slowly. Don't do anything stupid." He took a step forward, and again pressed the muzzle of the gun against Cameron's temple.

Blake tentatively came forward and removed the second pair of handcuffs.

"Cuff one of his ankles."

Blake leaned over and did so as gently as he could.

"Thread the other side through that gap under the seat, and cuff his other ankle."

Blake had to lift Cam's feet up a bit to make it work, and once the second pair of cuffs was securely attached, Blake stepped back. It was an extremely uncomfortable position for Cam, but he stifled any sounds, knowing it pleased the deputy to hear his cries of pain. He tried to move, but found he was completely incapacitated.

"Now, aren't you a little curious what I plan to do with *you,* Mr. Jackson?" Brady taunted, removing the gun from Cam's head and advancing slowly toward Blake.

"Let him go, Brady. You and I can work this out. It has nothing to do with him. Let him go. Please," Blake pleaded.

"It has *everything* to do with him! He stole you away from me with his money and fame, giving you everything you *think* you want! But it's turning out to be not a good night for Fuller, huh? First he saw his wife get murdered by her own father, and now he'll watch his boyfriend getting fucked, and fucked good. So sad." Brady laughed.

"Brady, what the hell are you saying?" Blake asked, recoiling from the words he just heard.

"I'm saying that I'm gonna screw you into next week, right here, in front of your precious new boyfriend. Let's see how *he* likes seeing the man he loves getting laid by someone else."

The flatness in which Brady said those awful words struck Blake more than the meaning of them. His blood ran cold as he realized Brady felt no remorse about what he was doing, and had obviously thought this out beforehand.

"If you think I'm just going to sit here and let you do that, you're crazy," Blake finally said, his tone steel.

"Oh, that's exactly what you're going to do. Unless you want me to shoot him?" Brady swung the lethal weapon around and pointed it at Cam. He cocked back the hammer.

Cam's eyes grew large, but he said nothing.

"No! Don't!" Blake yelled, holding up his hands. "Okay, okay, I'll do it, but promise me you won't hurt Cameron. Promise me, Brady!" he pleaded, defeated. "You'll let him go afterwards?"

Brady grinned evilly, and released the trigger. "You better fuck like a snake, then. *Convince* me. Now, roll over. You're going to love this, I know it," Brady said as he reached down with his free hand and undid his pants. He wiggled his hips back and forth, and the trousers fell to the floor. He wasn't wearing any underwear, and his erection, now freed, was standing stiffly at attention. "Yeah, look at it! It's been too long since you got fucked by this, Blake."

Blake looked at Cam, then at the gun in Brady's hands.

"Do what he says, babe. Just do what he says," Cameron said in calm, soothing tones. "It's going to be all right . . ."

Frustrated and angry at being so helpless, Blake slid over to the side of the bed closest to Brady.

Brady stepped out of his pants, and then slid the shirt off, one arm at a time. "Come on, baby. Let's get it on!" He reached out and man-handled Blake's shoulders. He had incredible hand strength, and he flipped Blake over easily. Blake was face down on the bed, his face buried in the rumpled pillows.

"Yeah . . . that's what I want to see," Brady snarled, climbing up onto the bed himself. He crawled up between Blake's legs, and using his knees, pushed Blake's legs further apart. "Get that ass up in the air, boy!" he commanded.

Blake shifted his head to the right and stared at Cam, who had tears in his eyes. Feeling completely helpless, he turned away from the man he loved. He couldn't look at him while this was going to happen.

"Yeah, nice ass! *Mmmm,*" Brady muttered as he grabbed his cock and placed it up against Blake's ass. He cupped one hand and spit into it.

Blake grimaced. He held his breath and waited for the exact right moment. He knew that Brady always used one hand to guide his cock and the other to cup his own balls as he entered a man. It was his routine, and it never varied. He would have to put the gun down to do that.

Brady didn't disappoint.

He dropped the gun, just for a second, so he could push inside Blake. At the moment Blake felt the gentle bounce of the gun on the bed, he reared back and slammed his body weight into Brady, who was caught totally unawares. He was knocked off balance and fell back. Blake, now on all fours, sprang forward and scrambled out of the way, quickly turning around to try and grab the gun. But Brady's fall backwards had twisted the sheets around, so the gun was covered and Blake couldn't see it.

"You motherfucker!" Brady roared as he slid off the bed, hitting the floor hard with his head and shoulder.

Blake jumped off the bed and thrust his arm under the bed frame to try and find the bat he kept hidden there. He had a tentative hold on it when Brady, now back on his feet, charged at him. In order to get out of his way, Blake let go of the bat and jumped back up on the bed. He leaped down to the other side, opposite Brady, who was scrambling to climb over the mattress.

"Blake! Run! Call 911!" Cameron shouted, straining to free himself. "Run! Get out!"

Blake glanced at Cam, and realized he had to get out of the room. He didn't want to leave his lover alone with the enraged deputy, but their only chance was if he got away and summoned help.

Blake ran out the door and down the darkened hallway. Brady roared in anger again, and ripping the sheets and bedding up and around, searched for his gun. He found it quickly, and raced out the door after Blake.

The second he was out of the room, Cameron renewed his efforts to get free. He swung his legs out and back as hard as he could, and was relieved to hear a cracking sound coming from the old chair.

He redoubled his efforts.

He was rewarded with a solid snap, and he felt his feet swing out freely. He had broken the rail between the seat and legs of the chair, and now his feet were loose, though still cuffed together. He slid out of the chair and fell to the floor, writhing around in great distress. He strained to bring his legs up high enough to pull his arms over his butt and up under his thighs.

He had to get his hands in front of him. That was crucial.

Blake ran down the short hall and straight into the kitchen. He snatched up the cordless house phone and frantically began punching in 911. He was shocked to get a recording telling him to wait just a moment, that someone would be with him shortly.

Brady flew into the room, and seeing Blake's form clearly outlined by the kitchen window, leapt at his former boyfriend. He crashed into Blake with such force that the cordless phone popped out of his hands and sailed across the room. It impacted with the hard slate floor and broke into several pieces.

Blake and Brady smashed into the kitchen table and knocked it over with a huge crashing noise. The revolver again flew out of Brady's hands, and slid across the slate floor, coming to a stop under the refrigerator.

"Rand! Rand! Call 911!" Blake screamed at the top of his lungs as he struggled to break free of Brady's grip.

Brady laughed. "Rand can't hear you right now," he grunted as he manhandled Blake down onto the floor.

"Why? What did you do to him, you sick son of a bitch?" Blake screamed, still thrashing to get free.

Brady got a hold on Blake's right arm and twisted it up behind his back, just as he had been trained to do at the police academy. Blake groaned in anguish, and Brady dragged him to his feet.

"Settle down, now. Settle down! This will go a lot easier if you don't try any stupid stunts like that again!" Brady warned, pulling Blake over to the countertop by the doorway.

"What did you do to Rand?" Blake repeated, dreading the answer.

"Oh, nothing too serious. He's my alibi. I just slipped him a little something that will make him sleep through the night. Tomorrow he'll wake up a little groggy, and he and I will discover the terrible scene here," Brady calmly explained. "If I let you go, will you behave? Not try anything foolish?"

"Yes! Yes, anything you say! You're breaking my arm!"

Brady released Blake and watched him rub his now-sore arm.

"Jesus, Brady! Why? Why are you doing this?"

"It's so easy for you, to just wipe people out of your life." The deputy moved a step closer. "I've got a bulletin for you. I knew all about you and Cameron-fucking-Fuller. I knew the first night he stayed over here after that 'romantic' dinner at Kate Mantalini's. I knew that he gave you that fucking truck! I knew you went to Hawaii to be with him! Did you think you were fooling *me?*" he spat out.

Blake tried to make sense of what Brady was saying. "It's true? You *were* spying on me? On us?"

Brady just grinned.

"You spied on us?" Blake repeated, the realization that it was true breaking his heart.

Brady got even closer. "I *am* a deputy. It's what I do. I follow and watch people. You never even knew."

"Does Dillard know what kind of man you really are?" Blake retorted archly.

Brady's eyes narrowed to slits. "I see someone's been talking. Yeah, Dillard was a convenient lay, but that's all. I told you, you weren't the only one to play around."

Blake realized he didn't know this man standing in front of him. It was as if a complete stranger had inhabited Brady's body. A vague suspicion flutter around Blake's mind, and when it crystalized, Blake began to become very afraid. "How did you get that dent on your car?"

Brady kept grinning. "I think you know how."

"You tried to run me over! That was you! What the fuck, Brady! Why? Why would you do that?" Blake felt his pulse racing, and he tried to slow his rapid breathing.

Just keep him talking, he told himself. *Just keep him talking.*

"I just wanted to scare you. Keep you on your toes. It worked." He laughed.

"I don't know who you are anymore!" He felt something wet on his leg. He jumped, startled.

It was Joe's nose.

"Hey, Joe!" Brady cheerily called to the dog. "Come here, big boy!" The big dog did as he was asked, and he happily walked over to Brady's side and sat down heavily. Brady rubbed his head. "See? Even your dog loves me."

"Brady, you could have killed me! I barely got out of the way!" Blake said. *Just keep him talking,* he reminded himself. *Stall for time to think of something you can do!*

"No. If I had meant to kill you, you'd be dead. Although I did think I killed you when I shot up your house that night. But, alas, I didn't. Imagine my surprise when it turned out I'd shot Rand's boyfriend. I guess it was a temporary insanity thing. I was so incensed that you went to Hawaii with that guy, I didn't know what I was doing. I'm glad you weren't there, now. I think just watching you freak out about it was even better. And who did you turn to for comfort? Little ole me." He just kept scratching Joe's head. "Ironic, isn't it? I think I kill you, and you show up, needing my shoulder to cry on. Priceless."

It was all just too much for Blake to handle. He had so completely misjudged the man in front of him.

"Oh, my God. I think I'm gonna be sick." Blake started to hyperventilate and he bent over so he could breathe better. He wrapped his arms around his stomach and tried to calm down. "You almost killed Sam!"

"Fuck him." Brady took a few steps closer, and towered above the hunched over form of his ex-boyfriend. "If you're gonna hurl, go ahead. I'll think you're weak, but, whatever."

"Who gives a shit what you think?" Blake said, standing tall again.

Brady drew back his right fist and punched it forward, hitting Blake squarely on the right jaw. Blake's head whipped back and smashed into the wall behind him. Stunned, he crumpled to the floor.

"Don't ever talk to me like that again, you hear me? Now, get up," Brady snarled. "I said get up, you pussy!"

Blake was literally seeing stars. When his vision cleared he struggled to get up. "What did you mean when you said Rand was going to be your alibi?" he asked when he was up on steady feet again.

"Because I'm going to kill your new boyfriend. After I fuck you, of course. I want him to *watch* us make love. Then I'll shoot him. Then I'll shoot you. It'll look like a murder-suicide pact between two gay lovers. No one will think twice about it. Poor Rand and I will discover your dead bodies tomorrow."

"No one would buy that! It's insane! No one will believe that I'd kill anyone!" Blake protested, his stomach churning, his jaw sore from the punch he'd just received.

"Oh, but, just like on *CSI,* the evidence will prove it. They'll find the murder weapon in your hand, put there by me after you're dead. And don't forget . . . your fingerprints are all over those handcuffs now." Brady looked triumphant.

Blake knew he was running out of time, and options. He completely believed that Brady was capable of killing him and Cameron. He had to do something, and do it fast, if he was going to save them both.

"Fuck you!" Blake yelled, making the decision to act. He charged at Brady, hoping to catch him off guard and knock him down. But it was like hitting a wall, and Brady, who had somehow sensed the attack, curled up his fist and with a strong uppercut punched Blake so hard he actually lifted up off the ground before falling to the floor like a sack of stones.

"You promised you wouldn't try anything," Brady gloated.

Blake shook his head a couple of times to clear away the fog. His lower lip was bleeding, and he thought he might have lost a tooth. Brady's hands roughly grabbed his shoulders and dragged him to his feet. Brady slammed him up against the wall, lifting him off the floor for a brief second. He leaned in so close that his face was only an inch away from Blake's.

"I've been your lap dog for too long, my friend. Good old Brady, that was me! Always there when you needed a shoulder to cry on, but you left as soon as you got what *you* needed. Never a thought about me. Do you know what a mind fuck that is?"

Blake found he couldn't turn away from the officer. The words cut him like a knife, because he knew they were true.

"You look good scared, you know that? It's turning me on," he said with an ugly leer. He churlishly grabbed Blake's right arm and bent it back so that Blake had to spin around, or risk a broken arm. Brady reached up with his other hand, and placing his hand behind Blake's neck, pushed him down so that his chest was now resting on the kitchen counter, his ass sticking out.

Blake struggled against the hold, but before he knew it, Brady had pressed his crotch against Blake's naked ass, pinning him into the counter. Brady never let go of the back of Blake's neck.

Joe, having seen Blake and Brady wrestle around before, thought nothing of this assault. He lay down, promptly going to sleep.

Blake's face was smashed down onto the cool tile countertop, and he couldn't get any traction to pull away. The blood flowing from his split lip smeared on the counter, and his face got covered in it. He was amazed at how strong Brady was. He could feel his legs getting pried open by the pressure of Brady's weight against him. He felt the the deputy's hard cock press up between his ass cheeks.

In a last ditch effort to get free, he thrashed about as hard as he could, trying to yell for help at the same time. But, because his face was pressed into the counter, it came out muffled and garbled.

Brady spit down onto his throbbing cock. "Yeah, you want this big dick! I know you do. You've needed someone to show you who's boss for a long time," Brady rambled, adjusting his stance, so that the angle was right for pushing into the struggling man he had pinned down.

Blake could feel Brady's barely wet cock start to penetrate him, and the pain was indescribable. He cried out in agony, but the sound was muted by his face-down position.

"Open up, baby . . . let me in," Brady taunted, thrusting his hips forward, entering his ex another tiny bit. "Always kept me at arm's length, didn't you, baby? Not now, huh?" He grunted, then bent over and started licking the trapped man's back.

Blake had never felt so helpless. He started to cry. He was in pain, and absolutely powerless, and he hated the feeling.

This just couldn't be happening to him in his own house!

He heard a brief shout, and then a loud *thunk*. Suddenly, the pressure on his ass and neck was gone, and Brady let him go. Taking advantage of the lull in the assault, he spun around and brought up his fists, ready to fight for his life.

It wasn't necessary.

Brady was in a heap on the floor, a spreading puddle of blood mushrooming out from the back of his head. His eyes were open and unseeing.

Cameron stood in the doorway, frozen in place, the baseball bat in his still-cuffed hands. He dropped the bat in a clatter to the cold floor.

"Are you all right?" the designer asked, snapping out of his stupor as he awkwardly hopped to Blake's side, his feet shackled together. Blake's face was covered in blood, and it terrified Cameron.

"Yes. Oh, my God . . ." Blake thought his legs would give out, and he had to grab the counter for support

"It's over now, babe, it's over, it's over," Cam repeated in a rush, hyperventilating. He picked up a kitchen towel from the countertop and reached his manacled hands up to wipe Blake's face clean.

Blake felt his strength return and he stared down at the motionless deputy on his kitchen floor. "Brady's not breathing." He kneeled down and felt for a pulse. He didn't find one. "Oh, God. Cameron, he's dead!"

39

In the weeks following the tragic death of Suzette—and the less tragic death of Brady—the media firestorm was incredible. The tabloids quickly dubbed the deaths the "Fashion Victim Killings" and splashed increasingly sensational stories about the principal players on the front pages. All aspects of the lives of those involved were exploited and reported on. The mainstream media, while only slightly less cruel, still focused intently on Cameron and Blake.

The duo watched helplessly as their images were plastered on front pages and magazine covers the world over, their lives dissected and held up for ridicule. They became known as the outed gay couple whose secret love affair caused the demise of two people.

The Los Angeles district attorney, seeing a way to garner free publicity for a future run as mayor, promised a full investigation in the "suspicious" death of a Los Angeles police officer, while at the same time pressing forward with murder charges against Silas.

But, eventually, even she saw that Brady's death had been a clear case of self-defense, and while the finger pointing lasted a while, Cameron was never charged with any crime.

Cameron and Blake were rarely seen in public after Suzette's funeral, which had taken place at a small exclusive cemetery in Upstate New York. They had taken to staying in at Cameron's large apartment on Fifth Avenue. Photographers and reporters staked out the luxury building and waited for the pair to emerge from their self-imposed exile. When they did venture out, it was usually under cover of night, and under the protection of Oscar and several bodyguards, as a few death threats from rabid extremists had been received.

Pacific Coast Highway cologne tanked.

The advertising campaign starring Blake had been halted almost as soon as it started. Blake's promised nationwide billboards and bus signs never materialized. His commercials never aired and *Esquire* pulled his cover shot and replaced him with . . . Travis Fimmel. The huge billboard on Sunset was quietly torn down, and in its place went up one for the new Ashley Judd movie. Both Bally's and Finlanda canceled his contracts, and the Hunk agency sent him a letter informing him that his newfound notoriety made him unemployable; regrettably, he had been dropped from their client list.

He put his small house, including furnishings, up for sale, because it now contained such painful memories. It was bought by an art director for one of the soaps after being on the market only two days. Blake put the remainder of his possessions in storage.

The scandal of the killings tainted anything Cameron Fuller, and sales dropped across the board. The once red-hot designer's products were now the object of derision, and most of the key department store chains dropped the lines from their stock. The stores on Rodeo and in Soho saw business drop ninety percent in the first quarter after the incidents. The opening of the London store was canceled.

The red ink began to eat up the black.

Silas, whose will left everything to his daughter and son-in-law, had suffered a fatal heart attack while being held in L.A.'s county jail, and died before he could change it. As Suzette's surviving spouse, Cam had been shocked to find he had inherited Silas's money. The enormous windfall allowed Cameron to help keep his company afloat longer, but after spending untold millions of his personal fortune trying to stem the flood of red ink, eventually he accepted the inevitable.

Cameron Fuller USA was forced to declare Chapter Seven bankruptcy. Cameron had hoped at least to protect his employees' futures by filing Chapter Eleven, which would have allowed him to restructure the company in a court-ordered fashion, but none of his vendors would go along with the required lowered payments. Loans were due, and called, and soon there was no other choice but to shut the doors.

The company known as Cameron Fuller USA ceased to exist one week and one day before the one year anniversary of Suzette Cabbott Fuller's death.

The liquidators had a monthlong liquidation sale at both the Soho Warehouse and Rodeo Drive stores. The huge "going out of business" banners that hung from both stores were photographed and ended up on the front cover of *People,* along with a story entitled "Cameron Fuller's Unfashionable Fall From Grace." The article brought renewed, and unwelcome, attention to Cameron and Blake, and gave what scant information could be dug up about their current lives.

The Soho Warehouse store was leased by Ralph Lauren to house his expanded Home Collection, and underwent a major renovation and transformation. The London store was turned into a Benetton.

The Rodeo Drive store was shuttered, and sat empty for months. The enormous building had been built specifically for high-end retail, but no national or private retailer could afford the obscenely high rent. Eventually the elegant building was torn down, and construction began on the upscale mini mall that was being built in its place.

Cameron decided to sell off the Tuxedo and Aspen houses. He knew he would never visit them again. He kept the New York apartment and the beach house in Kauai.

Over time, press interest in Cameron and Blake tapered off, and they began to be seen out and about in the city more. Sometimes they were spotted walking a large, elderly golden retriever in the park. Sometimes they were seen at a new Broadway show, or scoping out art at the numerous galleries. People were courteous to them, but always nudged each other and whispered behind their backs: "There goes Cameron Fuller and his lover, the ex-model. That scandal ruined them, you know."

Then, one day, they were simply gone. The large apartment was sold, and they became a question, "Whatever happened to Cameron Fuller and his boyfriend?"

40

The sunlight flooded the newly painted room, and Blake squinted, waiting. He was soon rewarded for his patience by the distant crowing. He smiled. He'd actually grown to love that sound. It felt comforting and like home. Stretching, he reached across the bed and felt the warm back of his partner of three years.

"Hey, baby. Time to get up," he whispered softly.

Cameron woke up and rolled over, faced Blake, and grimaced. "Ugh. Those damn roosters," he muttered.

Blake smiled. Cam said the same thing every morning.

"I thought you once told me they were easy to get used to. What happened?" Blake teased, reaching up and brushing away a stray lock of hair that had fallen into his face. He had let his sun-bleached hair grow, and it now hung well below his shoulders.

"I lied."

"Come on. Let's get up. You wanted to get the fence fixed, then plant those new bougainvillea along the west ridge. You made me promise to help."

"I did? I must have been insane. Can I plead temporary insanity?" Cam asked hopefully, not wanting to leave the bed. He now sported a salt and pepper goatee that actually made his masculine face even more handsome. He, too, had let his hair grow out a bit, and now it was sticking out every which way.

"Nope."

"Damn. Then how about a morning kiss to get me started?"

"Deal."

Blake leaned over and kissed Cam. Cam didn't let him go; instead, he reached across the bed and pulled him close. Soon they were making out like kids, Blake on top of his lover, his long hair tenting their faces together.

After the ex-designer slathered Blake with some lubricant, Blake began to slide in and out of him, and both men were amazed that this time was as awesome as the first time.

Their lovemaking had the added pleasure of being routine—comfortable and expected. They each knew what turned the other on, and the fact that they had built a life together through unimaginable odds made them love each other all the more. They gazed at each other lovingly while Blake's motions brought them close to climax. Joe Jr., or JJ, their nine-month-old golden retriever puppy, sat on the floor watching the action on the bed quizzically.

Neither Blake nor Cameron minded that their once perfect bodies had gained a few pounds here and there. Ripped abs and cut pecs weren't as important as they once were. Not that they had gotten fat; far from it. They both ran three miles every day down on the beach, and the guest room had been turned into a gym. Being perfect physical specimens just wasn't the be all and end all of their lives anymore.

After they both came, Blake lay down on Cam, and stayed inside, as was his habit. He gently rocked himself back and forth, his body weight pressing Cam down into the feather bed.

Cam, despite all he had lost, knew he had never been happier.

Except for one small thing.

They were on the bluff overlooking the blue Pacific when Cam finally broached the subject he'd wanted to talk about for weeks.

"Blake? Babe?" he called out. He was digging a hole in the ground on a ridge next to a steep gully. Swaying palm trees rustled overhead and the potted bougainvilleas he was about to liberate into the ground were a riot of hot pink, which stood out amidst all the green. JJ was romping through some nearby bushes, getting muddy red.

Blake, wearing only an old loose pair of Honolua Surf Company board shorts and no shoes, was beside the property fence. He had pulled his long hair back in a loose ponytail and had achieved a tan so dark he was often mistaken for a native Hawaiian. In his mouth were several nails, and he was hammering away at a loose plank. He was repairing the section of the fence that had blown down a couple of days earlier during a heavy windstorm.

"Whaa?" he struggled to say, and not swallow the nails. He looked over at Cam, and still felt the warm rush of love for the man. Cam was wearing flip-flops, faded blue jams, and a worn red T-shirt, and still he looked like a million bucks.

"I need to talk to you," Cam struggled to say.

Blake set the hammer down and spit out the nails. "You look so serious. What is it?"

"I need you to really hear what I'm saying, okay? Listen to me before you jump all over me, all right?"

"Hmmm. This doesn't sound good." Blake smiled.

"Just hear me out, that's all I'm asking."

"Okay." Curious now, Blake sat down on the grass and hugged his knees with his arms.

"I love you. You know that."

Blake nodded.

"And I won't do this if you don't support it, but, I have an opportunity."

Blake's eyebrows rose, but he said nothing.

"Dillard called last week. You know he lost the palimony suit, and moved to Los Angeles?"

Blake nodded again.

"He says there's a storefront on Rodeo that's available. Good sized, and reasonable rent for that street."

"Uh huh . . . ," Blake allowed.

"Blake, I want to go back. I want to start over. It's time. I feel like I still have something to offer, and I want to try it again. Only this time, I want you to do it with me. I lost everything before because I wasn't true to myself. I want to try it knowing who I am now."

A thousand warning bells went off in Blake's head. This was not a good idea. Every time Cam had even begun to mention going back to the mainland, Blake had refused to consider it. Their lives were here now, and that suited him just fine. He knew that Cam wasn't one hundred percent happy in Hawaii, but at least the locals here treated them with respect and friendliness.

When they first decided to move to the island it was as an escape. An escape from the rumors, the finger pointing, and the constant reminders of Cameron's great fall from retail stardom. As they integrated themselves into island life, they found that the vast majority of the people here couldn't have cared less what their story was. They were welcomed with open arms, and had built good lives here with a close circle of amazing friends.

Granted, the gay life here was almost nonexistent, but Blake was surprised to discover all he needed was Cam. They were each other's best friend, lover, and playmate. The days actually seemed too short to get in everything they wanted to accomplish. On the island, they were free to be who they were, and they both cherished that.

They spent their days working on the estate, which now was truly one of the most beautiful in all the islands. Blake oversaw a complete renovation of the house, while Cam became the landscape architect he surely could have been. The grounds had been turned into a lush wonderland of gardens, meandering paths, and koi ponds.

Money was not an issue for the couple, as Cameron had been spared financial ruin during the business bankruptcy. The company went broke. Not him. He still had a large portion of his personal fortune and some safe investments left.

"Cameron, have you forgotten what it was like for us back there? The press? The cameras everywhere? The awful lies they spread about us? I haven't. I don't ever want to live through that again!" Blake said emphatically.

"I know," Cameron quickly said, crossing over to his man. He sat down next to him and took his hand in his own. "But, sweetheart, I almost feel like I was run out of town. For what? For falling in love and trying to correct a big mistake? I love our life here, don't get me wrong. And if you really don't want to go back, we won't. You're my husband, and anything we do, we do together. I just think it's time for us to reclaim what was ours. Together. And unafraid."

Cameron had felt the pull to go back for some time. He hadn't mentioned his desire to Blake because he knew where Blake stood on the subject. But fashion retail was in Cam's blood. To deny that was to deny who he was. He wanted to start over, but smaller this time. More exclusive, and with a narrower product line. He had a thousand ideas, and was confident he could not only build back what he had but improve on it tenfold.

"Oh, Cam . . . I don't know." Blake sighed. "This is our home now. I don't want to leave it. I love it here."

"Just think about it, okay? And I'm not saying it's a permanent move. We'll go back and forth. Money's obviously not a problem."

Blake stared at the ground. He had feared this conversation, but now that it was here, he felt oddly calm.

"Blake, I need to do this," Cameron continued, serious. "I need to see if I can be the man I want to be, and still contribute something. I've missed my old life, I admit it. I've always told you I didn't, when you've asked, but, honestly, I have."

Blake raised his head. "I know. I know you have. I think I allowed myself to be fooled into thinking you were glad to be away from the business. But I guess I always knew you missed it," he admitted.

"We would be an unbeatable team! Your sense of style? My business acumen? The timing's right, I can feel it. Enough time has passed that I think it'll work. No, I *know* it'll work!" Cameron's enthusiasm for the project was apparent.

Blake looked out to the sparkling ocean and drank in the surf crashing onto the rocks a hundred feet below them. He took in the house, the place he had come to love as his home. Their home. He saw the gently curving gravel drive that gracefully met the road. He loved this place.

How could he leave it to go back to L.A. and face that turmoil again? But, with one look at Cameron's expectant face, he knew he would.

"Cam, if you really think this is what you need to do, then I'll support you wholeheartedly. I don't like it, and frankly I have grave misgivings about this. But you're my partner, my husband, and where you go, I'll go."

Cameron let out a happy yell and grabbed Blake, pulling him up. "Babe! You won't regret it! I promise! Thank you! Thank you so much."

The two men hugged while JJ barked at their feet, trying to join in.

41

Beverly Hills, California

"Are you ready?"

Blake took a deep breath, and nodded.

Cam signaled Kelly Gecko, the perky women's buyer from the old store, who was now his store manager, and she went to unlock the door.

"Okay, folks. Here we go!" Cam said loudly, beaming.

Blake noticed that one of the shirt stacks had tilted over in its bin, and he quickly straightened it. He looked up as the flood of people crowded into the store. He was stunned by the amount of people coming through the plate glass and chrome doors. He was even more surprised when he saw they were actually buying product.

The first thing Cam and Blake had done upon returning to L.A. was to go directly to the proposed store location and check it out. Dillard met them there with the real estate agent, and within the hour Cam had signed a two-year lease.

The store was located two blocks down Rodeo Drive from the construction site that was the old Cameron Fuller store. The new space was narrow, but deep, and held only two floors.

Blake convinced Cam to go a completely different way this time, not to replicate his last stores. This smaller place was designed to be sleek and modern. Flat cement walls with a hint of green were the exterior, with large plate glass display windows fronting the street. The front doors were recessed about ten feet from the front display windows, and large black awnings shielded the windows from the sun. The large rectangular sign above the awnings proclaimed this as the domain of FullJack, the new name of Cam and Blake's company, and store.

Inside, sleek cement floors supported dark wood display cases and vitrines, and high intensity halogen lighting made everything shine. The first floor housed the women's collections, while the second floor held men's.

Cam had pared down what product and fashion he wanted to showcase, and only his best designs were on display. He had shifted his style from preppy to a more clean and modern look. The silhouettes were less structured, fresher; the fabrics richer; and the tailoring was superb. The clothes actually cost more than his previous lines, but he felt they were worth it. He had spent months finding the right fabrics and setting up his factory.

The work had been arduous, but he had meticulously heeded his one promise to Blake. One week out of the month, they returned to Kauai to regroup.

They had bought a small, mid-century house up in the fashionable bird streets of Sunset Plaza in the Hollywood Hills. Their new neighbors were a movie producer on one side and a starlet on the other. While designing the new store, Blake had also redesigned the house, and now both projects were finally finished.

At first tentative about reentering Los Angeles, and Weho society, the two men soon found that they were welcomed back easily. Travis Church and Clay Beasley graciously gave them a welcome back party, and soon they had invitations to anything of note in town.

As the opening of the store got closer, interest in them became intense again, but this time it was as if they had paid some debt and were suddenly cool again.

Cam and Blake did a joint interview with Barbara Walters that was the highest rated program of the week. Other magazines and newspapers soon followed suit and proclaimed them the prodigal sons of fashion, and everywhere they went they were met with impatient questions about when the store would open.

Now that the doors were open, there was nothing they could do but stand back and let their employees do their jobs. Blake had started to point out minor flaws on the floor to Chelsea and Dusty, whom he had hired to run the visuals department, but he stopped when he realized he was beginning to sound a lot like Rafael.

"God forbid," Chelsea said in mock horror.

"Whatever happened to that ass, anyway?" Blake wondered aloud.

Chelsea laughed. "You don't know?"

"No. We've been out of the loop for a while, you know."

"Oh, my God! After the company folded he couldn't get a job! He finally he got one with the Big Q discount chain. Can you imagine? Rafael figuring out how to display polyester stretch pants?"

"Now, *that's* justice," Blake said.

"It gets better. He had a huge breakdown, and had to quit. Last I heard, he was in a hospital dealing with his . . . demons."

"Couldn't happen to a nicer guy."

"Oh, come on, have pity for the insane," Chelsea teased.

Blake gave her a playful swat on the butt, and went up the wide staircase to join Cam, who was gazing down at the fevered activity.

"Well, what do you think?" he asked as he reached Cam's side.

"I think we're back. We've already done fifty-eight thousand, and the day's only half done." Cam was beaming.

"I'd say we're a hit," Blake agreed.

Cam turned to face Blake and took him in his arms. "Thank you so much for this. I know you weren't sure about this whole thing, but you have made such a beautiful store, I couldn't be prouder of you."

"Aww, shucks, 'twern't nuthin."

"Well, start thinking about how we can template this store for a national rollout."

"What?"

Cam hugged Blake hard. "I've been approached by Dillard and some other investors. We're going national again. You're going to head up the design team."

"Jesus, Cam! We just got this one done . . . Of course, I already know how we can improve the design for the next one."

"I thought you might."

The two men stayed in each other's arms, whispering to each

other, oblivious to the eager customers milling about them. Eventually they stole away to their shared private office, and locked the door.

They didn't come out for over an hour.